ULTIMATE OBJECTIVE

J G HUTCHISON

This book is work of fiction. Names, characters, places, and incidents either are products of the author's imagination or are used fictitiously. The locations depicted in this novel are likewise described with a modicum of literary license. Other than historic figures, any resemblance to actual persons, living or dead is entirely coincidental.

ISBN: 1479218294
ISBN-13: 978-1479218295

ACKNOWLEDGMENTS

Ultimate Objective required an extensive amount of research, specialized knowledge, and an overdose of editing.

The Internet provided unlimited, but sometimes unqualified information. For more authoritative insight I turned to knowledgeable friends who love thrillers and work for food.

Hunter Malson, an avid firearms collector, offered insight on side arms and long guns.

Dr. Ridg Gilmer, a pathologist, provided graphic detail of combat wounds and traumatic stress.

Kudos to the aspiring authors in my critique circles who assisted with extensive editing of this manuscript.

Special thanks to my wife, Kathryn, for her patience and support.

"Four things greater than all things are,
Women and Horses and Power and War"

—Rudyard Kipling

". . . a lever long enough,
fulcrum strong enough,
and I shall move the world."

—Archimedes

PROLOGUE

Houston, Texas
Early December

Fear is the true nourishment of the soul, the rising tide of panic, a feast.

Lost in thought, Sheikh Qadr al-Masri rested his chin on his fist, staring out the window at roiling clouds over the Gulf of Mexico. He dismissed the risk of a failed mission, as danger and death did not faze him. The imposing Falcon Pharaoh avatar adorning the stabilizer on his Gulfstream V intimated his power, wealth, and everlasting life.

Astute application of financial leverage had provided him the opportunity to be the wealthiest man in history, a dream he had nurtured since his impoverished childhood. For inordinately long, he abided in smoldering silence while Western influence and meddling in the Middle East festered like malignant cancer. Soon that would change. American hubris had served the summons to contest. He vowed to avenge his mother's rape and murder, moving quietly in the darkness, like the desert wind. Unseen. Unheard. But *alive.*

A master manipulator distrusting all others, he tolerated neither failure nor imprecision. Those he could not command, he beheaded. He would let nothing stand in the way of total victory. Enshrouded in secrecy, his plan would shatter the US economy, kill thousands of stupid and arrogant Americans, and bring down the Government of the United States.

As though his destiny were preordained, fate had a way of stepping in. The scheduled meeting with the Senator was a godsend—if one believed in such superstition. Religious faith? Opiate for fools. Force and fear reigned over the world. He found it amusing that politicians were the same the world over, easily corrupted with *baksheesh*—the lubricant used to grease men's palms. Little did the Senator know that "campaign contributions" bartered for intelligence revealed an obstacle to the Sheikh's scheme.

He opened his briefcase, and studied the contents of the appropriated folder stamped *Top Secret, Omega Six*. After a last look at the photo of the FBI counterterrorism agent, he returned it to the folder and stowed the documents in his briefcase, snapped it shut, and spun the lock tumblers.

Preemptive force would be most expedient. My Spetsnaz bodyguards would not dare fail.

Pressure in his ears and the reduced drone of the twin turbines indicated his aircraft's descent on its final approach to Bush Intercontinental Airport.

So, now begins the torrent of destruction and chaos.

With a hint of a satisfied smile, he regarded his musky-scented companion—amber eyes flecked with gold, honey-blond hair worn long and falling loosely about her shoulders. She was taller by a hand, and held herself with the erect carriage of a dancer. Her haute couture ensemble revealed long sculpted legs, her crème de menthe blouse a hint of enticing cleavage adorned with Buccellati emerald jewelry—alluring elegance altogether worthy of a crown prince.

The enchantress caught his expression and set aside a current copy of *Brigitte,* a German fashion magazine. She pressed the button to return her seat into the upright position. Taking his hand, she laced her silky fingers with his.

Abruptly, the Rolls-Royce twin turbines spooled up. The G5 responded quickly and climbed in steep ascent.

"My apologies, Excellency," the pilot announced through the intercom. "Air Traffic Control rerouted our landing to an alternate runway due to patches of ground fog. There will be a ten-minute delay."

"Was ist los?" the Sheikh's companion queried in a husky voice.

"Es ist nicht von belang, meine Liebe." The Sheikh squeezed her hand, then checked the time on his Cartier Pasha watch. He turned his dark eyes out the window to the panorama below to take in the heart of America's energy industry—the *ultimate objective.*

A blanket of gray mist partially shrouded the Port of Houston and the encompassing industrial complex unlike any other in the world. Through scattered fog, sprawling refineries and overburdened tank farms cluttered the landscape, ships navigating the overflowing Houston Ship Channel that were topped off with volatile hydrocarbons —fuel for Armageddon.

Anticipation of the rising tide caused a tremor of energy to ripple through his body and brought a smile to his face. In his perception, the ground fog materialized as smoke billowing from a raging inferno.

Like the heartbeat of the living dead, the ever-present voice in his brain resonated—*Redemption is not a vessel to be filled, but a fire to be kindled. There can be no end without a beginning. But, the beginning of the end is near.*

One

The Port of Houston
Early December

Mist that crept off Galveston Bay, almost rain but more like fog, had delayed Kirk Magnus' helicopter lift-off. Roiling dark clouds over the Port cast ominous shadows on the scene below, and the throbbing beat of the rotor and the whine of the turbines added fuel to Kirk's foreboding.

Following crusty and the usual cryptic orders from the commander of Omega Six, his elite counterterror unit, he had only a vague clue of his mission objective, a late start, and a very bad feeling. Something was going down. Something *big*.

Leaning out of the helicopter into the bone-chilling soup, he squinted into the bleak sky to make out more of the panorama. A thousand feet below in patches of fog, a parade of container ships and tankers queued up in the narrow waterway to disgorge cargoes. Dozens of petroleum refineries, chemical plants, and a checkerboard of storage tanks loaded to the brim with crude oil, gasoline, and jet fuel saturated the landscape. Ten miles to the west in downtown Houston, cathedrals to commerce arose from the gray shroud like tombstones from a necropolis. *Two for the price of one.* The entire scene was a terrorist's wet dream.

The more Kirk scrutinized the landscape, the more ominous it appeared. Feeling something terrible was about to happen, he could almost smell the acrid stench of blazing skyscrapers, burning fuel, black smoke, and human flesh. A carefully planned attack on the Port of Houston had the destructive potential to incinerate thousands of people in a manmade hell. The destruction would send shock waves throughout the energy industry, and slash the American economy to beggar's pocket change. Kirk wondered if his surveillance and threat assessment was too little, too late.

There was a hand in the darkness that held a massive Molotov cocktail. And there wasn't a damned thing he could do about it. Fate had conveyed a colossal gift to wannabe terrorists.

Vibration from his iPhone shattered his thoughts. He retrieved the phone from a belt holster and read the text message from his commander.

"Omni bar at seven. Fell into a rabbit hole. Road-kill stewing on the front burner."

As close friends, he and Brett Brosnan often communicated in body language and cryptic lingo unique to their profession. Road-kill was their code for terrorists who needed a lethal dose of lead poisoning; rabbit hole implied an intelligence breakthrough.

When the chopper set down near the Houston Ship Channel, Kirk jumped out and raced back to the hotel. He found a vacant spot on the second level of the Omni Hotel garage. Glanced his watch.

Ten minutes late.

The bar was crowded for a Friday evening—legions of gorgeous women decked-out in alluring clothing and war paint that got the juices flowing.

The corner table in the darkened pub allowed him to keep one eye on the door, the other on a raven-haired beauty at the bar in a low-cut dress, flaunting mouth-watering cleavage. While nursing a beer, he brooded over her. She was a nine or ten on the fantasy scale, exuding natural self-confidence. A formula he found provocative.

Lust trumping anxiety, Kirk was nowhere near as agitated as he'd been moments earlier. Antsy, he checked his watch.

Should have been here by now.

Kirk thumbed the speed dial on his iPhone.

Five rings, followed by voice mail.

In their line of work, failure to respond to an encrypted phone call struck fear. It meant one of two things, and no one buried a dead battery.

His pulse quickening, Kirk keyed the GPS tracking app on his cell to discover Brett's location—the Omni Hotel garage.

Not moving.

Dreading the worst, he tossed a bill on the table, bolted out the bar, and bumped into a couple entering.

No time for apologies.

After racing through the lobby, he took the stairs two at a time, past the ground-level valet parking area to the second level.

Constructed in a rectangular spiral, the garage was packed solid with cars angled-in on sloping floors. He paused to allow his pupils to adjust to the dim light, then scanned the area, relying on peripheral vision to detect movement.

Nothing stirred—no suspicious silhouettes lurked in the shadows.

Halfway down the ramp, Brett's Government Issue Crown Victoria stood out from the luxury vehicle line-up. No one in the driver's seat.

From a holster in the small of his back, Kirk pulled a no-bullshit Heckler & Koch HK45 fitted with a laser sight. Held in a two-hand grip, he cautiously approached the vehicle, hair standing up on the back of his neck like hedgehog quills.

In a crouch, Kirk crept closer, skin prickling. From twenty feet, he recognized Brett's lizard boots—toes turned up. He inched toward the prone form lying between a black Mercedes SUV and the Crown Vic.

Brett's matted hair was pasted to the concrete slab in a pool of warm blood.

Kirk dropped one knee, then pressed his fingertips against his carotid artery.

Nothing.

Feeling a sharp pain in his gut, he stared into his friend's lifeless eyes and uttered a curse. Too often, good men were killed in action. But it never got any easier. It always felt like defeat.

Searching the body, he found Brett's wallet in his hip pocket, his Rolex chronometer still on his left wrist. He rolled Brett's body face down to determine the cause of death.

Two small-caliber bullet wounds tightly grouped to the back of Brett's head confirmed Kirk's worst fear—a double-tap—the signature of a professional hit man.

Somehow, the enemy had cracked the hard shell of their covert counterterror operation wide open. And Brett Brosnan would take his intelligence bonanza to his grave.

But this was no time for sorrow. Kirk thought if he lived long enough, that would have to come later. The enemy was on to Omega Six. He'd be next.

Unless he hunted them down, and killed them first.

An old combat injury in Kirk's lower back twitched from tension. He stood to relieve the ache.

What now?

Kirk was the kind of man who envisioned things before they happened. An adrenaline-induced sixth sense warned something malevolent lurked in the shadows.

Soft footsteps on the third level behind him. *Close.*

In a fluid move, Kirk spun toward the direction of the sound, his weapon poised. Instinctively, he dropped into a combat crouch. The cough of a suppressed handgun broke the silence.

Supersonic bullets cracked over his head.

Peering over the trunk of the Crown Vic, Kirk scanned the upper level, sweeping the HK45 laser in wide arcs.

He heard running footsteps, then the rev of a powerful engine on the third level. Tires squealed against concrete when a dark BMW turned the corner above him. Scampering for cover behind a concrete column, Kirk took aim at the driver.

Intense xenon headlights flicked on high beam blinded him. Unsure his target was the assassin he withheld fire.

As the BMW bore down, muzzle flashes from a suppressed automatic machine pistol erupted from the passenger window. Chunks of concrete and dust exploded off the column. Kirk dove for the deck next to Brett's body. Bullets peppered the rear ends of the Crown Vic and SUV, shattering windows and ricocheting off the ceiling. Broken glass cascaded across the back of his neck. Shredded metal flew in every direction. Rivulets of gasoline leaked from the SUV.

In a blinding flash, the gas tank erupted with a *whump.* Flames shot out the filler cap. Intense heat and a thick cloud of smoke set off the fire sprinkler system dumping an icy-cold deluge. Acrid fumes burned his eyes and filled his lungs.

The BMW roared past, guns blazing, and accelerated down the ramp. Squealed around the corner onto the ground level.

Fighting a wave of scorching heat and coughing from smoke, Kirk dragged Brett's body away from the raging inferno.

Now running, he clambered over the cable barrier that separated his level from the ground floor. Taking shallow breaths to avoid sucking in too much smoke, his heart thumping like a jackhammer starved for air, he headed off the BMW.

As the powerful car roared down the ramp toward him, Kirk "painted" the red laser on the passenger's face. Squeezed off a round.

The heavy-caliber bullet exploded out the opposite side of the assassin's skull in a spray of blood, brain, and bone fragments that plastered the interior of the vehicle. Shrieking auto alarms were set off by the ear-splitting report from his weapon. Burning rubber, the BMW raced past toward the exit. Kirk swung his handgun, leading the driver target and fired a three-round burst.

The auto's rear window exploded into thousands of glass shards.

The driver killed the headlights and blasted through the articulated arm, leaving a wake of splintered wood and twisted steel.

Tires smoking, the BMW tore off into the night.

Two

Quai d'Aranc
Marseille, France
Saturday Evening

Menacing clouds pregnant with moisture rolled off the Mediterranean and turned the sky into a blue-black bruise. Thor's rolling thunder foreshadowed a torrent of glacial sleet. Captain François D'Auberge cursed the cold front. Foul weather numbed the fishes' appetite, chased the sport fishermen to warm shelter, and cut off his income clean as a guillotine.

Charter fishing was his livelihood. It was all François knew and all he loved—that and his family. He earned a decent income when the weather cooperated; however, big-ticket engine repairs on his boat had set his finances back. Now, a family medical emergency.

Curiosity—that is all it had been. His grandson wanted to watch the cockfights. He had slipped under the tent, and was it his fault he was there when an argument broke out over a wager? No. But did the Persian hashish dealer consider innocent bystanders when he fired a gun at the gambler? Hell no! The bullet went straight through the cheater's side, and shattered Luc's kneecap. French socialized medicine refused to pay for corrective surgery and the necessary prosthesis. Without it his grandson would never again walk with a normal gait.

François dropped his chin on his hand watching rain splatter the cobblestone street, filling gutters with trash-filled runoff. The weather outside the leaded glass window of the Fishermen's Pub looked exactly the way he felt. Fucking miserable.

Gaslights mounted on ornate iron posts cast eerie shadows from office buildings, the fish market, a café long since closed, and a *boulangerie* giving off the smell of baking bread. Dressed in faux leather, two whores sought shelter in a doorway across the rain-slicked street, smoking.

A pair of bearded men meandered toward them, casting furtive looks over their shoulders. One of the whores cupped her ample breasts, and spoke.

François could read her lips. "*Bonsoir, messieurs. Churchez-vous une femme ce soir?*"

The taller man stared hungrily at the whore's breasts; the shorter man shook his head and spoke.

After a drag on her cigarette, she pouted and pointed to the pub with the glowing butt.

The strange men strode with purpose across the cobblestones toward the pub; heads hunkered into the wind and rain.

A moment later François watched the men enter. "Fucking Persians," he muttered. Glaring at them, he ground his cigarette in an ashtray.

The waterfront pub was dark, floorboards warped and stained from years of spills and who knew what. Conversations, boisterous a moment before, abated as other patrons stopped playing cards and dominos and stared at the newcomers. A patron at the bar spit on the floor. Another curled his lips and turned back to his drink. François' friends felt the same way he did. *Étrangers,* Persians in particular, were not welcome here.

As though casting about for someone, the interlopers checked out the patrons before approaching the bar. They purchased a bottle of cognac and carried on a brief conversation with the bartender.

The bartender wiped his hands on his apron, and pointed his chin toward François.

"*Merde,*" François murmured. He lit another Gaulois, and appraised the men as they approached his table.

Without invitation, the rude strangers took seats to face him. Their odor was pungent and sour—the stench of anxiety, or bathing no more than once in a blue moon. Ice-cold rain could scarcely wash off the smell of the Persian filth. François glanced at his watch. Late for small talk and the weather was not worth discussing. *What possible business could these men have?*

"I am called Saleh," the shorter man said in Farsi-accented English in an officious manner.

François flicked a cigarette ash into the butt-filled tray and glowered with undisguised enmity.

"*Casse-toi.*" He made the obscene gesture with a closed fist, thumb in the air.

The bearded men frowned, not appearing to understand.

"If you do not understand the French language, piss off," François snarled in English. He turned his gaze out the window in an attempt to ignore them.

"We wish to charter your boat for a fishing expedition," Saleh said.

François felt he should spit in the man's face for what the Persians had done to his grandson and his country. He did not intend to provide services for their pleasure.

"My boat is not available for charter."

"Why not? It suits our needs."

"Needs? My boat needs engine repairs."

As he removed the top from his cognac bottle, Saleh shifted his eyes toward his accomplice and said, "We took note of your fine boat in the slip at the marina. The operator informed us you are the best."

"Your flattery earns shit. I do not much like Persians, and the fishing is not so good." François extracted another cigarette from a pack on the table and lit it from a match, then turned his attention to the other interloper.

A dark beard half covering a jagged scar from the big man's left eye across his cheek bespoke brutality. Scarface had the feral look of a religious zealot, a sick fire in his eyes only his death would extinguish.

François sensed genuine danger. The warm pub now felt cold. Nonetheless, he was curious about the characters who cast dark shadows. As he studied them, he noticed Saleh grasped his liqueur bottle with a hand with only three fingers.

A horrible accident? Or telltale sign of a fucking Islamic bomber?

A chill skittered down François' back.

Saleh poured the cognac into an empty glass and slid it across the table. "We know your boat is available for charter and is in perfect order."

François cast a poisonous evil eye at the pair, wondering how they obtained that information. But engaging in dialog would further their aims.

"I drink my own liqueur and I refuse any comradeship or business with Persians," he said.

Saleh hunched forward, eyes squinted.

"Perhaps you need the business." A sinister inflection in his voice and demonic eyes burned into François. When the man spoke, he moved his head side-to-side like a flute-charmed cobra.

"I do not want your stinking business." François blew smoke into Saleh's face. "There are many fishing boats in Marseille."

"Our money is good," Saleh said.

"Good? Your people import drugs, disease, and poverty into France, polluting French culture. Mullahs preach hatred of the West. Muslim terrorists plant bombs and harm innocent citizens. *For what?* We've done you no harm."

Casting a quick sideways glance at Scarface, Saleh lit an acrid Turkish cigarette. He inhaled the fumes deep into his lungs and held them like a doper relishing a toke of cannabis. He appraised François through hooded eyelids.

"We pay two thousand Euros—two days." Scarface held up a pair of calloused fingers stained with permanent dirt. His breath stank like a bloated corpse.

"Kiss my ass."

"Old man." Scarface rubbed the tips of two fingers with his thumb. "Much money, the boat repairs, yes?"

"Boat maintenance? A normal expense." François waved his hand dismissively, then studied the ash on his fag. "The weather will soon improve and my *good* customers will return."

"The boy?" Scarface sneered. "He *needs* the surgery, yes?"

François gasped; outraged these men had performed a background check on him. *Fucking barbarian.* No wonder it was called filthy lucre. *Who the hell were they?*

He took a large swallow of his cognac, his hands shaking.

"Captain D'Auberge, we know a fellow Persian injured your grandson," Saleh said. "We are shamed, and we will pay well for your service. Four thousand Euros."

These men appeared much too eager to charter his boat. Mesmerizing flames in the pub's fireplace provided solace. An exorbitant fee would deter their interest, François reasoned.

"My fee is six thousand Euros. Cash in advance."

Saleh studied him as he poured a second cognac. He raised the glass in salute, threw back a slug of the liqueur, and replied. "*D'accord.*"

Merde. François sucked in a long deep breath and stared out the window at the driving rain. Prayers for good fishing weather had long since failed him. The money would help pay for his grandson's surgery, and as a matter of integrity he could not back out now. He sighed.

"Very well. What kind of fish do you seek?"

Saleh glanced sideways at Scarface, his nicotine-stained teeth appeared as his lips drew back. "*Le Grand Requin Blanc*—the Great White Shark."

* * *

Fifty kilometers South Southeast of Marseille, under cover of darkness, a French *Aérospatiale Tigre* assault helicopter hovered motionless over the afterdeck of the French nuclear powered submarine, *Le Terrible.*

Two seamen exited a hatch and positioned an infrared illuminator on deck, then waved to the blacked-out *Tigre.*

Seconds later, Maxime Devereaux, a French Foreign Intelligence agent exited the helicopter door and fast-roped onto *Le Terrible's* pitching deck. After he entered, seamen closed the hatch, and then the submarine slipped below the surface. The Executive Officer greeted the interloper with undisguised enmity, and led Max to the Sonar Room.

Within the soundproof enclosure adjacent to the Control Room, Max observed the sonar operators studying the "waterfall"—a video display of squiggly vertical lines representing digitally processed sounds picked up by *Le Terrible's* ultra-sensitive hydrophones.

An ominous bright blip matched the acoustic signature of SSK-635—the *Ayatollah Khomeini.*

"Lieutenant?" Max asked in a hushed tone. "What is the target position?"

Detesting the *Direction Générale de la Sécurité Extérieure* intrusion, the XO responded curtly, "Bearing two-one-six, range 20000 meters, depth 100. Diesels running to charge her batteries. She is on a direct intercept course with the sport fishing boat. Making five knots towing a noisy snorkel." He sneered officiously. "Sloppy seamanship."

Max addressed the smug officer. "A word of advice, Lieutenant. Never interfere with the enemy while he makes mistakes."

* * *

As the grey dawn broke, *Le Paillard* pitched and rolled gently in half-meter swells. With a mug of coffee in hand, François slid the cabin door open and stepped out onto a mist-coated deck to check out his seaworthy boat. He was proud of the beauty, felt affection for her. She was a part of his total being.

Le Paillard, The Swordfish, had served him well. She was an American-built Hatteras—the finest sport fisherman in the world. Constructed of sturdy fiberglass, the ten-meter craft was powered by a pair of reliable 400 horsepower Volvo diesel engines. A rakish flying bridge over the helm set off her sleek lines. An enclosed cabin contained a galley, dining table, and settee. The lower forward cabin was equipped with a head and sleeping quarters for six.

He spared no expense on maintenance and sophisticated radar, radios, sonar fish finders, and GPS navigation. Operating expenses were high, but he catered to wealthy tourists and fishermen who paid his fee without hesitation and referred others for good reason—a lifetime of experience at sea. He had many repeat customers. Soon they would return and his financial situation would improve.

It was a good life.

The cold front had passed and he looked about to assess the fishing conditions. Fog banks crept by, but weather reports indicated improvement. He knew the sun would burn off the mist, and the fishes' appetites would return. Soon he would be rid of these men.

Relieved now that the charter fee was in his daughter's hands, François relaxed. He set his coffee cup on the gunwale off the port deck, and reached into his slicker to retrieve a Gaulois. Resting his foot on a scupper, he took a deep drag on the cigarette, then stared out at the surface of the dead-calm sea in deep thought.

The mysterious strangers appeared too anxious to charter his boat. They paid an exorbitant fee, ignored his insults, and insisted on fishing near the limit of French territorial waters. Why? Great White Sharks fed closer inshore at this time of year. These men were novice fishermen, but still the situation did not feel right. Could they be up to something sinister? Drug smuggling perhaps? He wanted no part in that filthy business.

He hoped the cigarette and coffee would settle his nerves. Life did not get easier with creeping age.

Movement in the fog bank interrupted his thoughts. Radar showed no surface contacts within fifty kilometers. *Strange.* He squinted into the mist. *Something was out there.* When he opened the cabin door to fetch his binoculars, the Persians looked up and halted their conversation. Not that it mattered. François understood not a word of Farsi.

Saleh glanced at his watch and offered a nod toward Scarface, like that of a shrewd buyer at an auction.

François snatched his binoculars from the helm, and rushed out the door to the rear deck. Something moved out there. He raised the binoculars and adjusted the focus.

When the mists parted, a threatening black undersea monster emerged from the fog-shrouded sea 200 meters off *Le Paillard's* port quarter.

A submarine's ten-meter-tall conning tower, fitted with horizontal fins set forward amidships, loomed with periscopes and antennae, hinting at vast evil power that lie within the beast. As foaming water rushed off her decks, François made out the lettering SSK-635 on her conning tower.

"*Putain de merde,*" he gasped. The cigarette fell from his gaping mouth. *A Russian-built Kilo Class submarine.* He would recognize it anywhere. Twenty years as a naval officer and Cold War warrior he wrestled with those hated beasts. He knew that fucking boat belonged to the Iranian Navy and was a long way from her base in Bandar Abbas. She had no legitimate business in French waters. Relations between France and Iran were strained due to the rise in Islamic terror attacks. But this? This was an act of war.

SSK-635 must be on a reconnaissance or an attack mission.

François' heart ticked like an over-wound metronome. He had to radio a distress signal to the authorities and move *Le Paillard* before the Iranians discovered and sank her.

When he turned toward the cabin, he spotted Saleh signaling the enemy submarine with a high-intensity xenon strobe light.

Fucking enemy spies. A wave of terror surged though him.

François pulled a filet knife from his scabbard and brandished it before Saleh's face. *"You Persian scum. Get off my boat."*

Saleh laughed at him. "Fuck off, old bastard." Ignoring François, he continued to signal.

François' head turned like a turret toward the sub. Aghast, he watched as four seamen climbed out of a hatch on her aft deck. They inflated a rubber boat and lowered it into the water.

Those Persian seamen intended to board his boat.

His heart knocking hard enough to shake his chest and arms, he gave Saleh a shove and raced toward the cabin. At the helm, hands shaking, he fired up the diesels to make for safe harbor. The engines rumbled to life, throbbing.

Scarface charged up the steps from the forward cabin. "Stupid old man." He slammed François against a bulkhead. Grabbing François by his neck, he squeezed his windpipe with a fist the size of a bear's claw.

Unable to breath, a wave of fear eddied through François' body. He pissed his pants.

Scarface laughed and tightened the steel grip on his neck.

François wriggled and kicked to no avail. Flailing arms, they collided with the table. Scalding coffee spilled down his back. Cups clattered to the floor. Breaking free, he lunged for the flare gun mounted next to the helm.

Saleh punched his face.

François howled. He pulled the filet knife, and slashed wildly, narrowly missing the bastard's face, but slicing a gaping wound in Scarface's forearm.

Screaming, Scarface kicked François in the groin, doubling him over. The brute ripped the knife from François' arthritic fingers, and brandished it before his face, and snarling, *"Infidel swine."* Scarface drew the razor-sharp knife across François' throat.

A flood of pain forced him to cry out, yet he heard only a gurgling sound. His weakened legs buckled, and he fell to the deck, a great roaring in his ears.

Straddling François's prone body with his arms outstretched and an evil smile on his face, Scarface pointed the knife toward the heavens and screamed, "*Allah-u Akbar!*"

François's vision blurred. He had a ringing sensation in his ears, a runaway heartbeat, and an icy coldness inside. His body convulsed beyond his control. Delusional from a brain starved of oxygen, his last thoughts were of his grandson laughing as the boy run through a meadow, his spotted dog at his side.

* * *

Le Terrible prowled slowly at periscope depth with gentle swells lapping at her photonics mast, but the real-time image from the surface was far from gentle.

Maxime Devereaux watched a bulkhead-mounted display in the Control Room as SSK-635 submerged. The heat in his face reflected his revulsion and anger for the atrocity he had witnessed aboard *Le Paillard*. Close-up images of the inferno engulfing the Hatteras made him feel confined, bottled up in an iron coffin. Acidic bile boiled into his throat. Yet, there was little he could do to vent his rage; he had a higher calling. As one of DGSE's most experienced covert operatives, Max was on special assignment at the direct orders from the President of France. 'Maintain surveillance on the Iranian Ministry of Intelligence Service agents, identify their chain of command, and annihilate it—*sans réserve*.'

An attack on SSK-635 would satisfy the burn within his soul for revenge, but it would violate his orders, and risk unintended consequences.

"Merde," Max muttered. The sweat on his brow registered the crushing weight of the world on his shoulders. The chilled air within *Le Terrible's* Control Room added to his edginess.

He considered Captain Gerard Bettencourt's expression—jaw clenched, compressed lips, hardened eyes. Bettencourt was legendary for his take-no-prisoners penchant. During the height of the Israeli-Hezbollah conflict, his sub rammed a Russian Akula Class FBM while playing a deadly game of Blind Man's Bluff. In an embarrassing international incident, the smoking Akula surfaced in French waters. A cadre of fellow officers closed ranks around Bettencourt at the Naval Board of Inquiry, forming an impenetrable phalanx. The sub skipper commanded admiration and respect. He was no loose cannon, but something burned in his eyes.

Max felt a conflict boiling below the surface, but he was determined to maintain control of the mission.

Captain Bettencourt snapped, "Down mast." He grabbed the boat intercom. "This is the Captain. All hands, man battle stations."

Seconds later, dim red light bathed the Control Room. Normal crew chatter abated to muted tones and hand signals.

"Captain, what is your intention?" Max asked in a hushed tone.

Bettencourt ignored him and snapped another order. "Weapons, make Tubes One and Two ready with F-21 torpedoes."

"Mère de Dieu," Max cursed under his breath. He needed clarification of the skipper's intentions, and he wanted it immediately. "Captain?" he hissed. "What the *hell* are you doing?"

Bettencourt ignored Max and rested his hands on the navigation table, fingers fanned out, studying a tactical display. "Fire Control, get a range and bearing fix on the target. Designate her Echo One. Helm, make turns for five knots ultra-silent running. Take her below the thermocline."

Max shuddered. He realized Bettencourt prepared to engage the enemy submarine and hide below the thermocline—a layer of seawater of variable density that reflected sonar waves much as layers of variable air density created a mirage.

"Thermocline at one-twenty meters, Captain," Lieutenant Rousseau reported.

"Very well. Helm, level off at one-forty. Sonar, set active pinging for two-hundred fifty decibels. One ping only from our bow array on my mark."

Max had to convince Bettencourt to stand down, and do it with finesse.

"Captain, if you irradiate the enemy, they will know we observed her actions."

"That is exactly correct, Monsieur Devereaux. I want every goddamned seaman aboard that enemy boat to feel that ping and shit in his pants. I intend to rattle the fillings out of their teeth. Before we send her to the bottom."

"Active sonar will divulge the location of *Le Terrible* and invite counterattack."

"I intend to launch my weapons before the shit storm. As soon as that enemy boat levels off, I will run two torpedoes up her ass."

"You cannot do this. There are issues above your security clearance level."

Bettencourt glared at Max. "You display remarkable knowledge of submarine warfare, for a civilian," he spat. "However, I am in command of this warship, and care little of your issues. Those fucking Persian spooks just executed a French citizen, a retired Naval Officer. Furthermore, that Iranian warship penetrated French waters. An act of *war*."

"Captain—"

Bettencourt held up his hand.

Max noticed seamen in the Control Room eavesdropped on their altercation. He knew they resented civilians aboard their boat, especially covert agents. If looks could kill, his body would be in first stage of rigor mortis.

"Captain Bettencourt," Max whispered, "I do not wish to challenge your authority to command your ship. However, I must determine the intentions of those enemy operatives, and that sub. If you irradiate or sink her you will defeat my objectives and risk unintended consequences."

"Such as what?" the Captain growled.

"She may transmit a message before she is hit."

"That heap of Russian bear scat cannot transmit when she is submerged. I want to hear the death rattle of that rust bucket as she breaks up on her way to the sea floor."

"My intelligence indicates SSK-635 is equipped with a retractable towed antenna, and can transmit while submerged. "You must stand down."

Bettencourt's eyes flashed fire. He paced the deck in the Control Room, hands locked behind his back, head down. Anxious seaman watched his movement out the corner of their eyes.

Turning to Max he said, "I'll be damned if I ever run from a fight. And I detest spies."

"I am not your enemy. Listen to me. I intend to hunt these psychopaths and their leaders down. I need your cooperation. This is a matter of national security."

"National security? A hackneyed term." Bettencourt glared at Max for several seconds, then turned to Lieutenant Rousseau. "XO, weapons status?"

Rousseau elbowed Max aside as he approached Bettencourt. "Sir, Tubes One and Two are ready in all respects."

"Weapons, open the outer doors on Tubes One and Two," Captain Bettencourt ordered.

Blood hammered in Max's ears. "Captain, the enemy will hear the air surge if you launch your torpedoes."

"Perhaps. But it won't stop them, Monsieur."

Max bit his tongue, grateful for the pain.

"Captain, we have a firing solution on Echo One," Rousseau reported. "Range 7500 meters, bearing three-one-five, depth one-hundred, speed ten knots."

Bettencourt glanced at a pair of illuminated weapons status indicators on the bulkhead. "Very well."

Max blocked the Captain's path, arms crossed. "Captain Bettencourt, I demand you listen to me. The Iranians would never have dispatched the pride of their navy for a low-level operation to ferry spies. We believe the sub and those MOIS operatives are involved in a major terror operation. In addition to a full load of fuel, she took on a cargo of Semtex at Sevastopol. If you engage that boat we may never determine her objective."

"All the more reason to send her to the bottom of the sea. Now, Monsieur Devereaux, get the hell out of my way. You are interfering with my command." He pushed Max aside. "XO, match generated bearings and *shoot*."

"Aye Captain." Rousseau turned to the bulkhead and pulled out a pair of red trigger switches. He twisted the handles clockwise ninety degrees to arm the torpedoes, and jammed them in.

Le Terrible shuddered from the surge of compressed air that forced the torpedoes out of their forward tubes.

"Captain, Torpedoes One and Two away," Rousseau reported. He cast a smug look at Max.

The Weapons Officer reported, "Captain, both torpedoes are running hot, straight and normal. Closing on Echo One at five knots, silent running. Time to impact—one minute twenty seconds."

Max studied an icon-filled tactical display that represented SSK-635, *Le Terrible,* and the torpedoes. Numbers listed bearings, range, depth, speed, and closing rates. In a matter of seconds, the torpedoes' passive sonar would acquire the target, then the torpedoes would accelerate to the locked-on target at fifty knots, their screws screaming.

He had no choice but to disclose Ultra Top Secret intelligence. Stepping in closer, he spoke in a bare whisper. "Captain, the Chinese Navy extended the boat's conning tower to accommodate three vertical missile tubes. They are loaded with short-range Silk Worm missiles armed with tactical nuclear warheads. The warheads are fitted with doomsday detonators."

"Nuclear? The Iranian Navy would never authorize a launch of those weapons. Our retaliation would turn Iran into a heap of molten slag."

"Captain, that boat is under the command of *MOIS.* These people are fatalists. They want to be martyrs. If attacked, they may trigger the doomsday detonators. Are you willing to risk the lives of your crew to soothe your hunger for revenge?"

Max glanced at the tactical display. The torpedo icons started blinking red—their passive sonar had locked onto the target. A shrill beep sounded within the Control Room.

Bettencourt ignored it and paced the deck with his hands behind his back, glancing several times at Max with an evil eye fortified with poison. He cast a sideways glance at his XO, stopped his pacing and turned to Max, a belligerent scowl on his face. "Very well, Monsieur Devereaux. We shall maintain hot pursuit. But if I get an inkling that enemy boat poses the slightest threat to *Le Terrible,* I shall see to it the bottom dwellers enjoy a banquet." He turned back to his XO. "Disarm the torpedoes, cut the wires, and close the outer doors."

Lieutenant Rousseau looked at him in disbelief.

"You heard me," he hissed. "Stand down from battle stations." Bettencourt's voice was filled with pain.

Max let out a deep sigh of relief. Less than twenty-five seconds remained to torpedo impact. The tactical display showed grayed-out icons for the disabled weapons as they fell away toward the sea floor.

He had made an enemy for life, but avoided Armageddon—for now.

Shielded in the enemy submarine's turbulent wake, *Le Terrible* maintained hot pursuit of the *Khomeini* as she passed through the Strait of Gibraltar into the deep Atlantic. On December 7, five hundred kilometers off the Azores, the enemy sub surfaced to recharge her batteries.

Under cover of darkness, the enemy sub rendezvoused with the Liberian tanker *Calypso*. Max observed a fifteen-man commando team debark the tanker to board SSK-635. *Calypso*'s crew removed a tarp and off-loaded a midget sub onto *Khomeini's* aft deck. After supervising the transfer of twenty crates of Semtex from the enemy sub to *Calypso,* the pair of MOIS operatives boarded the tanker.

Khomeini submerged and headed west, destination unknown. *Calypso's* manifest disclosed her port of call in the United States of America.

The Great White Shark.

Three

FBI Headquarters
Washington, DC
Sunday Morning

Kirk collapsed into Brett's executive chair and gazed beyond the window at the US Capitol Building, illuminated with filtered winter sunlight. The Republic's neo-Grecian architecture looked peaceful and calm, in direct contrast to his bleak internal turmoil.

He sighed heavily as he sorted through the drawers and file cabinets in Brett's office, and packed his personal effects—photos, memorabilia, awards, and talismans. All removed, except the big man's brass nameplate on the door: Brett Brosnan. No title, no recognition. High risk, little reward. That went with the violent world of covert operations. One had to be content with blowing a terrorist's brain out.

But in a business where violence was met with superior violence, sometimes it went the other way. Brett took two small caliber bullets in the back of his head leaving stippled powder burns. The double tap—two shots fired in rapid succession, insuring the kill—a hit man's specialty. How and why? The boss was an ace at combat. Getting the drop on him would have required great skill and planning.

Kirk found no witnesses to the execution; no one heard a shot fired, and the garage, security video showed the assassin wearing a balaclava. The HPD medical examiner recovered a pair of deformed hollow point slugs from Brett's skull. Before FBI shut them down, Houston Police detectives found numerous 5.45 x 18 mm shell casings in the garage near the Mercedes and Brett's Crown Victoria.

A weapons expert, Kirk knew the Russian PSM, a knockoff of the Walther PPK, fired those unique center-fire cartridges. The handgun was a Russian Mafiya hit man's weapon of choice. The weapon had little knockdown defensive capability, but was easily fitted with a suppressor, and the compact size perfect for concealment.

Russian wet work. Strange. Omega Six never operated in the Soviet Republics. No one in his right mind, not extremists groups, druggies, or domestic organized crime, whacked a Federal agent because it drew an immediate and overwhelming response from a formidable body of able men and women.

The situation smelled like an open sewer in the Third World.

Brett kept his cards close to his vest until he owned a lay-down hand. He and Brett had better things to do than target assessment, like pulling triggers and directing Hellfire missiles onto high-ranking terrorists who had passed their expiration dates. Pencil pushers called it surgical warfare, but there was nothing sterile about their operation. Targeted killing was assassination. Since the US Government did not acknowledge wet work, officially their unit didn't exist. *What kind of crap had Brett dug his fingers into?*

Brett had a solidly built upper body with a fireplug neck, and a set of massive arms and hands. He could take a man apart without breaking into a sweat. Taking out such a man required exceptional skill of a determined executioner. Poorly trained, but highly motivated religious fanatics didn't fit the MO—jihadists preferred attacks with explosives, never going toe-to-toe.

The scenario of opportunistic Islamic terrorists bringing in hired guns made sense.

Why Brett? What the hell were you into? Was it a revenge killing, or a pre-emptive strike? What was the Houston Ship Channel surveillance all about?

Something stirred in the back of Kirk's mind, small tumblers clunked into place. Weeks earlier, his boss had alluded to a moonlight project. Something to do with oil. *What was it? . . . Oil trading? That was it. Some damned thing about oil trading. Who could keep up with that three-ring circus? Had Brett established a link between crude oil trading and terrorism? Maybe that was his rationale for the aerial Port surveillance.* His boss ran their operation in circumspect fashion and did not rattle easily. The connection had to be heavyweight to get him worked into lather.

Kirk cursed to himself with the conundrum. He felt a pang of guilt, and marinated in his sweat for several moments. He had uncovered nothing of import in Brett's desk and credenza.

Kirk's eyes settled on Brett's safe, but he didn't know the combination. He eyeballed Brett's laptop tied into its docking station that was protected with passwords and encryption keys. Frustrated with his inability to inspect the contents of the damned safe and turn the computer inside out, he deferred the task until Harvey Rucker, Director of Security could provide access.

Duty called. He had to pay his respects to the Brosnan family. With one last visual trace around the office, he rose to leave, disgusted and dejected. He hefted the cardboard carton, flipped off the lights, then snapped a salute to his former commander, mentor, and friend—a lion among men who had taught him everything he knew about covert operations, and serving justice.

There would be justice. He'd see to it, come hell or high Nile.

Deep in thought, Kirk ran a red light and almost missed the turn-off from Arlington Boulevard to Tyson's Corner. An angry motorist blew her horn when Kirk cut across lanes to exit.

Parking on the street was impossible. Word spread quickly within the clannish tight-knit community of active-duty and retired military officers. The wives' grapevine communicated bad news faster than flu virus in a kindergarten. He squeezed the Tahoe into the driveway adjacent to the Brosnan split-level that backed up to a duck pond surrounded by cattails.

After Kirk opened the garage door, he set the carton on the workbench. Emotionally spent, he collapsed into an overstuffed leather chair that needed donation to Goodwill.

Kirk rubbed his weary eyes and glanced around the familiar place. Cast-offs of twenty-one years of marriage lay about, leaving the garage filled with memories. A side-by-side twin stroller faded with age. Cardboard boxes filled with who-knew-what treasures. Suspended from rafters, a pair of matching his and hers Schwinn bikes Kirk and his late wife had given the Brosnan twins as Christmas presents ten years earlier. The 1960 Corvette he and Brett had spent evenings restoring, complete except for dual four-barrel carburetors and various parts cluttering the workbench. Brett would never hear the throaty roar of the potent engine and throbbing exhausts.

Lizbeth Brosnan's soft, harried voice interrupted his reverie and choked him up. "Kirk?" Her Surrey-accented diction and over-the-top vocabulary pealed like a foreign language in need of interpretation. "I noticed your motorcar as you pulled into the drive, and I prepared you a bite." She held a plate loaded with beans, cole slaw, deviled eggs, and snowflake rolls stuffed with Smithfield ham.

Kirk smiled wanly and moved to stand up. "Thanks, Liz."

"Please. Don't rise." The strong woman's hands shook as she put the plate on the workbench. She sat beside him on the rolled arm of the chair and placed a delicate hand on his shoulder.

She managed as always. But inside, he knew, she was an unraveling basket case. He hugged her in awkward silence, at a total loss for words. There was little else he could offer in comfort. For several moments, they sat in death's air, close friends indulging mutual grief.

"Will you not come inside and join us?" she said, pressing a wad of tissues to her tears.

"Liz, I just wanted to stop by for a few minutes to see you and the kids. You know I'm no good at small talk."

"I understand," she said in a hoarse whisper. "And thank you for your kindness."

"Mother?" Beth Ann, a leggy tomboy who had grown into a beautiful woman, stood at in the garage doorway in jeans and a University of Virginia sweatshirt. Her violet eyes with dark circles matched her mother's. She shuffled over and slid onto the other chair arm, then hugged Kirk in a tight grip.

The three of them sat in stillness. Beth Ann's quiet tears moistened one side of his face, her mother's falling soundlessly on the other. Liz passed the wad of tissues to Beth Ann, then took Kirk's hand. "I know how much you and Brett loved the Corvette. When things settle down, I want you to have it."

"Liz, sell it. It's worth over seventy thousand."

"No. Hear me out. I dearly loved my husband, and as much as I wanted him to tell me about his endeavors, he never spoke of them. Not one *word*. And I dared not ask. He lived two lives. I always knew his travails were clandestine. At times, Brett muttered incomprehensible things in his tormented sleep, and would awake with a start—"

"Liz, don't."

She stood and gave him an unblinking look that probed deeply into his soul.

"Kirk, you have that damnable Scots' thirst for blood. I am mindful of your enterprise, and I feel certain you will execute retribution. Take care."

This amazing woman worried about him while Brett's body lay on a cold slab in the Houston morgue. Throat constricted, Kirk tried to swallow. Nothing but dry spit.

"My husband was a courageous and honorable man." Liz rose to leave and tugged Beth Ann's hand. "I want to know about his sacrifice. I want to be cognizant of everything."

After Beth Ann and Liz left, Kirk scooped his untouched plate off the workbench and wandered aimlessly toward the pond. A spot in the bank reasonably clear of duck crap looked good enough to park his butt. He tossed pieces of a roll to a dozen mallards swimming in the pond, his emotions rumbling. Ravenous green-headed mallards waddled ashore and pecked at his ankles, begging for more food, making happy duck sounds—*tucka, tucka, tucka*. Not a care in the world.

Kirk nibbled at the ham sandwiches, feeding a hunger but not the emptiness. Only supreme justice, the assassin laying dead at his feet, would fulfill that. Kirk tossed the rest of the rolls to the ducks. Why should they suffer? He stood up, then strode purposefully to the house.

Beth Ann opened the back door when he climbed the stairs to the porch. The kitchen bustled with the sounds of food preparation. Like a Saint Patrick's Day Feast, but none of the joy. That the Brosnan family friends were throwing an Irish wake in the midst of a tragedy made their generosity and kindness all the more stirring.

Kirk approached Beth Ann. "Where's your brother, Honey?"

"The den." Her voice was a bare whisper.

Kirk felt uncomfortable and out of place in the crowd. Needing a clear mind for the duty ahead, drowning his sorrows in alcohol was unthinkable. He patted Beth Ann's back, then headed down two half-flights of stairs to find four young men in the den zoned out like zombies, the Army-Navy game on a big screen TV, sound muted.

Beth Ann's brother Mark, a fullback dressed in the distinctive grey uniform of a West Point plebe, set his beer bottle on the coffee table and rose to shake hands.

Kirk pointed to the laundry room across the hall.

Mark followed and pushed the door closed behind them with his foot.

Standing there in uniform, eyes blazing, Mark Brosnan echoed his father's likeness, demeanor, and raw intestinal fortitude when the big man had led a column of armor in combat against Saddam's venerated Republican Guard.

Air filled with choking yellow-brown dust and sulfurous smoke from burning oil wells left a vile taste in Kirk's throat. The tenor and tactility of war—friendly artillery rounds ripped holes in the sky, and thumped on dug-in enemy fortifications and armor. As the echoes of artillery faded, Apache helicopter gunships roared overhead. The distinctive scream of a Warthog's twin turbines rattled the fillings in his teeth. The hellish whistle of the incoming Iraqi 120 mm mortar barrage and the crash-boom of the explosions amplified by adrenaline came through in surround sound. Ground shudder. The pungent smell of burnt flesh. The stench of burnt cordite. Pain. Excruciating pain—*pain beyond description.*

Brett bit the edge of a plastic wrapper and tore open a sterile compress to close a gaping six-inch shrapnel wound that had split Kirk's back like a melon thwacked with a machete.

Kirk's commander had risked his own neck by breaking cover to pull him to safety, and had prevented him from bleeding out. Now he owed it to Brett's family—the family embodied by the young man standing before him.

If the Bureau followed normal procedure, Kirk knew the Deputy Director would assign Brett's case to an agent who had no emotional involvement, then he'd be deprived of the opportunity to hunt down his friend's killer. No way in hell could he allow that to happen. If the DD wouldn't come around, Kirk wasn't above turning rogue. To hell with the consequences. Kirk placed a hand on the plebe's shoulder.

A signal passed between them sealing the blood oath—a word of honor.

Mark flexed his fingers into fists, "Bring me the bastard's balls back in a jar."

No stranger to killing, in combat fire between separated adversaries engaged in ear-splitting battle frenzy or in face-to face in a death-lock embrace with the enemy, Kirk knew what he had to do. He was skilled at it. He'd plan it. He'd be cold about it. He'd exact retribution on Brett's killer the way his Scottish Highland ancestors had paid back the ruthless English invaders.

He'd cut their fucking guts out.

Four

FBI Headquarters
Washington, DC
Monday Morning

With itching bloodshot eyes and a jutting jaw that accentuated Kirk's steely determination, he strode purposefully past Brett's office headed toward the corner executive suite. There was never enough time, or evidence. He had slept six hours in the last two days, and his eyes felt like they had been skewered with toothpicks. He had little on the case, no more than a nagging feeling that Brett sunk his teeth into something before his death—something festering and about to erupt.

In the reception area, Hannah Morrison, the Deputy Director's secretary, studied him with puffy red eyes over her computer monitor.

"Kirk, you look like I feel. Can I get you anything? Coffee?"

"Black coffee and a couple of Extra Strength Tylenol, if you have them." At least the throb in his head wasn't a migraine.

"Go on in. I'll bring them to you."

Kirk rapped his knuckles on the door jam or the corner office, pulled the door closed behind him, and dragged his ass to a chair, looking wearily around. The office was decorated with trophy trout mounted on walnut plaques, and black and white landscape photos reminiscent of Ansel Adams.

Kirk had the highest respect for the DD, a no-nonsense crackerjack, a man's man who had seen a lot during his career. It showed in the lines on his face—canyons deep enough to guide a tour group through, and blazing gray eyes that advertised the intensity with which he operated twenty-four hours a day. He retained a Marine Corps high and tight buzz cut, a remnant from running PBRs up the Mekong River during the dark days of Viet Nam.

Walter pushed a pile of paperwork aside, slid his reading glasses to the tip of his nose, then rubbed his eyes with his thumb and forefinger. Reaching for his coffee mug, he looked at Kirk expectantly over the top of his glasses, a deep frown on his forehead.

Talk about being in the hot seat. Kirk's ass burned, and Walter knew how to grill meat. He wanted an all-hands-on-deck response to Brett's assassination, and Kirk had a hell of a time convincing the DD to shut that down. Now Walter wanted answers.

He had damned little to report on his investigation other than a hunch the hit was terror related. But his hunches proved uncannily accurate. He had to make his case to retain investigative authority and keep out everyone else, if for no other reason, national security. Searchlights and magnifying glasses, the last thing they needed. The media and political opportunists would have a banquet picking meat off the Omega Six corpse.

Hannah entered the office, set a mug of coffee on a napkin on the front edge of the desk along with the Tylenol.

"Anything else, just buzz," she said and patted him on the shoulder.

Kirk nodded thanks, popped the caps into his mouth and washed them down with bitter brew, wishing the literal and figurative headaches would go away. He looked into Walter's expectant eyes and heaved a sigh.

"As you know, Brett and I were off duty, taking a couple days vacation. Harvey Rucker provided the combination and computer passwords. Nothing in his safe offered a clue, but Brett left his laptop in the docking station on his desk. I decrypted his computer files."

Walter raised his eyebrows. "Anything?"

Kirk nodded. "A file folder called 'Benefits.' At first, I thought it was personal stuff. Pension and medical benefits. But when I opened a sub-folder, it contained incoherent, random notes. I spent all day and night trying to make sense of the stuff. I organized the notes chronologically, by topic, names, whatever."

Walter pursed his lips. "Must have been a bootleg project. We don't have an op by that name." Walter's voice sounded like loose gravel in the bed of a pick-up truck.

"He never filled me in either. Made me dig harder. I think he was working a tenuous thread and developing his thesis. That's why we never heard of it."

Walter nodded and set his coffee cup on a coaster. "Makes sense."

Kirk chewed the inside of his cheek. "From what I gather, he was brainstorming a theory people benefited from terror attacks."

Walter scratched an eyebrow. "How?"

"Islamic terrorists are funded with oil money. When the price goes up after an attack, they're doing the Watusi out in the street, running around with checkered flags on their heads, shooting holes in the sky with Kalashnikovs."

"Get to the point," Walter growled.

"Sir, Brett's thesis is that inside players were buying crude oil futures prior to terror attacks."

"Islamic terrorists buying crude oil futures?" Walter propped his elbow on the desk and rubbed his buzz-cut.

"That requires deep pockets and a level of sophistication damn few people possess. Pardon the pun, but they must have made a killing on nine-eleven. Jihadists are not the circus clowns the media make them out to be."

"If they have the will, they'll find a way. But, it doesn't fit with their MO—a slew of illiterate religious nuts running around blowing people up, mostly their own. Well-heeled Arabs, some educated in the West, a few in Bahrain and Dubai with oil trading savvy, fund those nutcases. If they were aware of an op going down, they'd load the boat with oil futures."

"Don't you think that'd be too damned transparent?"

"At first glance. Brett's files included some trading history. Crude oil is the largest commodity trading on the world's markets. The volume of contracts is immense—it's the needle in the haystack thing."

Walter sucked his teeth. Kirk had scored a point.

"Why hit Brett in Houston?"

Kirk leaned forward to drive the point home. "Brett had me pull an aerial surveillance over the Port of Houston. I don't believe in coincidence. In our line of work, it's a four-letter word. There's a connection. And I'm gonna find it."

Walter threw his glasses across his desk, then met Kirk's eyes. "Kirk, you're the best counterterrorism operative in the Bureau, but you're no homicide investigator. There are hundreds in the Bureau more qualified. I cut you some slack, but you're out of your depth here."

Kirk's temples throbbed. He had to lay down his hand, containing a single wild card. He leaned forward to drive his point home.

"Brett's hit was thoroughly planned and brilliantly executed. We have few solid clues. But, I have a theory. Suppose a deep-pocket closet jihadist, a guy with trading moxy, found out that Brett was digging around, asking questions. The designated hitter had to be professionally trained to get the drop on Brett. Terrorists are getting smarter, and it is becoming more difficult for them to move in and out of the US. They bring in a hired gun, maybe Russian Mafiya or former Spetsnaz or KGB. These people can move in and out of the US with impunity. They take Brett out with a pre-emptive hit."

"Pre-emptive? Why do you think that?"

"Counter counterterrorism." Kirk slashed the air with his hand. "They decapitate the commander of Omega Six so they can finish their mission."

"*Mission*? What kind of mission?"

Kirk rubbed a couple of fingers against his temple. "I smell camel shit, but I have no clue. The hit fits the profile of a man or organization that doesn't have a political or religious agenda. Or a private grudge. Maybe someone financed the perps' operations—a contract hit. Rich Arabs pump money into so-called Muslim charities that are al-Qai'da piggy banks. It wouldn't be much of a stretch for them to take it up a notch with inside oil trading. *Benefits.*"

Walter reached into his credenza and pulled out a package of Rolaids. He countered, "These fundamentalist Islamic psychos can be creative in ways we can't comprehend. I can't fault your brainstorming. That's one of your assets. But Omega Six is buried under so many layers of black, it looks like tarpaper. Explain how Islamic terrorists could penetrate that level security."

Kirk set his empty coffee mug on Walter's desktop, and took a deep breath. "Maybe they weren't Islamic terrorists."

Walter's eyes formed slits.

"I have reason to believe we have a mole," Kirk said. "A fucking traitor in our ranks."

Walter raised his bushy eyebrows.

Kirk said, "The bastards who killed Brett were waiting for him in the Omni Hotel garage. They knew he was going there. He was ambushed."

"How could they possibly know?"

"Only thing I can figure is they intercepted Brett's text message to meet me in the Omni bar. Our phones are encrypted, but that wouldn't deter KGB."

"God Almighty." Walter then pushed himself heavily out of his chair, and stepped to a window with a spectacular panorama of the Washington Monument. He turned to look at Kirk in disbelief, then returned his gaze out the window. After a moment, he took his seat at the desk. He leaned on his forearms with a grimace. Rubbed an eye with the heel of his hand, like scrubbing without water.

"This crude oil trading thing has the stench of the District after a two-month garbage strike. I'll buy into that theory, but the mole?" Walter shook his head. "I don't know. I shudder to think about it."

"Sir. I don't know I'm right. It's a hunch, or maybe a brain fart, but you know I've been through a few hairy operations. I survived on my wits and my sixth sense. Sometimes leaving the skin of my teeth behind. We can't rule out a mole. How else would they have known?"

Walter rubbed his calloused index finger against his forehead. "If Brett was investigating oil trading, it makes sense, but I'm still not buying. The recovered slugs and shell casings may be our first lead, but I'm not optimistic. Your theories are shot full of holes. Swiss cheese."

"I'm not sold on the scenario either. That's why I want to run it to ground."

If Kirk had any hope of hunting down Brett's killer, he would have to lay out his plan.

"I'm sure you realize bringing in the hounds might feel good, but that'll be the end of Omega Six, unless we head them off with psychological warfare."

Walter raised a skeptic eyebrow.

"Plant seeds of doubt and deception. The media usually get it wrong anyway, so we get HPD to spin the attack as an attempted robbery on a Federal employee. Have them disclose they recovered a couple of deformed .22 caliber slugs from the Brett Brosnan's head with no identifiable markings. Serves two purposes—gets the heat off Omega Six, and may fake out the perps."

Walter nodded.

Scored another point. "You know I'm tight with the CIA spooks. If we have a mole, I'll bury his ass six feet under."

The furrows on Walter's face deepened.

Missed an easy three-pointer. "Walter, this is a counterterrorism op. That's my bag. I want the goddamned job. I can keep a lid on it."

The DD sighed heavily. "Kirk, you have an uncanny ability to get inside the enemy's head. And you have a ruthless killer instinct. These fucking people need a dose of ruthless. But your political skills suffer, to say the least. Hoof in mouth syndrome. You have to put your brain in gear before you mouth off."

"Yes, sir. I'll work on it."

"You'd better." Walter tented his fingertips. "Effective immediately, you take the point. The General's moved you into Brett's slot as Commander of Omega Six. It's a super-grade position. Congratulations." Walter reached to shake hands.

"Thank you, sir. I just wish it were under better circumstances. Any restrictions? What are my rules of engagement?"

"Extraordinary measures are called for. There's to be nothing clean or neat about it. If you stomp on somebody's civil rights, we'll worry about that later." Walter pointed at Kirk. "Be creative and make them fear for their lives. Fuck them over . . . then terminate the bastards. Take care of that mole. And remember the Thirteenth Commandment. Don't get caught."

Kirk relaxed knowing he was in control.

"Brett was visiting a friend in Houston," he said. "Travis Buchanan, his college roommate at A&M—the CEO of Houston Energy Resources. HPD has already grilled him, but I want to interview him face-to-face. Maybe I can develop a lead. Something subtle might have fallen through the cracks—soft evidence like Brett's demeanor and behavior. Stuff like that."

Walter nodded with a contemplative look. The Deputy Director did not get to the top by acting stupid. He looked like he had another item on his agenda.

"You'll need a lot of help."

Kirk wanted people he could work with and trust. "Yes, sir. I wanna bring in a couple of our Russian and Arabic speaking agents and CIA Case Officers. Hunters. Target spotters, and shooters. Demo experts."

Walter ran his tongue over his teeth, and reached for the phone. "Hannah, send her in."

Hannah opened the office door and waved in an apprehensive-looking Asian woman. Dull black hair, thirtyish, decked out in a frumpy Hillary Clinton pants suit—a style selected by women who looked bitchy and sex-deprived. With her frightened wide-eyed look, emphasized with an overdose of mascara and eyeliner, she reminded him of a startled raccoon caught in a floodlit garbage can. Someone should teach her how to apply makeup. She could take half of it off and look twice as good.

The woman glanced at him, took a seat, and plucked at the crease in her god-awful pants suit. It appeared to be a nervous compulsion rather than a need to straighten the knife-edged crease. At least her nails weren't bitten to the quick.

"Michele, this is Special Agent Kirk Magnus," Walter said. "Kirk's now commander of Omega Six. Kirk, meet Michele Li."

Why the hell did he divulge Top Secret information to this waif? Kirk was in no mood to display social niceties, with terrorists on the loose in the US of A and his commander's body cooling in the morgue.

She shifted in her seat to face him.

"I'm pleased to make your acquaintance, sir." She offered a limp hand that felt like he had dipped his mitt into a bucket of shucked clams.

Walter turned to his credenza to pour himself another cup of coffee from a stainless-steel carafe.

Taking his cue, and having a gift for sizing up people in seconds, Kirk decided she was a woman who hadn't pulled her act together. But then, his record of reading women sucked.

"What are your bona fides, Miss Li?"

"I earned a BA in Psychology from U C Berkeley, Master's in Forensic Accounting from Georgetown, magna cum laude. I was the Assistant Secretary for Protocol in the White House after I graduated from the Academy."

"I see. What's that mean? The protocol business? In one sentence—more or less." Kirk cast a sidewise look at Walter.

Walter studied his fingernails, chewing on Rolaids.

The waif looked over a pair of goofy-looking half-glasses clipped to a black lanyard around her neck. "I expedite things."

"You *expedite* things?" Kirk rolled his eyes. "Can you be more specific?"

Her face reddened. "I put my contacts to use."

Kirk sighed and frowned at his boss. *A political animal. Jesus H. Christ.*

"Kirk, maybe you'd like to know about Michele's role here. She's going to be working with you."

"What?"

Kirk sat bolt upright. His experiences with women on the front lines ran south of appalling—women balked under kill-or-be-killed scenarios. He had lost three good men during a Desert Storm firefight when a female officer under his command fucked up. And it wasn't the first time he'd seen women on the front lines freeze when it was time to drop the hammer. This woman would be scared shitless with the first shot fired. He'd rather French-kiss a pit bull than work with another woman.

Walter wiped his hand over his mouth. "Michele's your new partner."

"What?" Kirk's head throbbed. He felt like he had the wind knocked out of him.

The waif packed a weapon and a badge of authority. But, she didn't have a fucking clue. "Walter, for Chrissake, I'm under deep cover. You know I like to work alone or at least with battle-hardened men. Sir, I gotta have somebody cover my six. But, a woman? An *accountant* with training wheels?"

Michele's face turned the color of pickled beets; Walter frowned.

Kirk took a deep breath and sighed. "I don't see Miss Li enjoying a free-fall night jump into Indian country packing a sniper rifle and sixty-pound backpack. She'll get her ass blown away."

"It's my ass." Michele stood. "I don't need to take this." Turning to Walter she said, "Sir, I see no need to continue this meeting." Michele looked mad enough to jam Walter's letter opener in Kirk's jugular.

With Michele's face flushed, Kirk couldn't tell if she was about to blubber or claw his eyes out. Sympathy would weaken his resolve to establish a relationship that had to remain as taut as a garrote. He turned his head toward Walter, eyebrows up, mouth hanging open.

The DD glowered at him.

"Michele, take a seat," Walter growled. He jabbed a finger at Kirk. "I don't want an attitude. I could send your ass down to the third floor to work Computer Crime. You don't get a vote on this one."

Shit. Kirk cursed his bad luck. "But she's had no covert ops training."

"Michele's White House title was a cover. She acted as the General's aide."

Caught off guard, Kirk knew the man referred to as "the General" was a four-star—General Gus Nance, the President's National Security Advisor.

"Ms. Li is well aware of clandestine operations," Walter continued. "She has personal and political skills you lack, and can handle some of your administrative burden. Maybe, temper your sexist attitude. You think you earned it, but you'd better get over it."

Kirk nodded silently. He cast a sideways glance at Michele, wondering how much damage her self-esteem had suffered during her White House stint. Politics corrupted everything, and everyone.

Well, she'd blend in with the wallpaper, no doubt about it, and he hated bureaucratic bullshit. Besides, he didn't want to get crosswise with the General, the man who called the shots for Omega Six.

"At least that makes sense," he muttered.

Walter glowered over the top of his glasses.

Kirk shrugged. "Sorry, sir. Should have 'recalibrated' my words." He made air quotation marks with his fingers.

"You'd do well to keep your politically incorrect comments buttoned up in your Jockey shorts. We're *not* negotiating. You're on the edge of burnout, and you have to come up to speed quickly to find out what Brett was into.

And what about his killers?

"Yes, sir." Kirk let out a deep breath.

"Alright then. Let's move on." Walter gave Michele a nod.

With her index finger, she pushed the glasses up her nose and turned to Kirk.

"Special Agent Magnus," she said, avoiding eye contact. "I'm certain you will find me competent."

Yeah right. He stared at her for a moment—*Minnie Mouse.* He had no time to babysit a timorous rookie. He pressed the heel of his hand to his forehead.

"Proceed, Michele," Walter ordered, rolling his hand in a 'get moving' gesture.

Her eyes flickered toward Kirk as she snapped open a brown leather portfolio embossed with the presidential seal.

"I've arranged for a Falcon 2000 for our use. Based at Andrews," she squeaked. "And access to a CIA Gulfstream V."

She's pissed and trying to get her act together. But, how the hell did she arrange rides like that? His usual transportation was commercial coach or a beat-up Crown Victoria festooned with aerials and hubcaps any moron would recognize as a cop car. Whenever possible he used his three-year old Tahoe that packed more heat and blended in. A G5 was good for overseas flights. *Good thinking.*

It suddenly occurred to Kirk that Walter had been playing him like one of those trout. The decision to promote him to command had already been made before their meeting; hence, Michele's being ahead of the game.

Walter and the General must have drawn the same conclusions as he—Brett's killing was tied into a terrorist plot.

Terrorized minds thought alike.

Kirk looked at Michele. "That's a good start," he grumbled.

Michele tucked her hair behind her ear and touched her lips with the tip of her tongue. "I've also arranged for the reassignment of Robert Childress and Ignacio Torres from the Newark field office to help with our investigation. I understand these men were former Army officers you recruited."

"That is correct. Cool Rob and Nacho shoot good, and blow up enemy," Kirk wisecracked.

She sucked her lips in and winced, then turned back to her notes.

"Any weapons or surveillance equipment you need, I can get from Quantico within a few hours. We can draw in additional manpower from the field offices and headquarters, as required. I've also arranged for Top Priority on this mission, and that includes forensics we may need."

We? At least it appeared she was on top of the administrative garbage heap. Kirk glanced at her portfolio. Michele's handwriting looked like a barnyard of chicken scratches—a sign of genius? Or idiocy?

"Miss Li, you are about to enter the lion's den without as much as a chair and a whip."

"It can't be worse than the White House," she said, meeting his eyes fully for the first time. "General Nance explained the risks to me. I joined the FBI for a purpose—to fight injustice and terrorism."

An idealistic cynic. Now that was a twist. At least they had two things in common. But, crawling in the dirt held more risk than pushing paper.

"Miss Li, in your *spare* time, I want you to develop proficiency in use of your weapon. I'll make arrangements to enroll you in a crash course in undercover field craft at the Farm."

"That's not necessary. I practice at the basement range twice a week. I'm qualified as expert." She removed her glasses, allowing them to dangle on the lanyard. "Camp Peary? Been there, done that. No tattoos to prove it." Michele forced a smile.

He studied her for a moment, wondering if he had underestimated the mousy-looking woman.

She shook the unkempt bangs out of her eyes and moistened her lips—a gesture he interpreted as one of confidence. She said, "I've set up a lunch engagement with a Mr. Travis Buchanan at the Petroleum Club in Houston at thirteen hundred tomorrow. I've also made hotel reservations at the Omni Hotel near the Galleria, in case we have to spend the night."

"No. You can't allow a crime scene to cool off. This won't wait another day. I want to meet with the Special Agent in Charge of our Houston Field Office—this afternoon. Tomorrow morning we'll meet with the ME to witness Brett Brosnan's autopsy. Afterward, we will inspect the crime scene, and interview the HPD detectives. I'll meet you at the Andrews hangar in two hours. From here on out, you are to have a bag packed and your service weapon with you at all times, a round chambered. When confronted with a threat, you are you use deadly force, without hesitation. Clear?"

"Yes, sir. Absolutely. I would like you to think of me as your administrative assistant," Michele said, her eyes steady on him. "I'll try to stay out of your way."

And a mind reader.

She sat back, closed her portfolio and removed her glasses, then placed her hands in her lap, fingers interlocked, posture correct.

Miss Prim and Proper. Kirk realized he misjudged Michele. The woman had the right stuff—balls in her panties.

So much for first impressions. Follow my lead, Michele, and you'll do just fine.

"Call me Kirk," he said, offering his hand again. He broke into a smile that did not hurt.

"Oh. Michele." She took his hand and held with a firm grip and a confident smile.

Walter stood ram-rod stiff behind his desk. "Alright. Any questions?"

"No sir." Kirk stood, and shook Walter's hand. "Michele? You ready to move out? Sounds like you're on top of things."

Special Agent Michele Li had aced the first test. But, the final exam was out in the field. Under fire.

Five

TransNational Energy Tower
Houston, Texas

With Kirk at the wheel on the Interstate 610 Loop, Michele cast an admiring glance. She found she had a hard time taking her eyes off the intriguing warrior. He was beyond brutally handsome—deep blue eyes that glowed with intensity, dishwater blond hair, rugged features—tall and broad-shouldered with muscles that were created not by machines, but by the weight of his mission. His smile seemed almost cruel at times, other times, reassuring. Under that casehardened veneer was a man worth knowing—a man with considerable depth of conviction—a real man. She felt safe and took comfort in being around him.

Outspoken, sexist and brutally honest, Kirk bought into political correctness with a wooden nickel. He was more spit than polish. She understood how women would be attracted to him, but he was the kind of man not many people would approach, unless they had to. Kirk was jaded, dangerous-looking, a take-no-prisoners loner, quick-tempered, and very smart. He wore a hard shell of hurt and loneliness, but she sensed an inner strength of kindness—a sense of raw determination and duty.

Kirk was unaware that she had worked indirectly for him, under cover in the White House. She realized he had tested her in the Deputy Director's office, when she had not been at her best—six hours sleep the previous two days, not even time to change clothes. Too busy expediting things for Omega Six.

A year earlier, Michele had caught a glimpse of Kirk when he and Colonel Brett Brosnan had slipped into the White House late at night to join the President and General Clayton Nance, the National Security Advisor—her boss. Kirk wore Class A uniform adorned with Delta Force insignia—a delta and lightning bolt superimposed on a sword. He wore gold eagles on his epaulets and a Distinguished Service Cross pinned to his left breast, complemented by a slew of ribbons and commendations called "fruit salad".

Two weeks later, Michele and the General sat transfixed in his office watching high-resolution satellite video. The Keyhole satellite zoomed-in on the remote mountainous village of Rahimyar Khan located in northwest frontier of Pakistan. The gray-tone infrared image showed a pair of Hellfire missiles launched from a Raptor drone as they bore down. The missiles took out fifteen Islamic Jihadists conferring in a *majlis,* along with their leader, the Taliban warlord, Mohammad Khan—Number One on the Omega Six Top Forty hit list. The attack was in retaliation for Haqqani's ordering a Jordanian double agent into a CIA base camp on a suicide mission. Michele's fiancé and four others were blown to pieces.

Kirk Magnus, an assassin's assassin, became her idol.

Kirk must have felt her stare. He took his eyes off the freeway crowded with Christmas shoppers, and glanced at her. "What?'

"Just thinking," Michele said. "I know about the DSC. I know about Haqqani. I know a lot about you. We think we'll make a good team."

"I know." Kirk pulled the rental car out of bumper-to-bumper traffic on Interstate 610 loop and exited for the Houston Galleria. After finding a parking spot in an underground garage, he and Michele stepped out of the car. His sunglasses fogged up.

"My god," Michele said. "And I thought Washington was humid. If I were wearing makeup it would have avalanched on my face."

Kirk laughed. "This city was built in the middle of a steaming swamp. Clothes and underwear are serious liabilities."

He checked out her readiness and attire. It looked like she had worked on her appearance. She had a well-scrubbed look, decent eye makeup, a white blouse, and blue blazer. A form-fitting skirt and stylish pumps looked good. *Was her SIG concealed?*

"You packing?"

Michele slung a Gucci handbag over her right shoulder. She patted the slight bulge in her handbag. "I'll shoot through it if I have to. Trick I learned from an Amazon at Quantico, named Carla Calabrese."

"Plan on it. After Brett's hit, we have to assume we're under surveillance. A little paranoia goes a long way." He opened the back door of the sedan to retrieve his jacket, then caught her eye. "Michele? I want to attend this meeting by myself, if you don't mind. It's kinda personal."

"That's OK. I understand. . . . When we find the perp, will you take him out?"

Caught off guard, Kirk remained silent for a moment, then said, "Yeah, I'll kill him. I owe it to his family."

Michele tucked her hair behind her right ear, took a deep breath and said, "Kirk, I want you to know, I've thought about this a lot." Her voice became husky. "I'm with you on this. All the way. It's personal for me too."

She turned and walked off toward the Galleria, heels clicking on the concrete.

Kirk made his way through the underground garage to the TransNational Tower elevator bank. He entered the open car, and pushed the button for the top floor—the Petroleum Club.

The elevator rose briefly and stopped at ground level. Two men stepped on. As the car rose to the 80th floor, he observed their reflection in the lacquered elevator brass panels.

An Arab with a groomed mustache and goatee that looked like they had been chiseled into place carried a Louis Vuitton alligator briefcase in one hand and rolled a string of black coral and amber worry beads in the other. Nattily dressed in a Savile Row suit, he sported a diamond-encrusted watch on his left wrist the size of a pizza. His watch and cuff links glittered like plundered treasure. The man lived a privileged life, used to having his way. Arrogant, firmly in control, and haughty, the regal-baring Arab was no pretender.

The distinctive bulge of a firearm in the other man's black leather jacket increased Kirk's vigilance. The thug had Eastern European features and a suspicious look with the sneer of someone daring disrespect. And the physique to do something about it. Kirk knew the type all too well. Russian Mafiya hit men—the type who would take a victim down for a price, and never lose sleep over it.

In twenty years of experience, he had never witnessed an Arab willfully associating with a Russian. Muslims detested the godless communist heathens.

Kirk's skin prickled. The situation was unique. But, so was Brett Brosnan's assassination. The Arab-Mafiya correlation had to be a sinister plot like something out of a Lee Child novel. He wanted to dismiss the conjunction, but he couldn't get it out of his mind. These customers warranted observation. He wasn't buying. He didn't believe in coincidences.

Kirk allowed the men to exit the elevator first and followed them down a plush corridor toward the Petroleum Club restaurant. The bodyguard murmured something unintelligible to the Arab, who nodded; then the bodyguard turned to his left and entered the men's room leaving his charge in the corridor.

Kirk followed the Russian out of need to relieve his bladder.

As they washed their hands, the man's close-set gray eyes met Kirk's in the mirror. His cold eyes portrayed utter indifference—the eyes of an experienced killer. His menacing demeanor suggested a former KGB agent or Spetsnaz—Soviet Special Forces. A hooked nose once broke a head with a bony crown, and hair like a five o'clock shadow.

When the bodyguard passed behind Kirk and reached for a towel from the neat stack on the granite counter, he brushed his hand against Kirk's back, signaling he was aware Kirk packed a concealed weapon. But then, half the population of Texas packed concealed firearms.

"Sorry," the bodyguard said in Russian-accented English. He lifted a linen towel off the counter, offered a second to Kirk with a hand the size of a Polish ham, a twinge of a smirk on his ugly mug.

"*Spasiba,*" Kirk replied, leaving no doubt he had made the Russkie. He wiped his hands on the towel as they eyeballed one another like bull elk ready to lock horns. *Mess with me comrade, and you'll have a half-inch hole going in your chest and one the size of my fist coming out.*

Kirk gave him a wan smile, tossed the soiled towel into the hamper, and walked out the door toward the restaurant.

The maitre d' led Kirk to a corner table offering a spectacular view of the city. A rugged-looking gent with a weather-beaten face like the Marlboro man rose from his seat.

"Kirk? I'm Travis Buchanan. First thing I want to say is I'm really sorry about Brett's tragic death."

Kirk shook his hand, which was broad, cool, and calloused, befitting Travis' image.

A waiter approached and took their drink orders.

"OK. What can you tell me?" Glancing around, Kirk noted the Arab had joined two other men at a table across the restaurant. He recognized Senator Howard Dreihaus, widely known as the Washington Weasel, seated at the Arab's table. The Arab's bodyguard stood at the entrance eyeballing patrons.

"Brett and I go back a long way. We were roommates at Texas A&M, but we hardly moved in the same circles. After graduation, he took a commission in the Army. I majored in petroleum engineering. I couldn't wait to get out in the oil patch and explore. I drilled a couple of oil wells out in West Texas, using friends-and-family money. The first well produced a puff of dust—"

"Huh," Kirk snorted. He liked the good ole boy stories, and had done his homework on Travis, but he wanted to keep the conversation on track without offense. There was a chance Travis would possess valuable intel. Kirk was determined to extract it.

"Lucked out on the second well. My company is now one of the most successful private petroleum outfits. We're active in the cash and futures markets."

Kirk's pulse kicked up. "You trade crude oil futures?"

"Sure. You know anything about commodity trading?"

"Enough to lose my ass if I tried it."

Travis chuckled. "Futures trading requires talent, steely nerves, and smarts. And deep pockets."

Kirk flicked his eyes toward Dreihaus & Company. "Did Brett ever discuss that business with you, or talk to your traders?"

The waiter appeared with their drinks. Travis knew what he wanted, but Kirk hadn't glanced at the menu. "Give me what he's having," he said.

"I took Brett down to our trading room and showed him around," Travis said, once the waiter left. "He spoke with a couple of my people."

If Brett had talked with those traders, Kirk reasoned, they could have mentioned the interview to anyone.

"Is it important?"

"I don't know yet. . . . When Brett was killed, what happened before that?"

Travis emptied four packets of sugar into his iced tea, and said, "Four of us, Aggie alumni, went quail hunting on my ranch in South Texas. When we returned, we had a few beers and grilled quail at my home. Afterward, Brett returned to the Omni Hotel. The one near the Galleria. Around midnight."

"So Brett talked with your people before you went on the hunt?"

"That's correct. We had lunch here the day he arrived, and then I showed him around my trading room. He had an interest in oil trading and *grilled me* during our bird hunt." Travis took a beat. "Damn, he was a hell of a shot."

After the waiter set out their poached salmon, Kirk leaned forward.

"Over my left shoulder, who those two guys are with Senator Dreihaus—the Arab and the fat cat."

"The beer belly dude with the beagle eyes and heavy jowls is Wade Connors, CEO of TransNational Energy. Wade's money put Dreihaus into State office years ago.

He seems to think he owns Dreihaus. Fucker's grown too big for his britches. It's no secret Dreihaus has aspirations for the White House. Those *hombres* are lower than tits on a warthog."

Kirk fought back a laugh.

Travis continued, "Those politicians show up here all the time grubbing for campaign cash, and promise favors they rarely deliver. I think that's all they do for a living. That and calling one another a liar."

"That's the only time politicians tell the truth. Lying is at the top of their job description. . . . I'm more interested in Ali Baba."

"I don't recognize him. Wade deals with Middle Easterners all the time. He owns a foreign subsidiary that trades with the Iranians. Got a slap on the wrist from the Feds for trading Iraqi oil under the UN Oil-For-Food fiasco. Wade was on a first name basis with Saddam. I will lay ten-to-one a sleazy deal is going down over there."

"How about the Russian muscle? The mutt in the foyer. *Don't look him in eye.* He's a pro . . . . Is it alright if I make a phone call from here?"

"Go ahead. No one will notice."

Kirk retrieved his cell phone, hit a speed dial number, and described the Arab and bodyguard to Michele. He asked her to call the Special Agent in Charge of the Houston Field Office, and send in a photo surveillance team.

Kirk picked at his lunch, mulling over the crude oil futures connection.

"Can you give me a tour of your trading room, and show me some typical trades. Talk me through them?"

"Tour's my pleasure." Travis smiled. "But, our records are proprietary. I realize you can subpoena them. But, I don't want them to become a matter of public record. My competitors would salivate over that information."

"Doubt I'll understand any of it."

"Kirk, I'll do all I can to ensure justice for those bastards. I want Brett's killer hung by the balls with barbed wire. I'd string them up myself, given half a chance. But, that ain't gonna happen. I'll show you whatever you think important. You can take copies, if you classify the records to keep them out of public eye."

"Deal." From the corner of his eye he watched Dreihaus rise from his table, then shake hands with Wade Connors and the Arab. Dreihaus scanned the restaurant before walking out with the Arab's alligator briefcase. Loaded with cash, no doubt.

Kirk and Travis returned to the oilman's office to continue their conversation, and review some trading records. He and Travis looked up from a pile of computer printouts when Michele arrived.

"Did the SAC get a photo recon team over in time?"

She shook her head and frowned. "Hung up in lunchtime traffic. Missed the party by fifteen minutes."

"Damn it." Kirk leaned back in his chair. "Dreihaus and that Arab are up to something."

"That's what I thought too." Michele brushed the bangs out of her eyes. "When it appeared the team wouldn't make it in time, I went into the lobby to hang out. The place was crowded with the noon rush, but I saw both men you described exit the elevator and climb into a stretch limo." She blurted, "I took a couple of photos of the men with my cell phone."

Kirk rolled his eyes.

"I thought it was important," she said, as though she'd read his mind—again. "I memorized the limo's license plate number."

"See anything else?"

"An attractive woman in the back of the limo waiting for them. Elegant looking. Honey-blonde hair."

Kirk fought back a smile. "Did you get photos of her?"

She brightened. "Only this one."

The Arab's shoulder blocked the woman's face. Her short skirt displayed long sculpted legs. *Nifty tits.*

Kirk chewed on the inside of his cheek. "The Arab dude doesn't impress me as the type who'd waste time and effort. He'd no more bring a bimbo to an important meeting than he'd take a sack lunch to a banquet. I think that long-legged babe is a player."

Michele took a seat at the table next to Travis. "I ordered the SAC to run down the license plate. We may get lucky and identify the passengers."

"Good work, Michele. Forward the photos to CIA. I got bad vibes from those two characters."

"That bodyguard gave me the creeps," she said.

"Personality of a used condom," Kirk agreed. He patted a stack of computer printouts. "Let's move on. Brett interviewed a couple of Mr. Buchanan's oil traders right before he was killed. There might be a clue in these crude oil transaction records. Do you understand commodities trading?"

"I have a portfolio of stocks and commodities, and I trade option credit spreads."

Kirk looked at Travis, who grinned and nodded approval.

Michele peered over the top of her half-glasses and said, "If there's something here, I'll find it."

"Alright. I suppose that's good enough for government work." Kirk shoved the stack of computer printouts across the table to her. "These are Mr. Buchanan's most recent crude oil futures records. Brett reviewed them after interviewing a couple of his traders. Take a look; maybe you can spot something."

Michele pulled out her leather portfolio and took notes in furious chicken scratches as Travis walked her through the documents. Kirk squirmed in his seat. He didn't understand a damned thing they said. His thoughts meandered over to the Arab-Dreihaus-Mafiya connection—snakes intertwined, copulating.

After thirty minutes of shuffling paper, Michele removed her glasses. She looked warily at Travis.

"What?" Kirk asked.

"Looks to me that Mr. Buchanan's firm has been trading on inside information," she said with a high timbre in her voice.

Veins bulged in Travis' neck. "There's an easy explanation."

"On al-Qai'da terrorist attacks?" Michelle asked.

That made no sense, Kirk thought. *Travis had already been vetted.*

"Ms. Li got it half right," Travis snapped.

"Then why the correlation?" Kirk asked.

"There's no way in hell we'd know of terrorist attacks in advance. We take positions based on fundamentals, technical charting, news, and market momentum," Travis said. "Sometimes riding on others' coattails."

Kirk took a slug of bottled water, allowing a few seconds for Travis to simmer down. "What is this market momentum stuff? The coattails business?" Kirk's voice was calm, reassuring.

"It's simple enough. The crude oil markets are highly volatile. When a large influx of orders comes in, it may indicate insiders taking positions before news breaks. Our proprietary software triggers alerts, and my traders react. If you have inside information, it's like sticking a fork in another trader's pie. Riding coattails of inside traders is the next best thing."

Kirk asked, "What causes the volatility?"

"There's no world-wide surplus crude oil production capacity. The slightest hiccup or the perception of a disruption in supply, spikes oil prices. A minor production upset could move oil up ten percent, doubling the value of a long position. There's ten-to-one leverage in crude futures."

Kirk let out a silent whistle.

"We import thirteen million barrels a day—over half our petroleum requirements. Little of it from nice places. And the competition for those barrels is fierce." Travis explained. "The US is addicted to foreign oil like a street whore strung out on crack cocaine."

Kirk stood and walked to the widow facing the Port of Houston. "What would happen if terrorists targeted our energy infrastructure, instead of oil supplies?"

Travis sucked in a deep breath. "That's the worst case scenario. We have the Strategic Petroleum Reserve to ease supply shortages, but infrastructure would take months, if not years to repair." He pointed to a wall-hung framed photo of the Port of Houston and the Ship Channel. "There are twenty-three refineries in the Houston area along with a network of buried pipelines that feed the markets. A terrorist attack on a refinery or a pipeline will fire up the price of oil within seconds. Severe damage will bring the US economy to its knees.

"Kirk, I can't think of a more vulnerable or high profile economic target. You can imagine what an explosive laden tanker carrying a million barrels of gasoline or jet fuel would do to the Port of Houston and the surrounding refineries."

A terrorist's wet dream. "There's damned little to stop it from happening. Despite Homeland Security's rhetoric, our ports are not secure. We can't board and search every ship." Kirk tapped his fingers on the tabletop. "Benefits," he murmured. "*Cui bono?*—who benefits?"

Travis shrugged.

Kirk slapped his hand on the table. "Travis, if your guys traded on someone's coattails, then we need to find out *who* is wearing that goddamned coat. Who the hell could have the kind of financial muscle to manipulate the crude oil markets?"

Travis pursed his lips. "Same question Brett asked when I pointed out the oil-terror correlation to him several months ago. The answer is international oil companies, states like Iran, Libya, organized crime, wealthy Arab individuals."

Kirk stared out the window at the downtown Houston skyline. *Wealthy Arabs and Mafiya.* He felt a stab of heat with the connection. "Al-Qai'da doesn't have that kind of scratch. Those trades originated from people in the know—or from the controllers who run the terror ops. Travis, how the hell do we track down inside traders?"

"That'll be tough. The daily trading volume is huge. A regulatory body called the Commodity Futures Trading Commission is supposed to monitor that, but it's a daunting task—unless they're tipped in advance. Maybe the New York Mercantile Exchange records would show where the trades originated—if you could dig them out of a mountain of information."

A perfect job for Michele. Kirk glanced at her. She looked apoplectic, her face flushed, hands shaking.

"Michele, you OK?"

She tossed the bangs out of her pain-filled eyes, and tucked her hair behind her ear. "Mr. Buchanan's records," she gushed, "show an influx of crude oil buy orders within the last two weeks."

"Goddamn it." Kirk slammed his fist on the table, his pulse pounding. "That's why they killed Brett. There's a terror op going down, and he was on to the bastards."

Six

CIA Headquarters
Langley, Virginia

Kirk had learned long ago to recognize when things came to a tipping point. They were far from it. He had a sense of foreboding and felt like he had crawled an inch on a hundred-mile hike. They were moving forward, but not nearly fast enough to rip the case open and spill its guts on the floor. Brett's assassination remained an enigma—a rotten onion wrapped in a riddle that would have to be peeled back, layer after layer.

Flying back from Houston gave him time to organize his thoughts. They had loosely tied Brett's assassination to evidence of an impending terror attack, possibly on the Port of Houston. *But how? And who was running the operation?*

The appearance of the regal Arab and his Russian bodyguard at the Petroleum Club piqued his sixth sense. Michele had earned her stripes with her brazen photos and a brain the size of a planet that she applied to those oil trades. Kirk shifted his eyes off the road and stole a quick glance at her.

New power bob and light touch of eye makeup reflecting renewed confidence from her achievements. So much for first impressions.

Kirk and Michele presented their credentials to an armed guard at a gatehouse. He studied their photos and faces before lowering the tire shredders and directing them toward the VIP parking lot.

Set back in the woods of northern Virginia, the imposing quadrangle was designed to intimidate America's enemies. It kept the Soviets at bay, but failed to deter terrorists hell-bent on cutting the US down to size. This time it would be different. Kirk was plenty pissed off and pumped up. Anxiety building, he felt as if he was closing in on his objective tightening a noose around the neck of the doomed.

They entered the lobby and walked across the famous CIA logo with its sixteen-pointed compass star, shield, and eagle. Michele strode beside Kirk as he approached a white marble wall engraved with names of fallen CIA operatives. He paused, and ran his fingertips across several well-worn names.

"Did you know any of these men?" she asked.

He pressed his lips together. "I can relate to all of them." His mentor's name, Brett Brosnan, would be another engraving on an anonymous stone monument.

They presented their credentials at the security desk, declared their weapons, and obtained visitors' passes. When they exited the elevator to the rarified atmosphere of the seventh floor, Dr. Jessica Masters, the Assistant Deputy Director, a Stanford PhD physicist, intercepted them. Her petite figure and shoulder-length platinum-blond hair did little to disguise her stature and daunting presence. Stylishly dressed in a navy-blue suit that clung to her curves, Jessica wasn't just photogenic, she was telegenic. Articulate and confident, she often handled CIA case officers on counterterror missions, and acted as the intelligence-gathering arm of Omega Six. In spite of pulling an all-nighter, her glacial ice eyes radiated acuity. They now flashed a warning.

Jessica gathered Kirk's hand to relay the portent of danger with a single word—a word she knew was etched deeply into the back of Kirk's mind—*"Incoming."*

Kirk's muscles tensed into rigid rocks, the scar tissue in his back tingled. Omega Six regarded themselves as tight-knit family— outsiders never privy to their secrets.

"Teddy Jeffers is sitting in on our briefing," Jessica said.

"*What?* You gotta be kidding me. He's just another Washington suit with a shine on his ass."

"Those were my thoughts, exactly. If he were any dumber, he'd have to be watered twice a week like a split-leaf philodendron."

"Who let that fucking dog out? Jessie, we can't have that mutt sticking his nose up our butt."

"The order was passed down from Sixteen Hundred Pennsylvania Avenue. President Omar seemed to think Jeffers could apply his Wall Street expertise to the crude oil futures transactions. Turns out that lawyer is in over his head, gasping for air."

The president surrounded himself with egocentric idiots who pretended there was no Islamic jihad. But you had to dig deep to find a bigger moron than Teddy Jeffers.

"Figures," Kirk said. "Teddy has a much depth as a puddle of piss. He wouldn't know a futures contract from a Mafia contract. You can't fix stupid."

"Or arrogance," Jessica said. "He attempted to manipulate me into holding *our* briefing in *his* office. The man deserves a lifetime underachievement award for bureaucrats with lobotomies."

Conniving asshole. "He's so crooked you could open wine bottles with him. You set him straight?"

"Ran him through the wringer," she smiled, "and hot pressed with a flat iron."

Kirk grinned, amused with Jessica's style.

Barely five feet and ninety-eight pounds, she hit like a heavyweight. Their close bond had been formed ten years earlier when she helped locate and disable a tactical nuclear weapon hidden by al-Qai'da operatives near the base of the Golden Gate Bridge.

"Let the General handle Teddy," Jessica said. "His presence is not the *bad* news."

Kirk frowned. "Huh?"

"Late-breaking intel." Jessica tugged Kirk's hand. "Let's go."

"You recording?"

"Of course. Be cool. Don't break the pottery."

"I'm good. I've quit rolling gutter balls."

Jessica led them into the sanctum sanctorum of the Operations Directorate—the clandestine arm of the Central Intelligence Agency. In the windowless dark-paneled room Deputy Director Walter Munford, General Gus Nance, the President's National Security Advisor, and Theodore Jeffers, Secretary of the Department of Homeland Security, sat at a conference table engaged in conversation.

As Kirk approached the table, Jeffers followed his movement, his pickpocket's eyes shifting, a dour expression on his fat lips. Hair rose on the back of Kirk's neck. After greeting Walter and the General, he didn't bother to extend his hand to Jeffers.

Kirk had Jeffers' number, along with his name and rank—stench. He eyeballed the DHS Secretary with contempt. There was a sneaky, ferret-like look about the bureaucrat, and he had a deep-seated hatred for the military and intelligence communities. Kirk mistrusted all politicians, but that sleazy narcissistic pencil pusher was a red flag. The former Wall Street rainmaker bought his office with 'campaign contributions,' and had a reputation for empire building, backroom dealing, and greasing palms. But, trafficking in classified information for political gain was the shyster's oyster. Jeffers had leaked deeply buried secrets to enhance his status. Kirk knew it, and Jeffers knew he knew it.

Kirk had crossed swords with Jeffers when the Secretary attempted to upstage CIA by passing intel to the *New York Times* of a covert op to take out high-ranking al-Qai'da leaders in Pakistan. As a result of the planted leak, the Taliban captured and beheaded a Pakistani informant and killed six CIA case officers. The spin-doctors at DHS disavowed their role. President Omar turned a blind eye. Kirk vowed never to forget it.

Taking a seat at the head of the table, Kirk made eye contact with General Nance, a wiry and reclusive intelligence officer who had served under numerous administrations, and was high on the short list of people who had unlimited access to the president. Highly regarded by powerful men who sought his counsel, a man known simply as "the General" could send chills down an adversary's spine with a simple gesture or facial expression. The General had recruited Brett and Kirk from Delta Force ten years earlier to form Omega Six. Only a select handful of people knew of the covert unit, or its mission. Now there was one more on the inside—the enemy within. *Jeffers.*

Kirk studied the man out the corner of his eye, half-expecting to smell ozone in the room. Jeffers had the habit of eye fucking everything in a skirt while he was checking to see if anyone was going to wring his fucking neck. Kirk wondered how soon it would be before the General eviscerated the jackass. Pieces of the puzzle were coming together, and now Jeffers presented a risk of it being ripped apart.

"Let's get started," Nance said.

Kirk reached for a tray containing a coffee pot and Danish pastries. "Jessie, anything on that Russian thug?"

Jessica slid folders across the table, stamped *Top Secret – Speculator, Eyes Only,* then said, "We forwarded a set of latent prints recovered from the limo to Interpol and SVU. Russian Intelligence matched them to this man—Ilya Borisov, a one-time Moscow Mafiya don and KGB operative." She keyed her laptop. The wall-mounted monitor displayed a formal portrait of Borisov in Soviet Army uniform—three gold stars and red stripes on his epaulets indicated colonel rank.

"Borisov graduated from Yuri Andropov's KGB charm school and later became the lead interrogator at Lubyanka prison, the master of ceremonies for torture and assassination. Interpol has been on his trail for years. Attribute several murders in Germany and Turkey to him. His trademark is a double-tap. Typical back-of-the-head executions with a Tula PSM 5.45 mm."

The cold finger of revelation went down Kirk's spine. *Identical to Brett Brosnan's assassination. There are no coincidences.* He stared at Borisov's portrait, his pulse pounding in his ears. *A dead Red.*

"Last night, I received a communiqué from French Intelligence that increases the scope and urgency of our investigation. Maxime Devereaux, Deputy Director of DGSE is standing by on a secure two-way video teleconference link." She keyed her laptop to bring up Max's face on a second wall-mounted monitor. "Max, please proceed."

"Feel free to interrupt if you have questions," Max said, in a French-accented baritone. He narrated a video displayed on a second monitor of the SSK-635's rendezvous with the tanker, *Calypso,* off the Azores.

Kirk's jaw dropped as he absorbed the intelligence. *It had to tie in with Brett's assassination and crude oil trading. But how?*

After Max finished his video presentation, the General set his coffee cup down, and leaned forward, a frown on his face. "So, the tanker took on fuel, four thousand kilos of Semtex, and the pair of MOIS spooks. Fifteen commandos offloaded a midget sub from the tanker onto SSK-635, then boarded here?"

"Correct. Elite Takavaran naval commandos," Max replied, "apparently taking orders from MOIS.

"And your intel indicates that Kilo is fitted-out with nuclear missiles?"

"Three five-hundred kiloton warheads," Max replied. "Our submarine, *Le Terrible* lost contact with SSK-635 in mid-Atlantic."

The General rubbed his forehead. "Disturbing, but the US Navy will have to locate and deal with her. Anything else on the tanker?"

Max pursed his lips. "*Calypso's* cargo manifest indicates her destination is the Port of Houston."

The conference room erupted with an entanglement of voices, arguing at cross-purposes. The dominoes went down one after another. Kirk had velocity and was getting battle ready. Sensing things were spinning out of control, the General rapped his knuckles on the table. "Anyone know where that ship is right now?"

"Port Authority claims she's at anchor twelve nautical miles off Galveston Island in international waters," Jessica said. "*Calypso* is scheduled to steam into the Houston Ship Channel within twenty-four hours."

Jeffers sniffed; his head tilted back rotating slowly. "I've got to brief the president on this, along with the National Security Council." He spoke with an officious sneer.

Here we go. Déjà vu all over again, Kirk thought. *Asshole is attempting to hijack our op.*

"You'll do no such thing," The General said, steel in his voice. "Your role here is limited to analysis of crude oil trading." He pointed a leathery finger at Jeffers. "Stay in your sandbox."

Jeffers stared at General Nance with angry eyes, looking like he was about to jump over the conference table. "I don't answer to you!" he snarled. "I'll have your head."

"Not if I have yours first." The General smiled. "I suggest you check out your environment. Sometimes the walls have ears."

Jeffers's eyes grew to the size of ice cream cones. "This is not the end of it."

"It'd better be." The General's acerbic voice was a bare whisper above the hum of the ventilation system.

Jeffers had the common sense of a rutabaga and was probably stupid enough to ignore the General's warning. But the DHS Secretary had the president's ear. He would use every legal gimmick his cadre of lawyers could dig up to short circuit FBI and CIA in an attempt to claim glory for his fiefdom. Kirk knew Jeffer's would fail with the counterterror operation, just as DHS failed to stop the Fort Hood assassin, and jockey shorts bomber.

Kirk caught Jessica's eye. "Let's move on. I'm anxious to see if all this ties in to Brett's assassination."

"There's a connection, and I'll build to it with what we have so far," she replied with a confident tone. "Michele's photos allowed us to confirm the identity of the Arab man—Sheikh Qadr al-Masri."

She keyed her laptop. The wall monitor displayed an array of photos of the Arab in Western and traditional dress as she narrated—the Sheikh shaking hands with diplomats and fretting over global warming with the pregnant chad presidential candidate. The last slide showed a portrait photo of the Sheikh in classic Arabian attire—an *Egal* white cotton head covering that flowed over his shoulders topped with a black corded *Shora* with gold bands.

"A Dubai citizen, al-Masri attended boarding school at Eton. Earned a Ph.D. in Chemical Engineering and a Masters in Finance from Cambridge University. Owns an engineering and construction firm and is on the inside track on large commercial projects in the Emirate. A student of religion and patron of the arts, he's passionate about Egyptian antiquities. Owns hundreds of Arabian horses, and enjoys falcon hunting. Net worth, fifty billion Euros. He's a generous philanthropist, and well-connected with politicians and heads of state."

"The guy has more sides than the Pentagon," Kirk said.

"True, but he manages to maintain a low profile."

"Not too low," Kirk added. "He lives the good life and keeps attractive female company. Any clue of the identity of leggy babe waiting for him in the limo? I think she's a player."

"Nothing on her yet. She's a mystery."

"The Sheikh hooked up with a notorious oilman at the Club named Wade Connors. They sat at a table in the restaurant with Senator Dreihaus. Afterward, the Sheikh passed a briefcase to the Senator. Ten to one it was loaded with something that had lots of zeros behind it."

"Magnus. You seem to have distain for our political leaders." His plump lips spat the words like they were last week's sour milk.

Kirk was tempted to tell the DHS Secretary to go fuck himself. But advising a member of the president's cabinet to perform an impossible act of self-gratification had to be timed just right.

General Nance's stone-cold glare at the shyster said, *"Sock it to the slimy prick."*

Kirk knew he could be physically intimidating with his swagger, muscular build, and penetrating look that showed absolutely no fear. He gave Jeffers 'the look,' and said, "There's good reason for it, *sir*." Kirk used the word as an insult, and offered the thinnest possibility of a smile.

Jeffers studied him for a long moment. A vein in his temple throbbed.

Jessica cast a side-ways glance at Kirk that said, “Cool the sarcasm.” She then cleared her throat, and said, “The Sheikh owns a high-roller stock and commodities firm—Falcon Trading Ltd based in Zurich. Minimum account deposit is one-hundred million Euros. With pattern recognition software, we traced the suspicious crude oil transactions through the New York Mercantile Exchange to Falcon Trading.”

Jeffers waved his hand dismissively, his lips curled into the practiced smile of a sleazy politician. “That proves nothing. Coincidence—“

“There are no coincidences,” Kirk replied. “Only idiots and dead men believe in them.”

Jeffers squirmed as if he had a bad case of hemorrhoids, ignoring Kirk he continued, “Brokerage firms generate the bulk of their profits from proprietary trading—house money.” The bureaucrat pumped out one useless tidbit after another, like string of tasteless sausage.

“That’s true,” Jessica agreed. “However, I wouldn’t rule out one or more of the account holders trading on inside information of pending terror attacks. Unfortunately, unless we can prove criminal activity, we may have a difficult time identifying them, due to Swiss banking laws.”

“Jessica? The General asked. “Do you anticipate any problem in hacking the Speculator’s database to identify the account holders?”

“No sir. We’ll burn through their firewalls without a trace of smoke.”

Jeffers bared nicotine-stained teeth the size of Chiclets. "You realize you're violating Swiss and International Law."

The General's piercing grey eyes seemed to dissect Jeffers. He pulled a cigar out of his vest pocket, ran it under his nose, then stuffed it between his lips, never breaking eye contact with the DHS Secretary. "So is terrorism," he deadpanned out the corner of his mouth. He pulled the cigar from his mouth and studied it. "What's your point?" The General had figuratively flipped a one-finger salute to Jeffers.

Without grasping the significance, the DHS Secretary said, "The CFTC, the Commodities Futures Trading Commission, is responsible for regulatory compliance."

"We know what it is," The General snapped, "and what they're supposed to do."

"They failed to detect the influx of trades," Jessica replied diplomatically, ratcheting down the tension. "Furthermore, Falcon's trades were disguised through proxies and were difficult to detect without hindsight. I'm sure you know crude oil is also traded on several international markets where the CFTC has no jurisdiction."

Jeffers shrugged.

The universal expression of incompetence, Kirk thought. "Jessie, anything else on the Sheikh?"

She nodded. "Qadr owns a security firm, Laarson Sécurité Limited, based in Brussels. Staffed with former Special Forces—Spetsnaz and Stasi. Ten thousand of them guard high-risk facilities around the world. Nuclear power plants and port facilities, including the Port of Houston. His personal bodyguards are former Spetsnaz. Flight plans indicated he arrived in Houston on his private Gulfstream V four days before Brett was assassinated. Two of the Sheikh's associates cleared customs on phony Ukraine passports. One did not leave the US."

The headless Omni Hotel shooter, Kirk thought. Body's probably a crab feast in Galveston Bay. "Bastard's arm has a long reach."

"The hand of hate," Michele interjected.

Stunned into silence, everyone around the table turned to face Michele. She looked to Kirk before continuing, encouraged by what she read as a supportive look. "It's not about money. Al-Masri has more than he could spend in ten lifetimes. It's about *power*. He's been planning this little shop of horrors for years. It is brilliantly conceived, and unlike al-Qai'da's mass murders, his op is designed to achieve *mass destruction*. It is the work of a genius. A megalomaniac. There's a lot to admire about the man, and a lot to fear.

"At age eight, he witnessed his mother's rape and murder by American oil field workers in Dubai. MI5 reports al-Masri has no criminal history, but they said the Sheikh was institutionalized in a psycho ward at Bethlem Royal Hospital in London for a period of three years."

Kirk rolled his hands in a keep-it-coming gesture.

Michele looked at a dossier, and read, "*Master Qadr al-Masri exhibits symptoms of auditory hallucinations, masochism, and delusions of grandiosity or persecution—a paranoid schizophrenic.*" She looked over at Kirk, and said, "I jumped in line and ran the Sheikh's dossier that Jessica provided by a profiler I know at Quantico. Dr. Metzler's take is that the Sheikh sees himself as the last rider in the *Four Horsemen of the Apocalypse*—Death. Angie Metzler says, and I quote, '*He's set to divine apocalypse upon the West.*'" Michele rubbed goose bumps on her arms. "Bottom line: Sheikh Qadr al-Masri is scary-smart. He's motivated by something other than religious zealotry—malignant venom. He *won't* stop until he fulfills his objective."

Kirk was swept off his feet by Michele's ability to take small pieces of information and draw stunning conclusions. Reacting with palpable excitement, Kirk's mind churned. "The Hand of Hate—that's good. Damned good. That Sheikh's psychological underpinnings are more nails in his coffin. Beneath that phony varnish is a loose thread. We tug on it, and his world will unravel."

The silence seemed to roar as Jeffers gave Kirk a stone-cold glare. He said, "Before you entertain that flight of fancy, we should consider another possibility. Sheikh al-Masri may have a legitimate gripe. We should encourage the Secretary of State to entertain behind the scenes negotiations."

Fuck you and the cayoose you rode in on, Kirk thought.

The General started to drive the nails home. "It's time to close the walls in on that bastard," the General said. "Max, can you put a team on the Speculator?"

"Most certainly. Our intelligence indicates the Sheikh financed the Semtex purchase. Some of it was utilized by Iranian jihadists on the aborted Louvre attack last year."

"Jessie? That Sheikh have any other business here?" Kirk asked.

Jessica tossed her platinum-blond hair over her shoulder. "The limo driver picked up both men and the woman at the Warwick Hotel. After his meeting at the Petroleum Club, the driver took them to Armor Holdings in Sealy, Texas. Around nineteen hundred, he dropped them off at the General Aviation Terminal at Bush Intercontinental Airport. Flight outbound direct to Cairo."

"Armor Holdings has a contract to build armor-plated mine-resistant trucks," The General interjected. "What was the purpose of his visit?"

Michele said, "Our Houston Field Office reported al-Masri toured the facility and ordered a half-dozen turbo-charged HumVees equipped with reactive armor and extended range fuel tanks. A rush order."

The General pulled the unlit cigar from his mouth, and cleared his throat. "I want to commend you ladies for outstanding work. We now have to develop a course of action to interdict that ship, and terminate the bastard—"

"Now hold on just a minute," Jeffers interrupted. "You've established no motive—

"Sir," Michele interrupted. "Falcon Trading is long *fifty* billion dollars in December crude futures. A mere ten percent increase in oil price will double the value of al-Masri's position."

Way to go Michele, Kirk thought.

"Tainted evidence that will not hold up in a court of law," Jeffers snorted.

Fucking jackass has all the answers. Kirk fulminated over Jeffers' stupidity. "We have more than sufficient evidence of his culpability, even if some of it is tainted. Do the math and calculate the probabilities. The bottom line is a license to kill. But how would *you* handle it, Mr. Secretary?"

"I'd arrest him as a suspect!" Jeffers's voice was shrill and intense.

"Arrest him? And lawyer him up like the Times Square bomber? Wouldn't it be better to throw some harsh words his way? When the shit storm hits, you'll find you're not in Kansas anymore."

"What's that supposed to mean?"

"He's surrounded by Russian Mafiya thugs who would burn you down and bag your ashes. That fucking

Sheikh wants to reduce this country to rubble, but he'll never see a day in court."

"It's the law."

"No it's not," Kirk snarled. "It's *war*. I got an agenda here, a real personal agenda. My hunting license is current, and there is no bag limit on holy warriors. There isn't a man on this planet who can hide from *real* American justice." Kirk pointed to the Sheikh's photo. "That son-of-a-bitch is a one-bullet problem. When I'm done with him there'll be nothing left but bleached bones and pocket change. Death solves all problems. No man, no problem."

"Ironic to quote Joseph Stalin," Jeffers spat, his eyes bulging. "Magnus, you're around the bend. We can't have half-cocked people with bad attitude running around the world assassinating perceived enemies."

Kirk refused to take the bait and blistered the DHS Secretary with a glacial glare overloaded with contempt. "Do you prefer *terrorists* running around killing innocent people? Downplaying or ignoring the threat, *Mr.* Secretary, is a very dangerous game. Even the captain of the Titanic tried to avoid the iceberg. And one more thing. We don't need your permission to run this op."

Jeffers looked on with obvious condescension. The vindictive prick was not accustomed to people talking to him that way. Kirk wondered if he had over done it, risking retaliation.

Tension hung thick in the air like Spanish moss in a swamp. But General Nance's lips offered a hint of a smile.

Jessica cleared her throat, and broke the ice with another avalanche: "Sheikh Qadr al-Masri is the nephew of the Emir of Dubai and is next in line for succession. He's also the Emir's emissary—an ambassador at large. Qadr has diplomatic *and* sovereign immunity under President Ford's Executive Order. A sanction is not an option."

Stunned breathless, Kirk's needle went into the red zone. After a deathly silence, he said, "Goddamn it. If the president doesn't change the rules of engagement *right now*, the Port of Houston is gonna burn to the ground."

The General rubbed his brow. "First thing: we need to take decisive action to interdict the tanker." His voice was cool, measured, and calm. "It won't be a cakewalk. Not easy to convince the president to countermand Jerry Ford's Executive Order. Assassination is political plutonium. Nobody wants to get near it, let alone touch it."

Kirk noticed everyone's head nodding, except Jeffers'. The man looked choleric—a scowl the size of a rotted melon on his oily brow. He would avoid the issue like stepping around dog shit on the sidewalk.

The General pushed his chair back and stood up. "Teddy, I want to remind you this intel is classified *Eyes Only.*" The General left no doubt of the ramifications. "I alone will brief the President. We've got a big clock on us." He pointed his cigar at Kirk. "Walter, we'd better assign this boy a mission before he bites somebody."

"Assault that ship?"

The General nodded. "Navy SEAL team before she enters port—pending White House approval."

Walter caught Kirk's eye. "Mobilize at the Little Creek amphibious base. Get moving!"

Seven

Burj al-Arab
Dubai, United Arab Emirates

"Excellent," a voice within his head said. *"Excellent indeed."*

Emboldened with his progress on the Port of Houston attack, Qadr studied a schematic diagram on an oversized computer monitor that displayed an array of icons representing natural gas and coal-burning power plants, hydro-electric and nuclear facilities—all interconnected by high-voltage transmission lines. The schematic and real-time data depicted the US Northeast Power Grid from Niagara Falls to the nation's capital. To anyone other than an electrical engineer, and few of them, the diagram would be meaningless. To Qadr, the pirated software was a lever that would move the world, his fulcrum, a nuclear power plant in New Jersey.

Years in planning, he had designed *Radburn* as a knockout blow that would destroy the US economy, panic the populace, and cause the American dollar to plummet. With 100 to 1 financial leverage speculating in Dollar futures, Qadr would attain unimaginable wealth.

And revenge.

He despised the Americans for their meddling and arrogance, selectively applying their principles. Now, he held the reality of his dream in his hands—the power to destroy, to emasculate, to kill—the power to bring America to her knees.

Qadr smiled, then allowed himself the luxury of a comfortable quiver. He closed his eyes and savored a sip of his thirty-year-old Madeira. Soon the screams in his head would cease.

The nightmares and screams had started when he was of six years, a time when the city-state of Dubai was a dirt-poor village. Unlike the larger Emirates, Dubai had no oil production, yet the American oil companies were relentless in their search.

They came at dusk in a lorrie while Qadr bathed in the warm waters of the oasis—four rough-looking oil-field workers speaking an incomprehensible language. Father tended the goats under the date palms; inside their tent, Mother made preparations for our evening meal of hummus and dates. After wandering about the oasis, the men discovered the tent and rudely entered their home, uninvited.

Frightened of the strange men, Qadr hid in the papyrus bulrushes and watched. Within moments, Mother screamed for Father. She ran out into the desert. Running, running, her *hijab* and veil gone. Her *abaya* stripped to her waist, her breasts bared.

A man with hair the color of straw caught her, and then viciously threw her to the desert sand. He dragged her back into the tent by her hair, struggling and shrieking in pain.

Father heard Mother's screams and charged out of the date palms brandishing his double-edged *jambiya*. Two men beat and kicked Father into unconsciousness, then slit his throat with the dagger.

Mother screams ceased. An eternity passed.

Finally, the men left, stealing the few possessions his family owned—prayer rugs, brass-cooking utensils, his mother's precious gold jewelry. After an interminable silence, Qadr made his way out of the bulrushes, his heart pounding.

Father's mutilated body lay outside the tent. Goats licked his blood. Inside, the sight of his mother's nude body shamed him. He stepped closer and saw a ligature tightly bound around her neck, her face a ghastly purple.

Too young to comprehend, Qadr fell to his knees and wept. That evening, Bedouins found Qadr, bathed in blood. They led him to his uncle, the Emir of Dubai.

For several months, Qadr refused to speak. Uncle sent him to London for psychological counseling and boarding school. Annoying men in white coats visited frequently, goading him to speak. He soon realized they reduced their visits when he told them what they wanted to hear. He wanted the men to leave him alone.

Qadr fondly remembered the day he met Hans Wei at the boarding school. Later he learned Hans's father, James Wei, had died years earlier, bequeathing an inheritance to Hans and his mother—a substantial quantity of stock in the largest casino in the world—the Venetian in Macau.

As a teen, Hans traveled the world enhancing his considerable athletic skills and fighting off women of every nationality. Qadr studied with furious intensity, and became fluent in English, German, Russian, and Arabic. With an engineer's mechanical aptitude and incisive logic, he developed an uncanny ability with finance.

Qadr smiled to himself recalling his introduction to Hans' mother. She leased a flat in London to be near Hans and recuperate from a nervous breakdown. Marta von Reich, a former dancer and actress married a wealthy Chinese businessman, but kept her maiden name for her stage persona. A German national, she struggled with the English language. On occasion, she invited Qadr to her flat to translate documents and help manage her bewildering finances. This was the sort of lucky turn for which Qadr had dared to hope.

In spite of their twenty-year age difference, Qadr lusted for Marta—a goddess who shamelessly flaunted herself in his presence. In short order, Qadr succumbed under the alluring beauty's considerable charms.

Marta introduced him to rough sex, to which he willfully surrendered, taking pleasure in pain. He discovered intense gratification as Marta tightened the leather collar around his neck when he was on the verge of orgasm. She kept him sexually satisfied, though somewhat bruised.

Qadr took another sip of Madeira and smiled contentedly.

Although Marta dominated him in the bedroom, he manipulated her every move outside. In short order, he gained control of her financial resources, to their mutual benefit.

He soon discovered another thing to his liking—the buying and selling of an article no one owned, nor ever intended to own—financial derivatives called "futures." It was a way of gaming in which the outcome was determined, not by chance but by the needs of the marketplace. Profiting required great skill to determine when prices peaked or bottomed. If a trader were positioned correctly, he earned far more money than if he purchased the commodity outright.

It only took a moment for Qadr to collect his thoughts when a vision came to him with unexpected force and perfect clarity—the commodity markets could be manipulated. If he came up with a workable scheme, he'd attain more wealth than he had ever dreamed. He could know its taste—a savory taste indeed. His life changed before him, knowing at that moment his greatness would begin. Soon the world would be in awe of him. The goal was within grasp. He understood the requirements. His grand plan to accumulate power and exact revenge came together like pieces of the puzzle.

Qadr planned his operations using a combination of intelligence and determination, connections in high places, suave conversation, humor, luck, and Marta's seed money. He boldly weighed the odds and placed his bets when they were overwhelmingly in his favor. He gamed the system and rarely lost. Prayer had nothing to do with it. What deity was there for him to pray to in the face of injustice? However, Qadr studied the Qur'an and could fake religious fervor when it was in his best interests to do so. His generous donations to "Islamic charities" fueled their terror attacks—to his benefit.

Studying the computer monitor, Qadr set his wine glass on desk, then keyed in a set of numbers. With a click of the mouse he highlighted a nuclear power plant icon on the schematic display, an exercise he routinely used to clear his mind of hatred and rage.

The simulation of a shutdown of the nuclear facility caused circuit breakers to automatically trip on transmission lines. In a cascade of color that branched from New Jersey, west to Pittsburgh, south to Washington, and north through Boston into Canada, other icons flashed from green to blinking red.

Total catastrophic shutdown.

The Americans paid too much attention to tree-hugging environmentalists who stymied power plant construction, and too little consideration to the stressed Northeast power grid. The political leadership had learned not a thing from the Great Northeast Blackouts in 1965 and 2003.

Qadr smiled to himself. He had the financial leverage, and now the fulcrum to apply pressure. The blackout, looting, and panic in the populous northeast, combined with the Port of Houston devastation would cause the American currency to plummet in value. Shorted American Dollar futures, leveraged at one-hundred to one, would instantly make him the wealthiest and most powerful man on the planet.

Qadr loved the privileges that came with success, but he exalted in power even more. Power at his fingertips. The power to destroy America.

He rolled his *misbaha* beads slowly between his fingertips. How many men throughout the ages have been in so unique a position to change the course of history with a sudden and catastrophic shift? How many men had the wisdom and courage to follow through on their plans?

"Soon. So soon," the voice in his head said. *"The Americans will pay, and Mother's screams will cease.*

Eight

Little Creek Amphibious Base
Virginia Beach, Virginia

A muscular seaman, wearing black BDU pants and a T-shirt emblazoned with an eagle's talons gripping a trident, waited on the edge of the landing strip. He introduced himself as Master Chief Petty Officer Harry Matlock. His grip felt like a two-ton hydraulic press. Impressive guy. CPOs, not admirals, ran the US Navy. One didn't earn the coveted rank by acting stupid, and Matlock commanded SEAL Team 10—the best of the best.

Kirk threw his bag and sniper rifle case into the back of the car and climbed into the front passenger seat. "Chief? What are your orders?"

"I'm to standby to lead a reinforced squad to assault that ship. We are to assume the crew are enemy combatants unless proven otherwise. Rules of engagement are to take them down by any means necessary, under your command, sir. What's your service MOS?"

"Army O-6. But, in my line of work I never wear a uniform. Or pull rank."

"Colonel—"

"Kirk."

"Kirk." Matlock glanced over and smiled. "We have an amphibious P-6M Seamaster loaded and standing by.

We'll set the bird down about five miles east of that tanker, and use a pair of silent running Zodiacs for our assault. We go in at oh-dark-hundred, after the ship's midnight watch change. The day crew should be asleep by then."

Kirk nodded approval.

"We've studied the specs and 3-D drawings of the ship. My men and I have been living in her for the last few hours, and have a good idea of potential hidey-holes for personnel and explosives. We're bringing German shepherd bomb sniffers, and we're also going to plant remote activated limpet mines on that tub, as a contingency."

"Sounds like a plan, but this is your op. I'll take out the strays."

"Stun 'em, stick 'em, gut 'em, and skin 'em." Harry grinned and keyed the ignition. "Welcome aboard. My men are anxious to meet you and get the details on this thunder mug of crap."

The SEAL commander was a welcome companion. Matlock acted like he could kick ass into the next century. The SEALs were an elite group that existed for one reason and one reason only: to go in first, go in fast, and take out the threat.

"What's your combat experience?" Kirk asked.

"Somalia, Bosnia, Desert Storm, and the last Iraqi go-around. My people took out a good portion of the Iraqi Navy. They are damned good, experienced in assaulting hostile ships. They're motivated and will insure those fucking terrorists burn in hell."

"Good. I'll give your men a detailed briefing."

"A detailed briefing?" Matlock let out a belly laugh. "That's an oxymoron. You that anal retentive?"

"Chief, anal is a first approximation. Mistakes or omissions cost lives."

"True enough," Harry snorted. "Been there. Done that. Bruises and scars to prove it."

"You don't look old enough for a Mogadishu vet."

Harry stuck his tongue in his cheek. "You look like you're in pretty good shape, too. I still do fifty one-handed pushups every day. Each hand. What are you packing in the gun case?"

"A Steyr .50 HS."

"*Whoa.* You good with that elephant gun?"

"I've never missed a target under fifteen-hundred yards. Thing is, call whatever you hit the target."

"What if they were running?"

"They died out of breath."

Matlock whistled. "Here we are. We have strip steaks, twice-baked potatoes, and Key Lime pie. Plenty of coffee. We board the plane here at 2100 hours."

Kirk and the Matlock poured over drawings of the ship, laying out strike positions and coordinating force movements until they had a minute-by-minute plan of their assault. Each part of the assault had a backup, every backup an alternative. The whole operation was a hazardous mission fraught with risks and hidden dangers. But that was the way he liked it.

After dinner, Kirk paced the floor of the ready room and checked the wall clock every five minutes. *Two more hours. Why the hell didn't Walter call?*

He prayed the politicians in Washington would get their shit together, and pass the order down. *Calypso* was due in port by 1600 hours the following day. They had no time to waste on Jeffers's petty turf wars.

Kirk grabbed another cup of coffee and checked out the SEAL team one more time. Some of the men in the ready room catnapped; others cleaned and lubed weapons that were already clean and lubed. Matlock drank coffee as he read the newspaper.

Cool dude. Kirk was glad he had drawn an experienced assault team leader who could think as well as act.

A seaman stuck his head in the door of the ready room. “Chief? Phone call. Secure line.”

Heads popped up. Every battle-hardened man in the room reacted as if pumped with adrenaline. They knew the drill all too well.

Kirk felt the juice as well. *This was it.* His iPhone chirped and he glanced at the caller ID—DD Munford.

“Kirk—”

“What the hell? Must have been a dropped call, Kirk thought. He hung up, and then his cell chirped again.

“Kirk, can you hear me?”

“Loud and clear.”

“Went through a tunnel,” Walter shouted. “Listen carefully. The Navy has been ordered to stand down.”

The news hit Kirk like an 18-wheeler. He could not breathe.

“You there?”

“Yeah.” Kirk took a deep breath. *Shit. What the fuck brought this on?*

“With the delicacy of the political environment, and Senator Dreihaus—”

“You’re breaking up. Repeat.”

“Dreihaus is threatening to impeach the president. And the administration is worried about setting off another international incident.”

“Dreihaus doesn’t know jack shit. He’s playing fast and loose with national security.”

“I don’t have time to go into your rant,” Walter responded. “Homeland Security claims jurisdiction. You cannot board until that ship enters US Waters.”

“God damn it. Can’t we cripple that ship? Foul her propeller?”

“We’d lose the element of surprise.”

At least that made sense, Kirk thought.

"You're orders are to take command and lead a Coast Guard boarding party to neutralize the threat. They have a counterterrorism unit based on Galveston Island."

"A *boarding* party? A band-aid fix for a bullet wound? Am I expected to attempt an arrest of these men—*terrorists?"* Kirk's voice dripped with disgust.

"You're in command of Omega Six because you demonstrate initiative. I didn't order you to arrest those terrorists. I ordered you to *neutralize* the threat. Do it."

Nine

Ellington Field
Houston, Texas

After the Falcon landed and came to rest on the apron, Kirk hustled off the plane, and climbed behind the wheel of an FBI Suburban. Escorted by a Texas Department of Safety cruiser, they sped down Interstate-45 under a full moon. Rapture for rambunctious lunatics, Kirk thought.

The boarding party business made him grind his teeth together. Kirk had Jeffers' number and wondered if the schmuck would leak information on their covert operation. He wouldn't put it past the man to place the Bureau and CIA into a compromising situation for personal gain. Kirk was forced to stay one step ahead of his own government.

Tension created pinpricks of light behind his eyes. The base of his skull ached—the signs of an imminent migraine.

Oh Jesus, not now. "What else could go wrong?" he muttered.

As though in answer, his cell phone vibrated with a "Life in the Fast Lane" ring tone. He glanced at the Caller ID—Jessica.

"*Calypso* lifted anchor and is underway toward the Houston Ship Channel ahead of schedule," she said.

Kirk cursed and hung up.

The flicker behind his eyes intensified, his vision closed in with an aura, the nausea began. If *the Bureau found out about his disability, they'd nail his ass to a fucking desk.* Only Jessica knew of his migraines.

He dug in an inner pocket, pulled out an Imitrex injector, bit off the top, and spit it out. With one eye on the freeway, he jammed the needle into his thigh through his BDU pants.

The siren on the DPS cruiser screamed as both cars flew over the Interstate-45 Bridge onto Galveston Island. They sped on their way toward the US Coast Guard Maritime Safety and Security Team base at the inlet to East Galveston Bay. Minutes later, Kirk entered the reception area. A seaman directed him to an office down a corridor. Commander Fernando Ramirez, commander of the counterterrorism unit, sat behind his desk sporting dress whites.

Either the Coast Guard had been blindsided by Jeffers, or Ramirez was clueless.

Ramirez rose to greet him, and shook hands.

"Commander, were you ordered to stand by with a team to assault and search *Calypso?*"

"An *assault?* DHS Headquarters ordered me to lead a boarding party to search the ship for illicit cargo. I understand you'll be in tactical command."

Illicit cargo? Jeffers played a dangerous game of semantics.

"I hope you didn't expect to be received by the skipper of that ship for a formal breakfast. You're likely to be centered in a terrorist's gun sight. Get into battle dress. You can't command from behind a desk."

Ramirez's face reddened.

"Has your team seen any action in a firefight?"

"We fired warning shots across the bow of fleeing narco Cigarette boats a couple times. My men are well trained."

Not for combat.

"Training is one thing, experience is another. Like reading a book to learn how to swim. You have to be immersed in blood to know."

"I take your point." Some frost in his voice.

"I want to address your men, immediately. We're out of time."

"This way." Ramirez led Kirk into the Ready Room.

Dressed in fatigues, a dozen Coast Guard looked up when Kirk and Ramirez walked in.

"Heads up, gentlemen," Ramirez ordered. "This is FBI Special Agent Kirk Magnus. He's in tactical command."

Kirk took a position at the front of the Ready Room, hands clasped behind his back, shoulders squared. He looked each man in the eye. Less was always more when it came to conversation and Kirk was not one for idle chatter.

"Gentlemen, listen, and listen carefully. *Calypso* is about to tie-up in the Port of Houston. There are enemy combatants on that ship. We are going to board her and conduct a thorough search for explosives."

Some men turned to look at one another. A murmur of excitement passed through the room. Bodies shuffled.

"We'll go in with full body armor bearing assault rifles, MP5s, shotguns, and handguns. Remove tracer rounds and jacketed or armor piercing shells from your ammo clips. Load up with soft nose hollow-points. We get in a firefight, we would not want to set that tanker afire, or be dinged with ricochets. Bring the bomb-sniffing dogs. Anyone know where that tanker will tie-up?"

Ramirez said, "She's headed to PetroMar refinery. Terminal C."

"Can you hail her and bring her about?"

"Not possible. *Calypso* is well into the Ship Channel. The waterway is too narrow and congested with marine traffic, and it's choreographed. We'll have to wait until she ties up at the terminal, then board."

"How long will she be taking on cargo from that refinery?"

"*Calypso* is delivering a cargo, not picking one up."

"*What?* Kirk felt like kicking himself. "What the hell's she carrying?"

"Refined hydrocarbons—seventeen million gallons."

And four thousand kilos of Semtex. "Jesus Christ on a raft," Kirk muttered.

"PetroMar imports those products from a refinery in the Azores to blend with their distillates to make gasoline and other products," Ramirez said. "*Calypso* makes a round trip every three weeks. No big deal."

"Commander, you ever heard of a Daisy Cutter—a massive fuel-air bomb used to defoliate jungles in Vietnam? They called it the MOAB—the Mother of All Bombs."

"Before my time." Ramirez crossed his arms.

"The MOABs use conventional explosives to vaporize liquid fuel a fraction of a second before it's ignited. Two Iranian Intelligence agents boarded that ship. They are demolition experts. They smuggled aboard four thousand kilos of Semtex. We can assume the *plastique* is set with a detonator. *Calypso* could explode with the force of a tactical nuclear weapon. With all those refineries and petrochemical plants near the Port, you can picture the rest."

The men nervously looked at one another. "Gentlemen, your mission is critical. We must locate and disarm the detonator on that explosive." He paused.

"Your orders are to treat the ship's crew as hostile enemy combatants. Terminate any asshole who looks or acts suspicious.

"I know you are worried, and you should be. These men think nothing of suicidal attacks. However, yours is not a suicide mission. To paraphrase the words of General Patton, your objective is not to die for your mission, but to see to it the other son-of-a-bitch dies for his."

A Master Chief asked, "What about the seamen aboard? They in on the op?"

"Affirmative, according to our intel."

"What's your combat experience?"

"I commanded an armored company during Desert Storm. Six years in Delta Force, ten in covert ops. Battle scars, no tats."

The Chief nodded. "Many of us have family living in the area. We'll follow your lead. Count on it."

"Good." Kirk scanned the determined faces in the ready room, and said, "I don't much like taking casualties. This is a no visibility on this Top Secret mission. And it isn't a cowboy movie. We won't give the enemy a chance to draw. My idea of a fair fight with terrorists is to engage with a Vulcan Gatling gun from a mile out while they're taking their morning dump."

Heads nodded. "OK, Gentlemen. Make me proud of you. There are hungry holy warriors out there dying for a taste of American hot lead. Let's give them a taste."

* * *

Kirk could never understand what went on in a lawyer's mind. Jeffers' politically motivated takeover of his op made as much sense as letting the lunatics loose in Bedlam. Unlike SEALs, the Coast Guard had little experience in armed conflict.

The panoramic view of Houston Ship Channel from the Coast Guard's *Aérospatiale* chilled him to the bone. Approaching the San Jacinto Battle Monument and the Battleship Texas, Kirk wondered if this battle would also be decisive.

What the fuck was Jeffers thinking?

"I've never seen such a concentration of refineries and petrochemical plants anywhere in the world," Kirk said over the roar of the turbines and rhythmic beat of the helicopter blades. "Biggest damned target I've ever seen. Those oil tankers in the Ship Channel can only add more fuel to the fire."

"Our dogs will detect the explosives."

"How soon will your men get here on the cutter?"

"Twenty minutes," Ramirez answered.

"Which of those refineries is PetroMar?"

Ramirez pointed. "Ahead on the other side of the San Jacinto Monument. South side of the Ship Channel. The seagull logo you see on the tanks? That's PetroMar. *Calypso's* tied up at their marine terminal."

Kirk focused his binoculars on the tanker's bridge. "There doesn't seem to be anyone aboard. Nobody on deck."

"The offloading process is automated," Ramirez said. "It takes two days to transfer the cargo. Most of the crew is probably ashore, hanging out in seamen's bars nearby, or renting hookers."

"My guess is those Iranian spooks are long gone. How many crew remaining aboard?"

"Bare minimum," Ramirez said. "Maybe a dozen."

"Any Americans?"

"There's a chance a couple of PetroMar people are aboard monitoring the product transfer. The harbor pilot would have already left the ship, and won't return until she's ready to cast off."

"Be a good idea to verify that, and order them out of there. Make up a good excuse. We don't want to warn tip our hand."

"Already done that," Ramirez snapped. More frost. "Commander Ramirez, I don't give a rat's ass about your fucking ego. This isn't an exercise to test your readiness. It's the real deal—as big as it gets. Think about your family back in Galveston. The people down there."

Ramirez gave Kirk an appraising look. "Sorry, sir. We're on the same page."

Better be. "She's really an odd-shaped ship." Kirk pointed. "What are those big spherical humps on the deck?"

"*Calypso* is an LPG tanker. The storage tanks are spherical-shaped pressure vessels designed to contain hydrocarbons under several-hundred pounds pressure."

"How'd you know that?"

"I studied marine engineering at Texas A&M on Pelican Island." Ramirez pointed. "Over near Galveston."

"LPG?"

"Liquefied petroleum gasses. Propane and butane."

Highly volatile liquids that would instantly vaporize. "Jesus H. Christ," Kirk muttered under his breath. *The situation couldn't get any worse.*

"If those men knew there was a bomb aboard, wouldn't they get the hell out of there?" Ramirez asked.

"Islamists are fatalists. Their expression is, '*Insha'Allah'*—God's will. Wannabe martyrs. If they resist or look at you cross-eyed, give them the opportunity."

"Roger that."

"You know a hell-of-a-lot more about ships than I do. If you planted explosives for maximum effect, where would you locate them?"

"Along the keel, directly under the pressure vessels, and the engine room."

Kirk nodded. “That makes sense. What weapons systems do you have aboard the cutter?”

“Two pairs of FN .30 caliber machine guns fore and aft, one M2 .50 caliber machine gun and one M-203 grenade launcher, aft mounted.” Ramirez pointed. “She’s about four miles out.”

Kirk raised his binoculars. The cutter kicked up a huge bow wake.

“She’ll tie-up alongside *Calypso,* then we’ll board,” Ramirez said. “The chopper will circle overhead as an observation post, and provide a fire-power backstop. My crew chiefs are manning a pair of miniguns back there.”

“What’s the wall thickness of those holding tanks?”

“Maybe an inch, inch and half, HY-80 steel.”

“That’ll stop the 7.62 mm rounds from the miniguns. Lay off the fifties and the grenade launcher. If we get in a firefight, we sure as hell wouldn’t want to rupture those tanks.” Kirk said. “Looks like we got the bases covered. You nervous?”

“Huh. Worse than my first piece of ass.”

“Concentrate on the mission. I’ll take the point. Cover my six.”

Ramirez raised his binoculars to glass the Coast Guard cutter. “The cutter’s in Crystal Bay. Should be here in fifteen minutes.”

Kirk glanced at his watch. “Too long to wait. Set her down. Have the chopper hover and cover us. Anyone comes on deck showing hostile intent, or attempting to flee, take them out.”

Ramirez turned to look at Kirk, eyebrows raised.

“Commander, we’re not taking prisoners. Clear?”

“Absolutely.”

The Aérospatiale circled once, then set down on the heliport. A pair of seamen jumped out with a bomb-sniffing mutt, and headed toward the bow. Ramirez led a blond, black-faced dog out the door. Biggest damned dog Kirk had ever seen. Attila looked like a black-faced, floppy-eared German shepherd on steroids.

Kirk slung a tactical shotgun equipped with a pistol grip over his shoulder, and allowed the brute to sniff the back of his hand.

Good dog. Better not do anything to provoke that monster. "He friendly?"

"Not to bad guys."

A seaman dressed in a greasy jumpsuit ran toward them, waving his arms angrily. Attila bared his teeth, letting out a low deep-throated rumble that made the air vibrate.

The seaman took one look at the snarling animal, and froze in his tracks.

Kirk aimed his shotgun at the man's chest, jerking his gun upward. "Hands behind your head. Identify yourself."

The swarthy seaman shouted over the whine of the helicopter turbines. "You no permission to land on ship. Why here? Get off ship."

"Farsi accent. Fucker's Iranian." Kirk pressed the shotgun under the seaman's chin while he frisked him. "We'll ask the questions. And you don't answer with a question, get it asshole? How many aboard?"

"Six. Sleeping in quarters. I am ship engineer. Captain is taking shore leave."

"The engine room, asshole." Kirk jammed the barrel of his shotgun into the man's stomach. "Move it."

When the engineer hesitated, Ramirez made a clicking noise with his tongue.

Attila let out a menacing growl, fangs bared, and more teeth than a shark.

The engineer stared wide-eyed at gnashing teeth, sharp fangs.

Good move. Looked like Attila did more than sniff bombs. Kirk though he could use a dog like that.

Walking through passageways and climbing down stairways, the engineer's eyes never left Attila's. The man's face perspired in spite of the cold air, sweating bullets.

Not good.

Attila smelled his guilt, and so did Kirk.

Filled with rusting pumps, tanks, plumbing, and four engines the size of boxcars, the engine room reeked of diesel fumes. Machinery rumbled, steam hissed.

Ramirez signaled Attila to search. Head down, the dog followed a scent, sniffing. A moment later, Attila sat facing a pressure vessel three feet in diameter, ten feet in length.

"Nitrates." Ramirez said.

Kirk jabbed his shotgun into the engineer's chest. "What's in that tank?"

"Fuel filter."

"Bullshit! A fuel filter without pressure gauges?" Kirk pointed with his shotgun. "Open that valve and draw a sample."

The engineer hesitated and cursed in guttural Farsi.

Kirk slammed his shotgun barrel on the man's shoulder. The Iranian cried out in pain, then reluctantly complied.

Nothing flowed out the sample drain.

Attila pawed the air four times.

"*Ah fuck.* PETN," Ramirez said. "Pentaerythritol tetranitrate—the major component in Semtex and C-4."

Kirk pointed his shotgun under the engineer's chin. "Where's the detonator?"

The engineer demonstrated the universal sign of incompetence—he shrugged his shoulders, waved his palms out, and mumbled curses in Farsi.

Kirk felt certain the man's curse had something to do with his ancestry, shit, or fucking. Maybe all. He lowered his shotgun, and fired a round of double-ought buckshot between the man's thighs. The blast took off part of the engineer's jumpsuit, and a tad of flesh near his genitals.

The engineer screamed, and stared at the blood soaking his leg.

"Next shot's a little higher. *Where's the fucking detonator?*"

The engineer spit another Farsi curse.

Ramirez hand signaled Attila. The huge animal let out a ferocious growl, fangs bared, straining at his leash.

Attila's bite would be worse than his bark. A lot worse.

Bug-eyed, the engineer cried out, "*Hold dog. Hold dog. Detonator in tank.*"

"Shit." Kirk retrieved his iPhone and hit the speed dial. "Jess. Our dog located the Semtex in the engine room. The plastique and detonator is sealed inside a welded tank. We can't get to it."

"Any wires or fiber-optic cable attached to the tank?"

Kirk crawled around the pressure vessel, searching. "Not a damned thing."

"Can you cut it open with an acetylene torch?" "Hold. I'll see if I can find one." Kirk pointed the shotgun at the seaman's genitals.

Suddenly, a low-frequency rattle overwhelmed the background hum of rotating equipment.

Kirk saw the engineer's demeanor change—his pain and fear morphed into a look of abject terror, eyes wide. Sweat poured down his face.

"What's that racket?" Jessica asked.

"Machinery, maybe. No. Wait a minute. . . . It's coming through the hull of the ship."

"Hold your cell phone against a steel surface. I need a better read. . . . That's not machinery noise. No harmonics. It's digital—an acoustic signal like that used to communicate with submarines while submerged."

"A signal? For what?"

"Kirk! They've just armed the device. Get out of there. Now!"

When Kirk turned to stare at the explosives-laden pressure vessel, the engineer bolted for the stairs.

Ramirez blew a silent whistle. Snarling, Attila lunged at the Iranian and knocked the man to the deck, his salivating jaws clamped around the Iranian's throat.

Kirk stepped over and shot the enemy agent in the chest.

"*Jesus.* What now?" Ramirez asked, agitated.

"Fall back. Hold the bird. I need a couple of minutes to disable the detonator."

"How?"

"Damned if I know." Kirk looked around and spotted a welding machine in an alcove. "Can you use it to cut into that tank?"

"I don't see how."

"Damn it. Can we scuttle this tub?"

"Won't work. Channel's only forty feet deep."

"Shit. Get the hell out of here!"

Ramirez ran up the stairs, Attila at his heels.

His heart thumping like a bass drum, Kirk searched the engine room, and spotted a reel of water hose connected to a pipe. *Deck wash down,* he thought. Kirk unreeled the hose, and connected the end to the drain valve on the pressure vessel. He turned on the water, tasted the drip.

Saltwater.

Looking around, he realized there was nothing more he could accomplish. Raced up the stairs onto the deck. Headed toward the heliport. Ducking under the rotating blades, he dove aboard. After donning his headphones and mic, he said, "I pumped salt water into the tank. Maybe it'll short out the detonator electronics."

"Maybe not," Ramirez muttered. "Let's get clear of this floating bomb." He circled his finger in the air, signaling the pilot to lift off.

The Coast Guard chopper leaped off the heliport, then nosed downward as it roared off, headed east.

"Where're we headed?"

"Port Authority heliport." Ramirez pointed out the windshield. "Other side of the Ship Channel. I've ordered an evacuation of the area."

"I hope we're not too late."

A minute later, the helicopter circled the Port Authority heliport. Out the starboard window, Kirk caught a glimpse of *Calypso*. He prayed that his half-assed procedure to disable the bomb would work. His skin tingled with premonition.

The *Aérospatiale* flared prior to setting the skids down on the pad. Suddenly there was a pregnant silence in the air, like the threatening stillness between the blinding flash of a nuclear weapon, and the blast that shattered the night sky.

Time slowed.

Kirk watched the hypersonic compression wave of superheated air approach. A fraction of a second later, it slammed into his chest.

Ten

Hermann Hospital
Houston, Texas

A shrill beeping noise penetrated Kirk's dream. He groaned and opened his eyes, attempting to focus on the ceiling. They hurt. His back hurt. There wasn't much of anything that didn't hurt. Felt like his head had cracked open. Something felt out of place, but he couldn't put his finger on it.

"Kirk? Kirk? Can you hear me?"

Michele's voice.

His view of the world came slowly into focus. He rolled his head. Michele stood next to his bed, blotting tear-filled eyes with a tissue. Behind her, an IV drip and an array of medical monitors beeping, drawing lines on cathode-ray tubes.

Jessica leaned over from the opposite side of the bed, touched his bandaged face, and said, "Your helicopter crashed and burned. Port Authority people pulled you out of the wreck."

A crash? His temples throbbed. He did not remember a crash. "Where am I?"

Jessica cranked the bed up. "Herman Hospital. In Houston."

As Kirk's vision cleared, he spotted Walter standing at the foot of the bed.

"Life Flight evacuation," Walter said. "The doctors say you'll be OK in a couple of days. You were banged up and have over a hundred stitches. No broken bones, deep cuts, or internal injuries. Body armor and your helmet saved you. I think you used up eight of your nine lives."

"How long have I been out of it?"

"Out cold for over a day," Michele said. "The doctors say that's the body's way of dealing with pain."

Kirk attempted to raise himself on his elbows, and winced. "Oh man," he muttered and fell back on the bed. "Walter, how're the Coast Guard who were on the chopper?"

Walter shook his head, lips compressed. "All gone," he responded in a gravelly voice. "The chopper exploded before the Port people could extract them from the wreckage. The dog leaped out and tied to pull Ramirez out of the burning wreck. Word is, he was out cold and buckled in."

Kirk struggled to rise on his elbows, straining to focus on Walter. "What the hell happened? All I remember is flying over the Ship Channel Bridge in the Coast Guard helicopter to the Port Authority building."

"You're lucky to be alive," Walter said. "*Calypso* detonated and leveled an area within a one-mile radius. Apparently, the blast occurred when your chopper was about to set down on the heliport. Their building was destroyed, but it deflected most of the shock wave that caused your chopper to roll on its side and crash."

Kirk's stomach knotted up, washed with sorrow, and pissed off. It wasn't the first time he had lost men in an operation. It was never easy. It only became harder to accept. Sighing he asked, "What's the damage assessment from the explosion?"

"Emergency crews are extracting bodies out of the rubble all over the Port area. Fires burning everywhere. The primary explosion set off numerous secondary explosions on storage tanks." Walter flipped his thumb over his shoulder. A muted TV mounted up on the wall displayed scenes of the carnage. "The sky looks as bad as Kuwait when Saddam set the oil wells on fire. Houston airports are shutdown. The blast blew hundreds of windows out of skyscrapers in the downtown area. Streets are covered with debris. The ship's twelve-ton anchor landed in a parking lot over a mile away. The body count may run in the thousands—"

"Aw, shit."

"Don't beat yourself up. You're not supposed to be a martyr."

Kirk studied Walter's face, but didn't say anything.

Walter continued, "The explosion hit the financial markets and unleashed a fear-driven free-for-all. The price of oil bid up to over two hundred dollars a barrel. A stampede of motorists quickly exhausted gasoline stocks throughout the country, creating fuel shortages everywhere, along with panic and violence. Trading curbs on Wall Street halted activity after a twenty-five percent sell-off. That Sheikh will undoubtedly use his profits to bribe politicians and fund the jihadists"

"Just like trickle-down economics," Kirk grunted. "Terrorism's good for the GDP."

The images on TV were worst than anything Kirk had ever seen in a combat zone, making it difficult to tare his eyes away. He had to think beyond the devastation and develop a coherent picture in his mind.

"What's the status of our op?"

Jessica said, "We hacked the Falcon Trading database. Verified the bulk of the trades were proprietary, to Qadr's direct benefit—a smoking gun."

"No surprise. What about the Iranian connection?"

"We identified two complicit accounts at Falcon trading—President Mahmood Esfahanian and General Iraj Reza, head of MOIS."

"The *President of Iran?* Anything else?"

Walter approached the side of the bed. "Tracers in Semtex residue found on shrapnel indicated it was from a lot produced five years ago and sold to Iran, the same lot identified by DGSE. This solidifies the Sheikh Qadr-Iran connection. This may well be state-sponsored terrorism. Iran's role appears to have been limited to logistics. We need to find out more. Naval Intelligence is on it."

"That goddamned submarine. We saw it coming." Kirk winced, and fell back onto the pillow.

"As usual," Walter said, "the politicians and media wag their finger at the FBI and CIA. They want us to protect them, but point the finger of outrage when they see what the job entails. Senator Dreihaus and his cronies are ranting about another Nine-eleven type intelligence failure. We could have interdicted the tanker out at sea. The administration caved in to Jeffers. To save face and buy time, the administration spun the terror attack as an accident."

Kirk moaned in pain. "Word will get out soon enough, and I want to get outta here."

"You're not going anywhere until the hospital releases you," Walter said. "You have a bad concussion. They're gonna hold you for observation for a few days."

Jessica said, "I'm staying here to keep an eye on you."

"Jess, any word on the *Khomeini?*"

"Nothing yet. However, the good news is that the President Omar rescinded Ford's Executive Order and conditionally approved the Speculator Sanction. We're good to go."

"Conditionally?" Kirk frowned. "What conditions?"

"There's to be little or no collateral damage, and the usual plausible deniability," Walter said. "The president wants distance on this. You are authorized to deploy whatever assets you deem necessary."

"I want to keep that dog—Attila. Never seen anything like him. What breed is he?"

"Anatolian shepherd. From Turkey. They're used in Africa to keep the big cats away from the livestock. He's at the vets, recovering from minor injuries. I want you to rest and recover for the job ahead. The President authorized the Speculator Sanction. We have a blank check to hunt that Sheikh down. A break will come. They always do. Criminals are never as smart as they think, especially psychos."

* * *

Kirk sat up in bed reading a Vince Flynn novel when Jessica walked into his hospital room.

"Any good?"

"Yeah, thanks. Better than *The Giant Book of Dirty Limericks*. This character? He knows how to kick ass." Kirk dog-eared a page, then set the paperback aside. "I gotta get out of here to go kick some Arab ass."

"Your physician wants to hold you for another day."

"Get me the hell out of here."

"How's your head?"

Kirk waved a bandaged hand dismissively. "Nothing but a dull ache. No more dizziness."

"Maybe they need a couple more X-rays."

"They take any more, my head'll start smoking."

Jessica laughed. "I understand you've been giving the hospital staff some flak about your breakfast."

Jessica could nag paint off the walls. "Quiche and fruit cup?" He pointed to the empty breakfast tray on a side table. "That's *girly* chow. Real men don't eat quiche. I need a couple Danish. And real coffee with real cream. My cholesterol demands a fix."

Jessica jiggled a Starbucks bag. "Two cheese and a Grande Latté."

Kirk scratched a dozen stitches on his left arm. “Gotta love spooks.” He flipped a thumb toward some electronics mounted on a rack next to his bed. “You monitoring my brain waves, or what?”

“Signal’s too weak.” Jessica vamped a set of perfect ivories with her sly smile. “Your yellowing bruises and itching means you’re healing.” She dug into the bag, and handed him a Danish. “Your nurse says you’re getting back to normal—hawking piss and vinegar.”

Kirk chomped into the cheese pastry, talking with his mouth full. “The cute brunette with the bangs? Bee-stung lips?”

Jessica arched an eyebrow, handing him the latté. “That’s her.”

“Can you get her back here? To kiss my boo-boos?” Kirk rubbed his lower belly, a grin on his mug.

Jessica rolled her eyes. “That’s the worst attempt at seduction I’ve ever heard.”

“Think it’ll work?”

“*No.* She’s a Candy Striper, only seventeen. Get dressed! I’m getting you out of here.”

“Then what?”

“Dubai. Max is on top of—”

“That fucking sheikh,” Kirk finished.

Eleven

Intercontinental Hotel
Dubai, United Arab Emirates

After a fourteen-hour direct flight from Houston on a CIA Gulfstream, Kirk and Jessica slipped through Dubai on diplomatic passports, and set up an operations base in a suite at the Intercontinental Hotel.

Dog-tired and jet-lagged, Kirk stared out the hotel window toward Qadr's headquarters on the top floor of the *Burj al-Arab*, the Arabian Tower.

"If I could get within fifteen hundred meters, I'd put a fifty-caliber bullet in that gold-plated fucker."

Taking a seat on the couch, Jessica tucked her legs under her bottom and said, "Kirk, we've evaluated that option. There's no way you could get past his phalanx of bodyguards. He has more protection than the President does, and those Spetsnaz have no rules of engagement. They neutralize any threat, real or imagined. We can't risk civilian casualties, and you're in no shape for combat."

"Yeah well, a Hellfire missile will turn Qadr into an extra-crispy critter."

"General Nance insists we finesse this and leave no trace evidence of our involvement."

"Like how? Stick him with a ricin-tipped umbrella?"

Jessica sighed. "Sometimes you're impossible, you know?" "Your tribal lust for revenge can only cloud your judgment. I wish you would get your mind off your anger and channel that energy into the job you're paid to do. If you convert your blood lust into sexual urge, you will be a better man. You love your guns more than your women."

"Guns never nag and complain."

"I can think of few other things they never do," Jessica said with a half-smile.

"Well, yeah." Kirk chuckled. "You got me on that." He walked over, and sat on the couch next to her. "What's your game plan for the take down?"

"Max has a twenty-man surveillance team on the Sheikh. They installed laser microphones on the roof here with line-of-sight to his office in the *Burj al-Arab*. We can pick up some of the conversation in there. We can't take him inside. Too many bodyguards, and he has a female house guest."

"The leggy blond? From the limo?"

"Hard to say. She stays in the living quarters located on the side of the building facing the Persian Gulf. We can't hear anything back there because of the angle."

"Pick up anything useful?"

"Maybe. We may have a window of opportunity. Qadr plans a falconry expedition in the mountains near the Omani border. He will probably take his entourage, horses, commissary, and bodyguards. We'll track him via Keyhole satellite and Max's ground surveillance, and then wait for a set-up."

Jessica could have the whole thing settled within hours. That feeling lasted for ten seconds.

"I just had an epiphany."

"Did it hurt, like a gas pain?"

"Funny. I'll get my gear ready for a helicopter insertion. All I need is one shot. That fucking Sheikh will be dead before his face hits the hummus."

"We don't have a chopper."

"Then we'll borrow one from one of the American oil companies."

Jessica shook her head. "No. My orders are specific. You're in no physical condition for field deployment. You ought to cover those bruises and stitches. You radiate ghoul vibes."

Kirk had fought in far worse physical condition. A few dents and dings wouldn't stop him. "These people around here? They'll get used to seeing body parts."

Jessica rolled her eyes. "I don't want you to pull any of your stitches, or some stupid Rambo stunt and leave us wide open."

"I want to kill that son-of-a-bitch. Up close and personal."

"What can possibly go wrong with a plan like that?" she asked sarcastically. "You could use some adult supervision. My orders are to keep an eye on you. I need brains, not brawn."

"For what?" Kirk waved his hand dismissively.

"Jessica's Rule: the Thirteen Commandment —Thou shall not get caught. I have a sophisticated set-up that will take him out. Minimal risk. No collateral damage. No telltale. I've actually done this a time or two."

"I don't have much confidence in tactics I don't understand. If you want to kill someone, zero-in on the target yourself. One bullet, one kill."

"Stubborn Scotsman."

"What's *your* plan of attack?"

"You act like you resent it."

"It's fine with me."

"Good. Because that's the way it's going to be."

"Lay it on me."

"Do you recall Qadr ordered six HumVees fitted with reactive armor?"

"Yeah. Stuff explodes outward when hit with an incoming projectile and neutralizes the impact."

"Correct. Reactive armor can also be detonated with a high-voltage charge of twenty-thousand volts. We convinced Gus Kaiser at Armor Holdings to install the plates inside out. We wired the GPS in the trucks into military satellite transceivers. When tickled with a charge from the ignition coil, the reactive armor will implode.

"Slick physics. For a pint-sized babe, you pack a wallop."

"Glad you think so. When Qadr takes his caravan into the mountains, all we have to do is watch and wait, then press the button."

"Sounds too damned easy. You know the Sheikh's security people will scan those trucks for bugs and explosives. They're good. Don't underestimate them."

Her smile evaporated, mouth flattened into a thin line. "You know me better than that."

"Sorry. I didn't mean to come across as a horse's ass."

She waved him off. "The transceivers are buried inside a sealed Delco battery. It would be difficult to detect them, and they require a ten-twenty-four bit encrypted digital code to activate. The GPS are always on, even when turned off, like TV."

"I'd prefer directing a warhead on his forehead from a Raptor drone."

"Poetic justice?"

"The Magnus maxim."

"The Houston attack juiced *al-Qai'da*. Tangos and insurgents in the Middle East are climbing out of their holes and pulling weapons from under their beds. All our drones are committed to Yemen, Iraq, and the 'Stans."

"OK. When do we bounce?"

"They roll out in the morning."

"You hungry?"

"Not really."

"Good. Let's eat."

At dawn, Max reported, "We have a complication. At the last minute, the Emir and three other relatives decided to join Qadr's falconry expedition."

"Shit," Kirk said. "We don't want to take out the Emir. He's one of the good guys. We have to trigger the device when the Sheikh is in his vehicle, but when the civilians are clear. Fat chance."

* * *

At fourteen hundred hours, Max called in on the tactical net. "The Emir and other guests leave on horseback into the desert. Qadr drives the lead vehicle east into the *Qara'* Mountains. Stand by."

"Communing with the Angel of Death on top of the world," Kirk said. "That'll make my day."

Jessica moved to the couch, toggling keys on her laptop sitting on a coffee table.

Kirk set a fresh pot of coffee and sandwiches on the table, and took a seat beside her. He anxiously watched a real-time image from a Keyhole-19 satellite on the laptop.

"The bird's over Bandar Abbas right now," Jessica said. "In a few minutes we should pick up the caravan when the satellite comes overhead."

Kirk poured two cups of coffee, and slid one across the table to Jessica.

"I have them." Jessica zoomed in on the targets—three vehicles entering a pass. "This looks good. The Emir's entourage is ten klicks away in the valley on horseback. Here goes." She keyed in a command relayed to a military communications satellite.

Frowning, she said, "I don't understand it. None of the transceivers pinged."

Kirk swallowed a bite of sandwich. "Any way they could be disabled?"

"If they installed a bypass switch on the GPS. But would they do that?"

"Borisov's no dummy. He'd know the GPS are always active. Maybe he bypassed them. Otherwise those vehicles could be tracked."

"Damn it. I never thought—"

"Neither did I."

"Any ideas?"

"Those mountains are no-man's land. Qadr is driving the lead Hummer. There is a chance he'll use the GPS to navigate that terrain. Keep trying. Maybe we'll get lucky."

"Luck can go both ways."

High on the mountainside, Max glassed the Emir's horses kicking up a cloud of dust as the hunting party galloped off into the desert. Two kilometers to the east, three of Qadr's vehicles rambled through the rocky pass below. At the base camp, a pair of bodyguards climbed into one of the HumVees.

Communications and command post, Max thought. He scrambled to set up a laser microphone. With the telescope, he aimed the invisible laser beam at the HumVee's windshield. Electronics converted the Doppler shift of reflected waves to sound in his headphones.

The HumVee engine cranked over, the background rumble partially drowned out the Spetsnaz conversation. Tinny-sounding Arab music on the radio.

"Turn on the heat," a man ordered in Russian.

"Look at this. The Americans. They are clever, but stupid. The capitalists sell sophisticated weapons and GPS technology to anyone with a fistful of mon—"

Kirk stared wide-eyed at Jessica's laptop as plume erupted at the base camp. "*Jesus H. Christ.* That IED you planted in the Hummer just took out a couple of Russian bodyguards. And a fucking horse trailer."

"And killed our stealth edge," Jessica said with a deep sigh. "The Sheikh will realize we're on to him and disappear like smoke. He'll be far more dangerous than ever."

"Then we'll have just have to figure a way to smoke him out and punch holes in his canoe."

Twelve

Burj al-Arab
Dubai, United Arab Emirates

Qadr had experienced a range of emotions and sacrifice on his journey from obscurity toward his ultimate destiny. Now, looking back at his successes, it was a trivial price. The attack on the Port of Houston had met all of his objectives. The financial markets plummeted, losses in the trillions of dollars, his gains from oil futures in the billions. It was not luck, that was for certain. It was only the beginning.

Memories of that cursed day when his family was slaughtered by the Americans came raging back, the day that sparked his rebirth. His life had taken on a far greater purpose than it otherwise would have. His chest swelled with pride knowing he was about to strike another mortal blow to his enemy—The Great Satan. He could see it all before him.

"Know your greatness," the voice in his head said. *"Your regal Arab heritage."*

Qadr's collection of ancient Egyptian artifacts became an obsessive avocation. Before him, the ancient papyrus scroll looked magnificent. His bribes to the archeologists paid off handsomely. Money was no object in dirt-poor Egypt, every hand outstretched. A gold death mask and alabaster sarcophagus would arrive shortly adding to his vast collection of Egyptian antiquities displayed in his office. These he shared with few.

He adjusted a halogen light at a raking angle to examine the thirty-five hundred year-old hieroglyphics etched onto the brittle parchment. Carefully interpreting the text and noting the numerous falcon and eye-of-Horus references, Qadr was stunned by the enormity of what lay in his hands. He instantly recognized the work as that of a scribe enslaved to the most powerful ruler of upper and lower Egypt—Horus, the Falcon Pharaoh and son of the winged goddess Isis.

As he studied the scroll, an ice chill hand touched his skin and goose flesh broke out over his body. Qadr read as if his hunger for knowledge would sate starvation. His heart hammered in his chest. He could not believe his good fortune. He had traced his bloodlines to the Falcon Pharaoh through curiosity more than superstitious destiny.

Qadr smiled inwardly, then took a sip of Madeira to savor the moment.

The unique warbling tone of the encrypted Iridium satellite phone on his desk interrupted his reverie. He glanced at the caller ID. Borisov.

"Yes?"

"A new report from the Senator."

"Excellent. It is of interest?"

"*Da*, but the Senator demands more money. Two million American dollars."

Qadr, the manipulator, would never allow himself to be manipulated. He pulled a manila folder from his desk containing a set of sexually explicit photos of Senator Dreihaus, and chuckled.

"Reduce the *baksheesh* by half, and leave a Mafiya calling card in his bed." Qadr slid the stack of photos across his desk. "The American Senator could use a lesson in manners."

Borisov glanced at the photos and laughed.

Qadr said, "The intelligence?"

"Omega Six has a new commander—a man named Kirk Magnus. An Asian woman named Michele Li assists him. We have photos and operations reports. This man Magnus, he is a former Delta Force operative, and is obsessed with free-ranging revenge."

*"Bloody hell."*Qadr heard the bitterness welling up into his voice until he could taste it. He tried to hold it back, but then vomited it out.

"Send two of your best men to lay bare their intelligence, then you know what to do. Do not fail me."

Still flush with excitement, the musky scent of the woman aroused Qadr before he heard the rustle of sheer silk. Actually, he was aware of her presence without hearing her. Long familiarity enhanced his senses. He didn't even have to look up to know she was there. In fact, he did not look up; he pretended to read the Omega Six operations reports.

Her delicate ivory-colored hand touched on his shoulder, a voluptuous breast pressed against his neck.

"All is well?" the sultry voice murmured.

"Yes, *meine Liebe.* All according to plan." He caressed her exposed breast, then ardently took a ringed nipple between his teeth, and bit hard.

"Oh, meine Gott," she moaned. "Come to bed now. *Schnell.*"

* * *

Qadr loved the view of the brightly lit City of Dubai from his elegant quarters. The city lights shimmered in the desert air and added to his sense of fulfillment. The Port of Houston attack was a complete success—oil prices rose over $100 per barrel. Feeling an overwhelming sense of power, he rolled his beads between his fingers as he gazed out the window.

Suffering and death meant nothing to him—he had purged empathy from his spirit decades ago. The power he felt before him was all that mattered, a power greater than any he had known before, reflected in his new office and living quarters that occupied the entire top floor of the Arabian Tower. To him, it represented the seat of ultimate power in the universe. It was appropriate he designed his 1,000 foot-tall headquarters building in the shape of a crescent—the symbol of Islam.

Things had progressed well. Very well indeed, he mused. Yet, there was more to come. Much more. He looked forward to Hans's briefing on the status of their next operation.

When his private elevator chimed, he turned away from the window, and walked toward the elevator.

Hans Wei, his life-long friend and co-conspirator, stepped out, smiled. He touched his left hand to his forehead, made a slight bow, and brought his hand down in an elegant arc. "*As salaam alaikum,*" he said.

Qadr beamed at the sight of Hans, an exceptionally handsome man having glorious golden eyes and gifted with superb athletic ability, looking the part. He could have served as Rodin's model for The Thinker, but Hans was no thinker—his prowess was of the physical nature. They loved one another like brothers.

"And may peace be with you, my friend." Qadr responded, then embraced Hans. They kissed one another on each cheek, right-left-right, then shook hands. "It is good to see you my brother. Come. Let me show you my new office."

Qadr led the way, describing his artwork and priceless collection of ancient Egyptian artifacts that would be the envy of the British Museum.

Hans paused near the elevator and pointed to a statue depicting a man with a falcon's head, holding an *ankh*, the ancient Egyptian symbol of everlasting life in one hand, and a crook, the symbol of power, in the other.

"The god Horus," Hans said. "History is made by great men. And the falcon. The symbol of your power. Magnificent, Qadr. Absolutely magnificent."

If Hans recognized the symbolism of the goddess Isis next to the left door, he made no indication. The winged goddess knelt before Pharaoh, arms outstretched in supplication.

"Please sit and tell me of our operations," Qadr said. "I am anxious for news of our plans. All is well?"

Qadr and Hans took seats on opposite sides of an inlaid coffee table covered with gold trays of dates, olives, braised goat meat, hummus, and pita bread. Qadr uncorked a vintage French Bordeaux, and poured the wine into Baccarat goblets.

"Pisces is on schedule," Hans said. He took an olive in his right hand and popped it his mouth. "The Persian agents disguised as employees completed the installation of the pipeline under the Delaware River to the island from an abandoned building located in the old steel mill. The air compressor and stockpiled raw materials are disguised as abandoned equipment and chemicals, cleverly hidden out in the open."

"Excellent. The Semtex?"

"The Persians offloaded one thousand kilos of the *plastique* from *Calypso* while she sat at anchor offshore Galveston. They buried half on the north end of the island, and the other half is hidden within the steel plant, along with the automatic weapons."

Qadr took a sip of wine and smacked his lips. "Perfect."

"The Iranian agents performed well," Hans said. "Pity, they have to be sacrificed."

Qadr shrugged. “Can anything be traced back to us?”

Hans spit the olive pit into his hand. “Impossible. The trail ends at MOIS headquarters. We leave no telltale footprints.”

Qadr nodded and smiled. Hans would have made a wonderful general, and he was the only man on earth that Qadr trusted.

“Hans, I don’t know what I’d do without you. I must tell you your account at Falcon Trading has tripled in value in a week.” He saluted Hans in a toast. “More wine?”

“Please.” Hans passed his goblet to Qadr.

“We must not become complacent,” Qadr said.

Hans sat back and crossed his legs. “Your strategy is brilliant. Pisces will serve to probe their defenses and as a diversionary tactic. *Pisces.* An appropriate name, don’t you think for the red herring?”

“Quite. The precursor to *Radburn*.” He held his wine glass up and studied the garnet colored liquid, envisioning blood.

Hans dipped a piece of pita bread into a gold bowl of hummus.

“My friend, I regret I could not attend your falcon hunt, as I needed to warm-up for the International Downhill ski competition. You had an enjoyable affair?”

“Very much so. However, there is one thing that troubles me about the falconry excursion.”

“Oh? What is that?”

“One of the lorries exploded, killing two of Borisov’s men.”

“What? Hans uncrossed his legs, and set his wine goblet on the table. “How in the bloody hell did that happen? This makes no sense.”

“Borisov’s men had swept the lorries for surveillance bugs and explosives. He is dumbfounded and cannot identify the explosive, or explain how it was planted.”

"Where was the Emir when this happened?"

"Uncle was in the desert on horseback with my cousins."

"Then the attack could not have been directed at the Emir. Any aircraft or suspicious men nearby?"

"The Saudis reported no aircraft or missiles in the area."

"American puppets," Hans said. "This was an attempt on *your* life. Somehow, an enemy planted a time bomb in that vehicle. Fortunately, it detonated when you were nowhere in sight."

"Do you think they know about me?" Qadr chewed the inside of his cheek and frowned. "Surely the Americans know nothing of our plan. Borisov assures me our communications are secure."

"Remember your own admonition, we must not become complacent. Perhaps the bomb was planted by Iranian spies."

Qadr took a long breath and rose from his seat, pacing. He rolled his beads between his thumb and index finger at a rapid clip—the amber and black coral beads snapped together on the *misbaha. Click, click, click.*

"But why? The Iranians require our assistance with the operation, and they will be paid handsomely. Their attempt on my life makes no sense, other than the fact the *Shi'ite* Persians hate *Sunni* Arabs. We have a common enemy, and the war has just begun. Mahmood Isfahanian and Iraj Reza made billions of dollars from the Port of Houston attack. They stand to make more from *Radburn,* far more."

"Qadr, I do not trust this General Iraj Reza. That man is unstable."

Qadr shook his head. "No. Not Reza, or Mahmood. They need us. . . . Do we have intelligence that suggests the Americans suspect we were involved with the Port of Houston attack?"

"None."

"We must know if the Americans are on to our plans." Qadr thought for a moment as he stared out the window into the blackened desert. He felt a sense of dread, and whirled to face Hans. "The bloody Americans had to be behind this attempt on my life. I want you to go to Washington at once to investigate. Ascertain the FBI intelligence. See to it they terminate the threat."

"At once. Any other concerns?"

"Is it possible the American National Security Agency monitors our communications?"

"Impossible," Hans replied, shaking his head. "We have an excellent communications system that uses advanced encryption technology based on a KGB model. If Sheikh Rahman succeeds in recruiting his lawyer as a go-between, it would add another layer of security. I do not see a way the Americans could have penetrated our communications, or know of our operations. I am certain of it."

"Perhaps. But even paranoids have enemies."

Thirteen

Federal SuperMax Penitentiary
Florence, Colorado

She sat waiting in the cold visitor's room. The place was always cold, regardless of the weather outside. Aisha Yassin took her usual seat in a partitioned cubicle, opened her briefcase, and pulled out a yellow legal pad and pen. Relaxation impossible, she fidgeted with a mass of gold jewellery on her pudgy wrist and felt for the bracelet that dangled Egyptian gold coins and a worn-smooth medallion bearing the profile of former American President, George H. W. Bush.

"I will never apologize." The words relentlessly resonated in Aisha's head.

The attack on the Port of Houston was sweet, but how much longer would her client live before she had an opportunity to fulfil her destiny to serve the jihad and exact revenge?

Rubbing the medallion between her calloused thumb and index finger, she felt another surge of anger and revulsion as she recalled the American President on *al-Jazeera* TV saying, *"I will never apologize for the United States of America. I don't care what the facts are."*

The President's comments regarded an act of cold-blooded mass-murder by the U.S. Navy warship Vincennes when it shot down an Iranian commercial airliner and killed 290 Muslim civilians during the Iran-Iraq War.

Aisha felt the attack was a sign of Western corruption and hatred of Muslims and a lack of faith in the true god, Allah. The Christians and filthy Jews had everything, the Arabs nothing. Westerners take and never give. *They would pay. They would pay in blood.*

With the white ceiling yellowed from age, puke-green wallpaper peeling off the walls, vinyl floor tiles worn through, she wondered if the authorities allowed the Visitors Room to run down to enhance the gloom of the prison. Humming transformers in the fluorescent lights that cast a harsh glare into the room added to her despair. Through the walls, she could hear voices competing and echoing. Steel doors banging. Shouted orders. A red light flashed on the security touch pad next to the door. A harsh buzzer sounded. Seconds later two men passed through a heavy steel door in the far corner of the room. The door slammed shut with a loud clang that echoed throughout.

Goose bumps rose on her burnished-pecan skin.

The burly uniformed guard took the elbow of his frail and elderly prisoner, and escorted him over to the cubicle as he had done dozens of times before, once a week for the last three years. They shuffled along, the prisoner's hands and feet shackled to prevent normal movement.

Aisha felt a warm flush as the blind Sheikh felt his way and settled into the cubicle. She cast a poisonous glare at the guard. He retreated to stand duty twenty feet away, well out of earshot.

Signed-in as Sheikh Abdel-e Rahman's *pro bono* counsellor, her visits were allegedly to appeal the blind cleric's life-term conviction for his role in the 1993 World Trade Center attack. She stared into the clouded eyes of the Sheikh, and wanted desperately to touch his hand, bow to his wishes, and please him. They exchanged greetings, and whispered in Cairo-accented Arabic.

Sheikh Rahman placed the palms of his hands on the bulletproof polycarbonate partition. She did the same as he recited a verse from the *Qur'an*— *"Let not the infidels deem that the length of days we give them is good. We only give them length of days that they may increase their sins. And shameful chastisement shall be their lot."*

Why had he always cited *Qur'an* verses that inflamed her anger? He knew she hated the *kafirs*. What could be his motivation? Sheikh Rahman was her spiritual leader, a kind, gentle soul, and she loved him. However, she did not understand him. He teased her without mercy by reciting ancient Egyptian riddles. What could be the purpose of his manipulation of her emotions with these verses and riddles?

She rested her elbows on the table and held her forehead in her hands.

Sheikh Rahman recited yet another riddle.

Aisha sighed, reluctantly answered, and said, "The riddle game is a bore and upsets me."

Sheikh Rahman shifted in his seat, and frowned in anger.

Why? What had she done to provoke him so? Her voice broke when she asked the purpose of his actions.

He did not respond.

Aisha rolled her eyes toward the dingy ceiling, ululating and moaning as she rocked back and forth.

Sheikh Rahman leaned forward and hissed, "It is for the Glory of Islam. *Think*. Think of the Glory. Pray to Allah for divine guidance."

Aisha's ritual included prayer five times a day, which began two hours before sunrise and ended with the last prayer at dusk. The traditional ritual included a second prayer at noon, when the sun reached its apogee. It was not yet time, but additional prayer was good.

She stared at the Sheikh's blind eyes in total desperation and confusion. She dug into her purse for her *misbaha,* closed her eyes and recited another silent prayer.

Dear Allah. I am your lifelong servant. I know I have been chosen to fulfil your word, as no man would ever want me. You saved my soul for service in your name, and to serve Sheikh Rahman. I pray to you to guide me so I will not fail to understand what he is trying to have me do for your glory. Give my humble spirit wisdom to fathom why he is angry with me when I want to serve him in your name.

Although blind, surely he saw how devoted she was to him and the righteous cause. Why then did he continue to taunt her so with these ancient riddles and provocative verses from the *Qur'an*? What was he trying to tell her?

Dear Allah. My whole life is dedicated to you and to Sheikh Rahman and I gladly lay it down for our cause. Please give me the grace to know your will.

Aisha closed her eyes to will her desire to be heard, to be granted the opportunity to serve. She did not know when an answer would come to her earnest prayer, but she had faith—the undying faith in Allah, her saviour. An answer would come. Allah never failed.

Thoughts and questions formed in her head. The riddles, what could they mean? What secrets did they hold? Perhaps it was not the content, but rather the process—the nature of the ancient riddles that held the key to understanding the Sheikh's anger. Perhaps he wanted her to use the riddles to communicate that which could not be said directly.

She turned her attention back to the Sheikh's hands. Entranced, she studied the hieroglyphics he drew. What was their purpose? What did they mean? Could it be that he did not play a game? What then of the riddles? No one but Egyptian intellectuals knew of the ancient riddles or even their meaning.

Aisha opened her mouth as if to speak, but words failed her as the revelation struck home. If no one but Egyptians knew their meaning, then could they not be used to pass secret messages for the jihad? The hieroglyphics? Another secret code?

Of course. How could she have been so stupid? Astounding. Simple, and clever. Sheikh Rahman wanted to pass a secret message by use of the riddles and hieroglyphics.

Her voice cracked as she asked Sheikh Rahman to recite another riddle.

Rahman whispered, "What is it which passes unseen but is not heard?"

Aisha felt an adrenaline surge. She knew the answer, and responded in a whisper. "A secret message."

Sheikh Rahman smiled.

Yes.

Sheikh Rahman wished to pass a message to her, an important secret message. She stared at him in wide-eyed wonder. He wanted to pass a message to their friends in *al-Gama' al-Islamiyya*—for the jihad.

Aisha's hands trembled. She was well aware that she could be imprisoned if she passed messages. And wasn't the act itself treason, punishable by a death? Yet, to die as a martyr was noble—a golden pathway to Paradise. She would not be denied her destiny.

Her heart throbbed as she scanned the room to locate the security cameras. She spotted a small unobtrusive camera in each corner of the room. The cubicle partitions and their bodies partially blocked the camera's views. *Excellent.* The authorities could not see. They could not hear. She stole a glance at the guard. He acted passive and rarely reacted, standing there, leaning against the wall appearing stupid and brutish with a contemptuous sneer, sucking on a toothpick.

Twenty feet away, Sergeant Winters caught Aisha Yassin's shifty gaze, and bit down onto his toothpick, eyes squinting. He hated that woman, because not only she was pug-faced — the bitch was arrogant, psycho, and always acted as if she had something to hide. Winters also had to fight the urge to strangle the fucking blind cleric—a so-called man of God. *Bullshit. That explosion in Houston was no fucking accident. Those two scumbags celebrated the fireworks, and they're up to no good. Sneaky bastards were involved, somehow.*

Aisha and the cleric were in intense hushed conversation with their heads angled down when Winters slipped in closer in an attempt to discover their intentions. He positioned himself near their blindside, knowing the ACLU—the American Criminal Liberties Union, would burn his ass if they discovered he violated their "civil rights".

Fuck 'em. Terrorists got no goddamned rights. Except burning in hell.

Winters did not understand a word they hissed to one another in guttural Arabic, but he knew psychos had vulnerabilities—if you knew where to look. Surrounded by nutcases in the maximum-security pen, he analysed them. He did know where to look.

For a long moment, Winters studied the pair. The cleric's hand gestures and woman's facial expressions were a *dead* giveaway. A chill run down his spine when he realized what he had witnessed—illegal message transfer.

Dead— the operative word. Winters smiled, rolling the toothpick across his upper lip with his tongue.

That bat-shit crazy bitch was gonna take a dirt nap.

Aisha had to determine the recipient of Rahman's message. She thought of a riddle, leaned close, and whispered, "Where does that which passes, end?"

Sheikh Rahman fought back a smile, then uttered his reply, "With a mutual friend."

Aisha fought to control her excitement, quickly thinking of another ancient riddle. "Where is a place that to name it is to destroy it?"

While attempting to hide his hand from the surveillance video cameras, Rahman used his finger to draw Egyptian hieroglyphics, followed by a crescent moon and a star.

Her heart leapt as she recognized the series of pictographs—the ancient symbols for the Kingdom of Egypt. Every Egyptian schoolchild knew them! And the star and crescent drawn were the symbol of Islam. Aisha now knew her destination and contact. She felt a surge of excitement as she continued to stare in awe at Sheikh Rahman's withered hands on the tabletop.

When she looked up, she noticed Sergeant Winters standing over Sheikh Rahman's right shoulder, a look of hatred in his eyes.

Dear Allah. Could he possibly know?

Aisha averted her gaze. A wave of terror rushed through her. Heart pounding as though she had barely escaped the hangman, her skin burned. Nausea overcame her. She could not breathe from a stabbing pain in the centre of her chest, and prayed she would not die from cardiac arrest before she fulfilled her destiny.

Finally, she caught her breath and took a few moments to regain her composure. The guard continued to stare back at her, rolling a toothpick in his mouth.

American fool. She glowered at him with the poisonous eyes of Cleopatra's pit viper.

Sergeant Winters retreated to his station near the corner.

Satisfied, Aisha rubbed the medallion between her fingertips and dreamed of her role in the Global Jihad. She knew her mission and her contact. She would not be denied. Aisha would taste the sweetness of revenge.

Pressing her palms against the polycarbonate partition, she met the withered hands of Sheikh Rahman. They chanted in Arabic, “Death to America.”

Fourteen

Rockies Road House
Florence, Colorado

Sergeant Edgar Winters, a/k/a T-Bone, was thick, muscular, and vibrating with energy like a Peterbilt truck with a hard-on. With his *Conan the Barbarian* physique, Winters projected menace—a good trait in cops. And counterterror operatives. The man had a fireplug neck and shoulders as broad as a hangman's gallows. With his wife-beater T-shirt and pressed Wranglers, he looked like a redneck, talked like a redneck, and dressed like a redneck. His scuffed cowboy boots looked like they had been scrounged from a slow-on-the draw gunslinger on the way up to Boot Hill. The Federal Maximum Security Prison guard and former Force Recon sniper had called the Denver Field Office saying he had information that might be related the Houston explosion.

Now Kirk sat in a corner booth facing Winters, who had picked the perfect meeting location. Noisy, dark, and crowded three-deep at the bar. Michele Li and Ignacio "Nacho" Torres were on the dance floor, watching for people who might be watching him. No sense taking unnecessary risks—Sheikh Qadr al-Masri would be out head hunting.

Winters nervously wiped condensation off the glass with his thumb, and said, "Maybe this isn't a good idea."

"*What*? If you have information, I *want* it," Kirk demanded.

"You don't understand. I think I got something on that fuckin' Sheikh and his A-rab bitch lawyer, but unless we go off the record, I can't say much." Winters rolled a toothpick from one side of his mouth to the other.

Kirk studied Winters for a moment. "Why's that? You bend the rules, or do something stupid?"

Winters grimaced and looked up at the ceiling. "Man, I don't wanna turn things inside out. I'd like to keep my job, you know? Instead of stamping out license plates."

Kirk let out a deep sigh, then turned his gaze out onto the dance floor. Nacho had an arm wrapped around Michele's waist, dancing to the Rolling Stones' *Satisfaction*. Dressed in a skimpy French T-shirt, black tights, and calf-high boots with three-inch heels, Michele's *feng shui* appeared to be in perfect order. Kirk then turned his attention to the prison guard.

Winters stared at his beer glass, and murmured, "Look man, we gotta keep this off the record, or it's no dice. I put nineteen years in a dead-end job, and I got a few more months to retirement. I can't jeopardize it. I wanna retire from this dead-end job and sell real estate with my brother-in-law." He spread his hands out, palms up. "You see what I'm sayin'?"

Kirk leaned on his forearms. "Sergeant, I didn't come all the way out here to buy you a beer, or to bust your ass. I don't make arrests. I hunt down nasty people, not decorated war heroes. We're off the record. You have my word on that. And, I don't like wasting my time." Kirk wiggled his fingers inward, palm up. "Let's have it."

Winters rubbed the two-day beard stubble on his chin, then said, "Under the circumstances, anything I tell you may be wrong, and I don't know what the right circumstances are, either. . . . To make a long story short, my lieutenant has been gunning for me. Several of us took the test for lieutenant at the same time. I know I aced it, but he cheated, and one of the other guys ratted him out. Fucker pulled in a political favor to snag the job, but he still blames me for the snitch."

Kirk knew the drill, but he would have to milk Winters from an oblique angle. "I understand. How'd you get a funky nickname like T-Bone?"

"NCAA Wrestling. One of my patented holds. Scholarship at Colorado State. Name pissed me off at first. Now, I kinda like it. Never did like Edgar."

"Why didn't you put the asshole in headlock and flatten his face?"

Winters forced a laugh and leaned back in the booth. "Putting the hurt on him would be too easy." He stroked his mustache, leaned forward, and looked into Kirk's eyes. "What would *you* have done?"

"Wrongs need to be righted. It's a matter of personal honor. I'd bide my time and plan a way to get even when the opportunity arose."

T-Bone stroked his mustache. "So, what's with the bandages and bruises. You anywhere near Houston lately?"

Kirk's eyes riveted on the sergeant. "That's not open for discussion." He signaled the waitress for another round, then addressed T-Bone. "Maybe you colored outside the lines. No big deal."

"I feel like I can trust you to do the right thing. That's all I ask."

Kirk nodded. "Fair enough. Go on."

"OK. Here's the deal." T-Bone cast a furtive glance around the bar, and spoke a notch above the din. "I handle some bad-asses over there in the pen. Serial killers. Mass murderers. Psychos. Like that. They all have a chilling Charlie Manson nobody home look in their eyes."

"Sounds typical. Dark energy is the biggest mystery in physics and psychopathology."

"Yeah, but that bitch Sheikh Abdel-e Rahman uses for his lawyer? That stone-faced bitch stared me right in the face. *Nobody* does that. I'm telling ya, her needle ain't pointin' north."

Kirk wondered how the sphinx-like woman could be a threat. "Tell me about her."

"She's always dressed to kill, so to speak, in a black *abaya* and a color-coordinated *hijab* that shrouds her face. If she lived in Gaza, she would have already strapped a bomb around her waist filled with nuts and bolts. Her ovaries rattle whenever I escort the Sheikh into the room. Bitch would fit in well with the rest of the Loony Tunes in the Florence Pen."

Kirk took a deep swallow and drained his beer. "Yassin's in love with the blind geezer? What makes you so sure?"

"I'm fascinated by those sociopaths and try to figure out what makes 'em tick. I read their case files in the prison library."

"Not many people have that kind of intellectual curiosity."

T-Bone placed his big arms on the table and leaned forward. He spoke in a conspiratorial whisper. "Yeah, but some of those records were sealed."

Kirk rocked back. "I never heard that." He took a beat, then said, "Rules were made to be bent. I probably would have done the same thing. How did you do it?"

"I hacked into the database to find out why the lawyers copped plea bargains on some of those psychos." T-Bone bit his lower lip and looked down at the table for a moment, then gave Kirk a questioning look. "If any of this gets back my lieutenant will bar-b-que my *cojónes* for breakfast."

"I've given you my word. It won't."

A waitress strutted over to their booth lip-synching the music. She was poured into skin-tight jeans with a blouse knotted at the waist.

Nice moves, nifty tits. Kirk admired the view, and raised an empty bottle. "Two more Coors and a double order of buffalo wings."

"Gorgeous redhead," T-Bone remarked.

"If you want trouble, hook up with a redhead. They're descended from Celtic warriors—hell hath no fury like a redheaded woman scorned."

"Speaking from experience?"

"You know the cliché, 'Once bitten, twice shy'." *Get it back on track.* "I understand you're a Desert Storm vet."

"Nothing I like to brag about."

"You ever lose sleep over it?"

"Nope. Never, ever. They were armed enemy needing a smoke-check. The sniper's motto, 'When in doubt, let Allah sort it out.'"

T-Bone had visited hell and spit on the fire with contempt.

"Self-preservation. Works for me too," Kirk replied.

T-Bone let out a sigh of relief. "You know. I feel I can trust you to do the right thing, and that's all I'm askin'. You see what I'm sayin'?"

"Calling in was the right thing. You may be a hero."

"Most heroes I've known are *dead.*" T-bone's voice was funereal.

"What dirt do you have on the lawyer?"

"That explosion in Houston keeps me awake at night. I've seen things that indicate that fuckin' Sheikh and that lawyer lady may have been involved in it."

"*Things?* What things? Suppose it was a terrorist attack, then how'd they fit in?"

"Kirk, don't try to bullshit me. I've been watching those two dirt-bags, trying to figure out what the hell they were up to. That bitch has an evil aura—nothing but anger and hatred in her eyes. She comes in every Monday morning, and they pray together. Following the Houston attack, they did the Terrorist Tango. A minute later, she looked like she was about ready to blow a head gasket from over-revving her motor. I wondered what the blind bastard said that got her panties wadded up. They whisper in Arabic, real sneaky like."

Kirk waved his hand dismissively. "Lotta lawyers act that way."

T-Bone glanced around, tightened muscles in his shoulders and neck, his body language projecting something big league. "Yeah, but that ain't the *bad* news," he said in a deepened voice.

Kirk frowned. "What the *hell* are you trying to tell me?"

"Like I said, I study these psychos. I noticed Rahman used his hands sometimes to make lots of gestures and finger-painting on the table, like this." T-Bone cupped his left hand and used his index finger to draw pictures. "At first I figured the Sheikh's use of his hands made up for his blindness and all, you know?"

The waitress dropped off two bottles of Coors and a heaping platter of spicy-hot chicken wings. He poured the beer into their glasses and watched the foam rise. "They up to something?"

T-Bone gnawed on a wing and nodded. "Wait 'til you hear this. . . . I kinda snuck up behind the Sheikh to see what the hell he was doing with the finger painting. They were so engrossed in their conversation they didn't notice me move in. Too close for ACLU comfort. Know what I mean?"

Kirk thought he could use a man with that kind of initiative. "You have a set of brass balls the size of the Wall Street Bull. Weren't you concerned she might file a complaint?"

"I was more worried you'd rat me out." T-Bone grabbed another wing.

"Not my style, but that's damned good detective work. You should have joined the FBI."

"No kidding."

"Did you hear anything they said? You understand Arabic?"

"Sounds like they were gargling with gasoline." T-Bone swallowed a slug of beer. "Anyway, when Aisha Yassin looks up and sees me standing there, she looked like she was passing a gallstone the size of Gibraltar. Bitch got gall all right, and she's dirty. What convinces me is I'm sure I saw Rahman draw Egyptian characters on the tabletop."

Kirk wiped beer foam off his mouth with the back of his hand. "Characters?"

"You know? The bastard's finger painting. The hieroglyphics."

"Hieroglyphics? So what?"

T-Bone stroked his mustache. "That bitch's bio says she was born and raised in Cairo, and I know that fuckin' Sheikh ran the local terror network called, *al-Gama'a al-Islamiyya,* before the Egyptian government ran his ass out of the country. Those two would know all about hieroglyphics. It's in their blood."

Where the hell was this headed? "Tell me more about the hieroglyphics." Kirk slouched in the booth feigning nonchalance.

"I don't understand all I know about them, but those Egyptian characters are distinctive. I recognized a couple, and looked 'em up on the Internet." T-Bone took a long pull on his beer.

"Like what?"

"An ankh, a cartouche, and an evil eye. Ankh is the symbol of eternal life, a cartouche represents a proper name, and the Eye of Horus symbolizes a powerful dude, the Falcon Pharaoh—"

"The Falcon?" *Sheikh Qadr al-Masri's trademark.* Kirk sat up, his blood running cold, nerves on edge. "You're certain?"

"I know what I saw, and there ain't nothin' wrong with my memory. I'm convinced they're passing secret code. Some kinda covert communication. Maybe a plot for another terror attack. My gut says Rahman had something to do with the Houston blitz."

Kirk felt a cold tingling premonition of disaster. He wondered if al-Masri manipulated *al-Gama'a al-Islamiyya* and MOIS. Maybe Yassin and Rahman were the linchpin. If he could penetrate into their communications network, he'd pull the pin and watch the wheels fall off Sheikh Qadr al-Masri's goat cart.

"You have anything else to spill besides your beer?"

"I spilled my guts and I feel a whole lot better getting this shit off my chest. I hope it does some good. We shoulda fried that fuckin' Sheikh Rahman."

"He'll rot in prison, and from here on out, I'll know every move Aisha Yassin makes."

"Spoken like a true Desert Storm warrior." T-Bone raised his glass. "Skoal, brother."

* * *

Kirk had to scramble, hard and fast. He needed more help. T-Bone was a perfect candidate to fill a void. The big man had unloaded a hell of a lot of baggage at considerable risk to save innocent lives—a true patriot. Kirk decided to risk limited disclosure. He looked T-Bone in the eye for a few seconds.

The bruiser had a trace of a simper on his mug. It disappeared with the *Bad to the Bone* ringtone on his cell phone. He read the text message, then snapped the phone closed.

"My ex. She found the meaning of life and traded me in for a younger model. Bitchin' about the kids' custody again. Next time, if I find a woman I like, I'll just give her a house." He sighed. "Women are either at your feet or at your throat."

"They always get the last word in every argument," Kirk agreed. "Anything a man says after that is the beginning of a new argument."

"Ain't that the truth."

Kirk regarded T-Bone for a moment. "How would you like to come to work for me?"

T-Bone rolled his eyes. "You serious?"

"As a heart attack."

"Man, I only got a few more months to retirement."

"You have a lot of tread left. I admire those who know when to bend the rules and take measured risks. I need people who can think straight and act decisively in a crunch. I want a shooter I can trust to cover my six—a lead gundog."

"Kirk, I appreciate the vote of confidence, but I wanna send my kids to college. Get the ex off my back."

"With your service record and Federal guard service, I can bump you two grades to a GS 14. You'll be fully vested and draw a pension along with your FBI salary. The pay's not that great, but the parking and ammo are free. In your spare time you can peddle *Satanic Verses* to the ayatollahs instead of hawking real estate to housewives."

T-Bone raised his eyebrows. "You got that kinda stroke?"

"Anything I need, I get. I've reviewed your military records—the commendations and number of confirmed kills during Desert Storm. I need that kind of talent to back me up."

Kirk set his beer on the table. "Look. You feel the same way I do. Here's the deal. I run a covert paramilitary counterterrorism unit. I have a couple of smart women on my team along with battle-hardened Special Forces vets, like you. We don't much like making arrests, if you get my drift."

"Huh. Sounds like you have a lot of fun ducking bullets and bombs. And political brickbats." T-Bone remained stone-faced.

"Sergeant, you can lead the pack and have an unrestricted view of the world or stay hitched to a harness pulling a lead-sled while looking up your lieutenant's ass. I'm giving you the opportunity to do something that makes a difference and steer history on a safer course. The downside is you won't get any accolades. The political fat cats will express gratitude the way they'd thank street cleaners who follow horses in a parade. Your reward is just this." Kirk slammed the table with the palm of his hand. *"Satisfaction."*

T-Bone's eyes widened.

"'Some people spend an entire lifetime wondering if they made a difference in the world, but the Marines don't have that problem. This is your defining moment—a time that shows what kind of man you really are. Most people never get that chance." Kirk set his beer on the table, leaned forward, and dropped his voice to a bare whisper. "That tanker explosion was no *god damned* accident. You are a United States Marine. You can make a difference. What are you gonna do about it?"

T-Bone eyed Kirk for about ten seconds. "Kirk, not to put too fine a point on it, but you have a prodigious ability for bullshit that can only be topped by your brass balls. I kinda like that. . . . "How much time do I have to think about it?"

Kirk pointed at T-Bone's glass with a chicken bone. "Until you finish your beer."

Fifteen

Cairo International Airport
Cairo, Egypt

Michele's phone taps paid off. They discovered that Aisha Yassin had made travel plans to Egypt immediately after her last visit with Sheikh Abdel-e Rahman. From Denver, she connected with a KLM flight from Kennedy Airport to Cairo.

Kirk's buzz from T-Bone's intelligence offset the boredom and jet lag from a fourteen-hour flight on a CIA Gulfstream V direct from Denver to ancient city on the Nile. After slipping through customs on a diplomatic passport, he and Natalia Levi, the Mossad Chief of Station in Cairo, waited in a beat-up Volvo sedan in the passenger pickup area.

"That's her. Aisha Yassin." Kirk pointed. "The chunky woman with the black *abaya* and *hijab.*"

"What is this chunky?"

"American slang for short and fat."

Natalia's face remained void of any expression. Kirk wondered what went on behind her dark mysterious eyes—eyes that had seen a thousand lifetimes of death and destruction. From her sad expression, he thought with half her family blown to pieces by Islamic terrorists, it would be hard to smile. Natalia had a burning desire to stomp out the menace—like the terrorist bitch in black.

"Natalia, I have the gut feeling something important is about to go down here—activity that might help us determine the terrorists' objective."

"We shall see."

Kirk and Natalia watched as Aisha boarded a taxi. They tailed the cab to a squalid slum on the south side of the city. The cab slowed as it passed an ancient madrassa, an Islamic school of indoctrination for the faithful.

Aisha turned her head toward the mud brick building, as the cab continued down the rutted dirt street.

"Where the hell is she headed?" Kirk asked. "I thought you said she was going to that madrassa."

"The woman exercises crude field-craft. Her actions are a poor attempt to lose anyone following."

Kirk watched as the taxi dropped Aisha in front of a bakery a half-block south of the madrassa.

"How familiar are you with this place?" Kirk flipped his thumb over his shoulder toward the madrassa.

"This place serves as a safe house for *al-Gama'a al-Islamiyya*, the Egyptian *al-Qai'da* affiliate. Sheikh Omar Abdul-e Rahman was spiritual leader here before his imprisonment and exile for his role in Sadat's assassination and the Luxor massacre. The madrassa is a terrorist incubator and serves as their base of operations."

"*Damn it*. We need more firepower if there are Islamic operatives in there," Kirk replied.

"Two of my men follow. Are you armed?"

"I'm only packing an HK45 handgun."

"My men and I are armed with Uzi's and will cover you. Find a good vantage point and remain concealed in the shadows. These people are dangerous. I shall maintain surveillance. This woman, she will return."

Kirk took cover in an alley filled with putrid garbage, the stench of open sewers, and the smell of death and decay enhanced by the olfactory stew of burnt animal dung used for fuel—the incongruous blessing of the Third World. The temperature was over 100 degrees, accelerating the rot of a bloated dog that lay nearby, maggots crawling out of its ruptured entrails.

He squatted behind a wooden crate to wait for Aisha's arrival. Salty sweat poured down his face and burned into his eyes, as he focused a laser microphone onto a set of heavy wooden doors on the madrassa.

He made out what sounded like chanting prayers.

"The woman now leaves the bakery and walks to the madrassa," Natalia reported.

Aisha cast furtive glances as she walked down the dusty street. The neighborhood was not a safe place. The environment added to her trepidation with the meeting. She knew Ramzi Gonimah, Sheikh Rahman's designated head of *al-Gama'a al-Islamiyya* was ruthless, but she prayed for a safe welcome, and a role in the jihad. Her pulse quickened as she approached the madrassa and surveyed the structure.

A new roof of river reeds blanketed the crumbling mud brick building. It would have made better sense to fix the broken walls when they rebuilt the roof, but there were many things about her home country that made no sense.

She entered the courtyard through a classic Arabic arch adorned with a mosaic of lapis blue tiles. A lone date palm provided shade to a mangy-looking dog that dozed. The cur lifted its head when she entered the courtyard, then went back to sleep.

As she passed an open window, she saw about fifty teenage boys inside kneeling on prayer rugs, ululating and reciting *suras* while they fingered strings of worry beads. The sights and sounds brought back memories of her youth when she attended the madrassa for indoctrination into her faith.

A teenage boy approached her and asked if he could provide assistance.

She introduced herself.

He said she was expected, and guided her to her contact, a man she recognized. Ramzi had lost a lot of weight, and his beard was grayer than when she had last seen him fifteen years earlier. He wore a *kafiyah,* a red-checked scarf, tied around his neck, and a soiled white cotton skullcap. She never knew his nationality, as he had represented himself as Egyptian at times, sometimes as Kuwaiti, and other times as Iraqi. He disappeared for long periods. Rumors were he was a ruthless *al-Islamiyya* enforcer. Yes, she knew Ramzi had the blood of hundreds on his hands, Muslim and infidel. He was repugnant and of the lower cast, a man not to be trusted. Ramzi had the suspicious eyes of a cornered rat.

She greeted him with hesitation. "*Salaam alaikum.*"

Ramzi focused on her forehead, instead of her eyes—the Middle Eastern cultural male signal that women were beneath men. However, she had earned an American law degree and had something he needed. And she needed something from him. *Standing and respect.* In her eyes, they were equals, and she was determined to set the ground rules, albeit with care and finesse—the lawyers' way. A woman's way.

"The Prophet smiles upon us," he responded in Arabic. He took her arm and guided her to a small table in a back room lit by sunlight streaming through elaborately carved shutters.

The touch. He *was* cognizant of her stature. A women of the West, with Egyptian blood and fire.

The young boy poured boiling-hot tea from a Bedouin brass teapot into a pair of tall dirty glass tumblers, then retired from the room.

She tried to ignore the smell of Ramzi's sweat-soaked robe. "I have brought baklava," she said, a slight quiver in her voice.

"*Shukran.*" He reached for the paper sack, shooing blowflies.

They each took a slurp of the hot liquid as she surveyed the surroundings. A small ragged table and two chairs on the dirt floor, mud brick whitewashed walls stained from mildew. It was cooler in the room, some parts in deep shade.

Aisha felt a flush pass through her body. In feigned deference, she lowered her eyes, and placed her hands in her lap so Ramzi could not see them shake. Jihadists exposed no emotion.

"Aisha, dear child, you left Egypt as a young maiden and return as a woman with an American law degree." Ramzi's eyes gleamed. "And perhaps a message."

"An important message."

He leaned forward. "You have been groomed at great effort and expense. We observed your progress with pleasure. Excellent. Excellent indeed." Ramzi smiled. His breath smelled like camel dung. He stuffed the pastry into his mouth.

She shuddered. "It is my sacred duty as I am a faithful daughter of Islam. I thirst for Paradise." Aisha bowed her head for a moment.

"Faith yields redemption." Ramzi's eyes glowed.

"But Paradise must be a real place."

"Is it not the word of the Prophet Mohammed? He was a worldly man, yet he became the choice of God to deliver His Word. And to slay the infidels, is this not the word of the *Qur'an?* You must work hard. You must keep the faith. Your work will destroy the *kafirs* for the glory of Islam."

Sheikh Rahman taught Aisha everything about America was evil, degenerate, and in complete opposition to the true Muslim faith. How could she not fight against a society whose purpose was the complete destruction of Islam—a modern-day Crusade.

"Please forgive me," she said. "I know all this, and I pray to Allah for guidance and forgiveness. To die for Allah—life could have no greater purpose. I am dedicated to the cause."

Ramzi touched her chin. "Aisha, dear child. The Falcon ordered your training for a supreme purpose in the jihad. I, myself, argued against use of women, but the Falcon's logic prevailed. Westerners rarely see women as enemy."

Aisha nodded.

Ramzi's eyes flashed as he spoke in a whisper, "Are you prepared to serve *Allah?*"

Aisha's heart palpitated. "*Yes.* My heart is strong for the love of Islam. We have nothing, and the decadent Americans have everything, taken from us. When everything is taken from one's life, it makes life more valuable in the service of the cause, to die for *Allah* in the jihad. I have been sent by Sheikh Rahman, but I do not know the reason for my quest. "I must know my purpose."

Ramzi's scowl frightened her. Had she pushed too far? She fought to suppress signs of fear and tried to maintain a lawyer's stoic face. She knew the trained look appeared contemptuous to many, but hoped it was an asset.

Ramzi took a slurp of tea, then set the tumbler down on the tabletop and leaned forward. "Very well. You will speak to no one of our discussion, or face beheading and denial of Paradise."

Aisha nodded assent, and breathed a sigh of relief. She now knew she had gained standing.

"The Falcon has conceived of a bold master plan for the jihad. The Great Satan will be punished."

Aisha smiled, then retrieved a pen and small piece of rice paper from her purse. She scrawled Rahman's message in Arabic script, then slid the paper across the table to Ramzi.

Ramzi's eyes gleamed with the raging fire of a half-crazed zealot. He crunched the paper into a ball, inserted it into his mouth, and chewed it, then swallowed.

He blew across the top of the glass, then took a noisy slurp. "So be it. . . . We have excellent funding and many dedicated young martyrs. *Al-Islamiyya* has established underground cells within the United States."

"What is the mission?"

Ramzi laughed contemptuously.

She felt a surge of anger. Had she had been away from Egypt too long?

"You are familiar with the CIA Rendition operation?" he asked.

"I have never heard of this. What is it?"

"The CIA has certain reciprocal arrangements to avoid American laws. They kidnap their victims and send them off to foreign countries for interrogation."

Aisha cringed as she envisioned Uzbek thugs pulling out her fingernails. She had no tolerance for pain. "Very well, Ramzi. I concede your point. Please proceed."

"You know of the Bronx safe house?"

She nodded.

"We would like you to relay messages between Sheikh Rahman and other *al-Islamiyya* cells, including that in the Bronx."

"This I can do." She smiled.

"Excellent. We have developed hyper-secure communications using the Internet. Your role as Sheikh Rahman's lawyer shall provide another layer of cover."

Ramzi handed Aisha a sealed CD that looked like one of the ubiquitous promotions from America Online.

"This contains encryption software, your contacts' e-mail addresses, instructions for use of the encryption system, and an auto-install feature to load everything onto your computer. The messages are imbedded in graphic files that can only be coded and decoded with the encryption key on the CD. Guard this with your life."

"Allah willing."

"My child, you have been chosen for an important role in the jihad as the messenger for *al-Islamiyya.* You are the *Sword of Ṣalāḥ ad-Dīn.*"

The thought of *kafir* bloodshed made her arteries sing. A plan was in place, and she had a major role. Their attacks would not fail. They would punish the Great Satan.

"Insha'Allah," she said. "The *Sword of Ṣalāḥ ad-Dīn* will again draw infidel blood. It is the will of God."

"You must send the message to our martyrs upon your return."

"Allah-u Akbar." they chanted in unison.

Misery loves company, thought Kirk. He hoped Natalia was covering his back as he squatted behind the crate, disgusted and nauseated with the stench in the alley. Heat, leg cramps, and failure to make out a single word of Aisha's conversation in that damned madrassa, disheartened him. *Another dead-end stakeout.* His mind wandered.

He felt a presence that made the hair on his neck prickle. An instant later, a scraping noise from behind.

As he turned, he caught a glimpse of a red-checked *kafiyah* at the instant he was struck on the back of the head with a lead-filled sap.

Kirk dropped flat on the hard-packed dirt. A heavy knee in his back forced the air out of his lungs, his arms pulled behind him and bound tightly.

Two men, speaking Cairo dialect Arabic, frog-marched him down the alley and forced him into the back of a dusty vehicle, face down.

Kirk imagined a *shafra,* a curved double-edged knife with a rib in the middle, drawn across his throat.

"Halt, or I will shoot," Natalia snapped in Arabic. "Drop your weapons and place your hands against the wall, feet out. *Now.*" She aimed her Uzi at the armed gunmen in a menacing thrust. "Move quickly. Hands against the wall," she ordered, then backed toward the car, opened the door, and cut the plastic ties off Kirk's wrists.

When he rolled over, he saw one of the men pull the sap and charge Natalia. Kirk lunged out of the vehicle and head-butted the assailant in the face. The assailant screamed in agony.

Kirk slammed the heel of his boot into the man's chest, driving him back into the mud brick wall. The assailant slid down the wall, lights out.

The second man advanced toward Natalia, a spooky look in his eyes as he came up behind her. Kirk shouted, *"Natalia."*

She spun on the ball of a foot and cracked her Uzi down on the man's wrist, then chopped the back of his neck with the edge of her palm. He went down, a moan oozing from his lips.

Kirk and Natalia bound the men with Flexicuffs.

"Kirk, are you injured?" She felt the lump on the back of his head. "No blood. You shall have a headache tomorrow."

He felt his head and let out a low silent whistle. “Damn that hurts.” He winced, but he was grateful for her saving his ass. “Who are those men? They *al-Islamiyya*?”

Natalia held up her hand, then barked an order in Hebrew into her radio. Seconds later, her men converged, brandishing their Uzi machine pistols.

Kirk did not understand a damned word she said, but based on the tone of her voice and gestures, Natalia dressed them up, down, and sideways. He could have been captured by *al-Islamiyya* nutcases, tortured, and had his head whacked off. He owed her. If those fundamentalist Islamic nutcases in the madrassa had any inkling they would face her in hand-to-hand combat, they would be better off to slit their own throats.

Natalia turned to Kirk with an apology written all over her face. Before she could speak, a clean-shaven man, dressed in a crisp Egyptian Army uniform rounded the corner into the alley. He laughed in a deep baritone voice.

“Natalia Levi. You should let me know when you operate on my turf,” the man said in Arabic. “Those are my men. Please release them.” He rested his foot on the front bumper of the car, a Turkish cigarette dangling between his fingers. He had a glint in his eye, and the trace of a repressed smile.

Egyptian Army? What the hell are they doing here?

She turned toward him, then laughed for the first time in a husky and sensuous voice. “*Salaam,* Amad,” she responded in Arabic. “So good to see you, even under these unpleasant circumstances.”

“*Shalom*, my Lovely,” Amad responded, then pointed to Kirk. “Who is this man?” Amad dropped the cigarette butt to the ground, and snuffed it with the toe of a brightly shined shoe.

"Special Agent Kirk Magus," Natalia said in English. "Please make the acquaintance of Colonel Amad Suleyman, commander of *Al-Mukhabarat al-'Ammah*, Egyptian Intelligence and Security Service."

Egyptian Intelligence? This is getting weirder by the minute. "*As-salāmu `alaikum*," Kirk said. He extended his right hand; his left touched his head as he gave a slight bow. "Sir, I speak Arabic if you prefer. Call me Kirk."

"Very good, Kirk. Then please call me Amad." He spoke in clipped Oxford English, then reached to shake hands with a firm grip.

"Perhaps it would be best if we retired to Amad's office," Natalia said. "We need to leave here quickly before we are detected. My men will take over surveillance."

"Agreed," Amad said. "Let us go now."

Sixteen

Al-Mukhabarat al-'Ammah Headquarters
Cairo, Egypt

Natalia and Kirk sat at a small conference table in Amad's small office. Kirk held an ice pack to the back of his head.

Amad stood at the end of the table leaning forward, with both palms on the tabletop. He glanced at his two battered men who sat in chairs against the wall, and shook his head. He took a seat at the head of the table and crushed his cigarette in an engraved brass ashtray. Appraising Kirk with a raised eyebrow, he nodded. A signal—*I am in control and we are not on an equal footing at this moment.*

Kirk thought an explanation was in order, without apology. "Amad, my objective was to place that madrassa under surveillance, with Mossad assistance."

Amad pursed his lips. "We try to cooperate when it is in our best interest to do so. I'm certain you understand my position."

"Looks like we got off to a bad start." Kirk looked at the ice pack. "It's no big deal, really. My head's not bleeding."

"My men took a beating." He half-smiled and waved his hand toward his men, who sat scowling, one holding an ice pack on his wrist, the other to a bloody nose. "Two of my best men, subdued by a woman." He gave Natalia a licentious smile.

Who wouldn't? With her tightly curled dark mane framing an alluring face and a lickerish body, she was a knockout. A man could lose himself in her arms. He could have forgotten the pain in the back of his head.

"We should take training from Mossad." Amad folded his arms. "Now, please tell me the purpose of your surveillance."

Kirk could tell his polite request was no such thing. It was an order, plain and simple. Getting crossways with Egyptian Intelligence would be a real bad start, and he needed their cooperation. He trusted Natalia's judgment, and she knew these people better than he did. He looked to her for guidance. She offered a perceptible nod, eyelids slowly closing.

Kirk set the ice pack aside on the table, deciding to divulge what he thought Amad needed to know, nothing more.

"We had woman named Aisha Yassin under surveillance. She traveled from the United States to Cairo, and acts as Sheikh Omar Abdel-e Rahman's attorney. We have reason to believe she may attempt to pass coded messages from Rahman to *al-Gama'a al-Islamiyya* operatives—messages that may have a grave impact on the US."

"We know the Yassin woman, and Sheikh Rahman. We know them quite well. Aisha Yassin was indoctrinated in that madrassa during her youth. Sheikh Rahman is her spiritual leader, and poisoned her mind with Islamic fundamentalist rubbish. My government forced Rahman into exile after he instigated several terrorist attacks in Egypt. *Al-Mukhabarat* has had the madrassa under surveillance for years. My men detected your suspicious presence."

Kirk raised his eyebrows.

"You are aware, of course, these people are enemies of Egypt? They deserve to die for their crimes."

"I'm going to kill them," Kirk said. "Every one of them."

Amad exhaled smoke through his nose in a rush. "On Egyptian soil?"

"We all have a common purpose," Natalia said, "We must work together to defeat these terrorists, this evil. Whatever it takes."

"Indeed." Amad's leering smile flashed a hidden message.

Something hot was going on between them. Lucky bastard.

The briefing continued, then wound down to who-do-you-know small talk. Kirk was anxious to get back to the madrassa, and started to rise from his chair and offer his thanks.

Natalia touched his forearm, shifting her dark eyes toward Amad's injured men—hard men who suffered a humiliating beating.

"My throat is dry," she said. "I think we all could use a bit of refreshment and become better acquainted if we are going to work in unison."

"Yes, I quite agree." Amad grinned. Good teeth. Smart, good looking guy, hence Natalia's attraction.

Subtlety was not Kirk's strong suit, but he took the hint, and he could entertain, especially on Uncle Sugar's dime.

"Colonel Suleyman, I understand beer was invented in Egypt. Would you happen to know a good place where we can wash down some dune dust? Your men look thirsty. It would please me to offer some consolation to you and your men. I'm buying."

Natalia acknowledged his correct move by offering a hint of a smile.

Amad's men rose from their seats, eager for booze like Bedouin's who found the last oasis in the desert.

"I know of an excellent hookah bar. Local color, as they say, with a magnificent view of the Nile and Egypt's famous belly dancers." Amad had a glint in his eyes. "Perhaps we should first listen to the taped conversations in the madrassa."

"What?" Kirk's eyes widened. "You had the place bugged?"

Amad shrugged. "All is not what it seems. My men installed surveillance equipment when the Imam had the roof of the building rebuilt."Amad pulled open his desk drawer and turned on an audio recorder.

Kirk listened raptly as Aisha's conversation with Ramzi Gonimah played back. *"The Falcon has conceived of a bold master plan for the jihad. The Great Satan will be punished."* Then no sound, other than hiss for several seconds, followed by a noisy slurp and Ramzi saying, *"So be it."*

"What the hell happened?" Kirk asked.

"It appears the woman is no fool," Natalia responded. "She passed a message, perhaps in writing. We may never know the content."

Seventeen

Los Angeles County Museum of Art
Los Angeles, California

Restless sleep on the fourteen-hour return flight from Cairo, heavy freeway traffic, and excess coffee churning in Kirk's stomach contributed to his foul mood. Aisha's surveillance proved she was an operative, but he still did not know the content of the message she had transmitted to Ramzi Gonimah. He held out a thin line of hope, knowing hope rarely cooperated.

"Michele, I don't understand why you're so upbeat. All we know is Aisha made contact."

"We're making progress, and we know more than that. We had a gift from the intelligence gods with T-Bone's observations of Rahman's finger painting. After reviewing the old visitors room security videos, we thought they were poor quality and in need of an upgrade."

"An upgrade?" Kirk took his eyes off the heavy LA freeway traffic and caught her grinning ear to ear, her dark eyes sparkling, voice radiating confidence. Big improvement from their first meeting at Headquarters. She turned out to be a great partner, demonstrating initiative, intelligence, diligence, and following the rules. It helped balance out his long list of negative traits.

"We installed high-resolution cameras in the visitor's room, including one over the booth Rahman always uses. Aisha's last prison visit is in Technicolor."

"How'd you get past the prison officials?"

"I made a few calls to expedite things."

"That's great work, but be careful following in my footsteps. If the ACLU discovers your surveillance, they'll have a conniption fit. They use every trick in their convoluted rule book to accommodate criminals and go after the good guys."

"They won't know. Plausible deniability, and all that." She shifted toward him causing her short skirt to ride up her thighs. "I'll do whatever it takes." Her last comment had a sexy lilt.

"What about Jeffers? He in the loop?"

"Mushroomed—fed a bunch of crap and kept in the dark. He won't dare interfere again." Her eyes dug into his for a moment, then she rattled on. "Kirk, I'm confident we'll identify the terrorist chain of command, and their mission. With taps in Aisha's apartment and office, we can monitor her phone calls. As soon as she logs onto the Internet, we'll trace her e-mails and capture copies of *al-Islamiyya's* encryption algorithm. I have the NSA spooks standing by, salivating."

"That's good. Tell me about this guy you lined up to review the videos. He's vetted?"

"Of course."

"What's his claim to fame?"

"Dr. Winston Burdette is a world renowned authority on Egyptian artifacts language, and culture—an Egyptologist."

Kirk pulled into a visitor's parking space at the Museum, then turned to Michele and said, "Maybe we'll get something going here."

"A girl can only hope," she murmured.

Burdette's secretary escorted them into his office, then brought in a tray holding coffee, biscotti, fresh cream, and sweeteners.

Kirk checked out the surroundings. Danish modern furniture, three walls with overloaded bookshelves. A neat but crowded desk covered with computer equipment and dusty files.

Kirk guessed Burdette was in his mid-seventies. He was nattily dressed in a chalk-striped, double-breasted suit along with a red bow tie, and cordovan wing-tip shoes. Although small in stature, the man maintained a presence with his shock of wavy white hair and deep blue eyes that focused intently on anyone who spoke to him.

Burdette's secretary poured coffee into china cups adorned with a Greek motif, then withdrew. Dr. Burdette smiled at them, awaiting their opening.

Given a choice, Kirk preferred getting his boots muddied rather than scrubbing his fingernails for a damned tea party.

"Dr. Burdette," Michele began, "we appreciate your time to meet with us on such short notice. I suspect you are a busy man, so we will get right to the point. We're in a bind and could use your help."

Dr. Burdette took a sip of coffee then set his cup and saucer down on the table. "I'd be pleased to help in any way I can, Ms. Li."

"We'd like you to review a couple of prison surveillance videos to see if you can make out the depiction of Egyptian hieroglyphics from a man's finger painting."

"I believe I can do that for you." He appeared quite the enthusiast.

After Michele inserted a DVD into his computer, Burdette reviewed the video, jotting down notes, occasionally pausing to rewind. The black and white security camera videos were grainy and out of focus. He studied them for ten minutes in silence, then he raised his clasped hands and gently bumped them repeatedly against his chin.

"Dr. Burdette, what do you think?" Kirk asked. "Anything there?"

Burdette removed his reading glasses and pinched the bridge of his nose.

"Well, it looks as though the prisoner was trying to hide his finger painting with his left hand; however, I can verify that the man's sketching were hieroglyphic characters. Just what they mean, it's hard to tell as yet."

"Why? Can't you interpret what you saw?" Kirk asked with a raised eyebrow. "I don't understand why this should be so difficult."

Michele glared at Kirk, looking like she intended to claw his eyeballs out.

"It takes several pictographs to make up a word or a phrase," Dr. Burdette explained. "The written language is quite clever, but the pictographs have wide meanings, and portions were blocked."

Kirk sighed and stared down into his coffee cup. He rubbed his forehead. "Michele? Any chance the second high resolution DVD will show more?"

"Possibly. I haven't had a chance to study it. Why don't we allow Dr. Burdette to review both DVDs in their entirety? They contain over two hours of recording and will take some time. Dr. Burdette, would you need our assistance at this point?"

"No thank you, Ms. Li. It would be best if I worked alone on this, allowing me to concentrate. If you two young people come back after lunch, I might have more to report then." He smiled. "I'm sure you have better things to do with your time."

"That would be perfect, sir," Michele said. "To reiterate, this is confidential. We'll be back at two PM."

While waiting for the elevator Michele turned to Kirk. "What the hell did you think you were doing back there?" She had a hand on her hip and looked like she was about to club him with her Gucci handbag. "Dr. Burdette is not under your command. You need to exercise better judgment with people, especially intellectuals. Some take offense readily. He would have been within his rights to throw us out of his office. Where'd they send you to charm school?"

Kirk almost blushed. "Camp Peary, Virginia."

She tucked her hair behind her ear, and moistened her lips. Kirk noticed she did it each time she wanted to stress a point.

"Be patient. We're making progress."

Jesus. Minnie Mouse suddenly became an 800-pound gorilla—a primate in three-inch heels.

"I'll try to tone it down."

Michele smiled coyly. "Do you normally let women walk all over you?"

"Only when they're buck-ass naked. In high heels."

* * *

After abalone and a bottle of Charles Krug zinfandel at Marina Del Rey, Kirk and Michele reconvened in Burdette's office.

Burdette pointed to his notes with his glasses. "I gleaned more detail from the color video, especially the overhead view. I'm in the process of reorganizing the pictographs so that I can read and interpret them. Unfortunately, portions of his finger painting are impaired, so this may be difficult and somewhat time consuming. However, I will do my best."

"Dr. Burdette. If you can fill in the blanks with a best guess, then please do so. If there is anything we can do to help, please let us know," Michele offered.

"Would you have audiotapes of their conversation?"

Kirk shook his head. "Nope. Lawyer-client privilege. We can only keep an eye on prisoners in the visitor's room; we can't listen to their conversations."

"That's too bad." Burdette mused, tapping his glasses against his lower teeth. "I recognize the importance of this. I recall that terrorist's face from TV news. I wish I could read their lips."

Michele immediately dug in her handbag, pulled out her iPhone, and typed away with her thumbs.

"Got a plan?" Kirk asked.

"I'm sending e-mails to get my network cooking.

* * *

The following morning Michele and Kirk met with Burdett. Officer Farah Khoury, a lip-reading Arab linguist from the New York Police Department, and Dr. Angie Metzler, an FBI profiler out of Quantico's Behavioral Sciences Unit accompanied them. The psychological profiler was an expert in dissecting the psyches of monsters.

After introductions, Michele said, "Dr. Burdette, we can synchronize the overhead view with the facials, as Farah attempts to read their lips. Then you may be able to hear what they say as Rahman draws the hieroglyphics. Angie will interpret their body language. Perhaps this may put things in context."

"Yes." Burdette said. "That is excellent. I'm anxious to get started. We have a lot of work cut out for us here, and I have numerous references to research, but I'm delighted to help."

Kirk and Michele silently watched as Farah, Angie, and Dr. Burdette reviewed the videos.

Kirk finished his second cup of coffee and asked, "Do we have anything yet?"

Michele kicked his ankle.

Why do women do that? He shrugged, and vowed to keep his mouth shut.

"Yes." Burdette eyes hinted at success. "The color videos are of much higher quality. We can make out much of what they say, and we have extracted more from their body language. They speak in colloquial Arabic with some Cairo idioms, which I do not quite understand."

"I may be able to help with that, Dr. Burdette," Farah said. "I am from Cairo."

Kirk's spirit improved with the news. He cracked a smile and winked at Michele.

Burdette tapped his notepad. "Some of their conversation appears to be friendly chat. There's a bit of legal jargon, the recitation of *Qur'an* verses, prayers, and we detect something that appears to be a verbal sparring between those two using ancient Egyptian terminology, kind of like our Old English—Chaucer and the like. It appears they are relaying ancient riddles and answers."

"Riddles?" Kirk frowned.

"Yes. This may not be unusual. In many areas of the Middle East and some portions of Asia, educated people tend to speak obliquely, rather than directly as Westerners do. Riddles serve as a polite form of communication and can be entertaining. They also tend to obscure conversations from eavesdroppers."

They faced three computer monitors; one mounted high displaying the overhead view, the other monitors skewed so the facials of Aisha and Rahman faced one another. The setup was as though one were sitting at a table with the perps, listening to their conversation while they observed Rahman's finger painting on the upper monitor. Burdette compared notes with Farah and Angie, jotting Arabic script while drawing hieroglyphics on his pad. The man was in his element, and it appeared he was enjoying himself with the enigma.

Kirk squirmed in his seat, drumming his fingers on the table.

Michele placed her hand on his, mouthing, "Cool it."

Burdette caught Kirk's eye. "This is quite fascinating." He nodded toward Angie.

"It appears Sheikh Rahman is the woman's spiritual advisor," she said. "They are both intensely religious, if not fanatic. Aisha has strong feelings for Rahman. He appears laid back. She has an animal intensity—the angriest eyes I have ever seen. She knows how to hate. And Rahman is manipulating her."

Burdette said, "There were no legal issues discussed. But, we do have good fragments of some riddles, and a reference to the *Sword of Ṣalāḥ ad-Dīn*. I made out some hieroglyphics that referred to Pharaoh Ramses II."

Kirk knew the *Sword of Ṣalāḥ ad-Dīn* was Aisha's code name. But what the hell did those hieroglyphics say?

"Dr. Burdette?" Michele said. "What did the Ramses glyphs refer to? Did you interpret those?"

"Yes, I did. They referred to a famous tomb engraving of Pharaoh Ramses II. I will see if I can find a photo for you."

Burdette removed a large coffee table-type book from a stack on a bookshelf, and leafed through the color photos and text. "Here." He tapped the photo with his glasses. "From the Valley of the Kings."

Kirk and Michele studied the photograph of a stone carving showing pharaoh standing in front of a reed boat, spear fishing.

"I have no idea of the connotation," Burdette said.

"What was the context?" Michele asked. "I mean, what was their conversation at that point?"

Burdette scanned his notes. "The blind Sheikh relayed a riddle—'What is that which passes unseen, but is never heard.'"

"Huh. A secret message," Kirk blurted. "So what's the message?"

"Let's try to work it out." Michele logged onto the Internet, and took notes in furious chicken scratch.

Kirk looked over her shoulder. "What are you doing?"

"The Pharaoh standing in the front of the boat holding a trident might be a secret message. I'm looking at an array of synonyms."

"Synonyms? Synonyms of—?"

"Spear fishing." Michele continued to take notes. A moment later, she spun to face Kirk. Her face turned the color of a China doll, white and pasty—filled with horror.

"What?" Kirk couldn't make out a damned thing in her handwriting.

"The message is 'Kill the fish.'"

"Yeah. So?"

"The logical synonyms would be *Execute Pisces*. I'm certain it refers to an order—to execute *Operation Pisces*. We're out of time," she said, her voice raised.

"An order? To who?" Kirk asked. "Aisha is no field operative. She's unprofessional and emotional—a bad choice for a spook. It's terminal."

"She's the messenger—a cutout," Michele said. "That's clear from the *Mukhabarat* audio surveillance in the madrassa. Rahman's her handler. The computer files Ramzi Gonimah relayed to her certain encrypted messages that she is to forward to the terror cells via e-mail."

Kirk stared at the Pharaoh Ramses II photograph. *Hieroglyphics, ancient riddles, encrypted computer files, all under a lawyer's cloak. What do they fear that requires such a high level of secrecy?*

Eighteen

Michele's Townhouse
Georgetown, Washington DC

The sleepless flight to Andrews Air Force Base from Los Angeles left Kirk bleary-eyed. Turbulence and heavy rain created by a low-pressure area over the East Coast shook the plane violently. The long flight and lousy weather didn't bother him as much as it did Michele, but they both felt good about the breakthrough in the case. The tap on Aisha's Internet cable yielded a trove of intel—several e-mails and the *al-Islamiyya* encryption algorithms. The information was immediately forwarded to NSA for decryption.

The rain had ceased when he helped Michele climb into the passenger's seat of his Tahoe. She looked in the back of the truck and laughed. "Do you own a dog?"

"Why'd you ask?"

"The back windows are smudged with nose prints, and there's brown hair all over the seat. What's the dog's name?"

"Stryker. He's a big Belgian Malinois. Looks like a longhaired German shepherd. Used to be a narc's sidekick, but retired when his sniffer burned out. Smart lovable dog. A K-9 security service retrained him as a *Schutzhund*—a guard dog. He takes hand signals and commands in German. My neighbors take care of him while I'm gone. . . . Where to?"

"N Street, Georgetown."

Twenty minutes later Kirk drove into the stately neighborhood.

"This is it," Michele said, pointing to an elegant ivy-covered brownstone.

Kirk whistled as he pulled onto the brick driveway. "Michele, how can you afford this place?"

She laughed good-naturedly. "I don't own it, I'm the house sitter. When I started grad school at Georgetown, I rented the apartment over the carriage house." She pointed to the two-story garage. "When my parents came to visit, they thought the townhouse had potential for appreciation. Purchased it from an estate. The home and carriage house came furnished in authentic eighteenth century antiques and artwork—Andrew Wyeth and Jackson Pollack paintings."

"I'd like to see that sometime. I'm an American history buff."

Kirk opened the SUV back hatch and retrieved her luggage. Under the porch light, she fumbled in her purse for her house key, then turned to him.

"Kirk, I'd invite you in and show you around, but I have too much work to do. Thanks for the ride."

"Tomorrow, follow up with the spooks at the Puzzle Palace. Push all the buttons, step on toes, crack a few heads if you have to. This is no time for Marquis of Queensbury Rules. There is valuable intel in Aisha's computer files that may help determine the Sheikh's objective. We have a long way to go and a short time to get there. If you need help, let me know."

"This is a one-man job, best taken care of by a woman."

Kirk smiled. After his initial resistance to a female partner, he found Michele to be a relentless workaholic and a naive intellectual. She complemented his combat skills, but he worried about her safety.

"Michele, get some rest. I think the situation is shifting in our favor. That paranoid Sheikh will react when he feels the heat. Stay alert. Tuck your weapon under your pillow. Take out life insurance and shoot first." Kirk took her hand and offered a comforting squeeze, then departed.

Michele ached to reach out to pull him back to her. He was the most fascinating man she had ever met—brutally handsome, a patriotic warrior, out-spoken, and protective. A real *man*. Not one of those brown-nosing effete Washington pin-stripers.

Michele knew she was Kirk's match intellectually, and she was an attractive woman—she would have to be blind not to notice the male heads she turned. But she could not seem to get Kirk to see her as anything other than his partner. She was certain he was drawn to her. Wasn't their innuendo and flirting a clue? It had to be his move. She was coming to believe Kirk was married to the job—all signs indicated he was faithful to that barren wife.

It would be another restless night alone.

Swallowing her disappointment, she unlocked the door, keyed-in her security code, and stepped into the foyer.

Other than a couple of lights set on timers and the elaborate crystal chandelier glowing in the foyer, her home was dark. No sounds, except warm air hushing through the ventilation grates.

Something wasn't right. Michele scrunched her nose, sniffing.

The faintest tang of body odor and . . . garlic?

Goose bumps rose on her arms.

She withdrew her SIG, pulled the slide back with her left hand to verify a chambered round, and slipped off the safety. After removing her heels, she stepped further into the foyer with her heart pounding, the .40 caliber gun heavy in her hands.

Pale blue light in the study grabbed her attention.

Computer monitor.

Kirk was about to turn the corner when his iPhone vibrated. He glanced at the Caller ID—Michele.

"Kirk." Michele's voice faltered. "There's an intruder in my home!"

He felt a stab of anxiety. "Michele, listen. Walk back to the front door and step outside under the porch light. I'll be there in a minute."

"Hurry."

Kirk parked in a neighbor's driveway, and jumped out of the Tahoe. He drew his HK45 and scanned the area, searching for movement in the shadows, silhouettes in parked cars.

Nothing.

He hurried up the steps onto Michele's front porch. She held her weapon down at her side, fear registered in her face.

"What makes you think you had an intruder?" he whispered.

"My computer monitor was lit."

"So, what's it prove?"

"My computer is set to sleep after thirty minutes of inactivity. Someone touched the keyboard or mouse less than a half-hour ago."

"Shit," Kirk muttered. The intrusion was not a normal burglary, or the perp would have stolen the computer. And it took skill to bypass Michele's top-of-the-line security system.

"Stay here. Don't do anything. I'm going in."

She nodded, and raised her weapon.

"Don't hesitate to use it. Double-tap, center of mass."

The whites of Michele's eyes showed. "I don't want to drop a burglar."

"No burglar. It's a black-bag job. You detect a threat, neutralize it. Clear?

"Yes."

"Anyone in the carriage house?"

"Not now," Michele whispered. "The tenant is on semester break from Georgetown Law."

"Who else has keys and the alarm code?"

"My parents and my maid. That's all."

"No boyfriend?"

"No time for that."

"Wait here." Kirk slipped off the safety on his HK45. Uncertain of an intruder's intentions, he took no chances. He would kill the perp. After noting the time on his watch, he stole a quick glance through the beveled glass sidelights on the entrance, then inched open one of the heavy mahogany doors. He listened, searched, and sniffed for presence. His adrenal glands flooded his system with adrenaline, heightening his mental acuity and senses. Every hair on his body acted like an antenna, a feeling of being in the zone, perceiving what others could not.

Kirk took three quiet steps, stopped, sensed. Moved on, his weapon ready, light pressure on the trigger.

On a walnut executive desk in the study, Michele's computer monitor glowed. He swung his weapon in an arc, prepared to kill.

Study clear.

Dining, living room, and kitchen. *Clear, clear, clear.*

Kirk tiptoed up the stairs to the second floor. Two furnished bedrooms devoid of any sign of use. The master bedroom in the rear smelled of Michele's scent mixed with perfume—Opium, his favorite. A Chippendale tester bed with a frilly lace canopy, photos of her parents, an antique armoire. Nothing amiss.

Kirk descended the stairs and opened the front door.

"Is it OK?" Michele holstered her weapon.

"Yeah. Let's have another look around. Don't touch anything. Speak in a whisper. Clear?"

She nodded.

"Any artwork missing?"

Michele looked around the foyer and living room. "Doesn't look like it."

'Where do you keep your important documents and valuables?"

"In the safe. The study. This way."

The clock in the foyer beat eleven times, then Saint Michael's chimes.

Too early for a normal burglary.

Michele's monitor went to sleep and caught Kirk's attention. He glanced at his watch. Two minutes to drive back here, six minutes inside. The perp left just before they arrived. Had to be two of them, one on surveillance, and one to penetrate.

How the hell did the Sheikh acquire Michele's name and address?

"Check the safe," Kirk whispered. "Open it."

Michele pulled out a leather bound book on a shelf, and pressed a hidden button. An entire library section loaded with leather-bound books moved forward and rotated ninety degrees exposing a wall safe.

Michele stared at the tumbler. "They tried to access *the safe*." Her voice was shrill.

Kirk waved her quiet and made a finger over the lips gesture. He pointed to the ceiling and mouthed, "Bugs," he whispered. "How do you know?'

"I always spin the combination to the same number after I close it. It's off one digit."

Kirk pointed to a stereo system. "Turn on music."

She frowned, then turned on the CD player—Barbra Streisand—*Greensleeves.*

"Use a tissue to open it. There could be recoverable prints."

Michele dialed the combination, opened the door and removed a stack of papers in manila folders and a jewelry boxes loaded with a small fortune in precious metal trinkets, pearls, and gemstones.

She carefully examined each. "It doesn't look like anything's missing. Nothing's misplaced. Everything's here."

"Lock it." Kirk scanned the well-appointed study. A trove of classic leather-bound books, the smell of tobacco—a man's inner sanctum.

When he turned, Michele had the phone in her hand, dialing 911.

He ripped it from her hand. "What do you think you're doing?" he hissed.

"Calling the police," she whispered.

"No police." He pointed to the front door.

Kirk pulled the door closed behind them. "Michele, we're in a covert operation, and have to maintain a low profile. A little paranoia is a good thing. I think the enemy has us under surveillance. They were after intel."

"Oh, my god. But, I always encrypt my files. They won't be able to read them."

"Depends on how good they are at cracking the code. These people are not street thugs. More like KGB." Kirk punched a speed dial on his iPhone.

Walter Munford answered on the first ring.

"What's up?" he growled.

"Looks like a professional black bag job at Michele's. Need a forensics team."

"She good?"

Kirk glanced at Michele. "Just rattled. Me too."

"They toss the place?"

"They messed with her computer and safe."

"Team will be there in a half hour."

Kirk addressed Michele. "Munford's sending a crime scene team over. Ten to one our people don't find any prints. Maybe a couple of bugs and phone taps. We got a big problem." He stared out into space. "I'm convinced there's a mole in the Bureau. That fucking Sheikh knows who we are and where we live. He killed Brett, and he won't hesitate to drop us after he determines our status."

"Kirk, I'm frightened."

"Fear is one thing. You cannot let it grab you by the ass. I've been through the progression too many times. Fear mutates to fury." He took her hand. "Michele, concentrate on the mission. Use fear to your advantage. Allow your fiery rage to build. Intimidate and face down your opponent. Push back. They're out there, watching. If you want, I can spend the night."

"I think you know what I want," Michele said softly. "But, it wouldn't be a good idea. Not now."

Cool Rob and Nacho pulled up in separate cars, and swept the townhouse. They located sophisticated bugs in the study, kitchen, and master bedroom, along with phone and Internet taps. A six-man forensics team followed. After scouring the townhouse, they reported discovery of a one-inch blond hair found on the hardwood floor near the desk. No extraneous prints.

"Blond? Michele, have you had any people over here with blond hair?"

She shook her head.

"Friends, or maid service?"

"I have no time for a social life, and my housekeeper is Hispanic—black hair."

"Alright. Nacho and Cool Rob will camp out with you tonight. You need to get some rest. I got a feeling it will be big day tomorrow. We'll bait the enemy into the open using their own bugs, then I'll take care of that problem."

The man watching from a parked Range Rover down the street checked his Rolex Oyster and noted the time. He slid down in the seat as Kirk's Tahoe drove by, pressing the speed dial on his cell phone.

Nineteen

Kirk's Condominium
Arlington, Virginia

Kirk made his way through light traffic to his condominium off Arlington Boulevard. If the Sheikh's operatives were onto Michele, he reasoned, they would also have him under surveillance. He decided to bait them into the open, then take care of them.

Stryker sat on the kitchen floor wagging his tail, quivering with excitement. Kirk squatted, and scratched the dog's ears. If he were not on guard duty, Stryker would have rolled over to beg for a belly rub.

"Stryker. Wanna go for a walk?"

Kirk donned a Kevlar vest under his windbreaker. Stryker grabbed a leash and headed for the front door. Stryker at his side, they walked around the block. When they approached his condominium, Stryker let out a low growl. Hair stood up on his back, nose pointing.

Kirk detected a slight movement in the shadows off to the left and hand-signaled Stryker to silence. They made their way back. Inside, he retrieved a pistol-gripped Mossberg twelve-gauge shotgun and a handful of double-ought buckshot shells from his gun safe. He loaded five shells into the magazine as he climbed the stairs to the master bedroom, Stryker close behind.

Kirk studied the room for a few seconds. If they were Russian assassins, they would most likely use thermal night vision goggles.

He pulled back the bedspread, wrapped the electric blanket around pillows and covered them with the bedspread, turned on the blanket. He extinguished the bedroom light and examined the bed in the faint red glow from a clock radio on the nightstand. Satisfied with his deception, he checked the time, 2:33 AM.

Kirk sat on the edge of the bed facing the doorway. A nightlight in the hallway provided minimal illumination. He jacked a double-ought buckshot shell into the chamber, and waited. Stryker sat down beside him. Kirk stroked him behind his ears as the clock radio counted down, the minutes slowly passing by in deathly quiet.

Suddenly, Stryker stood on all fours, ears pitched forward. He let out a low growl; hair rose up on his back.

Kirk's pulse raced. He glanced at the clock—3:55. He donned his NVGs, signaled Stryker to take an attack position next to the doorway, then stepped into the closet leaving the door ajar.

Movement on the stairs . . . then down the hallway. Seconds later the intruder turned off the night light, plunging the hallway into darkness.

The intruder was close. *Very close.*

Kirk disengaged the safety with a *snick*, and aimed the shotgun at the doorway, chest height. Seconds passed that felt like an eternity. . . . He sensed the assassin's presence before he could make him out—a silhouette in the doorway. A silenced gun flashed and coughed, twice.

"*Packen!*—Bite." Kirk yelled.

Stryker let out a terrifying snarl and lunged at the intruder.

Kirk's shotgun blast cut short the man's scream. He racked another shell into the chamber, and listened for movement.

Nothing but Stryker's panting.

Kirk stepped out of the closet and flipped the light switch. Stryker sat, wagging his tail and licking blood from his face. A bloody patch of clothing and a large chunk of flesh torn from the intruder's crotch lay at his feet.

The three-inch hole in the center of the assassin's chest and torn crotch left a pool of blood that soaked the carpet. Gore splattered the wall.

"Fucking mess. Good job, Stryker." He patted the dog's head affectionately. "Good boy."

Kirk stood over the assassin, carefully eyeballing the corpse.

Tall, muscular, a Tokarev 7.62 mm pistol equipped with a suppressor in the man's right hand. Black jeans, hoodie sweatshirt, and sneakers.

After removing the intruder's night vision goggles and balaclava, Kirk looked into the face of death—grey eyes that looked like a pair of burned-out light bulbs, Slavic features with a flat face like a two-by-four. Blond hair.

Prying open the assassin's mouth, he examined his teeth. Stainless steel dental work. Kirk pushed up the man's left sleeve to examine his inside forearm. Hammer and sickle tattoo. Searching the body he found a German passport, an airline ticket, and three-thousand cash.

Kirk stared at the bullet holes in the bedspread, and hit a speed dial number on his iPhone. "Walter, sorry to wake you up. Got a messy body here. Stryker ripped the privates off the perp, and I blew his heart out with buckshot."

"You OK?"

"Yeah."

"Related to the black bag job at Michele's place?"

"Looks like it. Typical Russian stainless-steel dental work. Spetsnaz hammer and sickle tattoo on his left forearm. Packing a suppressed 7.62 mm Tokarev, and Russian NVGs."

"*More goddamned Russian assassins.*"

"One more thing," Kirk said. "He had a KLM return air ticket to Dubai. One of the Sheikh's designated hitters. Walter, we got a serious problem with that leak."

"How the hell could they have tracked you and Michele otherwise? We need to flush out that mole."

A mole. It was the foulest four-letter word Kirk knew, and being ex-military, he knew plenty. "One way or another, I'll take care of it."

"Do it clean. . . . Kirk, we have to crack that *al-Islamiyya* encryption so we know what that fucking Sheikh is up to," Walter said. "I'll ask the General to turn up the heat on NSA."

"Hold on that. I want to sic Michele on those spooks. She knows how to expedite things."

Twenty

National Security Agency
Fort George G. Meade
Laurel, Maryland

Frustration in Michele's mouth left a taste as sour as pickled pork. A foul temper caused a spasm to run through her, tying her gut into a knot, a sensation she felt too often lately. She received no response from her NSA contact regarding the decryption of Aisha's files, and she knew why—sexism and the old bureaucratic run-around. She had been through it during her White House stint.

Michele parked her Porsche SUV in a visitors' slot in front of National Security Agency headquarters. She enhanced her intimidation factor with a stylish form-fitting pencil skirt, matching jacket, and ivory chemise. She flipped down the visor mirror to check her subdued makeup and hair done without fuss. Well aware anger amplified every feature in a woman, her cheeks flushed—the effect worked to her advantage. Time to push back—*face down opponents.*

She cleared security, and made her way to the reception area of the Assistant Deputy Director of Operations. Admiring glances from men and women in civilian attire and military uniform enhanced her confidence even further. The confrontation was long overdue.

Breezing by the Assistant Deputy Director's secretary, she flashed her credentials and paraded toward the inner-office double doors.

"Ms. Li, you can't go in there," the secretary called after her.

Michele pushed the door open to the office, strutted in, and slammed the door behind her.

Neil Bergeron looked up from his paperwork, eyes the size of goose eggs.

"Michele, what are you doing here? My secretary's suspicious already. Christ. There'll be talk."

"This is official business." She dropped her FBI credentials in front of him, and took a seat.

The ADD gawked at her, his mouth hanging open.

"I want to know why you have not responded to my e-mails and text messages, Michele said. "And I don't want a load of bureaucratic bullshit."

"You know they monitor that stuff. They're toxic—"

Michele cut him off with a wave of her hand. *"Toxic?"* She leaned forward with a poisonous glare. "There was nothing toxic in my messages other than to expedite your analysis and deliver the report. *High Priority* means exactly what it says."

"Well . . . I wanted you to call."

Michele rolled her eyes. "I can't believe you'd risk national security in an attempt to seduce me." Her voice dripped with disgust. "You took advantage of me when I was at a low point in my life. I've changed."

"What's with the gun and badge?" he asked in a condescending tone.

She pointed to her credentials. "That's the badge of authority and I'm exercising it. I want a status report on the *al-Islamiyya* decryption and e-mails. My messages to you were not cryptic. *Are you that dense?"* she asked, with sudden fierceness.

"What the *hell* has gotten into you?"

"I've made a few changes in my life. We had a dalliance, and it's over. I'm fed up with your games. I want *that report*, and I won't tolerate another minute delay going through channels."

Neil looked on, lips pursed in a condescending manner.

Michele's eyes burned into his like black laser beams. "Don't push it, Neil or wind up filleting fish in Finland."

"*Alright.* Alright . . . calm down. Will you please take a seat? Can I get you anything?"

"Tea and Tylenol." Michele took a seat in front of the ADD's desk and crossed her legs.

"Where're your glasses?" he asked.

"Contacts." Michele tossed the bangs out of her eyes. "*Get me that damned report.*"

He raised his hands with a resigned sigh, then turned to open his safe. Neil passed a bound report, stamped *Top Secret – Speculator* across his desk. "You can read it, but you can't take it."

"Neil, I'm taking two official copies, right now. You are to immediately hand deliver a third to Jessica Masters at CIA."

"I can't do that. You know the protocol."

"I know all about protocol from the White House, and I know how to bypass bullshit and expedite." Michele pulled her iPhone from her handbag and hit a speed dial number.

"*Jesus Christ. Hold on. Hold on.* "

Michele terminated the call. "I assume you've reviewed the report."

"Yeah. The FBI Field Office in Denver forwarded computer files obtained from *al-Islamiyya* containing e-mail addresses and encryption algorithms. Piece of cake." He looked at her as though he expected a compliment.

She glared at him.

He gave up and continued, "Without the files and pointers, we'd be up that well-know creek, clueless. Their code utilizes a two-stage process. They transmit an encrypted e-mail that only includes the words *Al Mahtah* in Arabic script—"

"*Al Mahtah?* What's that mean?"

"It's another Islamic jihad slogan like *Allah-u Akbar.* Figuratively meaning, 'Death to America.' It is not a message, *per se.* The e-mail is a clever innocuous tickler informing the recipients to download a pornographic photo containing the message from a Danish web site. Her message read, 'Acknowledge,' signed *Sword of Ṣalāḥ ad-Dīn.*"

"A text message imbedded in a photo?"

Neil nodded. "Embedding text messages in graphic files is called steganography. Been around for centuries. Leonardo Da Vinci used it in his artwork. In computer files, text is hidden in the white space. We would not have penetrated their communications without those files."

"When did you break it?" She swallowed a Tylenol cap, washed down with a sip of tea.

"Late yesterday. We traced the e-mails to file servers in Moscow."

"Russia? Why do I have to wring this out of you? What about the e-mail account holders?"

"Determining the account holders took more effort. We worked all night tracking the e-mail pings across the Internet."

Michele uncrossed her legs and leaned forward, "The locations, Neil. Where are the cells *located?*"

"The Bronx, Cairo, Dubai, Tehran, and Trenton."

Michelle frowned. "Trenton? What the hell's in Trenton?"

Neil shrugged, holding his arms out, palms up—the international sign of incompetence.

"We decrypted everything except the MOIS message. The Iranian spooks use another method of cryptography. Looks like a one-time cipher pad."

Michele's heart skipped a beat. If NSA could crack the MOIS code, then they could determine the submarine's mission and location. "'Where's that stand?" She took a sip of tea.

"Working on it." Neil waved his hand dismissively.

She slammed her cup onto the saucer, splashing tea on his polished mahogany desktop. "God damn it. That's not acceptable!"

He held up his hands. "Keep your voice down. What's this all about, anyway?"

"You have no need to know. Status, Neil. The status?"

"It's hung up in bureaucracy."

"The *bureaucracy?* What are the obstacles?"

"Same old shit. Assets, people, priority, holiday leave." Neil shrugged.

"This is High Priority. Bring them back."

"I can't do that."

"Who can?"

"General Malson."

* * *

In the Assistant Deputy Director's reception area, Michele hit the speed dial on her cell phone to a number in the White House known to few. She spoke briefly, and then made her way to the top floor. From the elevator, an MP escorted Michele past another security post to the NSA Director's outer office.

Seated in the hushed room were a half-dozen 'suits' and high-rank military, all bearing anxious looks. A Navy captain in dress whites with a briefcase shackled to his wrist glanced at his watch.

Michele displayed her credentials to the receptionist and signed the log. “I have an appointment with Lieutenant General Malson.”

“Yes, ma’am. General Nance called a few minutes ago to clear your appointment,” the receptionist said. “Please enter, he is expecting you.”

She could feel several sets of eyes burning into her back that caused her pulse to kick up several notches. Sucking in a deep breath to draw enough courage to make her case, she entered the walnut-paneled office.

A barrel-chested man with a jutting jaw dressed in US Army uniform loaded with acres of ‘fruit salad’ rose from a desk the size of an aircraft carrier. General Malson’s beefy grip swallowed her hand.

“Ms. Li. Pleased to meet you,” he growled. “Have a seat.” Malson gestured toward a chair.

It sure did not sound like he was pleased. She took in his office trappings. His desk covered with multi-colored telephones, military wall plaques, old Viet Nam war photos, display cases filled with war memorabilia and weapons.

She caught herself waiting for the machine guns to open up.

Malson gave her a prolonged fish-eyed look. “What can I do for you?” he asked in an abrupt manner.

“Sir, I’ve just come from a briefing with your Assistant Deputy Director of Operations regarding the *al-Islamiyya* decipher.” Michele fought to control the high-pitched timbre of her voice.

He nodded curtly. “General Nance informed me you had a major role in penetrating their communications. Congratulations.” His voice had the chill of liquid nitrogen, gruff to the point of insult.

“I’m not here for congratulations.”

"Then tell me why you circumvented the chain of command and disrupted my schedule." His voice rumbled, and his eyes grew hard.

"Sir, sometimes intel falls through the cracks."

Malson raised an eyebrow. "Implying exactly what, Ms. Li?"

"I have information you need. There is another terrorist operation in progress, Operation Pi—"

"I sat in on General Nance's briefing. Get to the point."

Michele swallowed. "The Navy is trying to determine the location of an Iranian submarine, the SSK—"

"I'm well aware of that."

Michele's pulse pounded away. "There is something more."

"Oh?" Malson leaned closer; his squinting eyes drilled into her. "Go on."

She attempted to slow her breathing, licked her dry lips, then unconsciously tucked her hair behind her ear.

"We believe the Iranian submarine is involved in *al-Islamiyya's* operation." Her voice cracked. "Their leaders will need to communicate with that boat, and—"

"And when they do, Ms. Li, we will listen in. We deciphered the Iranian Naval codes years ago."

Michele realized this was the critical juncture when push comes to shove. Kirk's words resonated. *Push back.*

"Sir, we've determined SSK-635 is under the command of MOIS. Not the regular Iranian Navy." She swallowed. "Your ADD just informed me that MOIS use their own cryptography."

Malson stared at her for several seconds. His tongue made two full revolutions in his cheek before he looked down at his desk, licking and sucking his teeth in a prolonged moment of hushed silence.

She had given it her best shot and wondered if she had royally screwed up. Her career hopes twitched.

Malson had the power to ruin her. Whatever happened, her work in penetrating the enemy's communications network had felt as good as anything she ever had done.

Malson let out a deep breath, rocking back in his massive leather chair, pursing his lips.

"Ms. Li, most people quake in their boots when they enter this office, for good reason. I do not brook bullshit or tolerate incompetence. I'm sure you realize you put your career on the line by barging into my office. Now, having said that, you did the right thing in pressing your agenda. I admire your spunk. No wonder General Nance thinks so highly of you."

Michele had plenty of exposure to military people, and understood their cryptic and abrupt language. After disrupting Malson's schedule, he had given her a high compliment. It made her face flush with embarrassment.

Malson leaned on his forearms, frowning. "Ms. Li, if this old soldier offended you, then please accept my apology." His overbearing demeanor softened, along with his gruff voice.

She shook her head, reaching for her handbag. "Sir, your apology is not necessary."

Malson nodded and smiled for the first time. "I'll rearrange our priorities and put maximum effort into cracking the MOIS crypt immediately." He picked up the phone. "Mr. Bergeron, my office. On the double."

Michele breathed a sigh of relief. "How difficult is it? To break the code?"

"That may be a formidable task, but one that can be overcome with sheer force of will."

"Yes sir. I think I'm beginning to appreciate that."

* * *

"Here she comes." Cool Rob jammed the rest of an Egg McMuffin into his mouth. "Nacho, let's roll. We guard her with our lives. You dig?"

"Yeah. It ain't bad duty. Michele would look damned good on the cover of Playboy," Nacho said. "She's hotter than a *habanera*."

"Stick close to her. You lose her and the boss will burn our ass with a cellophane torch. Close it up, White Bread. *¡Vamos!* "

"Acetylene. And your *Español* sucks."

"Whatever."

Nacho and Cool Rob followed Michele's car out of the NSA parking lot as she headed toward the Baltimore-Washington Parkway. When she exited onto Route 50 East into the District, a green Ford Taurus pulled in behind her Porsche.

"She know we're tailing?" Cool Rob asked.

"Hey Robbie. How can you miss two good-looking dudes in a new Hummer? Besides, I blinked the headlights. She tapped her taillights. Smart babe."

"Yeah. An IQ that would light up the Big Apple. . . . Move in closer. You let three cars slip in behind her. When the man says stick on her ass, we stay close enough look up her address and kiss her booty. Don't let any more vehicles come between us."

"I know what I'm doing," Nacho said.

"That right? You screw up, you'll be burro bar-b-que. Cut in front of those other cars. Get on her tail."

Cool Rob shook the thermos bottle. "Any coffee left?" He unscrewed the cap as their Hummer slowed to stop for a red traffic signal.

"What the fuck?" Nacho exclaimed. "You see that? Fuckin' Ford rammed Michele's SUV."

Cool Rob craned his neck to see over the tops of the cars ahead.

A Caucasian male climbed out of the Taurus, and approached Michele's car, reaching into his jacket.

"Mutt's got a gun. BLOW THE HORN!" Cool Rob scrambled out of the Hummer, drew his SIG, and charged forward.

The man pointed the gun at the driver's window, and fired a double tap.

Michele screamed, and fell against the steering column. Horn blasting.

Cool Rob took a two-handed stance and fired at the perp. A spray of blood erupted from the assailant's pelvis.

The assassin bellowed, holding his hip. Opened the door and dragged Michele out of her car onto the tarmac. Climbed in. The Porsche Cayenne burned rubber and sped off through the intersection, tires smoking.

Cool Rob let off another shot. *Missed.*

"Nacho," he yelled. *"Take that motherfucker down."*

Nacho peeled out and gave chase through the mean streets of the Nation's Capital.

Cool Rob dropped to his knees beside Michele. Struggled to pull off her jacket. Blood seeped between his fingers. Blood-tinted bubbles at the corner of her mouth. A rattling gurgle from bullet holes in her chest below her left breast.

Twenty-two years in Special Forces and covert ops, he knew that horrible sound—sucking chest wounds that blew out foaming blood. *Seal them. Prevent her lungs from collapsing. Get help.*

Michele tried to raise her head. Shaking, shallow, rapid breathing, eyes rolling back into her lids. Going into shock. Bloody foam poured out of her mouth.

Cool Rob tried to swallow the lump in his throat. He cradled Michele's head in his hand, and pressed his palm against the bullet holes; looked around for help. A mob of homeboys dressed in cargo pants hanging down to their crotch, matching do-rags, and Air Jordans, gathered around to gawk—worthless cop-hating gangbangers.

"Somebody phone for help!" he yelled.

A black woman elbowed her way through. "Dear Lord," she said. The woman covered Michele's legs with a baby blanket, knitting needles protruding. She patted Cool Rob's shoulder. "I'll call 9-1-1."

"Stay with me Michele." Cool Rob said. "God damn it. Stay with me."

A large puddle of blood formed on the tarmac under Michele's prone body. Her eyes had that all-too-familiar glaze, staring at nothing.

Twenty-One

Kirk's Town House
Arlington, Virginia

The black-bag job at Michele's place, and a hit man's attempt on his life left no doubt in Kirk's mind that the Sheikh was on to them. Cell phone vibration interrupted his thoughts. He checked the caller ID and picked up.

"An assassin just shot Michele," Walter said. "She's dead."

Kirk felt like a bayonet twisted in his gut. "*Ah, Jesus Christ.* Where the hell was her security detail? I ordered Nacho and Cool Rob to stay on her."

"Followed four vehicles behind her. Witnessed the attack. Michele was returning from NSA. The shooter set it up like a carjacking. Cool Rob got off a couple of rounds. Busted the shooter's pelvis. Perp stole her car. Nacho's giving chase. I have got a Jet Ranger headed toward your place. Get on it."

"Where's he at?"

"District, southeast side, off US 50. Michele was driving a black Porsche SUV with dealer tags. Take him down," Walter ordered.

"I'm on it."

Kirk hurried out to the garage, flung open the back hatch of the Tahoe; grabbed his Steyr sniper rifle, a box of cartridges, and binoculars. He ran to the parking lot as the helicopter set down, threw his gear aboard, climbed in, and ordered the pilot to lift off as he strapped himself in.

"You got that shooter's car?" He adjusted his earphones and intercom to deaden the thunder of the helicopter's rotor.

"Nacho's on him. We're about two minutes out. He just crossed over the Anacostia River. Hauling ass. North."

Kirk knew the area—a run-down neighborhood. Cars waiting in line for gasoline would slow the assassin's getaway. He hoped it would not be long before they spotted the SUV.

"Damn it," the pilot said, "bastard shook Nacho."

"The shooter might be hung up in traffic. Take her up a thousand feet. That Porsche will stand out in this ghetto like a priest in a whorehouse."

The helicopter circled. Kirk scanned the streets below.

"Don't see her car," the pilot said.

"Son-of-a-bitch is out there." Kirk raised his binoculars and glassed the dilapidated buildings and crowded streets. "Circle around again."

Kirk recalled how he located Brett's body with the GPS tracking app on his cell phone. Michele kept her phone in her handbag. It might be in her car, turned on.

He pulled out his iPhone, punched Michele's speed dial, listened to the ring, then voice mail.

"Her phone's turned on." Kirk checked the coordinates. "Six blocks east, moving." Kirk slammed an ammo clip into the rifle, and chambered a round . . .

"Two o'clock," the pilot said.

Kirk raised his binoculars and spotted the SUV as it sped down a side street.

"I want a clean shot at that bastard. Stay out of his field of view. Drop down to five hundred feet. Approach from his left rear."

"Dealer tags. Bashed rear bumper," the pilot said. "That's him. . . . *What the fuck*? News chopper's hot on the SUV. They're jockeying for position."

"The hell with them. Move in. Put me on their blind side."

Kirk took position in the open doorway, squatted down on his right foot, left foot extended. He wrapped the rifle sling around his bicep and forearm, and centered the vehicle in his scope. "I've got him. . . . Easy. Easy."

Kirk sighted the scope reticle on the man's left ear. Let out a half-breath, and squeezed the trigger.

That is when the driver swerved around a DC Metro bus.

The .50 caliber round blasted through the SUV moon-roof, tearing a six-inch hole and spider-webbing the Plexiglas.

The assassin looked up at Kirk's chopper, firing his weapon to no effect. The SUV turned off the main drag, tires smoking.

"Pull ahead of him a little. I want that killer to stare death in the face." Kirk slammed another round into the breach, and reacquired the target in his scope. For a moment, he looked into the face of Michele's assassin, a face staring back that bore an expression of absolute terror.

Kirk squeezed the trigger. His bullet impacted into the assassin's head, the recoil from his heavy sniper rifle satisfied.

The SUV sideswiped a parked car, skimmed the curb next to a bus stop, then rammed into a telephone pole, shearing it off at the base, stretching power lines and telephone wires to the limit. Steam poured from the Porsche's radiator.

"You blew that fucker's head off," the pilot said. "Like smacking a cantaloupe with a mallet."

Kirk had to get to the SUV before the thrill seekers. "Find a place to set down. Hover over the top of that building."

Kirk leapt out the chopper door onto the roof of a tenement. Clambered down the fire escape. Dropped ten feet into the ally, then ran a half-block to Michele's steaming SUV.

Thrill-seekers had gathered around the wreck to gawk and scavenge. Kirk waved them away with his badge and the look of serious business, his handgun held at his side.

A wino staggered over. "Hey buddy," he croaked. "You got five bucks?"

The man reeked of body odor, stale puke, and who knows what. Disgusted, Kirk shoved him aside and raced toward the car.

Bloody gore and brains covered the interior. Dressed in black jeans and sneakers, the assassin was built like an armored personnel carrier. His weapon lay on the front seat—a Tokarev loaded with 7.62 mm copper-jacketed rounds. Kirk pocketed the handgun, then pulled up the man's left sleeve.

Hammer and sickle tattoo.

He searched the man's pockets, and discovered a throwaway cell phone, and a money clip containing an American Express card, New York driver's license, a Russian passport, and $1,500 US. The inner pocket of the assassin's jacket held a KLM return ticket to Dubai. When Kirk leafed through the ticket sleeve, a small slip of paper fell out and fluttered to the ground. He picked it up and stared at telephone numbers, names and addresses—Michele's and his. Digging into the assassin's jacket pockets, he discovered their FBI photo IDs.

"Son-of-a-bitch," he cursed to himself. *That fucking mole.*

"Sir! Sir!" a woman called out, heels clicking rapidly on the tarmac. "Nora Dhue, Fox News."

Aw, Jesus. Kirk slammed the SUV door, and turned to face an intimately familiar and unwelcome sight.

He had an intense, and some would say improper relationship with the investigative reporter who preferred her formal name in business. Nora sounded tougher than Misty—her nickname. She was a fox, but by nature, reporters were weasels.

Misty Dhue was a pain in the ass.

A muscular dude with a video camera on his shoulder jogged beside her, lights on.

Kirk raised his hands palms out, in an attempt to halt their recording. Last thing he needed was his mug on the evening news.

"*Kirk?* What? *What* are you doing here? What's going on?" Despite her shallow breath, excitement nipped her voice. Her turquoise eyes, enhanced by Maybelline, darted about the scene soaking up details.

"You tell me." Kirk's tone was flat. He forced the scent of her perfume from his mind.

Misty put a hand on her hip. "Why should I? It's my job."

"We're both in the information business, but I got the badge." Kirk smiled wanly.

Misty's scarlet lips formed into a petulant pout. She hesitated for a moment, allowing her demeanor to harden from disappointment to determination.

"We were videotaping lines at the gas stations when I heard the police scanner, and then spotted that SUV tearing up the road." She stepped forward, trying to steal a look over his shoulder. "So, what brings the FBI to a car wreck? This is going to be good, isn't it?"

Kirk backed up to block her view.

Bad move.

Misty shifted sideways to look past him.

"Oh, my god." She turned away with her palm over her mouth, face flushed. "I think I'm going to be sick."

Kirk put his hand on her shoulder. "You OK?"

She nodded. "Give me a second."

Recovering quickly, she straightened her skirt, fluffed her hair, and shoved a Fox logo microphone in Kirk's face. "No head? *It's prime time.* Tell me about it."

"Turn that damned thing off. You broadcast any of this?"

"Not yet. Reserved it for my evening news segment."

Kirk extended his hand to the cameraman. "The recording." Kirk wiggled his fingers, palm up.

"I ain't givin' you jack shit," the dread-locked cameraman snarled in ghetto jive. "You want it, you get a fuckin' warrant. We got Second Amendment rights—"

Kirk hammered his left palm into the cameraman's solar plexus, doubling him over.

"Give it up, asshole, or you'll exercise your rights in an emergency room."

"*Kadrick.* Better give him the recording, and get out of here," Misty said with authority.

The cameraman tossed a DVD to Kirk and sulked off, cursing under his breath.

"Sorry about that." Misty sighed. "Diversity. Good videographer and bodyguard; bad attitude." She shielded her eyes from the sun and looked up at the thumping beat of an unmarked helicopter circling overhead. "Is that your helicopter?"

"Can't comment."

"That says a lot." Undeterred, she shouldered him aside and looked through the SUV's open window. "You didn't shoot . . . ."

Avoiding her gaze, Kirk looked off into the distance, stone-faced.

"You *did.*" Misty spotted the airline ticket in his hand. "Was he a foreign agent?" Her eyes glinted with the elation of discovery. "Give me something I can use."

Kirk shook his head. "Dirty Laundry."

"What?"

"It's a line from the Don Henley song."

"My." Misty touched his chest with her fingertips, following the button line down to his belt. "The old song and dance. Next thing, you'll be quoting scripture. Kirk, there's something going on. You're tap-dancing, and there's no music."

"You're too damned smart for your own good."

Misty smiled. "I'll accept that as a compliment."

Fox News regarded her as the most captivating personality and brightest star on the set. Kirk regarded her with respect and admiration. Misty relentlessly rooted out information from numerous sources. When required, she played off her sexuality and stunning looks.

Her strawberry blonde power bob glistened in the sunlight. Makeup concealed freckles across her nose and cheeks. But a six-figure wardrobe could not camouflage her curves. She was high-maintenance, tenacious, and hot-blooded. When she had an orgasm, neighbors at the Watergate headed for the bomb shelters.

She stepped in close, looking hungrily into his eyes. She pretended to brush something from his hair, then let her index finger trace his earlobe as she slowly brought it down.

"Anything you can give me? Deep background, no attribution?"

If Kirk were in a better mood, he would have enjoyed her flirtation. Instead, he shook his head. "Not even off the record. National security."

She backed up, her hands on her hips, eyes on fire. "Kirk, what are you hiding?" She pointed to the wreck.

"Who is . . . was that man? You shot him from the helicopter, didn't you? Why?"

"That's four questions." Kirk sighed deeply. "You never quit, do you?"

The smile on Misty's lips looked like a knife ready to cut loose. "Do you?"

"What do you think?" Kirk glanced over her shoulder at the milling crowd of belligerent gawkers. "Misty, you'd better leave. It's not safe around here."

Sirens screamed in the distance.

"You're prevaricating. I'm not leaving until I find out what's going on. There's a plum here, and I'm going to pick it."

"No plum. More like a rotten mackerel in the moonlight. Listen, the thing is . . . if you knew about it, your life would be in danger."

Her eyes widened, not from fear, but with the realization that she was onto a scoop. Misty had her heels dug in, and Kirk knew she would soon discover Michele's assassination and tie it to the car chase and Brett's hit. He had to deflect her interest.

Kirk knew she despised corruption in all forms and had no fear of powerful men. She would wade into a minefield to bring down perfidious high-ranking politicians. One came to mind—a corrupt senator who had aspirations for the White House—a man who fraternized with the Sheikh. Kirk wondered if Dreihaus could be the man indirectly responsible for Michele's assassination.

Light bars flashing and sirens wailing, a pair of DC Metro police cruisers raced down the street, approaching. He had to act fast.

"Look . . . I'll make a deal if—"

"I'm listening," she cooed.

"—you forget what you saw and heard. Maybe, I'll give you an exclusive on something bigger."

Misty smiled. "No maybes, Kirk."

"Alright, no maybes."

Misty pressed her body against his, and kissed his cheek. She murmured, "You'd better call me. Soon. I have the patience of a sinner and I'm no saint. But I *can* restore your will to live."

Her warm breath lingered in his ear as she strutted off.

It was a tempting visual, and Kirk had a hard time taking his eyes off her derriere. After Michele's assassination, he wondered what made him even think about having his "will to live" restored. Adrenaline hangover? Or just half-crazy with lust for revenge?

Kirk looked at Michele's photo ID he held in his hand. Two of his partners taken down in cold blood.

A wave of anger and revulsion raced through his body—a lust for revenge. Restoration would have to wait.

Twenty-Two

Kirk's Town House
Arlington, Virginia

Dog tired with his heart filled with sadness, Kirk entered his kitchen from the garage. Images of Michele Li flashed in his mind. She was smiling and saying, "*We'll make a good team*." He vowed to get even, but had to remain alert. No telling if the Sheikh had more heavy hitters out in the darkness. He had to gain an edge.

Stryker greeted him with a whimper, running in circles, wagging his tail. Grateful for the distraction, Kirk knelt to stroke his dog's ears. He decided on a plan to draw an assassin into the open.

"Stryker, wanna play Frisbee?"

The Belgium Malinois' ears perked up, tongue hanging out, panting in anticipation.

They exited the front door and ambled to a park that was popular with the locals. A soccer field abutted a jogging trail that wandered along the edge of the woods. Dusk, an overcast sky, the air cold.

Kirk tossed the Frisbee.

Stryker gave chase and jumped to catch it, then returned wagging his tail. He sat at Kirk's feet, begging for another Frisbee toss, never tiring. Several joggers ran by on the trail.

Moments later, Kirk felt eyes boring into his back. His skin prickled, hair rose on the back of his neck. In his peripheral vision, he detected movement—a man dressed in a dark jogging suit leaning against an oak tree at the edge of the woods, stretching.

Could be a neighbor. Or a dog lover. But joggers normally did their warm-ups near the parking lot.

Kirk spun to toss the Frisbee again, taking a quick look at the jogger. Registered the man's features in his memory.

Blond hair, maybe six feet, athletic build with fluid motions that maintained absolute control with the surety of a yoga master. Looked familiar, but Kirk could not place him.

Stryker begged for the next toss with his wagging tail.

Kirk spun, making another toss to take a second look at the jogger.

The man had faded into the darkness. Too slick, Kirk thought. He had to be one of Qadr's men.

Kirk and Stryker trotted back to the condominium.

After throwing on a flak vest and grabbing a set of night vision goggles, Kirk slipped out the back door, leaving Stryker on guard.

After scouring the park and neighborhood for an hour, he returned. Kirk pushed open the front door. Stryker nowhere in sight.

Kirk made a double-clicking noise with his tongue.

The dog did not come running.

Fear-pumped adrenaline amplified every sound—a car driving by, the clock ticking on the fireplace mantel in the living room, his pulse pounding in his ears. Kirk pulled his weapon, slipped off the safety. In silence, he searched, tormented by what he might find. The hallway and living room silent as he looked about. On tiptoe, he made his way up the stairs.

Study clear.

Down the hall to the master bedroom. Kirk picked up the coppery scent before he before switched on the light.

Stryker lay in Kirk's bed—in a pool of congealed blood, his throat slit, eyes wide open.

A fist of grief punched Kirk. His throat tightened up like a pinched straw, his breathing labored. Fury boiled over. Hot fury, but what he needed was cold at its heart—cold as malignant cancer.

Only a pro could have neutralized a guard dog trained not to bark or growl, but to maul and immobilize. Kirk knew the slaughter of his pet, following the murder of his partner, were meant to break his will.

But the Sheikh's plan was wrong. Dead wrong.

Remembering the cell phone he had confiscated from Michele's assailant, Kirk brought up the call history—three to the same number.

He hit redial . . .

"Yes. What is it?"

Male. Not American English—German-accented with a precision that was unique to those who were foreign born and well educated. Kirk burned the voice into his memory next to the visual image of the jogger in the park.

"I killed two of your men. Buckshot in the chest after my dog ripped one of your men's balls off. The other lost his head from a fifty caliber round. When I find you, I'm gonna mount your head on a pike." Kirk snapped the phone closed.

Some cruel fuck, not far away, exulted in his power each time he killed. Anger percolated through his body like superheated lava, jacking him up for a knife fight that was sure to come.

* * *

Kirk's cell phone vibrated. He ripped it from his belt holster. "Magnus."

"An hour ago," Jessica said without prelude, "NSA intercepted traffic from *Sword of Ṣalāḥ ad-Dīn.*"

"Where's Qadr? I'm going after him, even if I have to hunt him down from Dublin to Dubai on my own dime. And this time I'm doing it my way. Where is he?"

"Max has him under surveillance. In Munich."

"Munich? What the hell's in Munich?"

"Looks like a pleasure trip. He plans to drive to Garmisch and ski with a friend—a former Cambridge University roommate named Hans Wei."

"That German downhill ski bum on the TV commercials?"

"That's him."

Kirk's face and neck burned. "I had a feeling I've seen that guy's mug before. Kraut stalked me in the park. He slit Stryker's throat."

"He killed your dog?"

"I'm taking the first flight to Munich. The Sheikh and his roommate are dead men."

"No," Jessica said. "NSA traced Yassin's e-mail to a safe house in Trenton called Simmons Enviro Services. The MOIS spooks are holed up there, and coordinating an attack with the Bronx jihadists.

Kirk, they are mobilizing. Target and timing, unknown. It doesn't matter when, or how, you kill that Sheikh. But, you have to identify and neutralize the threat. We're out of time."

Twenty-Three

Simmons Enviro Services
Trenton, New Jersey
December 22

Identify and neutralize the threat. Sounded easy, but you had to dig a mountain of dirt to uncover the evidence. An educated guess was all Kirk had, and that was not good enough.

At dusk, he and T-Bone slouched in a rental car parked a half-block from the Simmons safe house.

The building squatted between industrial derelicts. The liver-colored building backed up to the Delaware River under neon glow of the *Trenton Makes, World Takes Bridge*—a wart in the limelight.

T-Bone scanned the building with his binoculars. "I don't understand why we don't end it and blow their heads off right now. There's only two of 'em. You whack one, I'll take the other."

"Not yet," Kirk replied.

"Then what're we doin'?"

"Racial profiling."

T-Bone stuck his tongue in his cheek, and snickered. "Never hurts to apply more redneck intellect, and two pounds of pressure on the trigger."

"We can't move until we determine their objective," Kirk said. "Besides, if we take them out now, the Sheikh will send in replacements. Life is cheap in the Middle

East. When they leave to grab something to eat, we're gonna pull a black-bag job."

"We get caught; it's time in the Club Fed. You don't wanna be on the other side of those bars as a prison virgin fightin' off a squad of tail-gunners. They lay a lotta pipe in there."

"You volunteered for this," Kirk reminded him.

"What was I thinking?"

"We'll bug and toss the place. They've gotta have a computer for the e-mails. I need you to hack it."

"Sounds like fun, but what if they got that shit-hole booby trapped?"

"Your insurance paid up?"

"Right before a barium enema . . . . Here they come."

Two men in dark windbreakers exited the building, furtively looking about. It was the first time Kirk got a look at the MOIS duo.

"You see that? T-Bone said. "That scar-faced scumbag's a scary-looking motherfucker. Eyes like a croc on *Animal Planet*. I'd like to get him in a scissor lock, and jam a knife into his eyeball."

"You that good?"

"Damned right. Smart too. Never hurts to have more brains on the job."

Kirk chuckled. "You'll get your chance."

Both Iranians climbed into a Ford Econoline van, the rocker panels eaten out by salt. The truck backed out of a parking space in front of the building, then continued down the street, Cool Rob and Nacho followed, maintaining surveillance.

"You ready?" Kirk asked.

"Semper Fi." T-Bone raised a clenched fist.

Diesel fumes in the night air along the waterfront, spiced with industrial phlegm, overwhelmed Kirk's senses, stinging his eyes. In the rear of the safe house, a chain-link fence topped with razor wire enclosed a loading dock. A lop-sided gate hung on a hinge.

T-Bone and Kirk squeezed through the opening.

Kirk popped the lock on the back door with a lock-pick gun, then yanked open the door.

"Slick," T-Bone whispered. "Gotta get me one of those."

Inside the condo, they moved fast. Kirk found the light switch.

A dozen cockroaches skittered across the floor. The office was a seedy wreck outside, the inside begging for fumigation and flame cauterization. Peeling lead paint and flaking asbestos appeared to be *de rigueur*. Along the back wall, a couple of soiled cots, a scabrous sofa against another wall, crushed cigarette butts on the floor—unfiltered Camels.

Figures, Kirk thought. He opened a chipped-enamel refrigerator filled with Colt 45 Malt Liquor and fermenting pizza—enough to gag a maggot. The office reeked of rancid grease, and body odor.

"Christ," T-Bone said, scrunching his nose. "These fuckers ever bathe or clean-up? For people who claim to hate pork, the place is a pig sty."

"Martyr's paradise."

The computer monitor and telephone sat on a scarred wooden desk. In a corner, a TV equipped with a built-in DVD player sat on an early Salvation Army table. Kirk lifted the lid off a shoebox next to the TV, and poked through a stack of DVDs.

"Huh. Porn collection. '*Girls Gone Wild, Deepthroat, Wet Head—*'"

"Could be do-it-yourself instructions for beheading infidels," T-Bone quipped.

Kirk tossed the videos into the box, then pulled out a drawer on nightstand between the cots to find two clips loaded with 9 mm ammo, and an open package of Trojan condoms.

"They bring any hookers back here?"

"Those two spooks would fuck the crack of dawn. Brought back low-rent pussy they picked up in sleazy bars, or when they were out looking for a nighttime snack."

"Wouldn't want a blowjob on an empty stomach." Kirk closed the drawer and looked around.

"Toss the desk and you hack that computer while I plant the bugs."

Kirk withdrew a screwdriver, then moved toward a ventilation register.

"Phone records here," T-Bone said, "show a dozen long-distance calls to the Bronx safe house. Several calls to a number in Roebling. Never heard of it."

"Small town ten miles downriver. An abandoned steel mill there that hasn't been used for over thirty years. EPA Superfund site guarded by rent-a-cops. Nothing but contaminated soil, run-down buildings, and rusty machinery." After planting the bugs, Kirk reinstalled the last screw into the ventilator cover.

"Find anything else?"

"Yeah. Why would these spooks rent an air compressor and a drilling rig? Receipts in the file here. Man, I smell something. There's a horse under this pile of shit."

"Have Jessica follow up on those phone calls and equipment rentals."

Kirk stood on a chair and drilled a small hole in the sheetrock ceiling. He inserted a tiny video transmitter through the hole, and then pressed the fisheye lens in place. Stepped down and admired the job.

"Good enough for government work." He checked out the video on his cell phone, and studied the image of his head.

"That abandoned steel mill?" T-Bone said. "Sounds to me like a good site to hide a bio lab. Or maybe a staging area to stash the Semtex for the Big One."

"Al-Qai'da made two attempts on the World Trade Center and a failed attempt on the New York City tunnels. Pisces might be a second attempt on the tunnels. We're gonna toss that steel mill. Tonight."

T-Bone inserted a flash drive into the computer to copy the files. "I bypassed their password. Shitload of porn downloaded on the computer from that Danish web site. Copies of e-mails from *Sword of Ṣalāḥ ad-Dīn*. Some other encrypted stuff. . . . I got it all."

Kirk installed a bug into the telephone wall jack. "Forward that stuff to NSA." He pointed. "Search that file cabinet I while finish up."

T-Bone rose from the desk chair, and pulled out the top drawer of the file cabinet.

"Booby trap!" He recoiled as though he had fallen into Indiana Jones' snake pit.

"Huh. Don't think so, or we would have bought the farm." Kirk peered into the drawer. "Might be."

"It thought you were an explosives expert."

"Hope so." Kirk patted T-Bone's shoulder. "Remote controlled IED. Probably Three Fingers' handiwork set to cover their tracks after they complete the mission. I'll take care of it. Photograph the documents."

Kirk removed the device from the drawer and studied it for a moment—looked like a brick of buff-colored Play Doh with an embedded cell phone. He removed the phone SIMM chip, then replaced the IED into the drawer.

T-bone wiped his brow. "What woulda happened if somebody dialed the wrong number?"

"Insha'Allah."

"Insha'Allah—God's will. Problem is gods are like cops. Never one around when you need 'em."

Back in their car, Kirk's cell vibrated. *Cool Rob.* He read the text message, then stowed his iPhone.

"Change of plan. We're blowing off the steel mill tonight. The rat's nest in the Bronx is scurrying with activity. Six Arab tangos headed out in a Dodge Intrepid, over the George Washington Bridge toward the Jersey Turnpike. It's going down. Nacho and Cool Rob are in hot pursuit. We need more firepower, pronto. I'm calling in reinforcements."

Kirk hit the speed dial and spoke to Walter, then hung up. He stared out the window at the Delaware River, and sipped cold coffee in silence. *First, he springs Michele on me, now this.*

"Something wrong?" T-Bone asked.

"The Deputy Director authorized the Hostage Rescue Team to take tactical command of the op."

"What? We're the ones who busted that Sheikh's op wide open."

"Makes no difference," Kirk said. "We couldn't pull enough manpower together in time. HRT is a mobile assault team. Twenty-four operatives are inbound on a pair of Black Hawks equipped with miniguns."

HRT was set up to do one thing and do it well—rescue hostages and take down terrorists. Problem was a female lawyer who might be predisposed to attempt an arrest, risking her life and that of her men, commanded the assault team. Making matters worse, Deputy Director Munford was not aware that Kirk and the FBI's HRT commander were estranged lovers.

Twenty-Four

FBI Tactical Operations Center
The State House
Trenton, New Jersey

With a call to the White House, Kirk had commandeered the VIP recreational facility as an op center. The Black Hawks would draw little attention as they ferried men and material into the heliport, security was excellent, and the facility was located close to the Simmons safe house.

At twenty-two hundred hours, the thundering beat of a pair of UH-60 Black Hawk assault helicopters broke the false calm of the star-lit sky. Kicking up a whirlwind of leaves and debris, the choppers set down. Black-clad HRT operatives unloaded an arsenal of weapons, night vision equipment, body armor, flash-bang grenades, secure communications gear, and loads of computer equipment—an impressive display of firepower—enough to start World War III.

Kirk recognized the hardened look of combat veterans: confidence and hunger for action, and a need to prove they could handle anything thrown at them.

Among the clatter of weapons, T-Bone strode into the ops center, and pulled up a chair next to Kirk. "We just intercepted a phone message to the Simmons safe house. Came from the guard shack at the Roebling steel mill. They spoke in Farsi—*'Oh two hundred.'*"

"Looks like you had the steel mill pegged. Nine tangos directly involved with the op so far. Firepower's in our favor; we know the target and time, but we have to locate that Semtex. We sure as hell don't want to host another disaster." Kirk glanced at his watch. "Six hours. Spread the word to the team leaders."

"Will do." T-Bone pointed to a satellite photo. "I'm gonna drive down to that steel mill to find a sniper hide that'll give me a bird's eye view of the mill and that nuke."

Kirk finished off his coffee, then turned his attention to the HRT Commander—Mary Margaret O'Malley—Type A hellcat on steroids.

They say of all the things that drove men nuts, nothing topped a passionate woman, and when trouble comes, she will have red hair. Hot-tempered and hot-blooded, Maggie O'Malley's lovemaking was like calling hell a mild warming trend.

Passion ruled and ruined. Their three-year affair ended following an intense argument. But he retained strong feelings for her. He was still in love with the bitch.

Maggie had limited knowledge of the enemy operation, and even less of his role commanding the Omega Six hunter-killer team. He had to bring her up to speed quickly. But, Maggie had been avoiding contact, raising his slow burn to incandescence. They needed to communicate—in private.

Maggie had to know he observed and weighed her every move, but Kirk was determined to set their personal differences aside for the sake of the mission.

Maggie's fiery temper befitted a flaming mane worn down to the middle of her back in a wind-tossed style. She was used to men's stares, and she could be aloof and cold as Freon. Thirty-three, two inches shy of six feet, with a lithe body kept in shape by third-level jujitsu workouts. She had a feint scar on her left cheekbone inflicted when a Nazi skinhead tried to punch her photogenic face in. She wore the battle damage like a badge of honor.

He always liked women with scars, but could never figure out why.

Judging by her posture, she exuded unerring self-confidence—one of the things he found most attractive about her. But most of all was her emerald eyes. There was a time when those orbs made him feel like the center of the universe.

Maggie possessed uncommon intelligence and superb leadership ability—talent he knew would be tested to the limit. Most of the HRT were experienced street cops and Special Forces vets, but Maggie had limited street and no combat experience. He questioned if she was up for an engagement with suicidal, battle-hardened warriors that was certain to come.

T-Bone leaned toward Kirk, whispering in a conspiratorial manner. "Your radar's been locked on to that Celtic temptress ever since she stepped off the chopper. Can't blame ya. She's got a nice set of cupcakes, a world-class ass and red hair right down to it. Babe's been sneaking ganders, but avoiding you like you're infested with sand fleas."

Kirk frowned. "What do you mean?"

T-Bone chuckled, then rolled a toothpick across his lips. "Kirk, you can't BS an old bullshitter. What'd you do to her?"

Kirk stuck his tongue in his cheek. "We had a thing going."

T-Bone stroked his mustache. "So, she's the one. Looks like you two hate each other. Or love each other. She shoot you down?"

"Something like that."

"I know the feeling. She's got a hard body. I betcha she could crack walnuts between the cheeks of her ass."

"Yeah, and she can crack more heads than Harley Davidson." Kirk tuned T-Bone out, and watched Maggie toggling keys on her laptop.

She studied satellite images of Trenton and New York City, then zoomed in on the Roebling steel mill. A few minutes later, she turned her concentration to a complex of buildings located on an island across the river from the mill.

"Newbold Island," She murmured, tapping her fingers on the tabletop. Maggie turned and caught Kirk's eye. "Do you have any idea what's on that island?" She pointed to the satellite image with a pen. "What are those large white dots?"

Damn. His focus was on an attack in New York City. It never occurred to him the nuclear power plant might be the terrorist's objective.

"They're nuclear reactor containment buildings," he said. "The Newbold Island Power Plant. Twenty-five hundred megawatts."

"*Mother of Christ.*" Maggie advanced to the front of the room with an authority that only the bold, or stupid, would question. "Heads up. Everybody. *Now.*"

All conversation ceased, every eye glued on her. Although her men outweighed her by a hundred pounds, something about her presence and air of steely resolve made her intimidating. She radiated a mixture of fire and ice.

"A nuclear power plant is located on an island in the Delaware near the steel mill ten miles downriver," she announced. "It has to be the terrorist's objective. This may have nothing to do with New York City, or that steel mill. I want a hot line to the operator of that power plant. We're going to turn out the lights on that nuke."

"Maggie, hold on a minute." Kirk interjected. "Shutting down a reactor normally takes several days. An emergency shutdown is quicker but it may damage the reactor core. The utility will balk at that. And we can't show our hand."

Maggie held her fists on her hips, her eyes boring into him. Knowing her, something like Vesuvius was about to erupt.

"How do you know that?" Freon in her voice.

"DHS target assessment, and I've visited the plant. Nukes have federally mandated emergency procedures for terror attacks, but it's mostly bureaucratic blather about airliner crashes into the reactor containment buildings. Regulations restrict plant guards to handguns. They'd be no match for a determined enemy armed with automatic weapons and explosives."

"Maggie," one of her men called out. "The utility's Operations Manager is holding."

She took the call, her pale skin turning mottled.

"Problem?" Kirk asked.

"You might say that," she snapped. "Unless the president declares a national emergency, the utility refuses to shut down either reactor. Due to high demand from Christmas lighting and seasonal heating the power grid is maxed out. The utility authorized their emergency protocol, guards on alert, maintenance people herded into a secure building.

"This attack was timed to perfection. What else do you know about that plant?"

"The operators are in a secure vault, but the maintenance crew, security guards, and dogs are vulnerable. A double chain-link fence with razor wire on top surrounds the entire facility. While the reactors are hot, the operators remain in the control room. They're safe, but we have to get the other personnel out."

"Why do that if they're in a secure building?"

"Explosives. Those Iranian tangos aren't planning a Greenpeace demonstration."

Maggie gave him 'the look'—hands on her hips, one foot forward, head cocked. "Some of you know Kirk Magnus." She nodded toward him. "His team uncovered the terror plot. He'll brief us as soon as I get back."

She didn't ask; she commanded and turned her back as though she expected unquestioned obedience. Kirk clenched his teeth in a grimace, his blood simmering.

He turned and spoke in hushed tone to T-Bone. "Coordinate our communications with the HRT base ops commander. Name's Carla Calabrese." Kirk pointed with his chin at an Amazon as she strutted into the room in black BDUs and tactical boots. Carla had traffic-stopping looks—black wavy hair down her back, sensuous dark eyes, a face that a model would kill for. She smiled at Kirk and twiddled her fingers at him.

T-Bone took a hard look and blurted, *"Holy shit!"* The pectoral muscles in his Grateful Dead T-shirt bulged with a lungful of air. "I'd like to cut me a piece of that."

"You'd be better off thinking about fucking jihadists instead of Carla. . . . I'm gonna lay out the ground rules with Maggie." Kirk stood to follow Maggie O'Malley as she sauntered out of the room. "Get my mojo working."

"Mojo?" T-Bone muttered to himself. "More like a mullet rising for the bait."

* * *

Maggie was smart enough to take advantage of the trove of Top Secret intel that she knew he possessed.

By baiting him in the ops center, Kirk realized Maggie was pushing an agenda. But at what purpose? He had to clear the air, brief her, and establish his role and the rules of engagement. And he had to do it with finesse. In private.

Seconds after the ladies room door closed behind Maggie, Kirk pushed it open and swaggered in. Arms crossed, he eyeballed her from head to toe.

With a fist on her hip in tomboyish daring, Maggie smiled. "So, Secret Agent Man," she murmured. "Is your visit personal or professional? What's on your mind? You didn't follow me in here to seduce me." Her lips formed into a suggestive pout.

Maggie had always used that intimate address as a teasing term of endearment.

Without warning, the moment turned awkward. Sexual tension in the air was palpable. Kirk could smell it, like ozone after a jolt of lightning.

"No." He grinned. "But it's a nice thought."

Maggie lowered her eyes, then returned his gaze. "Kirk, I'm sorry I couldn't visit you in the hospital after the Houston explosion. I wanted to, but I couldn't get away."

"Would have been nice, but I understand."

"Walter informed me you wormed into the terrorist's communications network."

"We got lucky."

"I suppose you could call that luck, but from my perspective, I'd call it an intelligence coup leading to a good result."

"Michele and T-Bone did the heavy lifting. Look, I realize my men and I couldn't take down a dozen tangos without risking casualties. I needed firepower. The decision to shift tactical command to HRT went above my pay grade."

She glared at him and snapped, "I don't play politics. My orders were to assume tactical command this op, and I don't want interference."

"Interference?" Kirk gave her a hard look, to which she cocked a challenging eyebrow. "Maggie, you haven't a god damned clue of what's going on here. The deck is

stacked against you. You're a card shy from a Royal Flush, and I hold the Ace of Spades. Fact is you're stuck with me. I don't have leprosy, and you won't break out in warts or have your skin slough off working with me. I'm not gonna fade into the fucking woodwork."

"I expected as much. Talk to me."

Kirk leaned a shoulder against the tiled wall, and nodded his head in the direction of the ops center. "This op is controlled by a wealthy Arab Sheikh. He used Russian contractors—Spetsnaz. There are an unknown number of operatives inside the steel mill, a couple of Iranian MOIS spooks here in Trenton, and fifteen complicit jihadists located in a Bronx safe house. You'll need our insight and the additional firepower."

"I admire you for backing your people, but your men are dressed as though they were attending a cocktail party."

"What?" Kirk had a two-day beard, and pointed to his tactical boots. "Do I look like I'm dressed for a high school prom?" He sucked in a breath of hardball resentment. "We know the effects of firepower, and we *damn* sure know how to use it. We've seen our share of death and destruction. And I've paid the butcher bill a few times. I've got a score to settle."

"I know." She gazed into his eyes for several seconds. "I saw you at Brett's funeral, but didn't approach." Her voice softened. "I knew you were hurting, and you had that blonde TV reporter anchored to your arm. Walter informed me about Michele and Stryker." Maggie touched his arm. "Kirk, I'm sorry for your loss."

Kirk looked away for a second or two. "We need to annihilate these people."

"You don't take prisoners, do you?"

"What's the point? You don't either, from what I've heard. You blew that Nazi's heart out."

Maggie sighed. "Kirk, your personal quest for payback may cloud your judgment and jeopardize the mission."

"*Personal?* This is far bigger than you realize. I hope you're not planning to arrest those terrorists. You'd better plan on a combat engagement—going in with guns blazing."

Maggie valued organization and rules, one of the reasons she rose so fast in the FBI. But that Girl Scout mentality was also her weak link. He knew his strength came from skirting the edges of the rule book, and that was also his weak link.

"My men can handle anything thrown their way. They're the best trained assault force on the planet, and—"

"Do tell," Kirk said sarcastically. He balled his fists on his hips. "I'm not interested in a pissing contest. We have a hell of a lot more experience in combat operations, and valuable intel you need."

"That may be true. But it's late in the game to integrate forces under my command. Your men do not know my style and may resent a female commander. Obviously, you do."

So, this is what it was all about. The basis of their estrangement. Maggie's perception of sexism.

Kirk never took his eyes off her. "What's your style got to do with it? They'll be under my command."

She glared at him. "For a man with so much talent, your knowledge of women is lacking. There is room for only one commander. I won't compromise it."

"*Compromise it?* What the hell's that supposed to mean? Don't you think we'd be better off watching each other's back than going at one another's throat? I have familiarity with the terrain that may prove valuable to you."

"Like what?" she said, cocking her head.

"Those tangos are on the water for a reason. Had it occurred to you they might use boats for an assault?"

"That makes sense if they're headed to an island. So?"

"So. I have a pair of Zodiacs at the marina, ready to go."

"Good. Some of my men were SEALs. They know how to handle watercraft. I'll take them off your hands."

Kirk rolled his head toward the ceiling and expelled a deep breath. "Before you get your Irish worked up into lather, consider this: I used to live around here. That island was my old stomping grounds. I also know what's inside those buildings in the steel mill across the river. When I was a kid, I sneaked in a few times to check it out. Stole a couple of souvenirs."

"So, what did you steal?"

"Hunk of wire rope used to build the Verrazano Bridge. To be honest, I thought those New York bridges, tunnels, or subways would be the Sheikh's target. They wanna another bite out of the Big Apple."

"That explains how you missed the nuke. . . . What else are you withholding?"

Maggie had no need to know of the mole, or his determination to destroy Sheikh Qadr al-Masri and everyone involved in the monster's plot. Kirk had faced her flare-ups, but he restrained himself from making a difficult situation even harder. He held her gaze with forced serenity, if not disappointment.

"Maggie . . . I thought you knew me better than that. And you, of all people, should know better than to demand intel for which you are not cleared. When, and if, you have a need to know, you'll be brought into the loop."

"Whose call?" she asked in an authoritative tone of voice.

"Mine. Or the White House—if I'm dead."

“Oh.” Maggie sucked in her lips. “It’s that bad?” she murmured.

Kirk hesitated for a beat. “Worse.”

“Dear God.” Maggie took a deep breath. . . . “Alright, I want you to ride shotgun on the chopper so you can give me a rolling intel update on the players and terrain. I plan a stealthy aerial assault. The door gunners aboard the Black Hawks will provide backup firepower. Take twelve of my men to slip onto the island with the Zodiacs, to cover our helicopter insertion.”

Satisfied with his tactical objectives met, and pleased that he would be in a position to protect her, he responded, “That’ll work.

“There’s one more thing I need to tell you. Those two MOIS spooks in the Simmons safe house are commanding the operation. Our intel indicates they planted Semtex on the tanker they blew up in Houston. Taggants match that of explosives planted at the Louvre last year.”

“Oh, boy,” Maggie muttered. “I had no idea these operations were connected.”

“That’s what I’ve been trying to tell you, without telling you. We have to keep this compartmentalized.”

“Anything pertinent to the steel mill or the nuke?”

“The spooks have been active in that steel mill for a couple weeks, allegedly drilling soil borings.”

She frowned. “Soil borings?”

“A cover. The property’s for sale. One of Sheikh’s companies has an option on it. The soil tests are supposedly due diligence. But that sure as hell is not why they’re in that mill. We think the mill’s a staging area.”

“Staging? For what?”

“At first, we thought it was for an attack on New York. The spooks smuggled one-thousand kilos of Semtex off the ship while it was anchored off Galveston.”

"One thousand kilos?" Maggie blew a silent whistle. "Where is it?"

Kirk shook his head. "They may have a cache stashed somewhere in that mill, or on Newbold Island. Looks like they plan to use it to make New Jersey glow in the dark."

"I had no idea. . . . Kirk, I want hard evidence of their intent. We need to see the explosives."

"Evidence? For Christ's sake, they already blew up half of Houston. These people are fatalists. They think committing suicide in the act of killing infidels is an honor."

"Don't you think I know that?" she barked.

Maggie wound a rubber band around her ponytail, donned an FBI ball cap. "We'll take them out if they attempt to transfer the explosives into the nuclear plant. Otherwise, we maintain surveillance."

"God damn it! We are not gambling with penny-ante stakes. These people are not rational. They're fatalists and will have a cell phone detonator baked in the cake. Take them before they hit the speed dial. A thousand kilos of Semtex makes one hell of a pop. You mess with it and you'll cook in the gravy. If that shit storm comes down you won't be able to dig your way out with a steam shovel. We can't let this become a bigger deal than it already is. We have to end it."

"The end does not justify the means."

"Tonight, it does. When was the last time you were on an op and everything went down just as planned?" Kirk crossed his arms. "We're supposed to do nasty shit to nasty people. Pre-empt and you won't host a disaster."

Maggie gave him a frustrated shake of the head. "Machiavellian ruthlessness is not my style, and I believe in justice—"

"Justice? You'll get justice in the next world. In this one, you have to shoot first." Kirk held up his hands.

"Maggie. Combat is an orgy of disorder. Sometimes you gotta play judge, jury, and executioner. War does not determine who's right, only who's left. Doing the hard thing is the right thing. Usurp their initiative. Annihilate them before they can press the god-damned button."

"That's where we differ,' she snapped. "You tore up the rulebook, burned it, and then ran off the reservation. I believe in rule of law."

Maggie, I hope you're not planning to arrest those terrorists so the DOJ can lawyer them up! Dead enemy can't beat the system on a technicality. They'll never come back to haunt you. Take my advice. Never go to a gunfight with a knife."

"I'll take your recommendations under advisement."

Maggie checked the load on an ammo clip and slammed it into her SIG. She racked the slide to chamber a round, then holstered her weapon. Glanced at her watch, then looked Kirk in the eye.

"You have three hours to brief our teams and prepare for the assault."

* * *

Kirk exited the ladies locker room and barely avoiding mashing into Maggie's sidekick, Carla Calabrese.

That would have felt good.

Carla's T-shirt fit more snugly than the FBI would have liked. Her tits entered a room before she did. Beneath her unflattering BDUs dwelt a Gold's Gym body. At six feet even, she was so gorgeous men who saw her literally froze in their tracks. In another era, she could have served as Al Capp's model for *Stupefyin' Jones.*

Stupefied, he froze in his steps, staring at a set of mountainous fleshy bumpers that looked like they had been ripped off the front end of a '57 Chevy.

She and Kirk looked at each other for a few seconds, and then she laughed huskily. “Was it good for you?”

“Never better.” Kirk grinned wickedly.

“That T-Bone?” she purred through pouty blood-red lips. “I’d spread him on a cracker.”

Her hard-as-nails Brooklyn accent made her more cop-like. Ruthlessly efficient, and Flatbush street savvy, Carla had a wild toughness and packed a SIG Sauer P229 on her left hip, a nasty stiletto she lifted off a Columbian narco runner on her right thigh. Equally adept with both weapons, she preferred the knife.

Brassy and vivacious, Carla’s lusty innuendo and double entendres left vapor trails. He admired that in women.

Twenty-Five

FBI Tactical Operations Center
The State House
Trenton, New Jersey

The makeshift ops center was a hornet's nest of activity—weapons preparation, men huddled over power plant drawings, nervous chatter. Gathered around a large marked-up satellite photo of the nuclear power plant, Maggie and her team leaders grilled Kirk as they laid out their assault plans.

"Something going on in that steel mill," Kirk said. "A guard there called the Iranian spooks. We'd better establish a contingency."

"Nothing of strategic interest there," Maggie replied. "The nuke is their objective."

Kirk's iPhone vibration interrupted. "Activity in the Simmons safe house."

"What's the situation?" Maggie asked.

"Cool Rob's maintaining surveillance. They prayed their last to Allah, then moved out in force, armed with AK-47s. Six Arabs along with the pair of Persian spooks climbed into their vehicles. I'll send Nacho to the marina to warm up our Zodiacs."

Maggie's pulse kicked up when Kirk answered another call five minutes later.

"Cool Rob followed the tangos to a warehouse that fronted the Delaware River," Kirk said. "They humped a pair of Zodiacs out of the building and launched them. They're warming up the outboard engines. It's time to roll out."

Adrenaline pumping, Maggie strode to the front of the ops center. "OK. Everybody, listen up. The enemy plan to commence their operation at oh-two-hundred. After we infiltrate the target, move into your assigned positions." She pumped her arm up and down, fist clenched, signaling her men to move out.

Clad in Kevlar body armor and black BDUs, Maggie and Kirk trotted toward the command Black Hawk. With a SIG P229 strapped to her thigh, and a 10mm MP5 submachine gun and night vision binoculars slung around her neck, Maggie was dressed to kill.

She had unwavering faith in her ability and that of her men, and she was determined to stick to her principles. There was no way should she could justify preemptive action to take out a perceived enemy, especially on US soil. That was murder, plain and simple. She needed hard physical evidence of their intent—explosives.

With Kirk aboard the chopper, she was confident he would be in no position to interfere with her objectives. Lugging a Steyr sniper rifle equipped with a night vision scope, Kirk was on a death hunt, out for revenge.

"What do you plan to do with that elephant gun?"

"I hunt big game." The iron-hard look of assurance that came from heavy experience showed in his eyes.

As the powerful Black Hawk turbines spooled up, Maggie tightened her harness, and studied Kirk out the corner of her eye. Maggie knew he would watch every move she made. She didn't need additional pressure, yet she felt comforted by his commanding presence and experience. She knew little of his covert operations, but she suspected the former Special Ops snake eater snacked on the most dangerous serpent—the king cobra. Kirk had no fear of helicopter and parachute insertions behind enemy lines. He thrived on it. The man was a noble savage—protective, vindictive, and internecine.

The tactical net snapped. "Red One, Cool Rob. The tangos launched and boarded a pair of Zodiacs. They're all armed with AK-47s. One Persian spook and three Arabs in each boat. Eight total. Three Fingers has the point."

"All Team Leads, Red One," Maggie said. "We have eight tangos so far and at least one collaborating security guard at the steel mill. Let's go." Maggie gave the pilot a thumbs up.

With a roar of turbines, a pair of Black Hawks lifted off, and headed south in wide formation over the Delaware River, their running lights blacked out. With her night vision binoculars, Maggie watched the enemy Zodiacs as they approached the north end of Newbold Island. The black Delaware River and dense forest on the island closed in.

Maggie watched the tangos continue down river past the nuclear power plant, then turned east toward the Roebling steel mill. This was an unexpected turn of events Kirk had predicted.

Wispy clouds filtered silver moonlight, casting coal-black shadows in the once great industrial enterprise situated on the banks of the Delaware River astride the Pennsylvania Railroad tracks. T-Bone thought the Roebling steel mill seemed like a stage set for a tragedy.

At oh-dark-hundred, a uniformed guard patrolling inside the steel mill perimeter stopped to take a piss, then lit a cigarette. After he moved on, T-Bone broke cover, and ran across the railroad tracks in a crouch. He retrieved bolt cutters from his knapsack, and cut a slot in the chain-link fence. Slipped through into the pit of industrial decay—more scrap iron than that lying on the bottom of Pearl Harbor. If the Delaware Valley was the mid section of the Rust Belt, then the Roebling steel mill was an iron oxide buckle.

T-Bone's objective, a water tower shaped like an oblate spheroid on stilts looming one-hundred feet above the ground. Hand-over-hand, lugging his backpack and weapon, he climbed the rusted ladder, hoping like hell a rung would not break under his weight.

On the catwalk that surrounded the massive tank, he set up a sniper hide, then surveyed the mill with his night vision binoculars. The mill had to be a staging area to attack the nuke—a perfect opportunity for the takedown.

"Man, this is gonna be somethin'," T-Bone murmured to himself. "Those fuckin' Islamic whack jobs are martyrs in the making.

"In position," T-Bone reported. He waited and listened to the chatter on the tactical net. The Black Hawks were closing in like raptors with infrared telescopic vision and deadly Gatling gun claws.

Minutes later, he observed eight tangos as they pulled a pair of Zodiacs up on the bank. The enemy slipped through the darkened facility like illegal aliens wading across the Rio Grande in the dead of night, headed right toward him.

He slammed a .50 caliber round into the chamber, and watched as Cool Rob's assault team stealthily followed the tangos.

"T-Bone, what's in that mill," Maggie snapped into the tactical net.

"A dozen abandoned buildings loaded with rusting machinery spread out over two-hundred acres. Six rent-a-cops patrol the perimeter. Hourly cycle. Place is an industrial graveyard loaded with hidey-holes. No electric power for lighting. I'm set up for the kill."

"We'll take them down in the mill," Maggie said. "But, we have to identify the explosives before we open up. Hold fire for my order."

As Maggie's Black Hawk circled out of audible range, T-Bone reported, "A plant guard rendezvoused with the tangos near the north entrance of the big building, five-hundred yards south of my position."

"Kirk, you know what's in that building?" Maggie asked.

"The Open Hearth. Brick-lined furnaces to melt steel. Structure's about one thousand feet long by two-hundred feet wide by a hundred feet high. Open on both ends, railroad tracks down the middle, overhead cranes."

"I got a clear view inside and see a couple of rail cars in there," T-Bone said. "Tangos are moving inside. Guard's standing watch on the north end."

"Alpha. Set down by the river, advance to the north side of that building. Take cover.

"Bravo. Move in on the south side.

"Cool Rob, cover Bravo's six. All teams confirm when in position."

The tactical net snapped with terse orders and observations, the tension in the air palpable. T-Bone rested a finger on the trigger guard of his Steyr sniper rifle observing activity inside the Open Hearth through his night scope. Battery powered lanterns used by the enemy illuminated skylights as the enemy moved deep into the building. The inside was as dark as a coal bin. But his thermal imaging night scope turned night into day.

"The Iranian spooks are giving the orders and standing watch. . . . The Arabs are removing material from a furnace—ten heavy mil spec crates. . . . Lowering the crates down onto the mill floor near a rail car. . . . Czech markings—Semtex."

That was all the evidence Maggie needed. "Team Leads, Red One. Weapons free. Open fire on my command."

Kirk slammed a .50 caliber cartridge into the chamber of his rifle, and thumbed the safety off.

"Red One, T-Bone. I got Scarface sighted in."

"Hold for my mark."

Seconds later, Maggie's Black Hawk hovered over the Pennsylvania Railroad tracks located 400 yards outside the east plant perimeter. Gunners in both doorways released the safeties on their 7.62 mm multi-barrel Gatling guns.

"Standby. . . . Open fire!"

A second later, T-Bone's .50 caliber round blew Scarface's head into pink mist.

Maggie's teams opened up with their FN assault rifles and Heckler & Koch MP5 submachine guns.

Caught in crossfire, three Arabs and the rent-a-cop dropped in their tracks. Remaining enemy returned automatic weapons fire in every direction at unseen targets.

Injured enemy shrieked in pain.

Three Fingers yelled a command, then made a run for a side entrance, and escaped into the blackness.

"T-Bone, take Three Fingers," Kirk ordered.

"Lost him."

"Elevation!" Kirk called out. He unbuckled his safety belt, then knelt in the doorway next to the mini-gun operator. Raising his night vision binoculars, he searched for Three Fingers in the massive complex.

"I've got him," Kirk said. "Hauling ass toward the river."

Maggie followed Kirk's rifle aim as he squeezed the trigger. The heavy bullet thundered out of the Steyr barrel. A red splatter burst out of Three Fingers' chest as his mangled body tumbled through the air.

"Tango down!" Kirk announced.

Even with her earphones in place, the report from his sniper rifle was deafening.

The tactical net indicated total chaos inside the Open Hearth. Terrorists fired at shadows while attempting to take cover. T-Bone watched as an Arab, partially hidden under a rail car, wired the Semtex. With no pretense of deadpan cool conveying everything was under control, T-Bone shouted, "FIRE IN THE HOLE!"

"Pilot, bank hard port!" Kirk ordered.

When the Black Hawk banked sharply, Kirk slid toward the open door. He grabbed a safety harness with his left hand, his right clinging to his sniper rifle . . . as his legs slid out the door.

The Gatling gun operator clapped a meaty hand on the back of Kirk's flak jacket, and jerked him back inside the chopper.

A second later, a bright flash followed by a thunderous shock wave, rocked the airframe. The Black Hawk rocked side to side, out of control. Red-hot shrapnel and debris thumped against the Black Hawk's armored bottom.

The pilot struggled to recover.

Stunned out of breath, Maggie saw a rail car blown end-over-end through the roof of the Open Hearth as if it were a toy. A massive mushroom fireball followed. The rest of the building collapsed on itself, steel beams reverberating from the shock wave.

Maggie snapped. "Teams report!"

Cool Rob reported a heavy piece of steel landed on an HRT operative and broke his leg. Maggie received no response from either of her team leaders.

"They probably can't hear," Kirk said. "My ears are still ringing."

"Carla. Send in the medivacs. Air and ground," Maggie ordered. "We may have men down."

"Copy," Carla said. "They're five out."

"Cool Rob. Move in on the north side and get a casualty assessment. I'll take the south side."

Maggie directed the pilot to set the chopper down in a parking lot. She climbed out of the chopper and ran toward what remained of the Open Hearth. The roof and sides of the building disintegrated, massive steel columns bowed outward. Kirk and two HRT followed, MP5's ready to take out any remaining tangos.

Maggie was stunned by the grisly scene. Massive piles of smoking rubble and twisted steel lie everywhere. Smoke rose through a gaping hole in the roof, a fifty-foot diameter crater in the center of the building. Fires burning. Structural steel glowing red-hot.

The shock wave impact zone formed pitiless boundaries between the spared and the doomed. Maggie shuddered from pained calls for help and the horrifying sounds of injured men. Two dazed and bloodied HRT rolled on the cinders in agony.

Her bodyguards located the rest of the Bravo Team—one unaccounted for.

Kirk called out, waving her over.

The smoking and deformed railcar lay upside down on a cast iron ingot mold, crushing it like it was made of paper mache—an HRT operative pinned underneath. Blood poured out of the man's nose, ears, and mouth—his chest crushed under the rail car.

Maggie looked down, breathless.

Kirk knelt beside the man and felt his carotid artery for a pulse. He looked up at Maggie, and shook his head. "He's gone."

Maggie had taken casualties on previous operations, but never a fatality. Her reaction was more emotional than she had ever imagined. She knelt beside her man in a pool of blood, and recited a silent prayer.

“Pete Townsend—The Squid, we called him. Former SEAL. Wife and two pre-school kids.” She gently closed his eyelids, then stood next to Kirk, then wiped blood off her hands onto her BDUs.

After-action reports poured in on the tactical net, and stunned her. Half her team took casualties. Cool Rob reported six men down on Alpha with severe injuries, no fatalities.

If she had followed Kirk’s recommendation to take the terrorists down before they had possession of the explosives, her men would be safe. But, it was no time for rehashing. Triage first—prioritize and treat the wounded.

While waiting for the medivacs and ambulances, the uninjured administered first aid. Quick action saved lives. They did their best to offer some comfort until help arrived.

“Maggie,” Carla said, “The blast knocked out windows within a five-mile radius. We’ve got media vultures circling. A call from the Governor’s office.”

“Fuck ‘em. Refer them to our Media Relations. Order the New Jersey State Police to secure the entire steel mill as a Federal crime scene.”

“Copy that,” Carla responded.

The staccato beat of Jet Ranger helicopter blades signaled the first medivac arrival. Maggie watched the paramedics stabilize the injured and load the seriously injured aboard. They zipped up Pete Townsend in a body bag and loaded his body into an ambulance.

Kirk took her elbow and tugged her away from the grisly scene. They walked toward the riverbank. In silence, they stared at the nuclear power plant.

"Just when you think you've received your ration of shit, you get another whopping helping. That Sheikh's busting our chops," Kirk said. "This is not the first time he's bested us. Something fishy about this op. Too damned easy."

"Easy? Half my men are down," she said, her face contorted in rage. "How the hell do you come up with easy? He's toying with us, showing us how smart he is."

"Outside of characters in movies, no one has ever been smarter than this. That Sheikh has an army of former Spetsnaz under his thumb. He didn't send them in to do the heavy lifting. This operation was not his primary thrust. Aside from the Iranian spooks, those Arab jihadists were rank amateurs. They were sacrificed."

She stared at him blankly.

Kirk nodded somberly. "Looks like a diversionary tactic—a probe to test our defenses and reaction. They named it Operation Pisces for good reason. It's a red herring. The Sheikh hopes we'd drop our guard after this head fake."

"Why would he do that?"

"So he could hit us with a sucker punch." Kirk pointed with his chin toward the nuclear power plant across the river. "Psychos don't go away. They hide in the darkness like anthrax spores. Waiting for a weakness, then they bloom."

"You're inside his head. How would you play it?"

"Time-honored military tradition. We pull a head number on him. We need to write a script for the media. Drop a few nuggets."

Maggie turned to Kirk and watched as he ran a hand over the back of his neck. His eyes were formed into slits, like those of a jungle cat on the hunt. She had seen that cold impervious look before. Kirk Magnus did not take kindly to defeat on anything.

They stood next to one another staring across the Delaware at the brightly lit nuclear reactor containment buildings.

Kirk murmured, “I’ll make sure I tell that fucking Sheikh how inconsiderate he’s been. Before I kill him.”

“Hold that thought,” Maggie replied.

Twenty-Six

MV Ocean Odyssey
Fifteen Miles SSE of Cape May, NJ
December 23

Chuck Hanson, a Texas A & M marine archeologist, sat in a high-back swivel chair in a dimly lit control room on the 300-foot ship as he lowered *Gertrude*, a tethered Remote Operated Vehicle, to the sea floor. Danny Waltrip, *Ocean Odyssey's* technician puttered at a workbench nearby, wiring and testing electronics.

The commercial archeologist's objective was to locate and recover $50 million in Double Eagle gold coins from the wrecked *SS Randolph*, an ironclad Union side-wheeler that had gone to the bottom during a winter storm in 1864.

Previous side-scan sonar and magnetometer surveys showed numerous anomalies within the search grid, and every one had to be checked out and logged into the database. The task was time consuming and tedious as hell—most of the time. But an archeological treasure find got the juices flowing. He was anxious to discover the treasure that lay below the gently undulating swells. He knew they were close. He could feel it, and it made the long boring spells easier to take.

Below *Ocean Odyssey*, the sea floor was a graveyard of sunken ships—a debris field covering twenty square miles. During World War II, German U-boats torpedoed dozens of Liberty ships and other merchantmen at the entrance of Delaware Bay when they left the port of Philadelphia laden with war material to supply the Allied armies.

News clippings of interviews with the survivors from the *Randolph* reported her position within the graveyard. Finding the needle in a pile of scrap iron would not be easy, and investor funds were running low.

When *Gertrude* hovered 200 feet off the sea floor, Chuck turned on the ROV's lights to illuminate the ink. Monitors displayed Gertrude's TV signals. With calm surface conditions, bottom visibility was excellent—over 200 yards at 550 feet, but his vision was blurred from fatigue. And excess caffeine didn't help one damned bit. This would be the last run of the season, and he looked forward to the Christmas break. Twelve more hours and he would be in front of his fireplace with his Annie and the twins, quaffing whiskey-laced eggnog.

The ROV's thrusters propelled it forward on its silent quest. Within minutes, *Gertrude's* lights illuminated the bow section of a Liberty ship on its port side, the stern section found minutes later 300 meters to the north. Chuck maneuvered the ROV to his next target located 1,000 meters northwest. Another WWII merchantman—a tanker lying upright in its grave, a massive hole blown in the port side. Chuck worked the joystick.

Gertude crept along the length of the wreck, then around the bow to the starboard side. Chuck spotted the ship's ID number draped with marine growth that looked like rusty icicles hanging from the wreck's deck and rails.

Suddenly, movement on the fringe of visibility caught Chuck's attention. Then a cloud of silt that looked like a subsea sandstorm rolled across the sea floor and over the tanker's deck killing all visibility. Chuck had never seen anything like it.

"Shit," he muttered, scratching his beard. "Wonder what the hell caused that. Current is only two knots."

"Mumbling to yourself again?" Danny quipped.

"Why don't you concentrate on the magnetometer readings?"

Chuck maneuvered *Gertrude* across the ship's deck in the direction of the debris cloud. He turned on another pair of high-intensity lights to penetrate into the murky seawater. He felt a sudden shiver of excitement and stared wide-eyed at the monitor when a patch of darkness coalesced into a massive shape.

"What the fuck? Danny, did you see that?" Chuck jabbed a finger at the monitor. "There, in the silt cloud, top left. You see that?"

Danny laughed. "School of whiting, some cod, and a couple of hammerheads. You pour Jack Daniels in your coffee again?"

Must be hallucinating from fatigue.

Chuck ground his knuckles into his eyes. "There was something out there. I'm going to move closer for a better look after this murky shit dissipates."

Resting his feet on the console, he took another swig of lukewarm coffee, staring at the monitor. When the current swept the cloud away, he dropped his feet to the floor and leaned forward, squinting. "Something's down there on the sea floor." Danny rolled his swivel chair closer and pointed to the monitor.

"Dark shadow. I can barely make it out. I'm going down to check it out."

"Hot damn!" Danny exclaimed. "It's an outline of a paddle wheel in the sand. *The Randolph*. We're rich. We're fucking rich!"

"Not yet. The ship broke up in a storm. The hull can be anywhere. But it's probably close." Chuck picked up the intercom to the bridge. "Skipper, you better get down here quick. Got an anomaly on the sea floor. Looks like it might be a wooden paddle wheel off the *Randolph*."

A moment later Jake Nicolas, a retired Navy Commander, opened the man-way to the ROV control room. He came up behind Hanson. "What do you have, Chuck?"

Chuck tapped the monitor with a pencil. "Twenty-foot diameter side wheel, partially buried in the muck. Matches the *Randolph's* drawings."

"Any magnetometer readings nearby?"

"We haven't checked yet. Danny, you picking up anything?"

"Yeah. Man, this is weird. Strong signal. Maybe three thousand tons of iron and it ain't mapped in our magnetic or side-scan sonar database."

"Signal's too strong for an iron-clad steamer. Where?" Jake demanded.

"There. Four hundred yards, bearing seventy-three degrees."

"Better have a look," Jake said.

Chuck maneuvered *Gertrude* slowly above the sea floor, her lights illuminating the ink. He caught movement in the background—a large dark object.

Danny blurted, "What the hell is that?"

"Too small for a surface vessel." Jake pulled up a chair next to Chuck, and leaned in for a closer look. "Zoom in. . . . Outline of a submarine. You sure it moved?"

"Yeah. Something kicked up a cloud of debris. Maybe when the sub settled on the sea floor. Probably exposed *Randolph's* side-wheel."

"Move in slowly."

As *Gertrude* maneuvered, the distinctive shape of a submarine emerged in the murk.

"Son-of-a-bitch!" Jake exclaimed. "I see it with my own eyes and I still don't believe it. A Russian Kilo."

"Russian? The Russkies never came this close. Not even during the Cold War. We're in US territorial waters." Chuck wiped his brow. "We ought to get the hell out of here."

"What about the *Randolph?"* Danny groused.

"She's not going anywhere," Jake said. "Let's see if we can identify that sub. Move *Gertrude* in closer."

"Man, this job doesn't pay enough for amateur spying," Chuck whined. "What if they hear her thrusters?"

"Their sonar's not likely to discriminate her thrusters from *Odyssey's* rumbling generators. . . . She's in mint condition. Clean painted numbers—SSK-635. Danny, Google that," Jake ordered.

"Strange. The conning tower is not typical Kilo class."

"Skipper, the Russians sold that boat to the Iranians in 1996," Danny said. "Got a photo on the Internet of her passing through the Suez Canal."

Jake studied the photo. "Conning tower was kosher when they took delivery." He stood up and paced the deck for a moment. "Mahmood Isfahanian and the mullahs are stupid enough to pull a stunt like this. I want to find out what that sub is up to. Move *Gertrude* closer. Slow and easy. We don't want spook the sub skipper. He might overreact."

"Aw man. I don't like this Rambo shit." Chuck dug his fingers into his beard, scratching.

"Where's your fucking patriotism?" Jake snapped. "Move in another fifty meters. . . .

"Look at *that.*" Jake pointed to the monitor. "On her after-deck. Zoom in. *Holy Christ.* The mother sub is piggybacking a *midget.* That goddamned sub has to be on an assault mission."

"Skipper," Chuck said, "we should kill *Odyssey's* thrusters and get the hell out of Dodge before they blow our ass out of the water."

"Not yet. If that sub's on a hostile mission, the skipper won't attack for fear of discovery. We're only ten miles offshore. That skipper has to maintain a stealth edge." Jake paced the deck. "We can't radio the Coast Guard, but ComSubLant has to see this.

"Danny, set up the secure Iridium satellite phone so we can e-mail the videos to Norfolk, ASAP. Chuck, bring *Gertrude* up to five hundred. . . . Circle the boat and get overheads of her, bow to stern. . . ."

Chuck pointed to the conning tower. "You're the naval architect, but it looks to me like three hatches behind the conning tower."

"Too big for man-ways," Jake said. "Looks like the Iranians extended the conning tower for missile launch tubes. Russians did that on the K-129 that went down near Hawaii."

"Missiles? You think—"

"I don't know what to think. But one thing's for sure, those whack jobs are up to no goddamned good. They slipped that boat past our undersea surveillance system. The Navy probably doesn't know she's penetrated into US waters."

"Skipper, I feel like Custer at Little Big Horn," Chuck said. "We ought to sneak out of here before we get scalped."

"Negative. ComSubLant will probably dispatch a fast-attack sub out of New London or Norfolk. We'll sit tight and keep an eye on that goddamned pigboat until the cavalry arrives. I have a feeling Uncle Sam will deliver a Christmas present to the Islamic Republic of Iran."

Twenty-Seven

FBI Tactical Operations Center
Trenton, New Jersey
December 24

After visiting their injured men at the hospital, in silence Kirk and Maggie returned to the ops center. Maggie was demoralized after one of her team leaders was killed in action; four men remained in intensive care with internal injuries, others with broken bones, shrapnel wounds, burns, lacerations, ruptured eardrums, and bruised egos.

Kirk pulled into a parking spot along the river. He cleared his throat. "We need to talk. Privately."

They climbed out of the car and strolled toward a promenade along the riverfront. Kirk turned to Maggie and said, "I know you're going through hell, but I've a feeling you will come out the other side. You'll heal, and become stronger and tougher."

"And jaded?" she asked.

"If you're lucky."

A Black Hawk roared overhead.

"That's one of ours," she said.

"We're relocating to McGuire Air Force Base. Better facilities, mobility, security, and it'll keep the media and political grandstanders at bay."

"You issued orders without consulting me?" Maggie hurled out her words. "You'd better have a damned good explanation."

"Security's weak here and the situation is critical. I had to issue orders above your level of authority—"

"What? You still retain a sexist attitude toward women in authority."

"There are a few things about this operation that were above your pay grade, and a few things you don't know. I don't work for the Bureau. I hide there. My authority and mission orders come directly from the White House."

"Don't patronize me," she snapped. After a moment of glaring at him, she spoke in a barely controlled voice. "Tell me what you can."

"My unit is a small cadre of Special Forces vets drawn from the Special Forces, the Bureau and CIA. Totally off the books. We terminate high-ranking enemy operatives."

"Assassins?"

"Covert termination specialists." Kirk rested his hands on a wrought iron railing, gazing out at the Delaware. "We have the firepower to counter the Sheikh's steel mill operation. I called for reinforcements. Munford mobilized HRT."

Maggie studied Kirk's eyes for a moment. "Kirk, I apologize for thinking less of you."

"Apology accepted, but not necessary."

"If you respected women the way you venerate your weapons, you might find a meaningful relationship."

Kirk nodded. "HRT was better suited for the mission. You and your teams are capable, but now you're down fifty percent. I had to exercise my authority quickly to reinforce our defense."

Kirk kept an eye on a man dressed in a jogging suit as he approached. The guy appeared more interested in

Maggie's ass. Kirk couldn't blame him. Dressed in form-fitting jeans, a green turtleneck, and blazer, she'd stop a column of Abrams tanks dead in their tracks.

Without turning to the sound of footsteps, Maggie slipped her hand onto the butt of her SIG.

Paranoia can be contagious, Kirk thought.

After the jogger had passed, Kirk continued. "FYI: Yesterday, a treasure-salvage firm spotted an Iranian sub fifteen miles off Cape May. She was hiding in a ship graveyard off Delaware Bay in six-hundred feet of water. The sub is piggybacking a midget. Fifteen Takavaran commandos aboard the sub—Iran's A-Team. There are nine more tangos holed up in the Bronx safe house, and possibly other operatives undercover locally. Our intel indicates the Bronx bunch will reinforce the commandos when they attack the nuke."

"We don't have the firepower to counter a threat of that level."

"That's why I need all of your able-bodied men. And you have to lead them into combat."

" We have to neutralize that warship."

"A SEAL Team Ten out of Little Creek is to take care of the sub and assist with our defense of the power plant. They know the scope of the operation. SEALs were mobilized to assault the tanker before the damned thing blew up in Houston."

Maggie frowned. "How did a SEAL Team assault on a merchantman fail?"

"Never happened. Political turf wars fucked things up."

Maggie responded with an expression of visceral and moral disgust, her forehead knotted, lips turned down at the corners. "Bureaucratic arrogance and stupidity."

Kirk said, "SEALs jumped saturation divers on the sub. Planted acoustic-activated limpet mines on her hull and welded the missile hatches closed. They're headed to McGuire on choppers, loaded for action."

Maggie turned toward the State House, and stared at the golden dome. "A military op on US soil. They'll haul our asses before a Congressional Committee."

"Only if we fail. They'll be under your command, disguised as FBI."

"Are you making me the scapegoat?"

"It's my ass on the line. . . . Not as nice as yours."

She raised an eyebrow. "Maybe we can talk about that later." She offered a half-smile.

Kirk considered her overture as a couple being towed by an ill-mannered yellow lab passed along the concrete walkway. After the dog people passed Maggie looked evenly into Kirk's eyes. "I have to bring in HRT replacements, and coordinate with the SEALs."

"We don't have much time. NSA intercepted an order from The *Sword of Ṣalāḥ ad-Dīn*. They plan to hit the nuke at oh-two-hundred tomorrow night."

Twenty-Eight

FBI Tactical Operations Center
Trenton, New Jersey
December 24

Carla, T-Bone, and Cool Rob sat around a table in animated conversation studying a large satellite photo of the Roebling steel mill and Newbold Island. Attila raised his head and trotted over when Kirk and Maggie entered. Kirk petted the big Anatolian shepherd and pulled out chairs for Maggie and himself.

"Find anything?"

"We brought in a couple dogs to search the steel mill for nitrates," T-Bone said. "No explosives in the abandoned mill, just rusting equipment and pallets loaded with drums of chemicals. Forensics is running tests on samples. Looks like the mill was a staging area to stash Semtex."

Kirk stared at the satellite photo for a moment. "We still don't know why the Iranian spooks were operating a drilling rig in the damned mill. If that fucking Sheikh is shrewd enough to throw out a red herring, he's also smart enough to have a contingency plan. I have a feeling the spooks' activity is related to the nuke assault, but I don't see a connection—"

"Connections here," Cool Rob interjected. He tapped a spot on the satellite photo circled with grease pencil. "Attila sniffed out Semtex buried on the north end of the island. Ten crates of the shit. Tracers in the explosive matched residue from the tanker and steel mill. It's all from the same lot."

"How'd you leave it?" Kirk dangled his arm and stroked Attila behind his ears.

"Hauled the shit off, covered our tracks, and laid out sniper hides and tactical positions to whack the motherfuckers. When they come back to get it, they *gonna* get it."

"Good work, Robbie—"

Kirk's cell phone vibrated. He listened for a moment, cursed, then hung up. "Jessica said Hans Wei's plane just landed at Philadelphia International Airport."

Maggie asked, "Do you think Hans is involved with the Sheikh's operation?"

"No question about it. I'm convinced he commanded the assassins who killed Michele and slit my dog's throat. I spotted him stalking me. Son of a bitch is here on a mission." Kirk drummed his fingertips on the tabletop for a minute. "I'm going after that fuck. Put a dent in the Sheikh's Bentley."

"Keep your head down," Maggie said.

The Falcon thundered down the runway with Kirk riding in the copilot's seat. At 35,000 feet, the horizon glowed pale orange, a portent of things to come. Weather forecasts indicated the unseasonably warm weather would end on Christmas Day. A massive Arctic cold front was making its way down from Canada, squeezing the high-pressure warm front in God's grip. A perfect storm in the making.

That's all we need.

Kirk wondered what possessed a man like Hans Wei to become an assassin. He had everything going—fame, fortune, good looks. His mother suffered a nervous breakdown. Maybe Hans inherited a defective gene, or was corrupted and manipulated by the Sheikh.

The twin turbines' pitch dropped as the aircraft lost altitude, interrupting his thoughts. He craned his neck over to look down at the Delaware River and Betsy Ross Bridge, the Philly airport dead ahead. In spite of the gasoline shortage, last minute Christmas shoppers flooded the highways.

The pilot set the sleek aircraft down smoothly, turned onto an apron, then rocked to a stop. A Philadelphia Police Bell Jet Ranger sat nearby with the rotor turning, a uniformed cop waving.

Kirk yanked open the door and threw his Steyr into the back of the helicopter. "Take her up," he yelled over the turbine whine." He strapped in and adjusted a set of headphones as the chopper lifted off.

"Where's the suspect?" he asked.

"Mr. Wei's plane landed over a half-hour ago," the police officer riding shotgun said. "He rented a green Range Rover with a ski rack. We have an APB out on the vehicle, but it's going to be hard to find at night, especially with this traffic. A cruiser headed south on I-95 thought he spotted a vehicle fitting the description headed north."

"That's a safe bet," Kirk said. "Roll up I-95 to see if we can spot the car."

"I never saw anyone jump through hoops like this. Who the hell is this guy? A mass murderer?"

"Not yet. Fucker's probably headed toward the Betsy Ross Bridge to New Jersey. The toll booths are on the Jersey side, right?"

"Yes sir."

"Good. Halt all traffic across the bridge. We may get lucky and trap his ass."

"We can't do that. There's gotta be over a hundred thousand people out there right now, wanting to go over that bridge."

Kirk pulled his cell phone; speed dialed the White House and spoke for less than a minute.

As his helicopter approached the bridge, he could make out a massive traffic jam on the bridge and its approach.

The cop riding shotgun turned to face him. "How the hell'd you pull that off?"

"I can't tell you that. Search for that car. . . ."

"Down there!" the cop pointed out the right side. "On the bridge."

Kirk raised his binoculars to the vehicle. "I can't see inside. Set the chopper down on the vacant westbound lanes. Back there where he can't see us."

Kirk leapt out the chopper door, ducked under the rotor, and jogged toward the Range Rover. Leap-frogging from one stalled car to the next, he closed on the enemy. At fifty yards, he pulled his HK45 and held it concealed next to his leg. He cautiously approached from the passenger side of the Range Rover, scanning for a threat.

Dark tinted windows in back, and rear passenger side. He realized he could not see inside, but the driver could see out. In a crouch, he crept on the passenger side. He popped a look through the front passenger window.

Kiddy seat in the back. A soccer mom. *Shit.*

Kirk retreated, and trotted back the chopper.

"Dead end. A last minute Christmas shopper. Let's keep looking."

The Jet Ranger circled for another half hour.

Disgusted, Kirk gave up. "He's probably holed up in the Jersey Pine Barrens by now."

Hans, I'm coming for you.

Twenty-Nine

FBI Tactical Operations Center
McGuire Air Force Base
Christmas Eve

The ops center was a flurry of activity. Large screen computer monitors mounted on the walls, banks of computers and secure communications equipment being set up and tested, FBI agents in huddles laying out tactical plans, team leaders on the telephone coordinating with the SEALs.

Kirk spotted several fresh faces—HRT replacements.

At midnight, Kirk retreated to his room in the Bachelor Officer's Quarters, and sat in bed studying satellite photos of Newbold Island and the nuclear plant. Team leaders had marked locations where they thought the enemy would breach the plant perimeter and attempt to set charges on the containment buildings. They had baited the trap with an audacious and well thought out plan, but it did nothing to calm his nerves. Traps sometimes ensnared those who set them. He had to avoid the pitfalls of anxiety and overconfidence. One could lead toward paralysis, the other to stupidity. Still, he could think of no setting more conducive to their assault. He was as familiar with Newbold Island as his martial arts moves, and like him, Maggie was anxious for payback.

A tap on the door interrupted his thoughts, then the doorknob turned.

Maggie slipped in carrying a cup of coffee, and handed it to him.

He pushed the maps and photos off his lap and patted the bed. "Thanks. Take a load off. Things quiet out there?"

"Carla's holding down the fort. Everyone else is in the field or racked out. We just got word from Harry Matlock that *Khomeini* blew ballast an hour ago and launched the midget. It's underway to the nuclear power plant. ETA is oh-two-hundred tomorrow. Matlock set up operations at the utility's marina this side of the river. SEALs are tracking it. I didn't realize those midgets had that extensive a range."

"Intel shows it's equipped with lithium-ion batteries and a small diesel generator, like a hybrid car. They'll also take advantage of the incoming tide."

"That midget sub equipped with a radio?"

"Maybe." He shrugged. "Why'd you ask?" Kirk took a sip of coffee, and offered it to her.

Maggie touched his fingers when she took the cup from his hand. First time they touched in two years, Kirk realized. A wave of heat rushed through his loins as he studied her reaction. He wondered if her contact was inadvertent.

She took a sip of coffee, holding the mug in both hands. "They'd use encrypted communications. Maybe there's a codebook aboard. Kirk, we have to capture that mini intact. If we can decipher the MOIS code and identify their chain of command, we can avoid a wholesale slaughter of innocent civilians when our military counterattacks Iran."

"Good call. You know the old saw; two heads are better than one. That's why I need you."

Maggie set the coffee cup and her iPhone on the nightstand, and looked into his eyes for a moment.

Kirk wondered what was going on inside her beautiful head.

Maggie moistened her lips and lowered her eyes. “Kirk, I want to apologize for overreacting to what I thought was criticism of women in authority. It was the basis for our intense arguments. You were right, and I was off base. If I hadn’t been so stubborn, I would have followed your advice and taken the enemy out as soon as they entered the steel mill.”

“There’s no percentage in second guessing yourself.”

Maggie shook her head. “Your combat experience proved valuable. If you had not ordered the chopper pilot to bank when the terrorists set off that Semtex, we might all be dead. Losing half my unit and my best team leader was bad enough.” Maggie reached for his hand, and sucked in her lips. “There’s something else bothering me, Kirk. I doubt I’ll have the courage to ask this again. . . . Is it too late for us? Will you have me? I’m willing to compromise if you will.”

“Maggie, I want you too. More than anything.”

“This may be our last chance to be alone, and I have to take it.”

“Here? It’ll get complicated. Maybe we need to talk about it.”

“If I wanted to talk, I would have worn underwear.”

Her eyes took on that satiny crème de menthe green signaling that she was ready. They held each other’s eyes for a long moment.

A pleasant throb passed through his loins. Then it got better when she ran her fingertips over his face, setting it afire. Then leaned forward closing her eyes. Their kiss was tentative at first, then deep. Her lips smothered his half-hearted demurrals. She pulled the clasp from her ponytail allowing her hair to fall around her shoulders.

"There'll be talk." The throaty tone of his voice gave away an awaking passion he could not fight.

"Carla will text me with a heads up if anything happens. It's Christmas Eve, and I'm not going to spend it in bed alone." She put her hand on the back of his neck and pulled him into a long hard kiss.

He saw it coming and went with it.

Maggie yanked her T-shirt over her head exposing her breasts. She rolled on top of him, her body pressed hard against his in an act of emotional desperation and reckless willingness to cross the line.

Neither of them paid attention to where they were, or what the next day would bring.

Thirty

Municipal Marina
Roebling, New Jersey
December 25

Cursing to himself in German after several passes along the riverfront, Hans failed to locate an ideal launch point for his kayak. The banks along the Delaware River were too steep, or fronted by private residences. With reluctance, he decided to use another option—the Municipal Marina.

Hans's mission was simple enough, but his profile as a world record holding surfer and downhill skier created the risk of attention. Many star fuckers recognized him from *Sports Illustrated* and his TV commercials. Nothing insurmountable. A light disguise should do the trick. His three-day stubble, dark sunglasses, and watch cap would suffice. And who, in this tiny village, would know him anyway? Life was about taking risks, and he thrived on the adrenaline rush more than the fame.

Pulling in the parking lot late at 5:30 PM, he was surprised to find the marina active for a mid-winter day. Bright sunshine and unseasonably warm weather made some people act like those during a full moon—lunatics. Teenage boys water-skied in wet suits. Powerboats raced up and down the river.

He backed the Range Rover into a parking slot. After releasing the roof rack ties, he lifted and carried a kayak to the boat ramp, then flipped it into the water in preparation for launch.

Without warning, a young couple in a new powerboat roared into the ramp creating a wake that almost swamped his kayak.

Fools. Hans watched as the owner and his female companion struggled to maneuver the boat onto the trailer. Incensed by their interference with his business and schedule, Hans offered to help trailer the boat.

The stunning woman stepped aside and eyed him with palpable hunger. He knew the effect he had on her—a beating pulse, face flushed, and wishing her partner were in another place. This they had in common. The adrenaline rush from his mission increased his normally high libido. Pity. He had other commitments that were more arousing.

Hans wondered if she had recognized him, then dismissed the thought. All women acted that way around him, like rock star groupies.

When the boat owner walked around the vehicle to the driver's side, the woman slipped a business card into his hand. She whispered, "Hans, call me. I'd love to book you on a trip around the world." She ran her tongue over her blood-red lips, then tossed her dark hair over her shoulder and slithered into her vehicle without breaking eye contact.

As the driver towed the boat from the marina, the gorgeous woman looked longingly over her shoulder and waved.

Bloody hell. The bitch recognized him. Not that it mattered as he would soon complete his mission and he would be long gone.

Hans strolled back to the Range Rover to retrieve a duffle bag from the rear hatch. After stripping out of his street clothes, he pulled on a black wet suit, rubber hood, booties, and a life vest. A moment later, he waded into the water, climbed into the kayak, and paddled downstream against the incoming tide.

When he approached the bridge connecting the New Jersey Turnpike to the one in Pennsylvania, he reversed direction, and passed the marina. He glanced at his Rolex, then looked around. No one in sight.

Roiling dark clouds to the west signaled a cold front approaching. Air temperature would drop twenty degrees; the wind would kick-up whitecaps on the river. Perfect conditions.

Hans paddled toward the Roebling steel mill with the swift tidal current at his back. Within a half-hour, he reached the northern end of the facility. There, he pulled the kayak onto the riverbank, retrieved the duffle bag from the rear compartment, and exchanged his wet suit for coveralls. After covering the kayak with a tarp, he searched about for guards on patrol. After a guard had passed on his rounds, Hans climbed the bank and made his way through the blacked-out facility toward a large metal building located adjacent to the river.

Inside, he quickly located the air compressor and pneumatic transport equipment. The Iranian spies did a good job of smuggling and hiding the equipment, along with a hoard of rusty steel drums filled with chemicals cleverly hidden in the open.

Manhandling the heavy drums would normally be backbreaking work for muscular men as there were several tons of the materials, but Hans barely worked up a sweat dumping the powdered chemicals into the pneumatic feed hopper—two drums of aluminum to each drum of iron oxide.

At 9:30 PM, he fired up the diesel-powered air compressor. The roar of the engine broke the dead silence. Hans opened the valve on the bottom of the feed hopper allowing compressed air to blow the powder out of the hopper into the buried pipeline. He continued to replenish the hopper with the black and silver powders, one drum after another, getting into the rhythm, like skiing the gates on a downhill run . . .

"Hey! Who the hell are you and what are you doing here?" a uniformed guard shouted over the compressor rumble.

The fucking compressor noise probably carried outside the building. What a cock-up. The Iranians should have muffled the sound.

Hans set an empty drum on the floor, removed his gloves, and slowly turned to face the guard. Pointing to the logo on his jumpsuit he said, "Simmons Enviro Services. We have a deadline to finish this work tonight."

"You still didn't tell me what the fuck you're doing. What is all this shit, and where is it going? What are you doing with it? I heard that machine running."

Hans turned back to his task. "Call the guard shack to verify my authorization. I must complete this work, and then home to my family."

"Horseshit!"

Hans took two steps closer to the guard.

The guard unbuckled the safety strap on his weapon and stepped back. "Stay where you are!" The guard held out his left palm.

"Please. I do not want any trouble. I am a hard worker. My family needs the money."

"With that gold watch? You're no common laborer. Turn around and keep your hands were I can see them." The guard drew his weapon. "I don't trust those Bosnian refugees either. Nobody's supposed to be here." He fumbled for a radio clipped to his Sam Browne belt.

Hans raised his hands, palms outward, as if in surrender. "Please, I am an honest man." He slowly turned his back to the guard, hands outstretched.

In a flash, Hans spun about and kicked the weapon from the guard's hand. With a fluid motion, Hans drew an antique Boker trench knife from his leg scabbard. He slammed the weapon upward into the guard's chin. The force of his thrust made the tip of the blade penetrate the man's skull.

Hans withdrew his weapon and lowered the guard's limp body onto the grungy concrete floor. He stuffed the body headfirst into a steel drum, and clamped on the top. After covering the puddle of blood on the floor with iron oxide, he got back to work, angered with the disruption to his schedule.

When the inventory was depleted, he shut down the compressor. Time was 11:37 PM. Seven minutes behind schedule.

Good enough.

Hans crept out of the building. At the river's edge, he donned his wet suit and life vest, launched the kayak, and paddled downstream in the white capping river. A feeling of elation washed over his body.

Half an hour later, Hans drove into a rural area where he dumped the kayak. The Americans would never know what hit them. Qadr's plan was the work of a genius.

On the return to Philadelphia International Airport, Hans smiled to himself. He dug into his pocket and pulled out the business card the delectable woman had handed to him earlier—Nancy Vargas, Residential Real Estate Agent. The fantasy of the moaning beauty writhing under him made his balls ache.

Perhaps the next time—if her radiant glow were not enhanced by unnatural means.

Thirty-One

Tactical Operations Center
McGuire Air Force Base
2300 Hours, December 25

The cold front roared in like an Arctic express, rivulets of rain froze on the rattling windowpanes. Thunder rumbled. Penetrating cold made Maggie's bones feel brittle, and the shitty weather inflamed her anxiety. She walked over to a nearby table where Kirk sat cleaning his weapons.

"Aren't you worried about the weather? The Black Hawks? Won't ice ground them?"

Kirk shook his head. "All-weather aircraft. They'll fly through this crap. But you better wear your Gortex girdle. This electrical storm is carrying wind gusts up to forty-five miles per hour, and it'll drop snow tomorrow. Maybe a foot or more."

"The weather doesn't bother you?"

"I'm more concerned about *you*." He reached out and touched her forearm.

"You OK?"

Hell no, I'm not OK. Maggie smiled wanly. "I work best under pressure."

She didn't know how he maintained his cool. For a man who demonstrated fervor in romance, when it came to adversity Kirk Magnus radiated sangfroid. He swam under the ice, then rolled in snow to dry off. She could use some of his equanimity.

Maggie put a brave face before her men, but it was akin to a polished suit of armor, better fitted for show than battle.

"Maggie, activity in the Bronx safe house" Carla called out. "T-Bone says the tangos prayed, then loaded duffle bags into a white Ford Econoline van and a beat-up Chevy Monte Carlo. Twelve of them. He's tailing on the Jersey Turnpike."

Maggie glanced around the ops center. Her men put their dirty jokes on hold, cocky attitudes tempered. Alert with energy and eagerness to get moving, like thoroughbreds at the gate.

"What's the situation on that midget sub?"

"Two hours downstream from Newbold Island, Carla responded. "ETA at the nuke, oh-two-thirty hours."

"Gut-check time," Maggie muttered.

After midnight, T-Bone reported both vehicles pulled up behind a run-down building located a quarter-mile south of the Simmons Enviro safe house.

"The tangos hauled two Zodiacs from the warehouse to the river," he said. "Loaded the boats with duffle bags. Six sex-starved camel fuckers in each boat. Don't see any ordnance, but something's in those duffle bags. Heavy shit."

"Copy," Maggie responded. "A pair of Zodiacs will meet you at the utility's marina. Get moving."

"Roger."

Maggie strode to the front of the ops center, her face set in a mask of grim determination. She scanned each man's attentive face, pausing briefly to look each in the eye. Special Forces spent a lot of time waiting, passing time in readiness. They were primed for action with an entire army's lethal capability.

"We took a dozen WIA in that steel mill, one KIA. Earth shoveled over Peter Townsend's coffin will serve his family no justice. But we will remember the Squid. We will remember him tonight. We *will* serve American justice." Maggie took a long breath. "Move out!"

Under the clatter of weapons and gear, the teams filed out to the waiting Black Hawks and ground transportation. Kirk could smell their cold sweat and adrenaline. He finished smearing green and black makeup on his face as Maggie approached.

"Kirk, can I have a word with you?"

"Sure." He pulled the slide back on his HK45 to insure he had a round in the chamber, checked the magazine and slammed it home, then dropped the weapon into his nylon thigh holster. She led him to her bedroom and closed the door.

Maggie looked into his eyes. "Kirk, if you ever had much faith in me, I could use a little now. I have a bad feeling about this op. I'm concerned about losing more of my men under our inane rules of engagement."

Kirk took her hand. "Maggie, if you have any weaknesses in your leadership skills, they're hard to spot. Your men would follow you into hell after that speech. My feeling is a good dose of audacity will make you more of a warrior than a worrier.

"The storm doesn't bother you?"

"Been through a lot worse. The storm will cover the Black Hawk's noise. The SEALs love this shit. Riders on the storm."

"Good. Just don't check out and pull a Jim Morrison on me." She laughed nervously. "Have to go. I don't want to keep my men waiting." She took his hand and pressed it against her heart. "Be careful, Secret Agent Man."

Kirk hugged her tightly. "I'd kiss you, but I don't wanna ruin my makeup."

The turbines on the Black Hawk helicopters screamed as the rotor blades turned faster and faster. A moment later, the powerful war machines lifted into the night sky headed west toward the black Delaware River, running without lights.

Visibility through the rain-swept windows was almost non-existent, landmarks washed out. The approaching storm unleashed a fury from the elements with frigid gusting wind that buffeted Maggie's chopper. Lightning struck incessantly, followed by crashes of thunder leaving continuous rumblings.

The external turmoil served to enhance Maggie's apprehension. Anxiety, but also a kind of rage to overcome the terror plot in spite of the rules of engagement.

In fact as her Black Hawk approached Newbold Island, her uncertainties and doubts, evaporated like spit on a boiling Bagdad sidewalk. She was determined to defeat the terrorists on her own terms.

When the choppers approached Newbold Island she slammed a magazine into her MP5 sub-machine gun with the palm of her hand, then did what she did best—take command.

Thirty-Two

Newbold Island
0200 Hours, December 26

Thermal night vision binoculars allowed Kirk to see through the freezing rain. From within the Black Hawk, he glassed the river and spotted the enemy Zodiacs in the middle of the Delaware, five miles north of Newbold Island.

Kirk's helicopter raced to the landing zone on the northwest side of the island and set down on the beach. He led his team deep into the forest to the site where the enemy had stashed the Semtex. Six of his men took cover in positions fifty yards from the hidey-hole. Cool Rob led another five-man squad one-hundred yards to the left and dug in—an ambush designed to catch the enemy in a deadly crossfire.

Kirk searched for a good observation and command post. Then he spotted a tall buttonwood that offered a good view of the hidey-hole and beach. Burdened with body armor, a thirty-pound backpack loaded with equipment, and a heavy sniper rifle slung over his shoulder, he lunged for an overhead branch and pulled himself up.

Fifteen minutes later the tactical net snapped. "Kirk, T-Bone. The tangos are approaching the beach. I'm laying back on the river two hundred meters. We'll come in behind them."

"Copy."

With his NVGs, Kirk watched the enemy unload shovels, lanterns, and AK-47 assault rifles. He counted twelve as they advanced through the forest to a small clearing where they had previously buried their Semtex. Eight formed a defensive perimeter. Four others used shovels to scrape the surface debris down to the sandy loam to recover their cache.

Payback time. Kirk was determined to kill every one of them.

"Standby for my mark!" he ordered. Kirk sighted-in a man issuing orders to those digging. "Open fire!"

For several seconds the chatter of FN assault rifles and returned AK-47 fire broke the howl of the gusting wind. Injured enemy screamed out in pain. Some broke and ran for cover.

Kirk squeezed the trigger. Missed his target.

Several of Ali Khalil's men screamed out and dropped dead around him. Ducking, he heard the crack of a heavy bullet as it passed his head. He turned and ran, stumbling through the tangled underbrush. The distinctive *crack-crack-crack* sound of a 5.56 mm FN assault rifle to his left. Muzzle flashes.

Kafir. Ali thought. *The Prophet Mohammed always provides.*

Ali crept behind the man. A flash of lightning illuminated a black face pressed against the stock of an assault rifle.

Ali charged. Slammed the butt of his AK-47 against the back of the man's neck.

The sound of AK-47 fire faded. "Cease fire! Cease fire!" Kirk barked. "Mop up. Head count."

"We got one friendly unaccounted for," T-Bone reported minutes later, agitated.

"Who?"

"Cool Rob."

Jesus Christ. From his OP in the buttonwood tree Kirk scanned the area with his night vision binoculars looking for a heat signature. Two hundred yards out, he spotted a tango frog-marching Cool Rob through the woods.

"I got him in sight, headed south. Toward the power plant."

With his NVGs, Kirk followed Cool Rob and the tango as they threaded their way through the forest toward the power plant. The tango gripped Cool Rob's flak jacket with his left hand, his AK-47 held in his right, pressed against Cool Rob's lower back.

Cool Rob was no pussy. He'd go down with a fight. Kirk realized he'd have less than a second before the terrorist would shoot his friend, if he resisted.

Options, Kirk thought. *Options.*

"Robbie, if you hear me, click your mic."

Click.

"I'm on him. On my command, fake tripping. Eat the dirt."

Click.

Kirk centered his night scope reticle on the tango's back. Range 400 yards. He placed his index finger against the trigger guard, his left arm supported by a branch. Set for the kill, he waited for a clean unobstructed target.

The tango forced Cool Rob forward, into a small clearing. Kirk applied light pressure to the trigger. "Steady, Robby. Steady," he hissed. "*Eat dirt!*"

Kirk squeezed off the round. The loud report from his Steyr rifle broke the sound of the gusting wind.

The .50 caliber round smacked into the middle of the tango's back. His torso disintegrated into mangled chunks of flesh.

Cool Rob clawed to his feet and waved. “Good shootin,’ Boss. I owe ya.”

“T-Bone.” Kirk ordered. “Run your boats down the west branch of the river to the nuke. SEALs will penetrate from the east side and neutralize the guards. Herd the guards and maintenance people into the generator building. Set up your positions. Wait for Maggie’s command.”

Single shots from handguns broke out as Kirk and Cool Rob climbed into a captured Zodiac.

“Martyrs meetin’ Mohammad,” Cool Rob quipped.

Kirk started the engine, and roared across the white-capping river toward the Newbold Island Nuclear Power Plant.

* * *

Gusting wind roiled the surface of the Delaware into whitecaps and spray, battering the stern of Kirk’s Zodiac. Lightning flashed across the sky, exploding in thunderous cracks. Freezing rain lashed down in a thick veil, chilling Kirk to the bone. Maneuvering a rubber boat in the middle of a river during an electrical storm had to be one of the stupidest things he had ever done, but there was a chance a copy of the MOIS one-time cipher pad was aboard that midget sub. They needed to break that code. Screw Thor and his thunderbolts.

Kirk killed the Mercury outboard in the middle of the river. Cool Rob took the oars to maintain position in the darkness on the river. It was 0230 hours and the enemy had not yet showed.

Maggie’s Black Hawk continued downriver to locate the midget sub. Her crew chief enabled the FLIR in the nose pod. Within minutes, the infrared image of the sub appeared on a display. She tracked the sub as it approached Newbold Island.

At 0245 hours, Maggie said, "Kirk, I have that midget on IR. She's submerged, three hundred yards southwest of your position. Passing the southern tip of the island. Your show. Good luck."

"Copy."

Kirk raised his binoculars, and scanned the surface of the Delaware.

Backlit from the bright lights within the power plant, the low silhouette of the midget sub appeared on the surface five minutes later. Hidden in the distance, Kirk counted fourteen Takavaran as they climbed out of a hatch. The commandos inflated rubber boats, and transferred ten mil-spec crates from the sub. Dressed in dark combat fatigues, they climbed aboard, then paddled their boats toward the power plant on Newbold Island.

"OK, Robbie," Kirk said. "Time to rock and roll."

Cool Rob sang, *"Mama got the rub board, sister got the tub. They're going round doing the rub-de-rub."*

"The Grateful Dead," Kirk chuckled. "That may be appropriate. Your turn for payback."

With the wind and waves at their back, Cool Rob dug the oars in and rowed their Zodiac toward the midget. Circling, he approached from the lee side.

Kirk threw a painter line over a cleat on the midget's hull, pulled his Zodiac alongside and tied it off. Burdened with body armor and weapons, he slipped out of the Zodiac on to the top of the midget. With waves rolling over the deck, he crawled on the slippery surface toward the hatch. Knelt on the deck and released the dogs. Lifted the hatch cover. Stole a quick look inside.

Wide-eyed, a commando looked up into Kirk's camouflaged face, then drew a handgun.

Kirk dropped a flash-bang grenade through the hatch. After the thump, he lowered himself into the smoke-filled iron coffin. The commando lay on the deck, blood pouring out his nose and ears, groaning. Kirk fired two rounds from his HK45 into the man's chest.

Ears ringing, he searched the body.

No documents. No ID. Nothing.

Kirk turned his attention to the communications module located immediately forward of the hatch. Nothing in the overhead cubbyholes but a Post-it note pad and pens. A pristine copy of the *Qur'an,* embossed with elegant gold script, lay on a small fold-down shelf.

Kirk had seen *Qur'ans* in destroyed Iraqi bunkers and T-72 tanks, but those were usually tattered, worn from use, and often bloodstained. He set the holy book on the edge of the shelf, and continued his search throughout the claustrophobic boat.

Duck walking in the heaving midget sub made movement clumsy, his stomach nauseous from the scene of blood, confinement, and vomit. Kirk searched for documents throughout the boat.

Nothing. Not a fucking thing.

Kirk made his way back to the forward hatch.

As he stepped over the commando's body, a wave rocked the boat. Kirk slipped in a pool of blood and knocked the *Qur'an* onto the deck with his elbow. The holy book fell open. A Post-it note stuck to a page.

Kirk picked up the *Qur'an*.

In the dim interior red light, he made out a series of random-looking numbers and letters on the Post-it—blocks of four.

The cipher pad. The letters and numbers had to come from the Qur'an.

Kirk quickly packed the codebook in a waterproof pouch, then climbed out of the hatch. He slid aboard his

Zodiac, leaving the midget adrift on the incoming tide for later recovery.

"You find it?"

"Yeah. Maybe." Kirk raised his binoculars and glassed the power plant.

Located on the southern end of the island, the plant loomed large and ominous—a technological marvel illuminated by quartz-halogen lamps that cast an orange glow. Within the facility, massive reinforced-concrete containment buildings shrouded stainless-steel pressure vessels that supported white-hot radioactive fuel rods—the target.

Enemy commandos set up defensive positions within the plant perimeter. Several Takavaran hauled crates through a hole in the chain-link fence. Czech markings. Enough Semtex to penetrate the four-foot thick containment buildings and destroy both nuclear reactors to create a Chernobyl-like disaster.

Problems were opportunities, Kirk thought. *With enemy focused on their mission, they won't know what hit 'em.* He passed the binoculars to Cool Rob.

"Those ragheads are full of themselves, ain't they? Let's bushwhack the motherfuckers," Cool Rob grinned.

"Probably ruin their day."

"It'll make mine." A lightning flash illuminated Cool Rob's grin, showing a gold tooth. He dug his oars into the black water with a powerful stroke. "I love a rainy night."

* * *

Kirk and Cool Rob pulled their Zodiac up onto the beach one hundred yards from the enemy boats. They gathered their weapons and crept forward through a wooded strip through tangled undergrowth.

Bordered by a twelve-foot-high chain-link fence topped with razor wire, the plant lay fifty yards ahead—two hundred acres, light and shadow—dozens of places for the enemy to take cover. Assaults on enemy positions always got the adrenaline flowing. The closer he approached the imposing plant, the more intense his senses. The hum of generators and cooling water pumps added to the sounds of atmospheric violence. Wind whistled through trees, rattling branches, freezing his hands and face. Cold crept up through his wet clothing to his spine. At the fence, Kirk dropped on his haunches to reconnoiter.

Forbidding signs that displayed radioactive logos, warned trespassers entry was not only prohibited, but also dangerous. Hidden in the brush, he studied enemy activity within the plant. The Takavaran were pros, going about their business, hell-bent on mass destruction.

A brilliant flash, followed by a thunderous earth-shaking blast stopped Kirk's heart cold. He hit the dirt. A second later he lifted his head, sniffing rotting vegetation on the rain-soaked ground, and the pungent odor of the ozone in the moisture-laden air. It sat on his chest like the fat lady, and she had not yet begun to sing. Lightning had struck one of the pylons supporting the 500,000-volt power lines, one-hundred yards from his position.

"T-Bone, Kirk. Sit rep."

"Ten tangos at the base of the containment building on the west side," T-Bone reported. "Four more set up a defensive perimeter. All armed with AK-47's. . . . They're opening the Semtex crates."

Kirk rolled his shoulders. He breathed in; breathed out. Payback was past due. Time to even the score with accrued interest.

"Robbie. I'm moving into the nuke. Cover my six."

"Roger."

Alone in the shadows, armed and dangerous, Kirk Magnus stealthily crept forward. Searching for prime targets to fill body bags.

"Lock and load!" Maggie snapped. "All Teams, standby for my mark. I'm moving into firing range." As Maggie's Black Hawk closed in, her crew chief flipped a switch in the cockpit to arm the miniguns—a pair of six-barreled 7.62 mm machine guns, mounted in the open doorways, capable of firing two-thousand rounds a minute.

"Standby. . . . *Open fire!*"

A pair of Black Hawks roared overhead, blasting out lines of thunderous orange-red flame, saturating ground targets with fire, creating chaos within the enemy from the torrent copper-jacketed bullets—music on the delivery end, Satan's organ on the receiving.

The report from a .50 caliber rifle blasted an enemy operative into the air, cart wheeling and lit up like a Roman candle.

T-Bone's handiwork.

Takavaran scampered for cover, returning fire at unseen FBI and SEALs with their Kalashnikovs. Ear shattering automatic weapons fire with tracer rounds lighting the sky like laser beams in all directions. Gravel and concrete fragments flew. The whine of ricocheting bullets filled the air with the deep distinctive sound of the AKs, and higher pitched sound of the FN assault rifles. Thousands of rounds flew back and forth, several cracked past Kirk's head. Enemy bodies lurched and twitched as if they were zapped with electricity. Screams of dying men.

Kirk spotted a Takavaran in the shadows, yelling into his tactical net.

The commander.

Steadying his left arm against the side of a building, Kirk centered the man's face in his 3X scope. Squeezed off a round.

Allah, make room for one more.

Kirk broke cover and ran to the shadows under a hyperbolic cooling tower. Shifted his eyes left to right. Hunting. He detected movement in his peripheral vision.

Under cover of a shed, a commando raised his Kalashnikov in the direction of a Black Hawk circling overhead. Kirk flipped the selector switch on his assault rifle to triple fire. Let loose, blasting a string of red blotches across the man's chest.

The whistle of the wind and the throbbing beat of the Black Hawks as they circled menacingly overhead could not drown out the screams of injured enemy. Charging forward, Kirk scanned for threats, shooting. Moving. Shooting. To his right, two black-clad men ran in the shadows, headed for the beach.

Kirk's voice came through on the tactical net with the practiced cool of a man who was used to talking and shooting at the same time. "Robbie. Two rabbits heading your way."

"Roger."

Kirk tracked one of the commandos and opened up with his assault rifle and nailed a double-tap in the center of mass. The man stumbled and went down, his body twitching. Kirk fired a third round into the enemy's head for style points.

Lying in wait at the breach in the chain-link fence, Cool Rob held fire and watched as the lone Iranian commando ran through the plant toward him.

Come to Daddy, motherfucker.

The commando dove for the hole in the chain-link fence. Crawled through the opening on his elbows and knees, gripping an AK-47 in both hands. He looked into a smiling black face with a gleaming gold incisor.

Cool Rob slammed an eight-inch, saw-toothed Ka-Bar tactical knife into the man's throat.

"Motherfucker," he hissed.

Cool Rob wiped the blood off on the man's parka, then murmured to himself, "Yea, though I walk through the valley of the shadow of death, I fear no evil, for I am the meanest fucker in the Delaware Valley."

As the gunfire faded, the only sounds were those of the wind and plant machinery.

Maggie said, "Cease fire. Get a body count."

"One unaccounted-for plant guard," Kirk replied minutes later.

"Damn it. Meet me at the heliport."

Kirk watched the Black Hawk circle the heliport once, then set down. Maggie jumped out of the chopper, ducked under the rotating blades, and jogged toward Kirk, an MP5 slung across her chest.

"Any friendly casualties?" she asked, still wired with adrenaline.

"We're good," Kirk said. "Nacho took a ricochet in the ass—time off with pay."

"Prisoners?"

Gunshots rang out.

Maggie snapped her head toward the report, her eyes wide. She turned toward Kirk and looked him fully in the face. He met her eyes and held them with dead seriousness, and regarded her for several seconds. Her compressed lips and frown manifested the conflict between her morality and legal background versus the exigencies of counterterror warfare. They had argued at length about the issue of executing prisoners. As commander, it was his call. He'd take the heat.

"Fourteen enemy combatants KIA within the perimeter," Kirk replied. "One KIA in the midget. No prisoners."

She grimaced, then nodded. "Alright. The cipher pad? You locate it?"

"In here." Kirk patted his knapsack. "They're using the *Qur'an*."

"Undoubtedly fighting for religious freedom," she said sarcastically.

"Shi'ite happens."

"Have you located the missing plant guard?"

Kirk shook his head. "We're conducting a building-to-building search."

Maggie nodded toward the reactor containment buildings. "Any chance this op's another red herring?"

"Not this time. The Sheikh sent in his A-Team. Damn good thing we stopped them. Dead in their tracks—so to speak. We need to inspect their demo set-up on the containment buildings."

"Right, and I need evidence. Hi-res stills and videos of the Semtex, and bodies."

"Lotta blood and guts over there—a vulture's breakfast."

"Let's get on with it."

"Maggie, wait. This attack wasn't a ruse, but there is something squirrely about it."

"What?" She froze, and turned toward him.

"I have this gut feeling, like we're missing something," Kirk said. "The piece in the middle that locks it all together. Jessie's intel indicates the AWOL plant guard lives in the same apartment complex as the rent-a-cop that T-bone took out in the steel mill."

"So? That proves nothing."

"They're both Muslim. Bosnians. They were wired in with the Fort Dix Six—the Bosnians who attempted to kill our servicemen on the base."

"Major Nidal Hasan's blueprint," she replied in a disgusted tone. "The perps are serving life to infinity at the SuperMax in Florence, Colorado."

"Sheikh Rahman's base of operations. Where it all began." Kirk gripped the hand and fore stock on his assault rifle. "Stay alert. I've a feeling the shit's about to hit the rotor blades."

* * *

Maggie and Kirk lowered their heads into the freezing rain and trudged south toward the reactor containment buildings along the east perimeter, scanning for danger. As they approached an open-sided structure covering a concrete pool filled with water, Maggie stopped at the edge. She pointed to an eerie pale-blue glow in the bottom of the pool. "What is that?"

"Cerenkov effect. Sub-atomic particles and gamma rays emitted from spent fuel rod bundles down there make the water fluoresce."

Maggie recoiled, taking two steps back. "They're radioactive?"

"Intensely. The fuel rods are still giving off heat from radioactive decay."

"My god. Why are they stored in the open?"

"No problem in boric acid solution. Water absorbs the gamma rays, boron tempers the neutrons."

"Doesn't temper my anxiety. Looks to me to be an accident waiting to happen."

"Call your congressman."

Kirk and Maggie passed five identical pools, glowing with blue light. Kirk raised his fist, signaling Maggie to halt. He pointed to a silver-grey mountain of sludge piled on top of the fuel rods in a pool.

"What the hell is it?" she asked, stepping closer.

"Beats me." Kirk stared down at the sludge. "I don't think that shit belongs in there."

"How did it get in the pool?"

"We better find out." Maggie followed Kirk as he circled the pool.

On the far side, Kirk discovered a four-inch diameter flexible pipe lying on the ground. An open end faced the pool, the other attached with a quick-connect fitting to a buried pipeline.

Maggie examined the set up. "Temporary set-up."

"The plant operator would never authorize a lash-up like that. The Nuclear Regulatory Commission would have a conniption fit. I wonder. . . ." Kirk turned and stared at the black buildings in the steel mill across the river. "T-Bone collected samples of chemicals he found over there and sent them to forensics. What'd he find?"

"No explosives. Steel drums filled with aluminum and iron oxide."

"Aluminum and iron oxide?"

"Yes. Forensics called it magnetite."

"Son-of-a-bitch." Kirk shook his head. "The Sheikh's contingency plan."

"What is?"

"Those chemicals are the components in thermite."

"Thermite?"

"Yeah," Kirk flipped his thumb over his shoulder. "That pile of sludge. The stuff burns with ferocious intensity, even underwater. If they had ignited it, the heat from the chemical reaction would have vaporized the fuel rods and released a torrent of radiation." Kirk shook his head partly in anger and partly in admiration for Qadr's engineering genius.

"Those Iranian spooks didn't drill soil borings in that steel mill. Ten to one they used a drilling rig to install a pipeline under the river. That flex-pipe is probably the tail end. The spooks rented an air compressor. Probably used for a pneumatic transport setup."

"Those spooks are dead, and—"

"Hans Wei. Had to be his mission."

In spite of the freezing rain, Damir Kovac felt cold sweat in his armpits. Hunkered down within the shadows of a hyperbolic cooling tower, he had watched the firefight in stunned silence.

How did they know? Did they know about his mission?

The mission had to succeed, even at risk of martyrdom. *Insha'Allah*—Allah wills it. Damir took a deep breath. When he crept out from cover, he spotted two heavily armed FBI agents inspecting his set-up. Perhaps they surmised the composition of the chemicals in the pool. He wasn't sure if he could kill them, but his duty was written in the *Qur'an*. Kill *kafirs*.

Quietly he crept through the shadows, staying close to the massive steel columns that supported the cooling tower. Closer now, moving by touch in the familiar darkness. He stood for a moment in the comforting hiss of the steam pipes. Then he drew his Browning Hi-Power handgun, verified the load—9 mm parabellum—deadly at close range. In silence, he moved forward, one column to the next. His shoulder brushed against a steel column.

There, exposed in the open, distracted with their backs toward him. Targets. *Time to kill.* A shot in the head would suffice. Easy at twenty-five meters. The man first. He'd shoot the woman in the face.

Damir raised his Browning and slipped off the safety. In a crouch, both hands on his weapon, he took aim.

Noise or movement, Damir never knew why the male agent suddenly looked over his shoulder. Their eyes met. With his heart knocking hard enough to shake his chest, Damir reacted and fired his weapon.

Kirk stopped in mid sentence, feeling a tingling sensation as though someone was staring at his back. He tensed and glanced over his shoulder.

Furtive movement in the shadows under a cooling tower, thirty yards away.

"Maggie!" Kirk raised his FN assault rifle toward a uniformed man who jumped out of concealment, and ran toward them, firing his handgun.

Bullets whined past Kirk's head. Gravel kicked up around them.

Maggie raised her MP5. Dropping into a crouch, she returned fire.

Ducking low, the guard raced toward the far side of the pool. He lobbed an object the size of soft drink can onto the sludge pile.

Maggie continued firing as the guard ran off into the darkened plant.

"Grenade!" Kirk yelled. He tackled Maggie, and covered her with his body.

A brilliant flash, like that of a giant arc-welder, went off under water. Within seconds, the entire storage pool lit up with retina-searing white light. Water erupted in a frothy flaming boil. A massive cloud of steam and white smoke poured from the open-sided building.

Kirk jerked Maggie to her feet. "Jesus Christ. Evacuate everyone!"

"We need to take him down!" She felt her leg, and came up with a bloody hand. "Bastard's not leaving this island alive."

Kirk saw blood on her left calf. "Fuck 'em! You're hit. The chopper. Now!"

Kirk held Maggie around the waist as they hobbled back to the heliport. After they clambered aboard, the Black Hawk rotors began turning, then it lifted off into a blanket of sleet cascading down at a forty-five degree angle.

Kirk and Maggie donned a set of headsets to drown out the helicopters racket and converse. He checked out her bloody calf. “How bad?”

“Stings a little.” Maggie pulled her pants above the top of her boot to check out the wound. “Damn it. I really hate getting shot.”

“Did I ever tell you I loved women with scars?” Kirk knelt to apply a compress to the open wound. “Bullet nicked your calf. Couple of stitches and you’ll be good as new.”

The Crew Chief asked, “What the hell went on back there?”

“Sandbagged by a sand snipe—that fucking Sheikh.” Anger in her voice.

Lightning flashed nearby, followed by a deafening blast of thunder. A tree exploded and tumbled over.

The kiss of death, Kirk thought.

When the chopper rose above the treetops, even with the sleet Kirk had to shield his eyes from the white-hot inferno. The conflagration lit up the night sky. A massive plume of white smoke poured out of the plant, leaving trail of deadly radiation across the east branch of the Delaware.

“Ah, shit. God damned disaster. Head north,” Kirk ordered. “Let’s smoke out the guard.”

The Black Hawk circled, searching the terrain through the sleet for heat. Kirk scanned the terrain with his thermal night vision binoculars.

Nothing.

“Head west to the lagoon,” he ordered. “Utility work boats are tied up there. Only way off the island.”

Kirk knelt in the helicopter open doorway, staring down into the trees. When the Black Hawk approached the lagoon, green tracer fire streaked. Bullets thudded against the armor plate. Kirk spotted two men armed with assault rifles in a small pleasure boat, one in uniform.

"Down there," Kirk aimed his weapon out the door, and fired, a trail of red tracers pointing to the target.

The Crew Chief followed Kirk's aim, directing the miniguns. A thunderous roar from the six-barreled Gatling gun drowned out Kirk's assault rifle. The lagoon erupted in a train of geysers that tracked toward the boat.

Flaming shards of fiberglass exploded into the air, followed by a fireball of gasoline that lit up the lagoon. Debris rained from a thick cloud of black smoke.

"Cease fire!" Kirk yelled over the roar of the chopper. "Let's get the hell out of here before we start to glow in the dark."

Thirty-Three

Tactical Operations Center
McGuire Air Force Base

As they walked in the door of the ops center, Kirk glanced at a wall-mounted monitor that displayed satellite imagery of the inferno. The steel and concrete roof over the spent fuel-rod storage pond had melted and collapsed. A plume of radioactive smoke covered a wide swath over New Jersey, passing north of the sprawling McGuire Air Force Base.

Jessica Masters walked over and greeted them. They took seats at a folding table. "If the enemy had succeeded, they would have taken down the entire northeast power grid. We had a partial success."

"Meaning partial failure," Kirk replied. "Hell can't be that hot."

Jessica said. "Heavy economic loss, but no friendly casualties. Rain will scrub the nasty cesium-137 and iodine-121 particulate fallout. The weatherman predicts six to eight inches of snow later that will provide an effective short-term radiation shield. Looks like the sheikh failed to account for the weather."

"Good thing."

Jessica continued, "State authorities ordered a massive evacuation. The real danger is panic when the media hype the threat."

"Count on it," Kirk replied. "That's why they call dirty bombs weapons of mass disruption."

Jessica sighed. "Why don't you save the self flagellation for the Iranians? We need to get back on track. Did you bring the cipher pad?"

Kirk dug into his backpack, then slid the waterproof pouch across a table to her.

Jessica leafed through the *Qur'an*. She studied the Post-it note, flipping pages back and forth. "It's all here. Correlated with chapter and verse in the *Qur'an*. NSA should now be able to identify the MOIS chain of command."

"Where's the Sheikh hiding?"

"Damascus. Mossad has a team on him. We can't touch him there."

Carla approached with a tray loaded with a carafe of coffee and donuts. "You guys OK?" She took a seat at the table, and poured several cups of coffee.

"Only a bruised ass and ego," Maggie said. "Kirk hit me with a flying tackle. Then I took a bullet fragment in my leg. No big deal."

Kirk reached for a mug. "Our op went down as planned, but the slick bastard blindsided us with that thermite. I sent T-Bone over to have another look in that steel mill."

Carla slid a cup of coffee and a donut on a napkin to Maggie and said, "SEALs took out the *Khomeini*. New York agents wasted every tango in the Bronx safe house. Sorry I missed it. I'm juiced for action. Up for some fucking revenge."

Kirk caught the look in Carla's flashing eyes. She was a pistol that needed to be gripped with both hands. He had in mind the perfect assignment for her.

"Looks like we caught a break," Jessica said. "Carla and I interrogated the power plant guards. "They're clean, except one dude who had fear written all over his face. He clammed up. Carla snapped a nasty stiletto open in front of his crotch. The guy couldn't talk fast enough."

Kirk snickered.

"Jesus Hernandez was his cover," Jessica continued. "Interpol had his prints on file. He's Indonesian. Name's Umar Sukarno. This wasn't his first rodeo. The bastard was involved with that Bali nightclub bombing. He left the country afterward. Entered the US and passed himself off as an illegal alien, and received free tuition at UCLA. Studied chemistry."

"Figures." Kirk rolled his eyes.

"There's more. Natalia informed me Umar had field training in a Taliban boot camp in Pakistan. He was indoctrinated by *al-Islamiyya* at their madrassa in Cairo."

"Cairo?" Kirk tapped his fingers on the tabletop for a moment. "Jess, let's haul his ass back to the Mossad safe house over there. Natalia Levi will wring every drop of sweat and information out of him."

Everyone looked up at the sound of a Black Hawk setting down near the ops center.

T-Bone walked in the door a minute later, removed his parka and flak vest, then took a seat next to Carla.

"I knew right where to look. Located an air compressor near the stash of aluminum and iron oxide drums we found earlier. Fuckin' spooks hid the stuff out in the open like doggie diamonds in a mountain of crap. Slicker than cat shit on a linoleum floor."

Kirk said, "Dogs would have never found thermite. They're trained to sniff out nitrates. That Sheikh set us up for a fall with his contingency plan."

T-Bone stroked his mustache. "Found a couple of other things over there."

Kirk looked up hopefully.

"Found bloody fingerprints on the lid of a drum. Uniformed guard stuffed inside. Stabbed right here." T-

Bone pointed under his chin with two fingers. "Big goddamned knife penetrated the guard's jaw right through to his skull. Cool Rob found this under a skid nearby." T-Bone flipped a gold disk to Kirk.

Kirk read the description on the medallion. "World Cup Downhill Ski Championship, 2002 – Innsbruck, Austria. The ski bum—Hans Reich Wei. Well, we now know his role in the attack, and that son-of-a-bitch slit my dog's throat."

"Bastard. I'll slit *his* fucking throat," Carla said.

T-Bone nodded slowly, and smiled.

"That man has everything," Maggie said. "Athletic ability, great looks, wealth, fans galore. You have to wonder what motivates him to kill. Has to be the thrill."

Jessica opened her brief case, and slid a dossier across the table to Maggie. "Hans and Qadr grew up together in London. Roommates at prep school and Cambridge."

Kirk squeezed the medallion in his fist.

"What is it?" Maggie said. She held out her hand.

He handed the medallion to her. "Gold keychain fob."

T-Bone said, "The Kraut probably lost it in the steel mill."

"Hans is Qadr's *capo*," Kirk said. "We're done here, but that Sheikh's wet dream is about to become his worst nightmare."

"How so?" Maggie asked.

"A little deception and misdirection." Kirk pointed to his temple. "We're gonna sprinkle a little fairy dust in a psycho's corn flakes."

T-Bone and Carla looked at one another and snickered, knowingly.

"Where are we going?" Maggie asked.

"You're headed to the infirmary." Kirk pointed to her leg. "Get that wound attended to. You're in no shape for another combat mission."

"I'll let you in on a secret, Kirk. Minor battle damage won't slow me down. We're in this op together.

"So tell me. Where are we headed?"

Thirty-Four

The Presidential Palace
Tehran, Iran
December 30

Mahmood Isfahanian dug into a rumpled jacket pocket to extract a package of Marlboro cigarettes. He flicked a gold-plated Zippo lighter embossed with the US Department of State logo, and stared at the flame for a moment. After lighting the butt, he deeply inhaled the acrid smoke, lost in deep thought.

The perquisites of being resident of the Islamic Republic of Iran were sweet and fortuitous. The Prophet Mohammad blessed Mahmood when Sheikh Qadr al-Masri approached him with the proposal. All that was necessary was to inform Qadr prior to any Iranian actions that would affect the price of crude oil, like closing the Strait of Hormuz. In exchange, Qadr advanced him 100 million Euros and invested the funds in a secret crude oil trading account with Falcon Trading in Zurich. No one would be the wiser. Over the last five years, Mahmood's numbered Swiss account had quadrupled in value.

Qadr's plan was ingenious, and hidden within the confines of the Ministry of Intelligence and Security. Fortunately, the Supreme Council had no knowledge, as the penalty was public hanging. Mahmood knew how to make the Great Satan bow to the power of Islam. The Americans defeated the powerful Iraqi Army in a matter of days, and could be formidable enemies, but they were weak in many ways. The Americans could never be defeated on a battlefield, but their openness was their Weakness. The country rotted from within due to politically correct leadership.

Mahmood tuned in Sky News and watched the fire burning in the Newbold Island Nuclear Power Plant. He took a satisfying drag on the cigarette. It was time for another clandestine meeting to plan the next phase of the operation. Soon, the nuclear weapons aboard *Ayatollah Khomeini* would destroy the American Capital. The payout from his currency trading would be astronomical when the US economy collapsed. *It will not be long before the Americans taste total destruction.*

Mahmood gazed out the tinted window of the armored Maybach sedan as it turned onto a side street bordering the imposing *Majmoueh Etelaat* building in Sultanatabad. The driver slowed, passed through an archway, and paused at the security post. The security guard glanced at the driver and waved the car through to the headquarters of the secret police.

Mahmood was proud of his legacy as former head of MOIS. As an operative and interrogator, he led students to capture the American embassy employees in 1979—a notable achievement that led to his presidency.

The building was notorious. Many reluctant visitors entered, most never left alive. Numerous underground holding cells in the building resounded with the screams of the damned. Cremation ovens ran around the clock eliminating the final traces of political dissidents and personal enemies. Human ashes fertilized the building's lush shrubbery.

After the luxury sedan parked in an underground garage, the driver and another guard stepped out of the car, opened the rear door and snapped to attention. Mahmood's bodyguards wore uniforms displaying the insignia of the Revolutionary Guards, and carried Makarov 9 mm machine pistols across their chests. They approached a set of thick doors on the top floor of the building. A pair of uniformed MOIS guards saluted and opened the inner sanctum of the second most feared man in Iran, General Iraj Reza.

Reza rose quickly from his desk and stood erect. The pretentious General packed a pair of pearl-handled Colt .45 pistols, and was not averse to using them to put a bullet in the head of persons deemed suspicious. Following his mentor, he used raw demagoguery under the guise of Islam to torture and execute political enemies and confiscate property in his quest for absolute power. Reza had seen countless victims suffer their dying breath in the underground chambers.

They kissed in the traditional manner, then took seats on facing couches separated by a cocktail table. Reza poured tea as Mahmood glanced around the familiar office he formerly occupied. Reza stroked his bushy mustache, dark eyes shifting. He seemed nervous.

"So, General Reza. A status report on our operation, if you will. I do not have much time."

"Yes, Excellency." Reza's tone could not mask the fear in his voice. He was hiding something. "All is going well."

Mahmood reached inside his jacket and pulled out a pack of Marlboros, retrieved one and tapped the end on the top of his watch crystal while staring Reza down. "Sky News shows the attack was a success. Radiation scattered over the State of New Jersey. The Americans panic. US currency futures will fall precipitously and increase our net worth by billions of dollars. Reza, you don't appear happy with this news."

Reza swallowed. "Excellency. Our submarine has not reported in as scheduled."

Mahmood waved his hand dismissively. "The *Khomeini* was refitted by the Chinese and incorporates much of their Song Class stealth. She is ultra quiet and slipped through the American's defensive sonar perimeter with no problem. They could not know she was involved in the operation." Mahmood picked a piece of tobacco from his lip, his eyes moving with nervous tics sweeping the office as he lit the cigarette.

"Of course, Excellency. And the filthy Arabs, of course, will be blamed for the attack." Reza let out a nervous laugh.

"So. No contact?" Mahmood picked a piece of lint off his rumpled trousers.

"The submarine commander was ordered to report in after he retrieved the midget sub."

Mahmood frowned. "Perhaps the *Khomeini* is having communications difficulties."

Reza averted his eyes. "Unlikely."

"Your nervousness belies your sanguine response. Loose ends can lead to a noose around one's neck. Your solution to this problem, Reza?"

Sweat beads broke out on Reza's forehead. "Excellency, we must assume the worst. The Americans somehow discovered and destroyed our submarine."

Mahmood rubbed his thumb over the State Department logo on the Zippo. "How can that be possible? The *Khomeini* lay in hiding within the ship graveyard." He took another drag on the cigarette and belched out a puff of smoke.

Reza shrugged. "I do not know. Fortunately, the only other connection to us is through the *Sword of Ṣalāḥ ad-Dīn*."

"Sheikh al-Masri assures me the *al-Islamiyya* communications are secure. I myself am not so confident. You are certain MOIS communications cannot be penetrated?"

"My people assure me our communications are absolutely secure. We use one-time cipher pads."

Mahmood exhaled smoke out his nose. "And if the submarine were destroyed, the cipher pad would be destroyed as well?"

"That is correct, Excellency. The paper in the *Qur'an* dissolves in water. Do you think Sheikh Qadr al-Masri can be trusted?"

"As much as he trusts us," Mahmood said, waving a dismissive hand. "Our arrangements are a traditional marriage of convenience."

Mahmood stood and walked over to a Plexiglas enclosed model of the Newbold Island Nuclear Power Plant. He leaned on the clear plastic case, looking down at the model, snapping the Zippo open and shut.

"Continue to attempt contact with the *Khomeini*. We must find out what the Americans know."

"At your command, Excellency."

Mahmood faced Reza with a menacing scowl. "American political leaders are weak, like frightened lambs smelling blood when led to slaughter. However, when provoked the Americans can be redoubtable enemies. Reza, they have long memories."

"What is your plan?"

"When you establish contact with *Khomeini*, have her standby for my order to launch the nuclear weapons. If the Americans dare attack us, I shall give the order." Mahmood pointed at Reza with his cigarette. "The *Sword of Ṣalāḥ ad-Dīn* is a weak link. The woman is expendable.

"Reza, do not fail me."

Thirty-Five

Aisha Yassin's Townhouse
Florence, Colorado
New Year's Eve

Kirk had parked the Suburban between cars on the street fifty yards from Aisha's townhouse. Surveillance had to be the worst kind of duty. Sitting in a freezing car for hours waiting and watching, bored to distraction. He looked over at Maggie who was breathing softly, sound asleep in the passenger seat beside him, her breasts rising and falling. Reaching over, he brushed the hair back from her face to admire her beauty.

The touch of Kirk's fingertips made Maggie stir. She opened her eyes, stretched like a cat, then glanced at her watch.

"Eleven forty-five. We should be kissing and groping on Times Square as the ball drops, instead of this gig."

Maggie had reservations about Kirk's objective, and the bottle rockets and cherry bombs set off by neighborhood kids only increased her anxiety. She studied Kirk's face in the dim street lighting, priding herself on reading body language.

A calm anger emanated from him like the radiant glow from a blast furnace. What gave her pause was the risk of mission failure if he didn't temper his lust for revenge. Kirk would kill everyone who had a connection to Sheikh Qadr al-Masri. She had seen that haunted look of deep determination too many times not to recognize it. He'd play rough and do it on his terms. Their mission bordered on rogue. But nothing could stop Kirk Magnus.

Maggie reached for the thermos and took a sip of coffee, then said, "Kirk, it's not working for me. This woman is a minor player. Don't we have higher priorities? This rendition business can backfire on us if our involvement became known."

"What involvement?"

Maggie sighed. "I have no desire to testify before a Congressional committee. If they find out, they'll be calling for blood. Anyone's blood."

"Keep the faith. Believe in Budweiser and Jessie's Thirteenth Commandment."

Maggie groaned, and gave Kirk a skeptical look. "More Magnus rules for the main drag? What's the Thirteenth?"

"Thou shall not get caught."

"No kidding. Why don't we just arrest her and let the dominos fall?"

"Maggie, I don't need any more devils, or their advocates. My orders are to annihilate the enemy by any means necessary." Kirk pointed out the windshield. "That bitch was complicit in the deaths of three-thousand civilians. There is no chance she's going to walk away from this to a life of celebrity and public maintenance in Gitmo. I'll see to it she gets a dose of her own medicine."

"I'd drop her with a bullet if I had a chance," Maggie replied, "but I have reservations about kidnapping an American citizen."

"I don't. She's enemy."

"Kirk, you don't have to convince me, or make excuses for following your instincts. Just tell me where you see the benefit. The payoff."

"We have to take that Sheikh and his den of thieves out before the political whores shut us down. I know how Qadr thinks. He's cunning, but predictable, like a lot of psychos."

Maggie sighed. "He's done a damned good job making us look like hoodwinked halfwits."

"We're not giving him another chance. Qadr thinks he's invincible. He'll make a mistake, and we're gonna force it."

"How?"

"Aisha is at the heart of his communications network. We take her out and he'll be deaf, dumb, and blind. Paranoia will get the best of him. He'll stick his head up like a gopher, wondering what's going on."

"You're toying with a man with faulty wiring and internal echoes. Sometimes I wonder if you hear voices in *your* head."

"The voices in my head may not be real, but they have some great ideas," Kirk replied. "Aisha Yassin is bait."

"You think he'll bite?"

"Like a ten-pound bass. I'm gonna snag him and rip his throat out."

Maggie took his hand. "You don't have to worry about my commitment to the mission, but there will be hair on the walls if we mess this up."

"Keep the faith. . . . How's the leg."

"Itchy. Six stitches." Maggie looked into his eyes. "So? Tell me again how much you love women with scars."

Kirk grinned. "Show me yours, and I'll show you mine."

"Later," she laughed. "Let's get on with the job, then we'll take care of the dirty work."

"Sounds like a great plan." Kirk took her hand and kissed it.

"Lights are still on over there." Maggie nodded to Aisha's house.

"We have her place bugged and know her routine. She'll turn the TV off after the evening news, then nod off. After she starts snoring, T-Bone and I will move in. You and Carla keep a lookout and cover us."

"Where are they?"

"Parked in the alley, behind a vacant townhouse nearby. Ain't stakeouts fun?"

Maggie stared out into the night, and sighed. "I could think of better things to do on New Year's Eve."

* * *

The lights winked out in Aisha's bedroom at 0130 hours. Thirty minutes later, Kirk pulled his HK45, press checked the weapon to verify a chambered round, then spoke into the tactical net. "T-Bone. Time to rock and roll."

"Copy."

"Maggie. Stay here and keep a lookout." Kirk kissed her hand, then climbed out of the Suburban.

T-Bone crept out of the shadows and met Kirk in front of Aisha's garage door.

"Open it with the scanner," Kirk whispered.

When the overhead door rose two feet, Kirk and T-Bone rolled under. T-Bone immediately closed it. Kirk then used a lock-pick gun to release the dead bolt on the entrance to the kitchen. He hacked Aisha's low-end security system, then slowly opened the door, stepped inside. He turned left toward the living area; T-Bone headed to the dining room, their weapons drawn.

Silently, they crept up the stairs toward Aisha's bedroom. Inside, Kirk took one side of her bed, T-Bone the other.

Aisha lay in bed face up, snoring. Her eyes moved rapidly under her lids indicating she was on the verge of awakening. She rolled to face T-Bone, muttering incomprehensibly, her chest heaving. Opening her eyes, she focused on the Taser T-Bone held ten inches from her face. "Happy New Year."

Aisha let out a scream that could crack plaster.

T-Bone fired the Taser into her chest. The 50,000 volt dart squelched Aisha's howl. Her body convulsed, eyes rolling back in her head.

"Hold her down while I stick her with the needle," Kirk ordered. "She's in for a big surprise when she comes around."

"Man. I waited a long time for this."

"She's one butt-ugly bitch. If Islamic jihadists had a clue Mizz Yassin was typical of the seventy-two virgins in Paradise, they'd probably look for another line of work."

"No shit," T-Bone let out a belly laugh, then bound and gagged Aisha. He took her feet; Kirk took her arms.

As they humped her limp 200 pounds down the stairs, Aisha's nightgown slid up exposing her genitals.

"Ah man," T-Bone groused. "How come I always get the dirty end of the job?"

"Hey! Low man on the totem pole gets the terra firma view—"

"Of the *Grand Canyon*?"

Kirk chuckled. "Let's get out the hell outta here."

They hoisted Aisha's body into the trunk of her car. T-Bone took a last look, slammed the lid, and said, "Mission accomplished."

"*Kirk, company,*" Carla's agitated voice rasped over the tactical net. "Two men in dark clothing, wearing balaclavas. . . . Creeping up behind Aisha's place."

"They're not ours. Keep your sights on them," Kirk ordered. "T-Bone and I will take them down if they come inside."

"Roger. . . . They're attempting to pry the door—"

"Night vision gear?"

"Negative. *Handguns.*"

"T-Bone, hit the main circuit breaker on my signal. I'm gonna toss a flash-bang inside.

"Maggie, cover the front entrance."

"Copy."

"They're moving inside," Carla reported. "I'm closing in behind them."

"If they haul ass out of the condo, take them down."

"Roger that."

Kirk nodded to T-Bone, cracked open the door to the kitchen, then tossed the stun grenade inside, and pulled the door closed. A second later, the blast knocked the wind out of Kirk, leaving a buzz in his ears. He and T-Bone charged into the home.

Two men lay on the floor at the base of the stairs, moaning, semi-conscious.

"Cuffs. Hands and feet" Kirk ordered. "If they make an aggressive move, I'll shoot both of them."

After fastening the ties, T-Bone confiscated their weapons. He studied one for a moment, then handed the second to Kirk. "Ugly weapons."

"Mint condition Russian Tokarevs—7.62 mm. Professional silencers. These dirtbags are assassins. Wonder who they are and why they're here." Kirk knelt and ripped off their balaclavas.

Both men were swarthy looking, full beards, muscular.

"Man, I don't like people sneaking up on me. Specially ragheads. They after us, or Aisha?" T-Bone asked.

"We'll work that out."

Carla and Maggie charged through the backdoor with their handguns drawn.

"Who are they?" Maggie asked. She stood over one man's head, her SIG pointed at his face.

T-Bone riffled their pockets. "Nothing. No IDs."

Maggie said, "They're coming around."

In Arabic, Kirk ordered the men to identify themselves. One turned toward the other with a look of incomprehension, mouth open, frowning.

"We gotta find out what the hell they were doing here," Kirk said. "Maybe they're Iranian spooks."

Both men's eyes followed Kirk closely.

"These gutter whitefish know our lingo," Carla said. "Just give me a couple of minutes with these bum fuckers." She pulled her Italian stiletto, and snapped it open. "They'll talk, or I'll jam their uncircumcised weenies down their throats." Eyes flashing, she dropped to one knee, then sliced off the men's belts.

Both assassins recoiled and gave her frightened wide-eyed looks.

Kirk kicked one of the men in the ribs. "These scum abuse females for good reason. They're scared shitless of women."

"Maybe I should cut 'em a little." Carla let out a husky laugh. "Teach respect—an old Sicilian custom."

"Not yet," Kirk said. "I have a better plan. We'll put them on the plane along with the power plant guard. Turn them all over to Natalia. Mossad will wring out everything including their last drop of sweat."

"What about Aisha?" Maggie asked.

"She'll receive payback for services rendered," Kirk replied. "The Mossad Special."

Thirty-Six

Al-Mukhabarat al-Amma Headquarters
Cairo, Egypt

The oval table in the room was large enough to seat eight. Jessica Masters and Kirk sat beside one another, across from Colonel Amad Suleyman. A chalkboard on a wall displayed Arab script that Jessica could not decipher. Through a cloud of blue haze, Colonel Amad Suleyman took another deep drag on a Turkish cigarette, then belched out the acrid fumes.

"Dr. Masters, I am afraid my government will never acquiesce to a covert foreign counterterror operation on our soil." With his Sandhurst Military Academy accent, Amad voiced his concerns in crisp, authoritative King's English.

Frustrated with the Egyptian's resistance, Jessica could feel the heat rising in her face. She cast a sideways glance at Kirk. *Cool as dry ice.*

"Colonel, we've worked together many times, and have exchanged favors. We need one now. These terrorists have been hounding your government for years, and now they've attacked the United States. We would be doing *you* a favor by exterminating the whole lot of them."

"Perhaps," Amad smiled. "However, the political situation here is, as you might say, delicate. Egypt has a large and powerful population of fundamentalist Islamic zealots. These people excel at fomenting riots."

"You oughtta thin out that population," Kirk said.

Amad nodded slowly. "I quite agree. However, there are many in our government who are pacifists. They believe turning the other cheek is best."

"You're not the only one with that problem," Kirk said. He lifted a bottle of Sakkara beer and took a long slug.

Amad drew on his cigarette, and puffed a perfect smoke ring toward the ceiling. "I would like to cooperate, but my hands are tied."

Kirk set his beer down and rested his forearms on the table. "Amad. You have respect and influence within your government. Ask them to turn a blind eye."

"Perhaps if I knew more of your tactical plans? What can you tell me of your operation?"

Jessica relaxed a notch, knowing they were making progress, but she had no intention to divulge their plans. She pushed her briefcase aside, and leaned over the conference table.

"We have a high priority op in progress. Our governments are allies in the fight against Islamic jihadists. We *must* work together. This is why we're meeting with you."

"Yes," Amad said. "And I do appreciate what you call a heads-up. However, your proposal may have grave political consequences. Certainly you understand this?"

"Your government and ours have an opportunity to neutralize this threat."

Amad sighed. "Your strategy has merit. However, we cannot allow a foreign power, even a valued ally, to undertake a covert operation on Egyptian soil. Surely you understand our position?"

Jessica looked Amad in the eye for several seconds. "Amad, we can insure plausible deniability. These terrorists have been in the bomb-making business for thirty years. But, sometimes they make mistakes. . . . "

Amad nodded and smiled. "Yes?"

"If an explosion at the madrassa were made to look like an accident, would that satisfy your government?"

"There will, of course be many questions. An investigation."

Kirk interjected. "Off the record, we'll proceed with or without your cooperation. We're in a high stakes game, and we're sore losers."

Amad fingered his mustache. "Kirk, make no mistake. I want your operation to succeed, but I may not be able to convince my superiors." He shrugged. "Politics."

"All politicians can be bought," Kirk said. "That's why they're in public office. What can we do to grease the skids? What's their price?"

"I cannot recommend *baksheesh*, although they will have their hands out."

"How much?"

Amad took a long drag on his cigarette, then crushed out the butt. "Perhaps there is another way—a *quid pro quo*."

Jessica caught Kirk's eye, and offered a hint of a smile.

Amad continued. "We have another terrorist problem I wish to address. We know Hamas plans to subvert our government. The American NSA undoubtedly monitors their communications. I *want* the Hamas intelligence."

"NSA. No Such Agency." Kirk leaned back in his chair, and studied the beer bottle.

Jessica was frustrated with the men's hard line approach. She prided herself on her negotiating and interpersonal skills, and came up with a plan.

"Amad, I'm familiar with that intel. I recall little that would be detrimental to American interests in those intercepts. If we redact the transcripts, I believe I can make a convincing argument with our director of national intelligence to release them to you."

Amad nodded expectantly.

"If I set it up, can you sell the deal?"

The Director of Egyptian Intelligence smiled and reached across the table to shake hands. "I shall do my best."

Thirty-Seven

Mossad Safe House
Cairo, Egypt

Inside the walled compound, a two-story mud brick building hid small offices holding an array of telecommunications equipment, sleeping quarters for six Mossad operatives, and four cells for prisoner interrogation.

Kirk and Natalia peered through a one-way window to check on Umar Sukarno, asleep in his cell bound to a rusting mattress frame wired to a magneto like that used for World War II radio/telephone. A dripping faucet on a rust-stained sink contained rubber gloves and used syringes, the walls splattered with dried blood, the basement cell a veritable dungeon, reeking of urine and feces.

"Umar confessed to commanding the Bali nightclub bombing in 2002. He admits command of the nuclear power plant assault, reporting to Hans Wei," Natalia said. "He will awake from the sedative within the hour, and remember little."

"Anything from the Iranian spooks?"

"General Iraj Reza ordered the assassins to eliminate Aisha Yassin in order to sever the link to MOIS. They know nothing more. The IDF shall use them for prisoner exchange with Hezbollah."

Kirk's suspicions of the men's intent were confirmed. By sheer luck, he had saved Aisha's life. The irony of the situation was not lost on him. He planned to use Aisha and Umar as pawns in a deadly game of global chess to disorient, disrupt, and disable the Sheikh. For the first time since Brett Brosnan's assassination, he was on the offensive.

Through the heavy veil of a narcotic induced sleep, Aisha opened her eyes to discover she was naked and securely bound to a stainless steel gurney. Her mouth felt dry with a metallic aftertaste. In spite of the warmth, she shivered when she remembered the intruders in her home.

She closed her eyes and strained against her bindings, to no avail. An oily sweat covered her body. She prayed to Allah.

When Natalia and Kirk entered the cell, Aisha cast a venomous glare at him. "What have you done to me? What is this place? Release me at once."

Kirk swiveled his eyes around her cell. "I suppose you wouldn't want to hang around here too long. But, you don't have to worry about that," he said in a flat tone of voice. "Welcome to hell."

"What is the meaning of this . . . this criminal insult? I shall file a formal complaint—"

"Signed, *Sword of Ṣalāḥ ad-Dīn?*"

Aisha winced, and averted her eyes. "I demand a lawyer."

"Are your demands non-negotiable?" Kirk's deep menacing voice sounded like it came from the bottom of a pit.

"Insolent fool. You cannot speak to me in this manner."

Kirk crossed his arms and looked down into Aisha's pocked face and sweating armpits. "You violated the laws of the United States. Conspired to kill thousands of innocent civilians, and now you want those same laws to protect your lard ass. Ain't gonna happen. You're in Egypt—land of your birth, and you're gonna die here."

Aisha's dark eyes took on the look of a cornered animal about to be mauled and eaten by a predator. She struggled against her restraints. "I am an innocent of these preposterous charges. I have no knowledge of terror activities."

"You can't hide your lying eyes. You are in it up to your hairy armpits. We have it all recorded. Your meetings with Sheikh Abdel-e Rahman and Ramzi Gonimah. E-mails to the Bronx and Dubai."

Aisha's features changed into those of a demented killer. "*Kafir* fool. You know nothing."

"Right." Kirk smiled. "I never did learn how to fight nice. Especially with Jihad Janes. I'm fixing it so you and the Falcon can spend eternity together. You're gonna get a dose of your own fucking medicine."

Aisha let out a whimper, her chest heaving. "No please. *Please.* I will tell you all wish to know. Do not hurt me."

"Flat on your back, it doesn't look like you're in a position to negotiate. There's nothing you have that we already don't already know," Kirk said. "I believe you're familiar with the effects of radiation poisoning—vomiting, diarrhea, internal bleeding, and hair loss. Even your teeth will fall out."

Aisha struggled against her bonds. "No! Please." She made little strange noises in her throat, like a woman lost in a nightmare.

"Go to hell." Kirk nodded at Natalia. "Proceed."

"We shall grant you one last wish," Natalia said in Arabic. "You may wish you never conspired to commit acts of terror."

"My regards to the Falcon," Kirk snapped the single digit salute, and turned to leave.

Outside, Natalia barked an order into her radio. A moment later, a Mossad operative dressed in a bunny suit, facemask, and latex gloves appeared, struggling with a heavy lead jar. In the cell, he retrieved a plastic vial containing a syringe from the jar, then tied a piece of rubber tubing around Aisha's arm. Locating a vein with the syringe, he injected Aisha as she writhed on the gurney.

A scream poured from Aisha's mouth, and then died away into terror-choked sobbing.

Natalia said, "One microgram of polonium-210. An alpha emitter. The isotope is one million times more toxic than cyanide. However, the low dose will be slow acting. She will go mad. I do not think you want to witness the results."

Kirk nodded. "Got that right."

Natalia took a last look into the window. "Two days. Three at most. Do you wish to reclaim the body?"

"Negative." For the first time, Kirk violated one of his key tenets by targeting a female enemy. But Aisha Yassin was the exception—she had one redeeming quality; her death would advance his agenda.

In a deadpan voice, he added, "Dump her body at the entrance to the Falcon Pharaoh's tomb in the Valley of the Kings. I want that fucking Sheikh to read my calling card."

Thirty-Eight

Mossad Safe House
Cairo, Egypt

Umar Sukarno slowly recovered from a drug-induced stupor to find he was bound to a rusting mattress frame with plastic ties. A single light bulb hung from the ceiling and glared in his eyes. When he tried to move, he groaned and grimaced from pain. He spotted an IV drip connected to his arm along with numerous sensors taped to his naked body. A stainless steel cart next to the mattress frame held several syringes, containers of drugs, and an array of gleaming tools. The cell contained a collection of electronic instruments that recorded his physical and mental signs. He recognized the lie detector, and remembered little of his ordeal other than the excruciating pain from the torture. He was physically exhausted and hungry, but could think of nothing but a means of escape.

He could barely move his right wrist, but he detected slack in the left binding. Struggling with a great effort, he worked the plastic tie back and forth against the abrasive rusted metal. After an eternity, the tie snapped. He wriggled the frame toward the cart and retrieved a scalpel to cut the rest of his bindings. When he sat up, a wave of nausea passed through him. For several moments, he remained dead still, listening for movement outside his cell.

Cursing under his breath, he yanked the IV drip needle out of his right arm, and peeled off a dozen body sensors, swung his feet to the floor, and attempted to stand.

Intense pain soared through his spine. He slumped to the floor, and passed out.

When he regained consciousness, he slowly clambered to his feet. Nauseous and dizzy, he cautiously approached the heavy steel door to his room. He placed his ear against the door and listened for sounds outside the cell.

Nothing. He tried the door latch.

Unlocked.

Cracking open the door, he peered into the corridor to find it vacant. Slipping out of the room, he crept down a dimly lit hallway to another door leading to a stairs. The walls in the stairwell seemed to move, rotating slowly at first, then faster. Grasping the handrail to steady himself, he ascended a flight of stairs, then stepped into a darkened alley.

The stench of a raw sewage overcame him. He fell to his knees, and puked on bare dirt. Gasping for breath, he surveyed his surroundings. In the distance, he recognized the brightly lit minarets of the El Haq Mohamed mosque. Umar suddenly realized he was in a Cairo slum, not far from the *al-Gama'a al-Islamiyya* madrassa. His heart leapt. This was a place where he would find friends and sanctuary. Ramzi Gonimah would welcome him like a conquering hero.

He made his way through the darkened streets and alleys. Creeping though the shadows, he shivered in the cold night air. Within minutes, he staggered across a beggar sleeping in an alley. In need of clothing, he hit the man in the head with a brick, rendering the beggar unconscious. The man's clothes were not a bad fit, but the putrid smell was sickening. No matter. He was free to rejoin *al-Islamiyya* and set out for revenge against the Americans.

From the shadows, Kirk observed Umar as he worked his way through the slum toward the madrassa. *Couldn't be better*, he thought. The *Mukhabarat* bugs located in the roof of the madrassa would allow him to listen to their conversation.

"Jessie? Umar's in," Kirk announced into the tactical net. "Ramzi was surprised to see him. He ordered an assistant to round up the *Islamiyya* senior operatives for a confab. Looks like our bait is attracting the big fish."

Kirk counted six operatives as they entered the madrassa. "Ramzi ordered Umar to follow them to the back room. Sounds pissed. Ordered his men to bind Umar's hands behind his back."

Kirk listened:

"Force this traitor to his knees," Ramzi ordered.

"Why are you doing this, Ramzi? I have done nothing wrong. I swear to Allah. I followed my orders."

"Umar, you have betrayed the Islamic Revolution. Our mission has failed. The American President himself said an Indonesian guard who worked at the nuclear power plant tipped them with a telephone call. You were the only Indonesian working there."

"I swear to Allah, I followed my orders."

"*Liar.*" Ramzi slapped Umar. "The Americans knew of our intent. Our communications are secure. There is no other way the Americans could discover our operation."

"But, I have succeeded in my mission."

"*No.* You failed, and must be punished. We shall bath your body in pig's blood. You will be denied martyrdom for your treachery."

"No. Ramzi, please. None of this is true."

"How did you escape to Cairo?" Ramzi snarled.

Umar remained silent.

"Break his arms," Ramzi ordered. "Allow him to suffer. I, myself, shall behead this traitorous scum."

Kirk said, "We got a whole bag full of bad actors. Let's pull the pin."

"Copy," Jessica replied.

An hour earlier a CIA drone, called the Reaper, accelerated down a runway at Prince Sultan Air Base in Saudi Arabia and lifted off into the night sky, headed toward Cairo. Invisible to Egyptian radar, the stealthy drone made wide banking turns over the city, awaiting a signal.

Jessica and Natalia set up an infrared laser target designator on the roof of an apartment building nearby. Jessica adjusted the focus of the invisible beam, and locked onto the madrassa.

"Engage the target," she ordered.

A flight controller at Nellis Air Force Base in Nevada studying a real-time infrared display toggled a joystick to bank the drone. With the madrassa sighted in the cross hairs of an infrared image, he activated the weapons.

A pair of Hellfire missiles mounted on rails under the Reaper's wings acquired the painted target, dropped from their rails, one after the other, and accelerated in a downward trajectory.

"Twenty-two seconds to impact," the Nellis operator reported.

From his vantage point a block away from the madrassa, Kirk watched streaks of light flash across the sky like inbound meteors. A fraction of second later, he saw the missiles detonate on target. The ground shook beneath his feet, as a massive fireball rose in the sky. Rubble rained down.

"Tangos vaporized," he announced. "Let's go skiing."

Thirty-Nine

CIA Safe House
Zugspitze Mountain
Garmisch-Partenkirchen, Germany

The Tyrolean chalet set on a hectare of forested mountainside, offered dozens of high-level East German and Russian defectors a taste of Western luxury in years past. The irony of using the safe house in a war against one obscenely rich man was not lost on Kirk Magnus.

He slid open a glass door and stepped onto a deck to check the view of a cloudless sky frosted with stars and the western horizon bathed in blood red silhouetting a stunning panorama of the Alps. The lights in Garmisch twinkled 2,000 feet below. Floyd Cramer's *Last Date* played on the stereo.

The wooden deck, surrounded by bulletproof glass panels, was equipped with a charcoal rotisserie, tables and chairs, and outdoor radiant heaters. Bathed in steam and glowing light, a hot tub on the deck beckoned.

Carla and T-Bone frolicked in the foam with wanton abandon, their eyes glowing with lust. Carla's screwball antics only enhanced her street-tough sexy persona. Beneath her super-feminine façade, she was a pit-bull with Maybelline eyes and stiletto claws.

With robes covering their bikinis, Jessica and Maggie followed Kirk out the door and shuffled barefoot across the deck to enter the hot tub. Maggie caught

Kirk's eye as she twisted her hair in a knot. She dropped her terrycloth robe to the deck, then stepped into the boiling water.

A moment later, Max stepped out the door. "Good to see you, *Mon Ami.* Lovely evening."

"Almost perfect." Kirk basted sizzling Cornish hens on the rotisserie. "Where's that fucking Sheikh hiding?"

"Damascus. Our internal sources inform us he attempted to set up a new base of operations in Syria."

Kirk took a sip of wine, then set the glass on the rotisserie. "Max, we can't allow that to happen. Problem is we're restrained from operating in Syria, and he hasn't responded to my calling card. We gotta flush that son-of-a-bitch out."

"I quite agree. Jessica and I met with our counterparts with the National Security Directorate. The Syrians denied any knowledge of the Sheikh's presence in country. I displayed photos of him being greeted by Hassan al-Rashid at the Presidential Palace."

"How'd they react?"

"They feigned ignorance. Jessica busted their balls."

Kirk laughed. "Tough babe."

"Yes. Like a *baccarat croupier*, she laid down one photo after another of every Syrian operative working undercover in Lebanon. The NSD agents did not do well hiding their reaction. She told them these men would *disappear* unless NSD forced the Sheikh out of Syria within twenty-four hours. Her performance was magnificent. God, I love this woman."

Kirk glanced at Jessica. With her platinum-blond hair shining like a halo from the hot tub lighting, she looked like a movie star, acted like Mata Hari, and dished up poison like Lucrezia Borgia. The polonium-210 had been her idea.

Max caught Kirk's gaze. "CIA and NSA broke the MOIS code. We are listening to their conversations and reading their messages. The Iranians continue in their attempt to raise the *Khomeini* on the radio. Surely, they now assume the boat is lost at sea. The snowball is rolling. Next, the avalanche."

Kirk raised an eyebrow.

Max continued. "In a coordinated plan, the Pentagon is targeting the Iranian Presidential Palace, MOIS headquarters and all known nuclear facilities by aerial attack. The French Navy will take out the Naval Base at Bandar Abbas. We have dispatched our nuclear submarine, *Le Terrible.* She is underway from Brest to the Arabian Sea, and shall be on station within eight days. I leave tomorrow to lead my team in Teheran to identify and designate high-value targets. Dissidents and students are being covertly mobilized to overthrow the Islamic *régime.*"

Deep Purple's rock classic, *Smoke on the Water, Fire in the Sky,* rumbled through the speakers.

"A surgical strike with cruise missiles and smart bombs," Kirk said. "Time to rock and roll."

* * *

The fireplace radiated warmth throughout the den but did little to warm Kirk's psyche. Lying on a bearskin rug next to Attila, he rested one elbow on the floor, fondling the dog's warm ears while contemplating a cold move.

Dressed in green silk pajamas, Maggie padded barefoot across the pine floor, then knelt beside Kirk.

"You've been staring into the fire for over an hour, and you're letting a candle go to waste, Secret Agent Man. Why don't you come to bed?"

Whenever Maggie was in the mood, she lit a candle in the bedroom. Romance was always in the back of

Kirk's mind, but his frontal lobes were burdened with thoughts of redemption.

She read him like pulp fiction, and she didn't like the plot of the story. Not one damned bit. Maggie had stress fractures in her demeanor.

"Are you going to take Hans out?"

"Hope you're not going wobbly on me." Kirk examined a half-drained beer bottle. "That guy's not going to die from the heartbreak of psoriasis. At least not until I extract information I need."

Maggie's forehead filled with torment. *"Torture?* You're going to torture him?"

"When Hans slit my dog's throat, he set the rules of engagement." Kirk took a long swig of beer, then shook the empty bottle. "Enhanced interrogation, with inducement."

Her face turned scarlet. "For God's sake! A CIA euphemism doesn't make it any better. You damned well know Bureau policy on that kind of thing. If the spooks want to do it, that's their business. But not us. Not *ever*."

"Maggie, I believe in the warrior ethic—meet force with overwhelming force. The moral high ground is saving thousands of innocent lives. I do whatever it takes. Sometimes I don't like it, but it's my job. His plane's due to arrive tomorrow morning at the Munich airport. I want you and Carla to tag him. Determine his routine. A couple more good-looking women eye-balling him would never be noticed."

Maggie sighed. "I really don't want any part of it. But, you'll do it anyway and never lose a night's sleep over it.

"What are my options? Hans is no empty suit. He's Qadr's *Capo*. Privy to information I need to complete my mission. I need your help."

Maggie shook her head. "What can Hans possibly have that's so important?"

"Info that will rock your world." Kirk jammed a poker at a log to renew the dying embers.

"Well, damn it. If you want my cooperation, better bring me in on it. You have the authority, and I have a need to know."

Kirk paused for a moment before he replied. "The Speculator Sanction's compartmentalized—buried deeper than nuclear waste at Yucca Mountain. Only twelve people in the loop. You're number thirteen—"

"Lucky me."

"One of the Sheikh's assassins, the perp who killed Michele, had copies of her photo ID and mine, along with addresses and phone numbers."

Maggie raked her fingers through her hair. "How the hell did they get that?"

"From the moment they killed Brett, I've suspected a mole within our ranks. I intend to extract the traitor's name from Hans."

"What makes you think he knows who it is?"

"When I was playing with Stryker, I spotted him in the park stalking me the night they shot Michele. Didn't recognize him at the time." Kirk stared into the fire for a moment. "There's evidence he commanded the Spetsnaz attack on Michele and me."

Maggie looked into Kirk's eyes. "Evidence? What evidence?"

"I recovered a cell phone from the Russian hitter who whacked Michele. The calls made on it went to same number. When I redialled it, Hans answered. I recognized his voice from his TV commercials—King's English, a slight German accent, self-confident beyond arrogance.

"Maggie, a thing like this, you get one chance and one chance only. Half-measures are not enough. I'm not letting that son-of-a-bitch get away. He slit my dog's throat."

"No wonder you're so hell-bent on revenge. But you can't keep going ballistic. When you take him down, you'd better plan right down to the gnat's ass. He's a celebrity, a national hero, and the media will go ape shit. The *Bundeskriminalampt* are ruthlessly efficient and will be on your ass like flies on manure."

"I don't have much choice. The stakes are too high. I'll put him through the wringer."

Maggie raised her eyebrows. "Kirk? Why would you risk everything torturing a prisoner?"

"This is the part in the movie where the plot thickens. . . . In Houston, I saw the Sheikh pass a briefcase to the Senator. Probably loaded with cash."

"You don't know that."

"There's no way to be sure, but I'm convinced. CIA traced another two million bucks from Falcon Trading to Senator Howard Dreihaus' campaign war chest. I don't believe in coincidences. Never have and never will. That Sheikh owns him."

Maggie frowned. "What could Dreihaus possibly offer of value to the Sheikh?"

Kirk sat up cross-legged, staring into the glowing embers for several seconds.

"He chairs the Senate Select Committee on Intelligence, and has access to redacted Omega Six op reports. He knows about the Speculator Sanction."

Maggie's posture stiffened. "Oh, my God." Her voice was barely audible. "I don't want to hear the rest."

"I'm not giving you that option. It's clear that Sheikh is trying to ruin our economy and bring down the US Government. There's a thin possibility that Dreihaus is an unknowing accomplice. But, if he's dirty, he's guilty of high treason and accessory to capital murder—three thousand four hundred and eighty-six counts."

"Maggie, I'll need unequivocal evidence of his complicity. Hans has it, and I intend to get it any way I can."

"I can't fault you for that. Then what?"

Kirk used a poker to stir up the ashes. "My orders are to terminate the traitor with extreme prejudice."

"A presidential candidate surrounded by Secret Service?" Maggie pulled her knees up against her chest, and hugged them. "Kirk, blowback can be fatal—"

"I have a plan for that, but right now I need to run Hans through the wringer. Sometimes the risks you take dictate the risks you have to take. I want your help."

A burnt-through log crumbed on the grate and fell into the ashes, startling Attila. Kirk petted the dog affectionately. Several moments passed in dead silence as they sat before the fireplace staring into the dying embers. Then Maggie leaned her head against his shoulder. He hugged her waist.

"We're in this together," she murmured. "Let's finish it."

"After I burn this bastard, I'm going after that Sheikh with a flamethrower."

* * *

Maggie and Carla watched the Citation X land at the Munich airport and taxi to the General Aviation Terminal. When the door dropped, Hans Wei stepped out of his plane with a pair of stunning playmates in tow that were barely over the age of consent.

They followed his Range Rover Garmisch. Crowds swarmed the picturesque ski resort. The World Cup Downhill Championship drew the best skiers on the planet, along with a mass of spectators, media types, and groupies hungering for a glimpse of celebrity, or a piece of the action.

After four days of surveillance, they determined Hans had many acquaintances in the village, but few friends. Late in the day, he frequented a skiers' hangout at the base of the slope called the Haufbrauhaus, a Tyrolean style restaurant and bar where he enjoyed bathing in the limelight, mingling with other patrons, signing autographs, and giving media interviews. He frequently picked up gorgeous women and invited them to his mountain lair for overnight fun and games. On the rare occasions when he was alone, Hans skied from the top of the mountain to his chalet, taking a treacherous shortcut down the back face through the trees.

"He's leaving the Haufbrauhaus alone," Maggie reported. "I can't believe it, but he didn't score a single babe."

"Copy," Kirk replied. "We'll tag him."

Kirk and T-Bone followed Hans on the ski lift to the summit. Fresh snow had fallen throughout the day, and a light wind kicked up flurries, reducing visibility. They struggled in deep powder to keep up with the athlete, skimming under snow-laden fir branches, jumping across crevasses and off twenty-foot cliffs.

Kirk and T-Bone slammed to a stop 100 meters uphill of Hans's mountain lair, their breath condensing in the frigid air as they watched him remove his skis and enter his chalet.

Cantilevered over a sheer cliff near the famous bone-breaking Kandahar ski run, the ultra-modern chalet looked like an impregnable fortress—thick granite walls, heavy timbers, large glass panels looking out over a massive deck perched 100 feet above the cliff face.

T-Bone pointed with his ski pole. "Those digs look like the mountain lair in that Alfred Hitchcock movie, *North by Northwest*. It'll be a bitch to break in."

"Top-of-the-line security system. An infrared laser perimeter intrusion, glass breakage, motion and heat detection, along with a deal to have the ski patrol run by his place periodically. But we didn't spot any bodyguards."

"Maybe he thinks he's invincible. Or has a death wish."

"By now, the Sheikh had to receive word of Aisha's demise. Wouldn't surprise me if he were hanging his friend out to dry. There's been no contact."

"Kirk, I know this is personal, but I still picture that steel mill guard's body in that drum. Makes me lose sleep. Why don't you let me do this guy? To me, he's just another target to be taken out."

Kirk leaned on his ski poles, staring down at the mountain lair through snow-laden trees. "Shooting him would be too damned easy, and would defeat my objective. I need to extract some information from him."

"What's Hans got that we need?"

"Intel that's above your pay grade."

T-Bone frowned. "You cutting me out of the action?"

"I need to confront him alone to extract the info. And deliver payback for slitting my dog's throat."

"That's cool. What's the plan of attack? How you gonna get in that fuckin' fortress?"

"His maid comes twice a week. When she disables his security system, we will log the key-code, and pick the lock. That bastard is gonna bathe in his own blood, instead of the limelight."

"Attaboy. Feel the revenge."

"Not yet. Not until I wring the shit out of him."

"Man, I hate it when they resist," T-Bone quipped.

"Not a great idea."

"What if he has women with him? He got a sweet tooth bigger than mine. Sometimes shags two at a time."

"That's the chink in his armor, and we're going to exploit it," Kirk stared off at the chalet, eyes narrowed.

"How?"

"Thought we'd start with our nutcracker—Carla's monkeyshines."

T-Bone let out a belly laugh. "That pun intended? Man, I can tell from the Dirty Harry squint in your eye, this gig's gonna be good."

* * *

The après-ski crowd was three deep at the bar, ski bums plying hordes of snow bunnies with booze in the Hofbrauhaus.

Maggie and Carla laid claim to a small table and hung their parkas on their chairs.

Carla removed the headband over her platinum-blonde wig, then rotated her fanny pack over her tummy. Looking down over her shoulder, she ran a hand over her butt to smooth a non-existent crease in the skin-tight Spandex ski pants.

"These pants make my ass look fat?"

Maggie let out a laugh. "Those honey buns of yours are rat bait." She nodded toward the opposite side of the bar.

Surrounded by media types and groupies, Hans held court in front of a floor-to-ceiling fireplace.

A waiter dressed in lederhosen arrived at their table. Maggie ordered two Lowenbrau drafts and a tray of Rostbratwurst, cheese, and crackers.

"He's surrounded by a pack of salivating women," Maggie said under her breath.

"Ummm," Carla purred. "No surprise. He looks like a hot lunch." She chomped into a cracker with a slab of Muenster on it. A few crumbs settled on her chest.

Maggie sniggered. “Carla, we’re going to slaughter that pig, not pork out on him. Hans has vital information we need to extract. He may be the fastest on the slopes, but his intellectual horsepower is bringing up the rear. Do the dumb blonde thing. Seduce him, and get him alone in his chalet. Kirk will handle the rest.”

“You think I look racy enough?” Carla brushed the crumbs off her chest, making her tits jiggle under her form-fitting sweater.

“*Titillating*.” Maggie laughed. “Those double-Ds will transform his brain into hominy grits, and harden his resolve—so to speak.”

Working on her night moves, Carla had overdone her mascara, eye shadow and liner. Her trademark bright red lipstick drew attention to a wide sensuous mouth. Under her micro-fiber turtleneck, she wore a Victoria’s Secret demi-bra that enhanced her bust-line and did little to hide her nipples. Her wavy blonde hair wig hung down to the middle of her back, complementing dark eyes that glowed like black onyx in the firelight.

“Buy you gorgeous creatures a drink?”

Oh, crap.

Maggie turned to look up into the faces of two grinning hunks, one proffering a bottle of schnapps. She slid her hand across the table and held Carla’s hand.

“No thank you. We’re taken.”

“Diesels.” The shorter man opined to the other. They did an about-face to troll the bar for easier women. The other muttered, “Whatta waste of first-class pussy.”

“Class act.” Carla laughed until her eyes watered.

“You sure you’re up for this?” Maggie asked.

“Damned right.”

“Good. The mark’s always on the prowl for strange nookie. When he makes eye contact, do the vamp thing.”

“The vamp. That’s my shtick.”

"We'll have you covered, but just make sure you don't put yourself in a position where he can shtick it to you."

"Questo non è un problema," Carla replied in Sicilian dialect, tainted with Brooklynese. "I'll make him an offer he can't refuse." She laughed darkly, patting her fanny pack containing her stiletto.

The zippered bag contained a covert agent's survival kit—a phony Canadian passport, Platinum American Express, 5000 Euros, a Walther PPK handgun with an extra clip of 9 mm ammo, her infamous stiletto, and a dozen Trojan condoms—lubricated.

In spite of Carla's over-the-top intelligence and integrity, she sometimes acted like a slut—hurling pulse-hammering sexual innuendo and flaunting a body that most women would die for. Maggie didn't know if Carla intended to put a bullet in Hans, knife him, or fuck him to death in a contest of burlesque over brawn. Hans outweighed her by fifty pounds, but she outgunned him by fifty IQ points. Carla Calabrese also had a few scalps under her belt.

Resting an elbow on the table, Maggie settled her chin on the back of her hand, casting a sideways glance at the hometown hero.

Hans signed an autograph, then took a long chug from an oversize beer stein while his eyes scanned the restaurant and bar. When he spotted them, he did a double take.

"Radar's locked-on," Maggie whispered.

Hans excused himself from his groupies, and immediately elbowed his way through the crowd.

"Oh boy," Carla whispered, "He's coming, and I'm ready, already."

Hans inclined his head, and took Carla's hand, raising it his lips. *"Guten abend, meine schönen damen."*

European manners. A cavalier killer, Maggie thought. "Please accept our apologies, Hans. Our Deutsch is as rusty as a torpedoed U-boat."

Hans raised his eyebrows, then laughed. "You are *Amerikaners*?"

"Canadians. From Toronto," Carla replied.

"I see." Hans ogled Carla and ran his tongue across his lips.

She shifted her body toward him. "Carla," she announced in her throaty voice. "No last name."

Hans frowned. "You are married?"

"Depends on who asks."

Hans grinned lasciviously, then gestured to a seat. "May I?"

"Go for it. You might get lucky." Carla batted her eyelashes seductively, and pushed the chair out with the toe of her boot. Carla had an irresistible voice, slightly husky and breathy.

Maggie offered her hand. "I'm Gillian Saint John, like the actress, but spelled with a G."

Hans pursed his lips. "Ah, yes. The James Bond spy movie, *Diamonds Are Forever*. But, surely, you are no spy."

Don't bet on it.

"I myself, love women with red hair." He fondled the flaming mass on Maggie's neck.

Maggie smiled demurely, and reached over her shoulder to catch his hand, then stroked it. She ran her eyes over him seductively, thinking. *I myself, would* love *to put a bullet in your heart*.

"We watched the World Cup competition," Carla said. "Awesome. You set a new Garmisch record. Four-thirty-one. Congrats." Carla slammed a high five with Hans.

"*Danke*. Do you compete?"

"I like it a little rough," Carla replied. "Don't you?"

Hans sucked in his breath. "Indeed."

She bit off a piece of sausage, then leaned forward and pressed the remnant between Hans' lips.

He caught her hand and licked her fingertips. "Delectable. May I have another taste?"

"*Wurst,* or best?" Carla laughed huskily; her double Ds resonated. Before he could respond she blurted, "Hans, real men take what they want."

He choked on the sausage, then hefted his beer stein, thumbed the pewter lid open, and took a long gulp. After several seconds, he replied, "I love women with a sense of humour."

"More than one at a time?" Carla arched an eyebrow. She reached over and took Maggie's hand. "We prank together."

Hans's eyes widened, then he ran his hand over his mouth, brow furrowed, as though contemplating a tough decision.

"Ladies, I would be delighted if you would join me this evening at my chalet. The view of the mountains is magnificent. From my hot tub on the deck, we can watch the moon rise, enjoy a selection of the finest wines, and work out the kinks."

Working on the kinky.

Hans lowered his hands below the table. "My bed can accommodate three." He ran his hand up Maggie's thigh causing a tremor of sexual heat to flow throughout her body.

Oh, my. She patted Han's hand. "A *ménage a trois?* My mother would be so proud." Maggie scooched her chair back, and stood.

"You guys can lather up and have all the fun. I think I'll go outside and roll in the snow to cool off."

* * *

Twilight settled over the Alps, and a gusting wind swept snow off the mountain ridges into swirling vortexes. The brutal cold enhanced Kirk's shiver of anxiety. For over an hour, he scanned the peaks and slopes with high-powered binoculars searching for a hint of Hans' bodyguards. Other than ski patrol now clearing the slopes of last minute stragglers, there were none.

Either the Sheikh was keeping his bum-fuck buddy in the dark, or Hans was relying on the hordes of people that surrounded him for protection. That strategy failed when Carla set the hook.

With his binoculars, Kirk watched as Hans and Carla approached the summit on the ski lift.

"Looks like Superman's taking the snow mobile. Carla's clinging to him like poison ivy on barbed-wire. T-Bone. Stay in the trees and cover her."

"Roger that. Have his head in my scope."

"Maggie. Establish a lookout a hundred yards uphill from the chalet. I'm moving in."

"Copy. On my way down."

Within seconds, Kirk's lock-pick gun released the tumblers on the entrance door to Hans's chalet, then he disabled the security system. Taking care to avoid leaving snow or water tracks, he climbed an open staircase that led to the master bedroom.

From within the darkened room, Kirk watched the snow mobile zigzag across the moguls, headed down the ski run toward the chalet. A minute later, a door slammed. He heard Carla's husky laughter, the stomping of their boots to remove snow.

Snapping a look over the balcony, Kirk watched Hans peel off Carla's turtleneck and grope her breasts.

Shit. She's carrying it too far.

Moments later, Hans led Carla up the stairs to the master bedroom. When he entered the darkened room and reached for the light switch, Kirk stepped in front of Hans with his arm extended, gripping a sparking Taser.

Startled, Hans raised his hands in a defensive move. "*Was—*"

The weapon let out a soft pop. A tiny dart sent 50,000 volts into Hans's chest, short-circuiting his nervous system, triggering uncontrollable muscle contractions. His legs buckled. Hans collapsed to the floor spinning into unconsciousness, his face contorted in pain.

"He tried to ball me in the mudroom." Unabashed, Carla adjusted her breasts in her bra. "Nailed my ass to the wall. The guy's as virile as Sonny Corleone."

"You had to fight him off?"

"Uh, no. I kinda liked it—"

"Jesus—"

"I had to lure him up here." She laughed huskily.

Kirk sighed. "Carla, you're a real piece of work."

"Yeah. But, I'm also a great piece of ass. Besides. It's all in a *day's work*."

Kirk shook his head. "OK. Let's get on with it. Hope this doesn't take long."

"It won't. Not with my help." Carla smiled.

Kirk dragged Hans across the bedroom and lifted him by the armpits onto a sturdy Bavarian oak armchair. "Let's strip him."

Kirk pulled Hans' sweater over his head. Carla knelt before the assassin, pressed the button on her stiletto and slit Hans' ski pants and boxer shorts open. She yanked them off, then stood with her hands on her hips looking down at the assassin.

"Wow! What a fucking waste."

"Pun intended?"

"I'll say. He's got the flowing lines of a thoroughbred racehorse—

"And hung like Secretariat," Kirk finished.

"Oh, baby!" Carla raised her arms above her head, gyrating her hips like a stoned groupie at an AC-DC rock concert. "Give me fifteen minutes with him."

"What for?"

"Bragging rights?"

Kirk rolled his eyes, shaking his head. He didn't know if Carla was half serious, or half nuts. But it wouldn't pay to have the zany Amazon as an enemy. When bottled up she was unstoppable, when uncorked Carla was merciless.

Hans let out a moan.

"He's coming around." Kirk quickly bound Hans' arms and legs to the chair with plastic ties. "Get out of here. I got this choreographed for shock and awe." Kirk pulled a tactical mask over his face.

"Shock and awe?" From ten feet, Carla whipped the stiletto. The knife buried itself in the wooden seat, quivering between Hans' thighs.

"Works for me, every time." She let out a throaty laugh. "Sure you don't need help with that?"

"I'm sure."

"OK." Carla turned toward the hallway, and twiddled her fingers over her shoulder.

More than half nuts.

Kirk took a seat facing Hans, waiting until he regained consciousness. A moment later, Hans swivelled his head, blinking like a toad that just crawled out of a primordial bog. His eyes settled on the stiletto between his legs.

"*Wer zur hölle bist du?*" Hans struggled against the Flexicuffs. "*Was wollen sie?*"

Kirk leaned forward, and rested on his forearms on his thighs. In a deep voice he said, "It doesn't matter who I am. What matters is what I want."

"Get the bloody hell out of my home!"

"Maybe I should have let Carla cut your balls off."

Hans went bug eyed. "What is it you want?"

"I wanted a challenge and was hoping you had more brains than the village idiot. Your handiwork left a dirty trail."

"Handiwork? Explain this."

"A fan recognized you at the marina in New Jersey. Nancy Vargas ring your chimes?"

Hans averted his eyes. "I know nothing of New Jersey." Hans forced a laugh.

Kirk pointed to the ceiling. "Eyes in the sky. You paddled a kayak in the Delaware River near the steel mill, knifed a guard, and transferred thermite into the nuclear power plant on Newbold Island. Thousands panicked. Innocent people died."

Hans strained against his bonds. "The *Bundespolizei* will be here in minutes."

Kirk laughed menacingly, "No they won't. We hacked your security system. Nice setup, but not good enough. Nobody can help you now."

Hans's eyes widened. "I am very wealthy. I shall pay you anything you ask to release me and leave at once."

Kirk shook his head. "Not a chance. I'm gonna deal with you on *my* terms."

"What is it you want?"

"A little information."

"I have nothing to say to you."

"Spoken like a man whose ass is up against the wall. Your downhill run for the gold was magnificent. Too bad it was the end of your career."

"What do you mean?"

Kirk reached into his parka and pulled out his handgun. "Recognize this? It's a no-bullshit Heckler and Koch .45 automatic." From another pocket, he withdrew a suppressor. "You know the athlete's mantra 'no pain, no gain'?" Kirk slowly screwed the suppressor onto the barrel of his handgun, without breaking eye contact with Hans. He knew there was a limit to the physical pain a human body could endure.

Hans stared at the large-bore weapon. "*What?*" His voice cracked. "What are you going to do?"

"Extract information. But first, I'm going to make sure you are properly motivated." Kirk ejected the clip, thumbed out a round and rolled the bullet between his fingers. "You ever see the damage done by one of these hollow-points? On impact, they mushroom to twenty millimeters. They'll make an elephant's eyes water."

The only thing worse than physical pain, was knowledge that it was coming.

Kirk reloaded the cartridge and slammed the clip home with the butt of his palm. "That one has your initials on it—HRW." Kirk retrieved a coin-like object from his pocket and flipped it into the air. "Same as those on this key-chain fob you lost at the steel mill."

Fear flashed in Hans' eyes.

"I really hate this, but I guarantee, you're gonna hate it even more." Kirk racked the slide to load a round into the chamber leaving the hammer cocked. "I don't have time to put up with your bullshit. Who killed Brett Brosnan?"

"Piss off. You will get nothing from me." Arrogance in his voice.

"I know you like to gamble. We can play my version of Russian roulette, or you tell me what I want to know. I'm a reasonable man. I'll give you time to make your decision. . . . You got five seconds."

"Go fuck yourself."

Kirk's radio snapped. "Kirk, heads up." Maggie said. "*Ski patrol*. Headed this way. Looks like two."

"How far?" He looked out the window, straining to see movement in the swirling snow.

"Two, three hundred yards. Barely make them out."

"When they get close, you and Carla head down the slope. Fake a nasty fall. Scream for help. Tell them you got lost in the dark. Lay on the charm and offer to buy them drinks. If they ain't queer, you're gold."

Carla laughed. "Roger that. How much longer before you're done?"

"Five minutes." Kirk watched the ski patrol pass the chalet, then returned to his seat.

"Hans, your boots are mired in deep shit. I want details. Who sent you? How did you know about the FBI counterterror operation in Houston?"

"I shall tell you nothing." He looked like he was about to burst a blood vessel from straining against his bonds.

"Wanna bet?" Kirk yanked his mask off.

Hans recoiled. *"You!"*

"Thought you'd gotten away with it, didn't ya? Time to even things up."

"Please," Hans begged. "I will give you anything you want. Millions of American dollars."

"I don't want your blood money. Talk fast, or you're gonna be condemned to a world of hurt. *Macht Schnell.*" Kirk aimed the red dot at Han's left knee. "You want to do it the hard way? Look at me, Hans. Look at the laser."

"What?" Hans voice cracked. "What are you going to do?"

"Extract information. An athlete's no good without his knees."

"You bluff." No conviction in his voice.

"I don't bluff."

The HK45 let out a muffled thump. The heavy bullet blasted fragments of bone out the back of Hans's leg, plastering his face and chest with body fluid and gore. Pulsating blood shot out of his thigh.

Hans convulsed, screaming, *"Uh, uh, uh."*

"It's going to hurt like hell in a minute, but no worse than stepping on a land mine. Your pain, my gain."

Kirk tied off Hans' thigh with Flexicuffs to stanch the bleeding, leaving his leg hanging by a thread of skin, baring gristle and white bone.

"Anything you want to tell me?"

"*Ahhh! Fick deine Mutter.*"

"My mother?" Kirk's anger raged. "I'm gonna fuck *you* over." He yanked Carla's switchblade from the seat. "What I really need is a nice cold slice of revenge." He lifted Hans's leg, and sawed the remaining tendons and skin, then dumped the leg onto his bloody lap.

Hans hung his head, staring down at the gory mess. He let out a half whimper-half groan, tears in his eyes. He had the frightened look of a man who had a noose around his neck. Kirk could smell the assassin's stench of adrenaline pumped fear—the smell when the guilty know they are about to receive just punishment.

He took his seat and aimed the laser at Hans's left kneecap. "Wanna go another round?" Hans' pulse throbbed in his neck. "*Please. No more.*" His plea came out in a strangled yelp. A glaze of oily sweat covered his body as the fight juice drained from him.

"Who are you working for?"

Hans averted his eyes. "Sheikh Qadr al-Masri."

"Good answer. Who killed Brett Brosnan?"

"Ilya Borisov," Hans gasped. "Qadr's director of security."

"How did he discover our counterterror operation?"

Hans hesitated.

"You wanna talk or take another bullet?"

"*No please.*" Hans moaned, barely conscious, head hanging down. "Borisov turned an FBI Agent named Harvey Rucker."

Rucker? The Director of Internal Security had access to Omega Six files. Qadr's long arm reached further than

Kirk had ever imagined. "How'd he know to hit on Rucker?"

"I do not know. He passed files to Borisov using a dead drop."

"Where's Qadr?"

Hans mumbled something unintelligible, rolled his eyes and passed out.

Going into shock.

Kirk broke an ammoniated cap under Hans's nose. *Wake up you bastard.*

"Where's Qadr? What's he up to?"

"Dubai. Casino grand opening," Hans response came out as a barely audible murmur. "He will kill you."

Kirk stood, and approached. "How?"

Hans' eyes fluttered closed.

Kirk's anger and hatred raged. His thoughts of Brett and Michele's assassinations, and Stryker's senseless killing forced his revulsion to a fever pitch. He had extracted some of the information he needed, but he did not feel good about it.

He passed the smelling salts under Hans' nose.

"Look at me, you murderous fuck. I'm also gonna even the score with that crazy Sheikh." Kirk grabbed Hans by the hair and yanked his head back. "Open your damned eyes."

When Hans raised his eyelids, Kirk stuck the stiletto under his left ear. "You slit my dog's throat. Your turn."

"Noooo!"

Kirk slashed the razor-sharp blade across the assassin's throat, silencing his scream.

Forty

Burj al-Arab
Dubai, United Arab Emirates

Qadr replayed the Al-Jazeera video showing Aisha Yassin's bloated body lying in the desert before the Falcon Pharaoh's tomb. Tourists panicked when the news agency announced the body was radioactive. This, Qadr thought, was the Americans' *carte de visite.*

Rolling his *misbaha* beads between his fingers, he had no feeling of emotion, only cold calculation.

The phone rang; security calling to inform him Borisov was on his way up to the penthouse.

Qadr's head slowly turned toward the elevator when it chimed.

Borisov stepped out with a blank look on his face. He strode across the large office, and took a seat at the desk facing the Sheikh.

"What is it? What did you find?"

"Hans is dead." Borisov slid a manila envelope across the desk.

Qadr released the clasp and pulled out a set of glossy 8 x 10 color photos of Han's mutilated corpse. "Where did you get these?"

"The *Bundespolizei* were not cooperative. My men broke into the medical examiner's office in Garmisch and riffled the files."

"It is obvious the American agents tortured him. We must keep this from Marta." Qadr rose from his chair, and walked purposefully toward the window facing the Hyatt Hotel across the causeway. "The enemy is closing in. We must act quickly."

Set the trap, a voice in his head said. It did not sound like his, but Qadr knew he had to listen to it, or risk having a manic spell.

As had happened so often in the past, he knew his instincts would lead him to a solution. It was there; he was near it. However, it remained out of his grasp.

He rolled his *misbaha* beads.

Click, click, click.

While on a falconry expedition, Qadr had discovered a large cavern in the *Qarā*' Mountains on the Omani frontier. Pakistani laborers employed by his construction firm had recently completed their fit-out of the temporary sanctuary. Equipped with utilities and provisions, it could shelter eight vehicles and support twenty people for three months. No one but him knew of it.

Without turning to face Borisov, Qadr spoke in a measured voice. "I shall proceed with the *Rub' al-Khali* evacuation. Mobilize your men, and execute *Ambuscade.* At once."

Forty-One

Tactical Operations Center
Hyatt Hotel
Dubai, United Arab Emirates

Two men dressed in maintenance jumpsuits with Hyatt logos, lugged heavy mil-spec containers onto the roof of the hotel. T-Bone and his spotter set up a laser microphone that received reflected signals attenuated by micro-vibrations from hard surfaces. They aimed the device at a window on top floor of the Arabian Tower, 500 yards across the causeway.

Moving quickly behind a parapet, T-Bone reassembled his Steyr rifle, mounted it on the bipod, and aimed the weapon at the Sheikh's office window.

Qadr and Borisov appeared life-size in his 25X scope, but a clean shot was iffy. Drawings indicated the windows on the Sheikh's headquarters were triple-pane glass that might deflect even a .50 caliber armor-piercing round.

"I'm in position," he reported. "Have them in my reticle, and can hear them good."

"Make anything out?" Kirk asked.

"He knows we whacked Hans, and he's fixin' to boogie into the desert. Hold on. Hold on. That fuck's looking right at me. My trigger finger's itchy. I think I can blow him away at this angle."

"*Negative.* He has information I need to extract. Let's figure out what he's up to."

"Your call."

Along with their funny accents, T-Bone had a difficult time deciphering words he didn't understand.

Ambuscade? What the hell's that?

On the floor below, Jessica sat at a table in the common area of their suite, using her laptop to redirect a pair of Keyhole satellites in preparation for the assault on Qadr's headquarters. Kirk stood at the window, binoculars raised. He tried to put himself into the mind of a man with the warped logic of a psychotic killer. With knowledge of Aisha and Hans' death, the Sheikh had to feel like a marked man. In a way, that was an advantage. But every time Kirk went operational, things went to hell. This time would be different. He had a crafted plan in place, overwhelming firepower, and a well-led and motivated assault force of HRT and Navy SEALs, staged for the assault.

He checked his watch.

Four more hours.

"Why don't you get some rest? Jessica was studying satellite images displayed on her laptop. "It's going to be a long night."

"I'm putting adrenaline ahead of sleep. You never know how things will break, and—"

A crackle of static on the tactical net interrupted Kirk's conversation.

T-Bone said, "Bad news. I just spotted a babe dressed like an Egyptian belly dancer in the Sheikh's living quarters. Hot-looking blondie."

"Damn it," Kirk grumbled. "That's gotta be his squeeze. We're going to flush out that royal piece of shit," Kirk said.

"Blowing the doors off and smoking up his penthouse with flash bangs won't go over well with the *Burj* management. How are you going—"

Thinking he heard a sound from Jessica's bedroom, Kirk reached for his weapon and raised his left hand to cut off her voice. He stepped toward the interconnecting door, his head cocked, HK45 pointed to the floor.

The door burst open. Four men, dressed as hotel staff, charged into the room bearing Stechkin machine pistols, the leader yelling commands in Russian.

As Kirk raised his weapon, a burly thug slammed his wrist with a gun barrel. Another Russian bludgeoned his kidneys with the gun butt, driving him to his knees.

"Down. Down," he yelled.

A third operative grabbed Jessica's hair, and threw her on the floor.

She kicked back, screaming.

"Spetsnaz," Kirk hissed.

The commander sent a sharp toe into Kirk's ribs. "No talk!" He pointed his weapon at Jessica's face. "Quiet! Do as I say or I kill woman."

Spetsnaz gagged Jessica and Kirk and bound their hands with plastic ties. They forced them out the door and frog-marched them toward the freight elevator.

In the basement, the Russians forced them into the back of a black Suburban with dark tinted windows. The truck sped out of the garage into the night, tires squealing.

Forty-Two

Burj al-Arab Hotel
Dubai, United Arab Emirates

The private elevator ascended rapidly toward the Sheikh's penthouse. When the doors opened, the gunmen shoved Kirk and Jessica across the threshold and onto a marble floor, hogtied, gags removed. Kirk wondered if they were going to star in an *al-Gama'a al-Islamiyya* version of a YouTube beheading.

The Sheikh's office was large and ostentatious, more like a museum than a place of business. Egyptian antiquities—sarcophagus, gold death masks, elaborate inlaid furniture, flashy gold fixtures—a display that exceeded King Tut's treasure filled the two-story room.

A life-size black onyx statue of a man with a falcon's head adorned with a gold sun disk, stood on the left side of elevator doors—Horus, the Falcon Pharaoh. A statue of a lapis and ruby winged goddess Isis on the right side faced Horus, kneeling in supplication before him, arms outstretched.

Powerful symbolism.

The Sheikh's obsession with Egypt antiquities explained his use of Hieroglyphics and ancient Egyptian riddles for a communications code.

Assessing the situation, he realized his operation had turned into a debacle. Kirk agonized over Jessica's safety, his mouth filling with the sour taste of defeat. *How the hell did they know?*

If he could get free, even for just a few seconds, he'd try to save her, and go down swinging. Kirk still had a weapon, the T-handled tactical knife tucked inside his left boot that the Spetsnaz had overlooked. But he couldn't get to it with his hands and feet bound, and he was outnumbered six to one with the bodyguards watching him closely.

Think. Damn it. Think.

Accompanied by Borisov, Qadr rose from his desk and stood before Kirk.

"So, Special Agent Kirk Magnus is it?" Qadr said in King's English, his five-second pause intended to project nonchalance. "You have an annoying penchant for survival, which is exceeded only by your irritating predilection for intrusion." He rested his fists on his hips, a hint of a cold smile playing at the corners of his mouth.

Kirk wanted to smack the sneer off the bastard's imperious face and jam it down his fucking throat. For a mass murderer, the Sheikh sounded like a Savile Row sissy—the worst kind of psychopath. Only thing missing was the lisp and swish.

"Why are you here? What is your mission?"

"Religious pilgrimage," Kirk replied.

Qadr laughed menacingly. "You are Christian. Dubai is a Muslim country."

"I was misinformed."

Borisov stepped on Kirk's cracked rib.

Kirk refused to let out a yelp. With grudging respect, he considered the man he had been hunting for over a month and realized how normal the Sheikh appeared. The only hint of his evil was the unblinking monomania of a psychopath, along with the flat dark eyes of a Mako shark. No question, the guy was a refined man one moment, a monster the next.

Who reigned superior in Qadr's head? Dr. Jekyll or Mr. Hyde?

"You are not so clever in hiding your intentions," Qadr said. "We had you under surveillance at the Hyatt Hotel. Borisov will hold you and the woman hostage until I make my way into the *Rub' al-Khali*. Then, you shall both be tortured, then shot."

"Sounds a like a plan," Kirk said. "Why don't you shoot yourself first?"

Qadr laughed, menacingly. "I admire one who faces the executioner with a sense of humor. However, you placed me in a precarious position. Therefore, I seek recompense."

"Why don't you release her?" Kirk glanced at Jessica. "She's my girlfriend. Just along for the ride."

Qadr raised an eyebrow. "Your lover studies satellite imagery? I think not. My suspicions are this woman is a CIA spy in your employ."

Kirk's spirits touched zero. His breathing was hard and painful from the kick in the ribs. He hated the helplessness, the sense of defeat, and the fact that he had been bested, yet again. He could feel the first symptoms of panic edging into his psyche. An inner coldness crept over him, bringing with it the acknowledgement he had somehow played into the Sheikh's hands. Drawing on his reserves, he commanded the feeling of panic to reverse into logical calm.

Qadr pointed at Kirk with a manicured fingertip, his eyes narrowing into feral slits. "You are responsible for my dear friend Hans's death. And you will bloody well suffer for that atrocity." Qadr announced it like the most reasonable man in the world. His actions appeared rational, but utterly insane. "Tonight I will recoup what is owed to me, with interest."

The Sheikh turned his attention to Jessica, and rubbed his hand over his mouth. "And now you, my lady, are quite beautiful. Exquisite. I observed your every move on our surveillance videos. You are one of the most alluring women I have ever seen." He licked his lips. "I should like to fuck you in ways beyond your imagination. However, time does not permit my fantasies. As hostage, you shall serve as insurance, allowing my escape into the desert."

"Just when you light my candle, you spoil the moment." Jessica replied. "I thought you wanted me for my body."

"Qadr. Was ist los?" a husky feminine voice called out. In the shadows of a darkened corridor leading back to the living quarters, her figure remained motionless.

Kirk studied Qadr's reaction to the mysterious woman. The scene was so surreal he thought the Sheikh could scarcely separate reality from bizarre visions in his head. A slight twitch in his eye indicated his composure had cracked.

What hold did she have over him?

Dressed in a sheer apricot-colored peignoir, a woman of startling beauty glided into Qadr's office. Her footsteps from three-inch high heels echoed off the marble floor commanding everyone's attention, her face eerily innocent of expression. Backlighting exposed her shapely hips, long legs, and full breasts. She was hard in all the right places, and soft in all the right places. Honey-blonde hair hung down to the middle of her back. Aside from the lines around her eyes, her striking features displayed ageless beauty. The bewitching goddess unhinged Kirk with her intoxicating presence. He had noted the woman's German accent and voice inflection, and recalled Michele's photo of the limo lady in Houston. The woman's eyes, a mesmerizing gold-flecked amber color, were identical to those of Hans Reich Wei.

Marta von Reich. Han's mother. Qadr's mistress? Maybe she was their ticket out.

Although Qadr was a master manipulator who knew the surest way into the souls of normal people, he could not hold Marta's eyes for more than a second. The guy had to make Marta believe her most secret fantasies about herself.

"*Mein Liebe,*" Qadr said. "The Americans are in Dubai. Borisov's men captured these enemy operatives. They now know of my plans."

"The *Amerikans?*" Marta cocked her head as though trying to understand. She shuffled before Qadr as though in a trance, her face taking on a wounded look, her eyes darkening to orange-red. She pointed to Jessica. "Qadr, you are again unfaithful to me, desiring to *fick this straßenmädchen* . . . this street whore. I heard you say it." In a traumatized voice, she struggled with her English. Turning, she gazed down at Jessica with an anguished sigh. Excruciating pain flashed in her tormented eyes. She shook her head; lips pressed together, shoulders sagging.

"This *fräulein ist wunderschön*, but it is her youth you desire. Do not deny it, Qadr. It is in your eyes." Her voice was a bare whisper.

Qadr placed his hands on her shoulders. "*Nein, Leibchen.* It is only you I love. No other." His voice was full of deceit. He kissed the tears on her cheeks. "We must leave at once. We shall have new life together in Syria. A life of wonders."

Marta remained motionless, a prisoner of love—a sex slave, used and abused.

Qadr turned to Borisov. "Secure my living quarters, the safe, and the office. One million Euros awaits you after I arrive in Damascus. I shall provide another million Euros to my loyal bodyguards who remain on post. As soon as these prisoners have served their purpose, you may have your way with them, and then you know what to do. These people have caused me a great deal of anxiety. Something I would dearly like them to regret."

Borisov advanced to Jessica's prone body with a menacing swagger He wore a smirk the size of a sickle blade on his lips. The tic in his left eye reflected his lust for unspeakable sex acts.

Kirk itched to press his thumbs against Borisov's throat until the Lubyanka Lunatic's eyes bugged out.

* * *

As soon as the elevator doors closed behind Qadr and Marta, an argument broke out in guttural Russian between the bodyguards and Borisov.

Borisov waved his Tula handgun menacingly, shouting orders. The bodyguards aimed their Stechkin machine pistols, their fingers on the triggers. They screamed back at him, pointing at the antiquities.

Outnumbered and outgunned, it appeared to Kirk that Borisov considered his limited options. Cursing, Borisov stood down and holstered his weapon.

Ignoring Borisov, the lead bodyguard ambled past toward a funerary mask mounted on an alabaster pedestal. The man removed the Plexiglas cover and snatched the glittering gold and lapis lazuli object from its base. A high-pitched alarm went off. Three other bodyguards ran off in search of loot.

Soldiers of fortune—no loyalty, in it for the money.

Borisov gazed down at Jessica with a miserable cheated look, like that of a eunuch at an orgy. His plans for her frustrated, he turned toward the walk-in safe around the corner.

Two bodyguards, lugging gold treasure, snatched Jessica by the arms and dragged her screaming to the elevator. Nothing Kirk could do for her, and imagining her circumstances would wear him down further. With his pulse pounding in his head, he needed to concentrate and find a way out. When he stressed his bound hands, a sharp pain racked his body.

Cracked rib.

In spite of the pain, Kirk struggled for the double-edged T-knife knife in his boot. Working his numb fingertips into the top, he felt for the handle. His sweaty fingers slipped. He wiped his hand on his pants and tried again, gingerly retrieved the knife and locked it between the heels of his boots, then frantically began sawing through the tough plastic ties binding his wrists.

A subsonic rumbling, almost too low to hear, vibrated though the marble floors. Seconds later, Kirk made out the distinctive beat of Black Hawk rotor blades in the distance. The muffled thump in the elevator shaft and the staccato sounds of automatic weapons fire on the roof indicated Maggie's assault was on.

Borisov ran around the corner into the office carrying a black leather valise in one hand, his Tula in the other, aiming it at Kirk.

T-Bone, take the fucking shot. Take it now!

* * *

Staged on a side street across the causeway from the Arabian Tower, Maggie's convoy of armored Suburbans awaited Kirk's 'Go' order. Maggie stared out the windshield at Qadr's brightly lit headquarters. With Carla at the wheel, she rode shotgun, two of her men in the back with Attila. His tongue hung out in anticipation, sensing the tension. They were all fueled with the scent of blood for the hunt.

"What do you think?" Carla asked. "Too damned quiet to suit me."

"This time, we're nailing that monster's ass to the wall."

The tactical net squawked.

"*Maggie.*" T-Bone barked, agitated. "Qadr's men captured Jessica and Kirk. They're holding them at gunpoint in the Sheikh's office."

A pang raced though Maggie's body that made her feel dizzy with nausea. The pulse in her ears roared like a run-away freight train. What-ifs blasted through her mind. No time to think, time to act.

"Move in," Maggie ordered. "I'm taking the penthouse elevator from the garage. Cool Rob, follow me. Nacho, get that chopper airborne, now!"

"Hold on a minute." T-Bone said. "Qadr led the babe into the elevator. He's hauling ass out into the desert."

"Where's Kirk?"

"On the floor, hogtied. The Sheikh's bodyguards are arguing with Borisov. . . . Goddamn it. A pair of Borisov's men snatched some loot and yanked Jessica into the elevator. They're armed with Stechkin machine pistols. I lost the other two bodyguards."

"Kirk alive?"

"I heard the Sheikh order Borisov to kill him."

"Take out Borisov," Maggie snapped into the tactical net. "Carla. Let's roll. *Go. Go. Go!*"

Carla raced over the two-lane palm-lined causeway to the Arabian Tower. As they approached the high-rise, Maggie spotted a convoy of HumVees and black Suburbans speeding out of the garage in their direction.

"*It's the Sheikh.*" She pointed. "Ram the lead vehicle. Lock and load." She jacked a cartridge into the chamber of her MP5.

At the last second, Carla killed the headlights, swerved over the lane barrier, and sideswiped the lead HumVee. The heavy armor-plated vehicle skidded and slid down the bank into the Persian Gulf. Maggie's

Suburban spun out, and came to a stop on the shoulder, a deflated air bag in her lap. The Sheikh's convoy sped by spraying automatic weapons fire. Her men busted out the side windows of their vehicle, and opened fire on the HumVee, now sinking in the black water.

Pinned down by automatic weapons fire from the Hummer and unable to advance she yelled, "Take them out."

Maggie's team laid down a withering torrent of fire with their submachine guns. Their bullets obliterated the driver. A passenger trapped in the back of the sinking vehicle tried to squeeze out a window. Carla ran down the bank, then crept up on the man's blind side. When the Spetsnaz stuck his head out the window, she lobbed a fragmentation grenade through it.

The vehicle exploded with a deafening *whump*.

"The *Burj!* Let's move it," Maggie ordered.

* * *

Maggie's convoy roared into the Arabian Tower garage. Her men poured out of their vehicles and spread out. Hunched over, Maggie and Cool Rob led their teams toward a pair of black Suburbans surrounded by Spetsnaz taking up defensive positions. Using hand signals, she ordered her men to advance and open up. Taking the point, the barrel of her MP5 spit orange flames, and bucked in her hands. Four enemy operatives dropped onto the concrete slab.

Maggie and Carla charged to the elevator. "Two of the Sheikh's bodyguards are on their way down, holding Jessica captive. We'll take them out here." She reloaded her MP5. "Robbie, take Attila with you to the penthouse fire stairs.

"Roger that." Cool Rob whistled, and the German shepherd ran after him.

Carla placed her ear to the elevator door. "It's coming down now."

"Double tap head shots as soon as the doors open."

Carla nodded and held up her hand. "Close." She dropped her hand, then stepped back raising her submachine gun.

The elevator doors slid open.

Stunned by the reception, a Spetsnaz yelled and sunk his hand into Jessica's hair. He jerked her off her feet and pressed his Stechkin against her chin.

The second bodyguard dropped the gold funerary mask, raised his Stechkin, and aimed at Maggie.

No one moved, then the doors closed.

Carla caught Maggie's eye, then hit the call button.

When the doors reopened, Maggie fired a double tap into the face of the man holding Jessica.

Bent over at the waist gripping the funerary mask, the other bodyguard looked up into the face of a towering Amazon. Carla kicked the Stechkin out of his hand, snapped open her switchblade and plunged it into his heart, twisting the blade. The Russian slid down the back of the elevator, eyes blank. She withdrew the bloody knife, then cut the plastic ties on Jessica's wrists and legs.

"You OK?" Maggie asked.

"Just shook up a little," Jessica said. "Borisov and four of his men are holding Kirk in the penthouse. We have to go to him." She grabbed a Stechkin, then checked the load.

"Jessie, stay here. You don't have body armor. Carla and I can take Borisov."

Maggie and Carla grabbed the two dead Spetsnaz by their shirt collars and dragged them out of the elevator, leaving a trail of blood.

As they rode in silence to the penthouse, each floor number seemed to stay lighted far longer than it should have; the time lapse between floors was a fraction of a second, but seemed interminable.

"T-bone, can you see Borisov?" Maggie asked. "We're ascending in the elevator."

"Negative. I think he's in the safe."

"Where're the other two bodyguards?"

"Lost them."

* * *

As the Black Hawk hovered above the roof of the Arabian Tower two dozen men loaded with assault rifles, grenades, and ammo slid down thick ropes onto the roof.

Three Spetsnaz charged out of the stairwell. Two of the men opened up with AKs, the third Russian taking cover. Nacho's miniguns on the Black Hawk blasted metal and stone turning two of the enemy into bloody hash.

The third Russian broke from cover, a long tube on his shoulder. He swung the weapon in the direction of the helicopter.

"RPG!" Nacho yelled.

The pilot banked sharply to avoid the incoming rocket propelled grenade as it trailed a plume of white smoke. It detonated against the side of the armored aircraft, leaving Nacho's ears ringing. Trailing black smoke, the helicopter veered off and headed back to the airport.

Nacho looked back to watch HRT lower ropes over the side of the building and rappel down to Qadr's office firing their assault rifles into the glass panes, shattering them into fragments. A dozen men charged into the Sheikh's office and quarters.

Cool Rob led Attila and his team to the *Burj* freight elevator. It rose slowly. They exited three floors below

Qadr's quarters, entered the fire exit stairs, then silently made their way toward the penthouse.

A door slammed at the top of the stairwell. Muffled Russian echoed.

Cool Rob raised his fist, ordering a halt. He knelt and pulled a small telescoping mirror from his backpack, positioning it to look around the corner. Pointed to his eyes, then raised two fingers, confirming he saw two armed men coming down the stairs. He drew his thumb across his throat, then hand signaled Attila.

In a blur of blond fur, the big dog charged up the stairs letting out a ferocious growl. Turning the corner with their MP5s raised, Cool Rob and company faced a pair of Spetsnaz struggling with a heavy aluminum chest. Seeing the big German shepherd, the Spetsnaz let go of the handles, and raised their Stechkins.

Cool Rob and his team laid down a hailstorm of hot lead with their MP5 sub-machine guns. Whining slugs slammed and ricocheted off the concrete walls echoing through the stairwell.

The Spetsnaz' mangled bodies dropped in the stairway above; the aluminum chest slid down the steps like a runaway eighteen-wheeler. It crashed on the landing at Cool Rob's feet with a dull thud. The lid popped open exposing a hoard of gold tola ingots embossed with the Sheikh's trademark, the Falcon.

"Leave that shit," Cool Rob growled. "Let's move."

At the top of the stairs, he signaled Attila to sniff for explosives. When the dog sat, nose pointed at the door, Cool Rob said, "Booby trapped. Blow the fucker in."

C-4 pressed into the doorknob and hinges, connected by det cord, blew the door off its hinges with a deafening thud. Cool Rob and his team charged into the office, their automatic weapons ready.

Borisov rounded the corner of the office carrying a black leather valise; the look on his face was one of rage.

Kirk managed to slice the plastic ties binding his hands, and rolled onto to his knees. He spun in a crouch, staring into the Russian's face.

Borisov's astonished expression morphed into an evil grin. He aimed the Tula at Kirk. "You are fucked," he snarled. A .50-caliber bullet cracked past Borisov's ear, exploding on the wall beside him. The marble wall disintegrated in a cloud of dust and debris leaving a two-foot crater. Rock chips blasted the side of Borisov's face. Blood ran down his neck, his mug mottled with oozing red.

Kirk folded his fingers into a rock-solid fist, and drove it into Borisov's balls.

Borisov doubled over, grunting.

Kirk kicked the Tula out of Borisov's hand just as he fired. He stared into Borisov's cold eyes before he drove his fist into the Lubyanka Lunatic's face.

Borisov swung the briefcase like a bludgeon and landed a sharp blow on Kirk's left shoulder, cracking the case open. Glittering gemstones and precious antiquities scattered across the floor. Kirk's knees buckled from the blow. He dropped to the floor. Recovering quickly, he found a gold and ruby encrusted *jambiyah* dagger on the floor.

With a poisonous glare, Borisov snapped open a switchblade and charged at Kirk.

Kirk dove forward, and rolled to the right to dodge Borisov's charge, then sprang up into an aggressive stance. He snapped a side-kick into the Russian's left knee. Borisov fell down on all fours. Grabbing the back of the Russian's head, Kirk kneed him in the face.

Borisov's howls echoed throughout the living quarters. He pulled a switchblade, snapping it open. "I have killed many. I kill you as well." His voice was a low-pitched growl as he took an aggressive shuffle step, hands in a combat strike position, acting as though he would slice Kirk's body into pieces.

Kirk turned sideways and slammed the heel of his boot into Borisov's face. Blood poured out of his nose, his face contorted with pain and rage, hoarse animal noises rumbling out of his mouth.

Kirk held the curve-bladed *jambiyah* in his right hand, cupping his left hand, wiggling his fingers. "Come on, you bastard. Spare me the smell of your shitty underwear."

Borisov growled and lunged forward.

Kirk sidestepped Borisov's charge, and slashed his left arm to the bone as he charged past. The Russian bellowed out in pain, staring at the gaping wound. Jets of bright red blood spurted across the marble floor. Borisov pawed frantically at the terrible wound.

Kirk waved the *jambiyah* in front of Borisov's face. "You're gonna die with the Shiekh's knife."

"*Yob vas.*" Fuck you. Borisov attempted an overhand stab.

Kirk blocked the Russian's weak thrust with his left hand. He kicked Borisov in the groin, then slammed his knee into his face. Broken teeth and blood gushed from Borisov's mouth, his jaw hanging at an odd angle.

Kirk looked down at Borisov for a moment, feeling the basic instinct of vengeance. He slashed Borisov's belly open. "Payback for killing my partner."

Borisov bellowed out in pain and fell to a kneeling position, attempting to hold his blood-slicked intestines from spilling out of his hands onto the floor. The Russian stared blankly at Kirk for seconds, then keeled over onto his face.

* * *

When the elevator doors opened, Maggie and Carla charged into Qadr's office prepared to lay down an overdose of mayhem. They found Kirk standing over Borisov's body lying in a pool of gore and guts, diamonds and emeralds, holding a bloody knife in his right hand.

"Nice work," Carla said. "Sorry I missed it."

Kirk handed the bloody knife to her and said, "Consolation prize."

Carla examined the curved dagger, then slid the curved blade under her belt, displaying the bejeweled hilt like a caliph at a slave bazaar.

Cool Rob and his team charged into the office.

"Whoa! Good thing I got here before you put the big hurtin' on him," he quipped in his deep baritone voice.

Feeling relief, Maggie touched the bloody knot on Kirk's forehead. "Thank God you are all right." She held him for a moment, her eyes closed.

"T-bone missed his shot, but saved my hide. You locate Jessie?" He asked, wincing from chest pain.

"Down in the garage. She's good. What the hell happened? You OK?"

"Got a cracked rib." Kirk pointed to Borisov's body. "That crazy bastard was about to rape her before his men mutinied."

"Shoulda cut his balls off," Carla replied.

"I drop kicked him good. They're ticking his tonsils."

Cool Rob winced. "Size ten tactical boots? That had to hurt."

"*Alright*. That's enough back slapping and cheesy gallows humor." Maggie said. "The Sheikh got past us. If we don't act fast, we'll lose him in the *Rub' al-Khali.*"

"Ain't gonna happen," Kirk said. "You and Robbie secure the quarters and office. Nobody gets in or out. We're claiming all this loot in the name of the US Government. Gotta be over a billion dollars worth of antiquities and loot here."

"I spotted the woman riding in the Sheikh's Hummer," Maggie said. "She in this? A coconspirator?"

Kirk pointed to the statues near the elevator doors. "Isis, the winged goddess, is the Falcon Pharaoh's mother. The Sheikh's big on symbolism. That blonde babe is Marta von Reich, Han's mother, and Qadr's mistress."

"*What?* She has over twenty years on him."

"Doesn't matter. If you saw her up close, you'd know why. She is a mother figure to him, and is a sex goddess. Along with the voices in his head, he has an Oedipus complex. But, he's holding Marta hostage. I'm taking the Black Hawk after the bastard."

"No go." Maggie shook her head. "Chopper's out of action. Took an RPG hit."

"*Damn it.*" Kirk groused. "If it wasn't for bad luck, I'd have no luck at all."

Forty-Three

Tactical Operations Center
Hyatt Hotel
Dubai, United Arab Emirates

Kirk pressed a bloody ice pack to the knot his forehead while Jessica taped up his ribs. It hurt like hell to breathe, and he had a splitting headache. But it wouldn't stop him, not for a second. When she finished, he took a seat at a table next to her watching anxiously as she connected her laptop to the Internet.

"How soon will that satellite be overhead?"

"It's over Afghanistan, but won't be over the *Rub' al-Khali* for another ten minutes. A second Keyhole follows thirty-seven minutes later. Period for the birds is ninety minutes, so we're faced with dead time, forty minutes every hour."

"You gonna be able to locate his convoy out in the desert?"

"Not with you breathing down my neck. Why don't you fix us coffee?"

"How about I just boil some water to get the hell out of your way?"

"Testy, aren't we?"

"I gonna kill that fucking Sheikh."

"Why don't you channel that anger into the job so we work this out. We won't let him get away. Not this time. I have his contingency plan figured out."

"How'd you do that? He's nuttier than a Christmas fruitcake."

"The road out of Dubai heads due south into the desert toward the mountains. I'm sure he's on it. It's the fastest route out of the city, and that desert is his playground. When I locate him, I'll order CENTCOM to put a Reaper drone up. We can take the convoy out with Hellfire missiles."

"Can't do that! Marta hasn't done anything."

"Kirk, *you don't know that*. You have a weakness for women, especially stunning six-footers with a lobotomy. If you had ogled Marta any harder, the vitreous humor in your eyes would have boiled, sending steam out your ears."

"I can't blame him for banging her brains loose, but the Sheikh's holding her hostage. She's *not* an accomplice."

"I can't make that leap. You saw the way he cowered in Marta's presence."

"I also saw how he manipulated her."

"We can't let that evil monster loose. That bimbo is expendable. I *want* to launch that Raptor."

Jessica's analysis was on the money, as usual.

"If I had access to a chopper I could cripple his convoy and isolate him in the desert."

She raised her hands, and let out an exasperated breath. "We can't deploy another Black Hawk in time to intercept him. Closest are at Bagram Air Base. Six hours flight time. The convoy may be out of the satellite's field of view by then, long gone in that wasteland."

"Shit." Kirk stared out the window past the lights of the city toward the desert and mountains in the distance, evaluating his limited options.

"Coming up to Iran," she said.

Kirk looked over Jessica's shoulder. Her laptop showed the satellite view of the bright lights of Tehran one hundred miles below; minutes later the dark Strait of Hormuz appeared, then the bright lights of the city of Dubai. She zoomed in, then panned south and located the well-lit paved road heading into the vast *Rub' al Khali*. After the satellite passed overhead, the image displayed the harsh blackness of the Empty Quarter.

"Where's the satellite now?"

"About a hundred klicks south of Dubai. I've toggled from visible spectrum to infrared. The heat signature from the auto engines should be easy to detect. Good contrast. Ambient temperature is near freezing out there."

Kirk sipped coffee and paced.

"I have them." Jessica pointed to blurred images. "Eight vehicles traveling over an old trade route one hundred twenty kilometers south of here. Doppler radar on the bird indicates the caravan is moving at eighty klicks per hour. A pair of Hummers are leading the convoy."

"Makes sense. They're equipped with satellite navigation." Kirk watched Jessica punch keys on her computer. "What are you doing?"

"They've crossed the dunes and are in a rocky wasteland in the foothills near the base of the mountains. No man's land. If they enabled their GPS, we can activate the reactive armor detonators on those Hummers. I have a ping from one of the vehicles."

"Which one, first or second?"

"The ping is most likely from the lead vehicle. Maggie said the Sheikh was in the second vehicle. We have to risk it."

"Hold on a minute. I need to think about this."

"We don't have a minute, and I've already thought about it."

Seconds later a bright plume flared at the head of the caravan. The convoy quickly diverted and raced by the flaming wreckage.

"I hope to hell Marta wasn't in that fucking truck," Kirk said. "I'll never live it down."

"We can't let this guy get away. I'm ordering up the Raptor at Prince Sultan Air Base."

"*Prince Sultan?* Hey. I just thought of something. Get General Nance on the phone."

Jessica handed Kirk the Iridium satellite telephone. "He's holding."

"General? We're not done yet. I need some help."

"We're monitoring the tactical net from the Situation Room. What do you need?"

"An Apache gunship, gassed up, weapons ready."

"That's a tall order. I don't see how we can get that kind of asset over to you in time to complete your mission."

"We sold a dozen Apache Longbows to the Saudis, with a training and maintenance contract. I heard they were located at Prince Sultan Air Base. That's only an hour away, flight time."

"You intel is correct, but The Kingdom will not cooperate with a US counterterror op on their soil."

"Unconventional warfare calls for unconventional response. We need to beg, borrow, or steal one of those gunships."

"That's devious, but the Saudi Minister of Defense owes me a few favors. Hold while I make the call."

Kirk paced with the phone to his ear, waiting.

"Kirk, it's a go. Where do you want that chopper deployed?"

"The heliport on the roof of the Hyatt Regency Dubai. I'm headed out in the *Rub' al-Kahli.*"

"Apache's can't carry passengers."

"I know."

Forty-Four

Rub' al-Kahli Desert
Saudi-Omani Border

Armed with an M230 30 mm chain gun and eight fire-and-forget Hellfire anti-tank missiles mounted on ends of the winglets, the hovering AH-64 Apache Longbow looked like death. Dressed in black BDUs and loaded down with body armor and his Steyr sniper rifle, Kirk waved the chopper down onto the heliport. Battered by the thunderous downdraft, he ducked under the blades of the gunship that bore the palm tree and crossed scimitar markings of the Royal Saudi Air Force. Moving fast, he yanked open the door, and climbed into the gunner's seat forward of the pilot, and tucked his rifle aside. He buckled his harness and gave a thumbs-up. After adjusting the helmet and intercom he said, "I'm Kirk Magnus." He flashed his creds over his shoulder. "What's your name and rank?"

"Major Duke Cunningham, US Army."

"What were your orders, Major?"

"A CENTCOM Lieutenant General requested a volunteer for a hot mission and told me to expect the unexpected. I was ordered to commandeer a fully armed and gassed up Saudi Apache, take on an O-6, and ask no questions. Which brings up a question. Colonel, what the hell's going on?"

"I can only tell you what you need to know."

"Fair enough."

"We're engaged in a counterterror op classified a few notches above Top Secret. You can dispense with formalities. Kirk works just fine. Duke, you've never met me, nor heard of me."

"I hear ya. If you don't mind my asking, what do you do for Uncle Sugar?"

"Kill people," Kirk deadpanned. "Our objective is a convoy of eight armored Suburbans and HumVees hauling ass out of Dubai. You get the target coordinates?"

"Programmed in. This side of the *Qarā*ʾ Mountains. That's Oman on the other side. If they pick us up on radar, the Omani's will jump a couple of Harriers and force us down."

"Don't need that heartburn. Kill your running lights and IFF transponder as soon as we're over the desert." Kirk glanced across the massive crescent dunes to the distant mountain range looking like a nicked knife that ripped the starlit sky. "Can you fly under the radar and hide in the background clutter?"

"A hundred feet off the ground if you want."

"That'll work. What's the ETA to target?"

"Fifty-seven minutes, give or take. You qualified on an Apache as a TFO?"

"A *what?*"

"Tactical Flight Officer. I drive, the TFO operates the weapons pod."

"No. You're going to qualify me, and show me how to operate the chain gun."

"You serious?"

"I'm perfectly serious. The honcho leading that convoy masterminded the attack on the nuclear power plant in New Jersey. He has a hostage aboard—a woman. We're going to single out his vehicle and waste the others. Talk me through weapons systems, and line up a couple of test targets for the chain gun."

"Man, you got my juices flowing. We can do this. The gun will lay down 300 rounds per minute where you designate on your helmet-mounted display. Effective range is 1500 meters. The depleted uranium projectiles will penetrate six inches of armor."

"Not much different than an Abrams. That oughta work."

Kirk looked down at the desert landscape illuminated by the full moon. After one-hundred miles of silvery crescent-shaped sand dunes and rocky plains, the stark beauty of the *Rub' al-Kahli* became hypnotic. Aside from the ever-shifting dunes, the vast desert was a forbidding and changeless wasteland on the map of the world. Few things survived in the Empty Quarter. Qadr dared it, and Kirk would see to it that he'd be swallowed up in it.

As the Apache approached the razor-edged *Qarā'* Mountains, his pulse kicked up a notch.

Duke broke the silence. "When we close in, we have to risk Omani radar exposure to clear that ridge line."

"Do it. I want to get close enough to identify the hostage. Lay back on the driver's blind side."

"Kirk, check your flight deck display. I have them on infrared. Range: six klicks at twelve o'clock. Another minute and we can take out the entire convoy with Hellfire missiles and the chain gun."

Kirk's scalp and forearms prickled. Eliminating the Sheikh from a distance was too goddamned easy, and he did not want to kill Marta. She was a merely a plaything in the Sheikh's harem.

As the Apache closed in, he focused his night vision binoculars on the lead vehicle. In the front passenger seat, Marta's blonde hair reflected moonlight. Kirk made out the dark shadows of two Spetsnaz bodyguards in the back.

"The target and hostage are in the lead vehicle, with two bodyguards. Come around ahead of the convoy to that rift at two o'clock. Drop down below their line of sight. When I tell you, elevate over the ridge and hover. Then turn on your running lights."

"*What?* That's nuts. It'll expose us to ground fire."

"Duke, you gotta be half crazy to take on this job. I want that bastard to sweat like a whore in church when he spots this gunship. When he reacts, I'll open up with the chain gun."

"A personal vendetta? What'd he do to you?"

"His men slit my dog's throat. I'm gonna kill him."

"With that sniper rifle?"

"With my bare hands, if I get a chance."

"Oh shit," Duke said under his breath. "Preparing to engage."

Coolness swept through Kirk's body. With the clock in his head, he timed Qadr's convoy.

"OK. Take her up to fifty feet, and hover. Hit the running lights. *Now*."

When the Apache stabilized, Kirk acquired his target at one-thousand yards and squeezed the trigger. The chain gun mounted under his feet roared from laying down a stream of 30 mm red tracers that illuminated the sky like a laser beam—the hand of Death reaching out.

Marta wrapped her arms around herself, rubbing goose bumps on her arms. She wondered how much longer it would be before they reached their hidden sanctuary in the *Qarā*ʾ Mountains. The Americans would search the *Rub' al-Khali* with their aircraft and spy satellites to no avail as their entire caravan would soon be safely hidden within the cavern. Thank God for her planning and insistence in building the facility in spite of Qadr's protests. In spite of his hubris she usually prevailed in their operational planning.

She squirmed in her seat, cold and in need of relieving her bladder.

"Qadr, *Ich bin kalt.*"

Qadr pulled his eyes off the rock and boulder-strewn desert. "*Liebchen,* our hiding place is not much further. Five kilometers perhaps. We will rest there, then continue our journey later to the safe house in Sana'a. Within a week we shall once more set up operations in Damascus."

"Sehr gut." Marta turned to glance out the window at the moonlit landscape. "Blinking lights in the sky, I see."

"Blinking lights?" Qadr said dismissively. "I think not. Those are twinkling stars,"

Marta pointed out the windshield. "*Nein, das ist ein flugzeug.*"

"Aircraft? Impossible! The Americans could never find us in the *Rub' al-Khali.* You are stressed and imagining things. Or perhaps the cold desert air creates an illusion—a mirage."

"*Eine* mirage? I am not a fool," Marta replied indignantly. "I do not imagine things. Stars are not red."

"*Red blinking lights?*" Qadr's voice cracked, a frown of anxiety formed on his face. He followed Marta's gaze, and craned his neck searching the sky ahead.

Above the desert off to the right, moonlight illuminated a whirling dervish. Hovering above the dust devil, what looked like a giant dragonfly spit fire out its mouth with a deafening roar. Qadr's HumVee shook from thundering explosions.

Qadr stared in disbelief at brilliant flashes of light in his rear-view mirror. His convoy was a smoking ruin.

Cursing, he slammed on the brakes; the vehicle skidded across the desert floor to a stop.

In the distance, he watched the menacing helicopter set down. Raising his night vision binoculars, a lone figure emerged from the cockpit seconds before the helicopter lifted off and flew out of audible range.

So, it comes down to this. Special Agent Kirk Magnus has somehow survived Borisov's poisonous tentacles.

With highly trained Russian Special Forces at his side, he held a three to one advantage. Qadr thought he would enjoy the kill. He ordered his bodyguards out, Marta to stay in the vehicle. They scrambled to the back of the HumVee to retrieve weapons. The Spetsnaz gathered AK-47 assault rifles, ammo clips, and grenades. Qadr pocketed a 7.62 mm Tokarev semi-automatic handgun.

Kirk snatched the Steyr, ducked under the Apache's pounding rotor, and ran toward a *wadi* in a crouch. Hidden in the gully, he absorbed the godforsaken slice of the planet. The terrain was rugged and loaded with ankle-busting boulders and gravel. A misplaced step could dislodge an avalanche of rocks. Stars shone with crystalline clarity; the moon cast an unearthly silver cloak over the rock-strewn desert. The gully offered concealment from the Sheikh's bodyguards, but Kirk knew the Russian Special Forces would run the same tactic.

Despite the cold night air, he was sweating. The chill clawed its way through his clothing into his marrow. Kirk wiped away all thoughts but the opportunity on the ground. Glassing the terrain with his night vision binoculars, he spotted Qadr and his bodyguards near the Hummer. The Sheikh had used Marta as a shield, and would now push his bodyguards forward as a sacrifice.

Kirk set his sniper rifle on its bipod; estimated the range and wind velocity—1,500 yards, 5 mph. He sighted-in the right rear tire of Qadr's vehicle, and squeezed the trigger.

The .50 caliber round smashed into the wheel hub, blasting shards of rubber and metal within inches of Qadr's legs. The loud report sounded across the rocky plain, violating the immense desert silence, and echoed off the mountains.

There was no way the terror mastermind could escape from the *Rub' al-Kahli*. Dubai was three hundred kilometers across the forbidding desert.

Qadr studied the damage. He shouted orders, but remained near the Hummer. His bodyguards ran off into the desert in opposite directions. Kirk knew they had to move in closer as their assault rifles were of limited use at long range.

Clouds passed across the moon, turning the desert landscape darker than twelve inches up a camel's ass. The Spetsnaz had to have night vision equipment, but what type—starlight or thermal?

Kirk picked up his weapon and ran down the *wadi*. After three hundred meters, he climbed atop the ridge, and scanned the terrain. Silhouetted against the cold black desert, he spotted a heat signature—eight hundred meters at ten o'clock. The bodyguard ran in a crouch, zigzagging toward Kirk's last location.

Moving fast, Kirk slipped a round in the chamber. His pulse raced as he set up for the kill. Lying prone with little exposed other than his weapon pulled tightly into his shoulder, he waited for the kill. When the Spetsnaz made a dash from one large boulder to another, Kirk led the target, exhaled a half-breath, and squeezed the trigger. The round ripped the man's torso in half. What was left would soon soak into the dry desert soil.

Suddenly, the air filled with the thunder of automatic weapon fire. Kirk scrambled to his feet and ran in spurts, staying close to the ground, then dove into a depression in the desert floor. He peered over the edge, following the AK-47 green tracer fire back to its source.

The bodyguard had to be using thermal night vision equipment. And he was now less than 100 yards away. At close range, Kirk's single-shot weapon was no match against an automatic assault rifle.

He crawled around a boulder, propelling himself like an animal, hands and feet working in concert. The sudden eerie quiet was in some ways more unnerving than the din of the AKs.

When he set his rifle on the lip of the depression, bullets tore up the desert floor, blasting rock chips and gravel into his face. Rolling on his back, he pulled a flash-bang from his web belt and tossed it, then shielded his eyes. With a blinding flash, the grenade exploded ten yards in front of the enemy's position.

Kirk aimed and fired. The bullet blew the top of the man's head off.

Qadr was now without protection, but nowhere in sight. Marta remained frozen in the passenger seat.

Kirk raced through the darkness toward the HumVee, skirting boulders prepared to dive behind one at the first sound of fire.

It came: five pistol shots in succession, bullets slammed into the desert soil, some whining past his head. He scampered behind a rocky outcrop, and stole a glance. Qadr hid behind a craggy boulder, a hundred meters from his vehicle.

Circling the Sheikh's position, Kirk crept to the edge of the rift. Loose shale spilled down, clattering at the bottom of the abyss.

Bullets zinged by his head.

Kirk pitched forward. The edge of a sharp rock caught him across the bridge of his nose. He cursed as blood spurted and coated his lips. Exhaustion and emotional strain flooded his battered body. He shook his head to clear the cobwebs, then laid his rifle aside. Creeping on his elbows and knees, he slithered toward Qadr's position.

Minutes passed. Progress seemed agonizingly slow. But every foot gained was a foot closer to his nemesis. Lust for revenge drove him on with a frenzy he didn't know he possessed.

Now accustomed to night vision, he spotted a shape crouched near the HumVee, thirty meters away. Kirk withdrew his HK45 and illuminated Qadr's lower spine with a laser dot. Crippling the bastard and leaving him in the desert crossed Kirk's mind, then he thought better of it. He wanted to look Qadr in the eye when he executed him—up close and personal.

A thunderous explosion from a burning vehicle lit up the desert landscape for a second, illuminating the Sheikh's profile. With the stealth of a hungry lion, Kirk inched forward, his concentration on the tritium dots on the HK45 gunsight.

"Toss the weapon," Kirk said quietly, but his tone carried the menace of death. "Hands on you head. *Now.* Move, or it's gonna hurt."

"Special Agent Magnus," Qadr hissed. *"Elif air ab tizak."* The Sheikh turned to face Kirk. Their eyes locked in a moment of loathing.

"A thousand dicks in my ass?" Kirk snorted a laugh. "If you want to live for another minute, you'll do exactly as I say." Kirk remained silent for several seconds, letting Qadr marinate in his sweat.

In the moonlight, the Sheikh's dark skin looked ghoulish as fear replaced the blood that drained from his face. For a half a second, Kirk thought about telling the monster why he was about to die.

"This is terribly inconvenient." Qadr's tone was condescending, dismissive, and contemptuous, yet his face contained a smear of anxiety.

"There will be no apologies for ruining your day."

"What is it you want of me?"

"Your balls." Kirk's cold voice belied his burning rage. "Where you're going, you won't need them." He lashed out and clamped the fingers of his left hand around the Sheikh's windpipe, cutting off his air.

Qadr's eyes rocketed wide. His arms flailed as he struggled to breathe, but his physical strength was no match against Kirk's iron grip.

Kirk cracked the HK45 across Qadr's forehead.

Qadr exhaled a muffled howl. Blood trickled down his face into his eye. "Release me," he gasped, "and I shall reward you with riches beyond your imagination."

Qadr had exercised the ultimate power of life and death, and he enjoyed it. Kirk saw it in his eyes, making his blood boil with hatred. Killing the crazy bastard wouldn't even cover the interest on the thousands of people the man slaughtered. He cranked down the vise grip on Qadr's throat, feeling his archenemy's strength drain.

"Would you care to speculate on the chance I'd take you seriously? I didn't think you were a fool, but what's my opinion compared to thousands of others? The difference between you and me is you manipulate people, and *I don't play nice.*"

Kirk tightened his grip, and jammed the HK45 against Qadr's groin. After a moment, he allowed the Sheikh a gulp of air.

Qadr's breath was rapid, his skin glazed with an oily sweat in spite of the cold. His eyes darting about as though searching for help that would never come.

"I have diplomatic immunity."

"Not in this corner of the world. You haven't been inoculated against lead poisoning."

"I have no fear of death. Death fears me. I am immortal." Arrogance in his voice.

"We'll see."

"I shall again be reincarnated as an embodiment of the Falcon Pharaoh."

"The Falcon? You been drinking the Kool-Aid. Last I heard he was a desiccated mummy. Hans is *toast*, and you're gonna be served up as vulture's breakfast, without the wrappings. You were born wet, naked, and hungry. Now, it's gonna get worse. Your high time is up, your Highness."

Qadr struggled in his iron grip. Kirk throttled the Sheikh's windpipe harder, cutting off all his oxygen. The look of panic spread on Qadr's face.

"If you prefer to live a few minutes longer, you'll talk."

The Sheikh nodded vigorously.

"How'd you turn the FBI agent?" Kirk released the throat pressure for a few seconds.

"Not FBI," Qadr choked out. "Howard Dreihaus."

Dreihaus? Not according to Hans. Something didn't compute.

"Better explain."

"You Senator solicited *me* with his proposition," Qadr gasped. "Intelligence for campaign contributions. Two million American Dollars."

Traitorous politician. A dead man walking. Anger raging, Kirk squeezed Qadr's windpipe harder and forced his HK45 tighter against his groin.

The look swirling in Qadr's espresso-dark eyes was of abject terror.

"That's *all* I want from you."

Kirk's bullet turned the Sheikh's testicles into tapioca. Warm wetness of royal blood soaked him as his Qadr's body lurched forward. He collapsed to the ground clutching his bloody crotch, writhing spasmodically, screaming curses in a guttural ancient language.

The Speculator would soon bleed out. Kirk felt neither remorse nor elation, but he would bury the memory as far down in his memory locker as possible.

* * *

The crunch of gravel behind him sent Kirk's senses into high alert. Before he could turn, the explosive sledgehammer blow to his back knocked the wind out of his lungs. He lost command of his legs, and hit the ground face first. Rolling onto his back, he looked up into Marta's glaring eyes.

Dressed in nothing but a skimpy negligee, she held Qadr's Tokarev, pointed down at his chest—the weapon's slide pulled back.

Empty clip.

Within seconds, oxygen starvation to Kirk's brain caused spots to form before his eyes. Round and round his thoughts went in a spiral with darkness at its center. Lying prone on the earth, his last vision was of Marta straddling him with a pallid smile on her face. . . .

Kirk slowly opened his eyes, feeling like he had been smacked between the shoulder blades with a broad ax. He wiggled his fingers and toes, then slowly rose to his feet, thankful the Kevlar in his body armor had saved his life. No telling how much time had passed. Two minutes? Five? Ten? It was hard to believe things had gone to hell so quickly. Why did she shoot him? And where did Marta and the Sheikh disappear?

Using his tactical light, he followed a trail of blood leading toward Qadr's HumVee, and discovered the

Sheikh's body lying motionless in a puddle of thick blood.

Kirk knelt and pressed his fingers against Qadr's carotid artery. Visions of Brett Brosnan's body on the garage deck flooded his mind. Things had come full circle, yet he felt no sense of closure.

Standing, he looked around. Marta was nowhere in sight. She had wandered off into the desert in a daze. He had to find her, and find her fast before she suffered from exposure.

Kirk searched the desert with his night vision binoculars. Outlined against the black profile of the *Qarāʾ* Mountains, he spotted Marta standing motionless on the edge of the rift. Her body and clinging peignoir glowed like a beacon in the moonlight.

With his chest screaming with pain, he trotted toward her. Approaching cautiously, he halted three feet away.

Standing on the edge of precipice, Marta gave no indication she had heard him approach.

Kirk absorbed her precarious position in one encompassing glance. In his second, the vision laid before him enchanted. There was more to claim his eye with every beat of his pulse. Moonlight reflected off her angelic face as though in a halo. A slight breeze swept the edge of the cliff and blew wisps of her flaxen hair back. Her sheer negligee billowed, enhancing her captivating figure. As she stood before him, he could feel the spice of her sensuality—that of a beguiling goddess.

Taken aback by the image of her overwhelming beauty, and disquieted with her vulnerability, Kirk broke out in a cold sweat. "Marta," he called softly.

She glanced over her shoulder at him. Her golden eyes had turned the color of burnt umber and looked hypnotic, as though in a trance and dead to his plea. Her moist lips parted, uttering no sound, offering only a tiny smile.

"I mean you no harm."

Marta slowly angled away from him toward the full moon hovering over the knife-edge of the *Qarā*ʾ Mountains.

Kirk knew she had difficulty understanding English, but his German language skills lay dormant in the recesses of his mind. "Please, take my hand," he murmured. "I will not harm you. I promise. I will take you home to Germany."

She remained transfixed, staring out at the full moon on the horizon.

Kirk shuffled forward, sending shards of shale clattering into the abyss.

"Marta. *Bitte, nimm meine hand.*"

With serene calm, she raised her arms out to her side. The sleeves of her gossamer peignoir fluttered in the breeze like the wings of Isis.

"Marta." Kirk reached out, his hand inches from hers, touching her sleeve. It took only a heartbeat before he realized the silken fabric had slipped through his fingers.

The goddess stepped off the jagged precipice, and appeared to hang motionless. Then she tumbled over the edge in mute silence.

Shining his tactical light, Kirk gaped at Marta's mangled body on the jagged rocks below.

The sight filled him with a wave of horror and grief. The lump in his throat felt like he had swallowed defeat in one giant gulp.

Epilog

Potomac Overlook Park
Rosslyn, Virginia
2300 Hours
One Week Later

Five minutes to midnight, Kirk dialed a well-known number with a throwaway cell phone he had purchased at a Stop & Rob.

Harvey Rucker, the FBI Director of Internal Security, answered after the first ring.

"I've been expecting your call." Harvey's voice was a hoarse whisper.

"You alone?"

"Yeah. Stacy and the kids are in bed."

"We need to talk. In private. Right away."

A moment of silence followed. "Oh, man. I've been losing a lot of sleep over this." Harvey choked up. "Is there a way out?"

"Meet me at the Potomac Overlook across from the Georgetown Reservoir. Take the park bench about fifty yards south of the parking lot off the GW Parkway."

From Arlington National Cemetery, the park wound northward along the west bank of the Potomac. Kirk pulled his Tahoe off the George Washington Parkway into a vacant lot shrouded in winter fog. When he opened the back door of his Tahoe to let Attila out, the cold night air condensed his breath into a cloud of misery. The air temperature had dropped well below freezing, turning the accumulated snow on the sides of the roads into an ugly frozen slush that matched his mood. The gut-wrenching mission had to be one of the hardest he had ever undertaken.

Kirk's footsteps crunched in the snow as he hiked to the rendezvous point. He found a place of concealment along the wooded riverbank, the brush thick under the shadows of tall trees. He waited, Attila at his side. The huge dog sniffed the air, his erect ears rotating, listening.

Heavy fog rolled off the river, dampening the sounds of passing autos on the Parkway. Traffic never ceased in the Nation's Capital. Within a few minutes, mist shrouded the woods, adding to Kirk's trepidation. Bone-chilling cold crept up his back, unsure whether the mission or frigid air gave him the shivers.

Tires crunching, a car pulled into the vacant parking lot. Seconds later, a door slammed.

Attila remained obediently quiet, every taut muscle quivering, eager. Kirk signaled with his hand. Like a blond phantom, the dog charged off into the night, invisible in the ominous shadows, standing guard over his master.

Kirk caught the sound of snow crunching underfoot. Through the trees, he made out Harvey's silhouette from the silver-blue moonlight as he approached the park bench. Harvey's heavy breathing condensed in billows of white condensation. Maintaining watch for several moments, he let out shallow breaths to conceal his presence. Although he fought to keep his temper under control, Kirk was a very angry man.

Ignoring the clammy chill spreading throughout his body, he withdrew his HK45, and screwed the silencer on, then slipped off the safety, leaving the hammer half-cocked. As he crept closer, he aimed the laser dot between Harvey's shoulder blades.

Up close, he snarled, "Don't turn around, or I'll put a fucking bullet in your back."

"I heard you come up," Harvey sniffed. "I'm not going anywhere. I've been expecting HRT to bust in my front door. I'm unarmed."

"You think it was worth it? Brett's dead. Michele's parents will never get over their grief. HRT took thirteen casualties, one KIA. An assassin slit my dog's throat. Those terrorist attacks killed thousands. What the *fuck* were you thinking?"

"I had no idea of the ramifications."

"How'd Dreihaus set the meat hook in you?"

"How did you find out?"

"Answer the fucking question."

Harvey sighed. "He called and requested a copy of our internal telephone directory."

"Your first screw-up was taking a call from that slime-ball. Didn't you smell a rat with him not going through channels?"

"I was flattered with his call." Harvey shrugged. "The request seemed innocuous, and it was hard to refuse. I mean, he chairs the Senate Select Committee for Intelligence and is running for president."

"BFD. Then what?"

"Then after I mailed it to his home, he wanted more."

"His *home?* You dumbass. You're the Director of Internal Security, and should have known that was over the top. I would have told him go fuck himself. You set yourself up. What did he pump you for next?"

"The Bureau organization chart, the one not for public consumption. He claimed his committee was investigating black ops."

Kirk pondered a moment. That explained how Dreihaus discovered Omega Six.

"Harvey, up until this, I thought you were a smart guy. The first rule of holes is when you find yourself in one, quit digging. Everyone knows Dreihaus has as much veracity as a used car salesman with no repeat customers. I'm still wondering how the hell you bought into his line of bullshit, and why you sucked up to the treacherous bastard."

"He offered to apply grease on an assignment I wanted—a berth as SAC of the Miami Field Office. Bastard knew I needed the money. Three kids in school. You know what the public schools are like in the District—dope, muggings, shootings."

"Typical fucking politician. Had it occurred to you the sleazy prick was on a witch-hunt? You promoted it by giving him Top Secret information."

"God, I'm sorry. I haven't been able to sleep. I'm a total wreck." Harvey rested his elbows on his thighs and lowered his head down into his hands. "Stacy doesn't know what's going on. She's nagging me to see a shrink."

Kirk took a deep calming breath. "So you sold out, and once the dirtbag set the hook, he turned the screws down. Don't you know it always starts out that way?"

"Dreihaus found out about the babe I'd been banging on the side." Harvey sobbed. "I couldn't risk my marriage. And we needed the money."

" How'd you pass the organization chart?"

"Dreihaus set up a meeting at Union Station at rush hour and directed me to put the envelope in my left coat pocket. I waited at the station for an hour. I never saw him. Later, I found a different envelope in my pocket containing twenty big ones."

"He used a professional cutout for the brush pass." Kirk shook his head. "Didn't that set off an alarm?"

"I was too damned stupid to realize I was in over my head. When I balked, he blackmailed me."

"How'd he shake you down?"

"He set up an offshore bank account in my name and wired money into it. A lot of money. I received a copy of the monthly statement in the mail."

"What else did he want?"

"Recent Omega Six operation reports. Photo IDs, addresses."

"And *you* delivered that shit to him? Did it occur to you Dreihaus was involved with terrorists?"

"I didn't have much choice. He had my balls in a vise." Harvey snorted and spit a wad of mucus. "One day I found an envelope in my car. It contained a dozen photos of my wife and kids. I thought about whacking the son-of-a-bitch."

"You should have. You would have done the world a favor." Kirk shook his head in disgust. "They used to hang traitors in public. Now they run for president."

"After Michele's assassination, there were many nights I thought about swallowing my piece. I had no place to go. No one to talk to. Not even my priest."

"*Bullshit.* You coulda come to me."

"I didn't know at that point if I could trust anyone," he pleaded. "What about Dreihaus? Does he get a pass?"

"Dead."

"Dead? How?"

"Nora Dhue's exposé on Fox News had him working away with his knickers down around his knees—photos of the pervert with underage boys on the Internet. District Police found his body a couple of hours ago in his garage. Mercedes engine still running."

"*Suicide?* I don't believe it. He was surrounded by Secret Service. You're the only one who could pull that off. Besides, I knew you had a thing going with that bitch. You sourced her. You were her *Deep Throat.*"

Kirk remembered the tracks of Misty's tears were real enough when he informed her of his reconciliation with Maggie. But they quickly vanished when Kirk showed her the photos on Dreihaus' encrypted web site. No dummy, she instantly realized she held the Holy Grail of Journalism in her hand—taking down a president or a candidate would lead to a Pulitzer.

She had kept her part of the bargain, and Kirk repaid his debt to her. And now, Harvey Rucker would have to settle his with society.

"You got bigger things to worry about. Harvey, it's over. FBI investigators found several encrypted e-mails to Sheikh Qadr al-Masri on the Senator's home computer. They've connected the dots."

Harvey broke down crying, wiped his nose, and sighed. "Dreihaus had a hundred-million dollar war chest and was set up for a run at the White House. If he made it, he'd be home free and have the world by the ass."

"Yeah. So did Sheikh Qadr al-Masri. The only thing left of it was the pucker when I blew his balls off."

For several minutes, both men's heavy breathing was the only thing that interrupted the eerie quiet, their breath condensing into a white vapor cloud in the cold air.

"We traced Dreihaus' wire transfers and discovered your Cayman Islands account. There is a crummy quarter-million in it. You sold out pretty goddamned cheap."

"Man, I'm really sorry."

"So am I, Harvey. So am I." Kirk had deep sorrow in his voice. "We been through a lot of shit together. You played a good game of handball, but you never beat me. You won't beat me at this game either."

Harvey blew snot into a handkerchief. "Kirk, I wanna make a run." He stood.

Suddenly, Attila charged out of the shadows, growling.

Kirk whistled. The 150-pound Anatolian shepherd skidded to a halt three feet in front of Harvey, his head thrust forward letting out long deep growls, fangs glistening, ready to tear a man's throat out on command.

"Holy shit!" Fear made Harvey's voice shrill, panicky. *"What the hell is it?"*

Frozen in place, he stared at the huge vicious-looking animal.

Kirk gave a hand signal.

Attila slowly sank back on his haunches, eyes glued on Harvey's crotch.

"You make another move," Kirk's voice dropped thirty degrees, "and I'll order my dog *eat* you. *Sit down*, you fucking traitor. . . .

"You sold out your country. You sold out the Bureau, and you sold me out. Now, *you* want a way out. You say you are sorry, or go to confession seeking atonement. It don't work like that. You had choices, and I'm gonna give you one more."

Kirk passed an unloaded Smith and Wesson revolver over Harvey's left shoulder. "Take it. *Slow*. Give me your wallet, and watch. Keep your wedding band."

Harvey dug into his hip pocket.

"We can take you in tomorrow with a coat over your head and the world media watching, or you take the bullet."

"Aw fuck," Harvey cried out with a short expulsion of breath. "What about my family?"

"You owe it to your family to do the right thing. The spin-doctors concocted a story that you got mugged on a stakeout. Stacy and the kids will receive survivor's benefits and life insurance. Harvey, don't fuck this up. It's your *only* way out."

"Man, I can't do it. I don't have the guts." Harvey shuddered like a condemned prisoner strapped on a gurney with a heart-stopping cocktail flowing into his veins.

A deep chill raced through Kirk's body as he ventilated his valediction—"Cowards always take the easy way out."

He tossed a .357 magnum cartridge onto Harvey's lap. "Harvey, don't waste the fucking bullet."

Kirk backed off into the woods, keeping the laser dot centered on the traitor's back. In the woods he turned to trudge back to his Tahoe. Frozen snow crunched beneath his leaden boots, Attila panting at his side, expelling hot condensing clouds.

Suddenly, a muffled gunshot broke the eerie silence, shattering Kirk's resolve.

Choked up with rage, remorse, and revulsion, he paused and lowered his head and uttered a one-line prayer for Harvey's family.

Kirk glanced back over his shoulder at the fog-smothered park, recalling some apropos words spoken by General George S. Patton.

"God deliver us from our friends; we can handle the enemy."

Turn the page for a preview of *High Treason,* featuring Kirk Magnus and his black ops unit in an action-filled sequel to *Ultimate Objective*. Soon to be available in paperback and e-book.

HIGH TREASON

J G HUTCHISON

Okracoke, North Carolina
April 15

The breeze off the Atlantic fluttered the sheer curtains over the glass door leading to the rear deck. Maggie O'Malley pulled the satin sheet to her chin and tucked her legs up in a feeble attempt to retain body heat. Her lover liked a chilly bedroom for hot sex, but his warmth had faded away. Chesty had left the bedroom while she slept.

Reluctantly, she threw back the covers, stooped to pick up her sheer black bra and panties, and set them on a chair cushion. Her new Victoria's Secret lingerie did the job. Maybe all too well. Chesty couldn't keep his hands off her, and things were moving too fast.

Hugging herself, she padded across the open bedroom to shut out the draft and dampen the sounds of the crashing breakers. As the cold front moved in during the night, the wind picked up and ruined an unseasonably mild spring day. In filtered moonlight the thunderheads to the northeast looked ominous. Over the weather-beaten deck, salt grass swaying on the dunes reflected her wavering feelings.

Maggie slid the door closed, leaned her forehead against the glass, and sighed. She wondered how she had allowed herself to get caught up in the illicit affair. Normally level-headed and introspective, her Irish temper sometimes overwhelmed her good judgment. Maggie's passion exceeded a temper as fiery as the flaming red hair hanging in waves over her shoulders. She was lonely and vulnerable when she met Chester Verhoeven, but still in love with Kirk Magnus, commander of a black ops counterterror hunter/killer team called *Omega Six*.

Kirk operated under a set of unorthodox rules that would have shamed Machiavelli, but he generated results like a one-man army. Contrary to normal canons of confidentiality, he held periodic coffee klatch meetings with Misty Dhue, a hot-looking Fox News investigative reporter and seasonal idolizer. Maggie suspected Misty had designs her man, and the jezebel often pumped Kirk for a scoop to air on her TV show.

Kirk's flaunting the rulebook and his indiscretion made Maggie furious. Their torrid on-again off-again romance had suffered another setback when the audacious bad boy pulled another shenanigan. Kirk circumvented her authority and poached one of her people to serve in his unit. Carla Calabrese, the Amazon warrior, was her closest confidant.

After Maggie's heated donnybrook with Kirk, the scoundrel stomped out of her home and never called to apologize. And she sure as hell wasn't about to call him, regardless of the longing in her heart. She realized they acted like flawed characters in a B-rated movie and felt certain he'd knuckle under. He always did. She knew he loved her as much as she loved the incorrigible bastard.

After three months of nail-biting dead air, Maggie decided to move on with her life. She had hooked up with General Chester Verhoeven, with reservations.

Chesty had all the right words, the right touches. He told her he loved her smile, her eyes, her athletic figure, her intelligence. She was attracted to him like iron to a magnet. Women of all ages threw themselves at him the way groupies tossed their panties on stage at a rock concert. No wonder. Chesty owned a warrior's physique—brutally handsome with a muscular body, intelligent blue eyes, and a wry sense of humor. In a uniform bedecked with medals, he radiated power and panache.

He was also a high-profile married man.

When Maggie fended off his advances, Chesty told her that his marriage was one of convenience—his socialite wife of twenty years preferred charity balls to the fleshy kind.

Lust did strange things to rational people. Late night seductive phone conversations led to a discrete rendezvous at a hotel in Norfolk. Candlelight, hand-holding, and four glasses of wine in the darkened restaurant shredded her inhibitions. Despite the risks and immorality, or perhaps because of them, they tore off one another's clothes in his hotel room.

This evening in his beachfront home, their second tryst was as memorable—seafood take-out enjoyed in front of the stone fireplace, several glasses of fine wine, pleasant conversation, and a round of lovemaking on the furry rug before a driftwood fire.

Chesty's voracious sexual appetite matched her own. His hunger had led to another round of lovemaking in the candlelit bedroom sending thrilling waves washing over her like the pounding surf. Now, she had second thoughts about their thunderous affair. They were juggling their careers like sticks of dynamite sweating nitro.

His muted baritone drifted to her from the study. She couldn't make out his words, and didn't try. Chesty ran the top job in the Pentagon. He received urgent calls involving national security all the time. The man had unbridled ambition and energy. He had even thrown his hat in the ring for a run at public office.

An unrecognized second voice startled Maggie, revving her senses to high alert. The conversation wasn't a phone call; it was a *meeting.* But Chesty had assured her absolute discretion. If their affair became known, the media would roast him on a barbeque spit. He'd survive, but once the media jackals got the scent of blood, they'd flush her job as Commander of the Hostage Rescue Team down the sewer. And a drawer full of commendations wouldn't help her.

Why did he violate her trust? Maggie's blood boiled; heat rose in her face. The urge to confront Verhoeven overwhelmed her, nudity be damned. She had a legitimate need to know the identity of the threat.

Maggie eased open the bedroom door and tip-toed down the hall to the study. In the dimly lit room, Marcus I. Heisenberg, Chesty's campaign manager, flailed his arms, yelping.

"Izzy," Chesty hissed, "I told you to keep your voice down."

"God damn it. Don't tell me you got another fucking bimbo back there. Chesty, you think with your dick. If the media catches you with your Jockey shorts around your ankles, it's all over. I didn't put my balls on the line for nothing."

Caught up in their argument, she took a deep breath and remained in the shadows of the hallway, cursing herself for a stupid affair with the indiscreet womanizer. It was hurtful and the last thing she needed.

"You're acting like a little old lady with a gerbil up her ass," Verhoeven snapped. "It's no big deal. The media gave Slick Willy a pass, and he had a stable full of women."

"Yeah. Only because he was a Democrat. But, I guarantee they'll skewer *your* balls on the front pages of the New York Times. If you want to win this election, you'd better sharpen your political skills and quit pissing in the wind."

"Quit worrying. You'll get the number two job, if we bag it. We need those additional funds to seal the nomination like a coffin lid."

"*Don't worry?* Are you out of your mind? You don't fuck with Jao. The Chinks have an unorthodox code of honor. They'll rob you blind, but still expect you to hold up your part of the bargain. His people wired the cash, and he demands the rest of the package. The drawings ain't worth the CD they're copied on without the W85 specs."

Chesty crossed his arms. "Tell that slant-eyed runt he'll get them after the election, when I have more flexibility."

"He's threatened to out me!"

"Quit whining. Two can play that game. I have DIA intel indicating Jao pinched off fifty million bucks of PRC money and stashed it in his secret Caymans account. The ChiComs will give him a cigarette and a blindfold if they find out."

Throat dry and pulse hammering, Maggie recoiled in horror. In less than sixty seconds she'd learned Chesty Verhoeven was not only a shameless heel and a despicable racist, he was also a reprehensible traitor—on a fast track leading to the White House.

She crept back to the bedroom, silently pulled the door closed, and crawled back in bed. Maggie shivered, not from cold, but trepidation. Sleep would be impossible. She'd have to fake it.

Loathing the thought of his touch and hating herself for allowing her predicament, Maggie knew she'd have to put on another act during the inevitable roll in the hay before breakfast.

Shag and gag would be a more apt description.

With her nails digging into her palms, she considered her limited options—burying Verhoeven's dark secrets under the dunes on the Carolina Outer Banks, or shouldering the moral obligation to do the right thing in spite of the awesome power she faced.

With a single word, Verhoeven could destroy her career. Or make her disappear.

There was no way out.

ABOUT THE AUTHOR

Jack Hutchison lives in Houston, Texas with his wife, Kathryn. He earned a Masters degree in Chemical Engineering from the University of Delaware, and was employed in chemical research and the oil & gas industry. He later founded a natural gas pipeline and marketing company based in Houston. Currently, he trades securities, enjoys fine woodworking, and reserves the early hours for creative writing.

Contact Jack at www.RedactionAction.com, the official website and forum for Kirk Magnus thrillers.

Made in the USA
Las Vegas, NV
06 March 2022

45152626R10216